Yours

LILA JEANNE ELLIOTT SYBESMA

Yours

the Civil War
a Love Triangle
and the Steamboat
Sultana

Indiana Historical Society Press | Indianapolis 2019

Printed in the United States of America

This book is a publication of the
Indiana Historical Society Press
Eugene and Marilyn Glick Indiana History Center
450 West Ohio Street
Indianapolis, Indiana 46202-3269 USA
www.indianahistory.org
Telephone orders 1-800-447-1830
Fax orders 1-317-234-0562
Online orders @ http://shop.indianahistory.org

The paper in this publication meets the minimum requirements of American National
Standard for Information Sciences—Permanence of Paper for Printed Library Materials,
ANSI Z39. 48–1984 ☺

Library of Congress Cataloging-in-Publication Data

Names: Sybesma, Lila Jeanne Elliott, author.
Title: Yours : the Civil War, a love triangle, and the steamboat Sultana / Lila Jeanne Elliott
    Sybesma.
Description: Indianapolis : Indiana Historical Society Press, [2019] | Summary: Told in two
    voices, in the early 1860s, Joseph struggles to escape his older brother's shadow and vies with
    him for the affection of Sarah, their neighbor who becomes a nurse and a spy during the Civil
    War. Includes historical facts and glossary. | Includes bibliographical references.
Identifiers: LCCN 2018024468 (print) | LCCN 2018056949 (ebook) | ISBN9780871954329
    (epub) | ISBN 9780871954312 (pbk. : alk. paper)
Subjects: | CYAC: Brothers—Fiction. | Love—Fiction. | Sultana (Steamboat—Fiction. | United
    States—History—Civil War, 1861-1865—Fiction.
Classification: LCC PZ7.1.S99 (ebook) | LCC PZ7.1.S99 You 2019 (print) | DDC [Fic]—dc23
LC record available at https://lccn.loc.gov/2018024468

Front cover: watercolor by Tom Cox
Back cover: blueprint by David J. Meagher

In memory of Anona (Elliott) Boone

Contents

Preface

"I saw that the men were jumping from all parts of the boat into the river.
Such screams I never heard, twenty or thirty men jumping off at a time,
many lighting on those already in the water, until the river became black
with men, their heads bobbing up like corks, and then many disappearing
never to appear again."

Joseph Taylor Elliott

It all started when my mother and I were sorting through family documents. She carefully placed a small, gray book in an envelope labeled "Elliott–Direct line" in a pile. "This book's about the boat disaster in the Civil War," she said.

Craving more information, I immediately reopened the envelope and leafed through the small booklet. "What disaster?"

"The *Sultana!*" she declared, as if I should know.

I wondered what the *Sultana* was, so I read the work written by my great-granduncle, Joseph Taylor Elliott. That little gray book was all it took: I was hooked on the *Sultana* story.

The *Sultana* was the worst maritime disaster in U.S. history. Almost 1,200 soldiers and civilians lost their lives. With President Abraham Lincoln's assassination and General Robert E. Lee's surrender at Appomattox Court House blazing across the headlines, the story of the ship's demise received little space in the newspapers of the day.

The boat, with a capacity of 376 passengers, was loaded with more than 2,100 people. Many of the passengers were soldiers, who after surviving some of the Civil War's bloodiest battles, such as Shiloh, Perryville, and Franklin, as well as the brutal prisoner of war camps Andersonville and Cahaba, were finally going home.

With the promise of being paid $5.00 per soldier, the *Sultana's* owners hastily repaired one of the ship's four boilers and headed north. Unaware of the aging boilers' condition and the danger presented by the overcrowding, the soldiers spent their last hours celebrating their new freedom: singing songs, playing tricks, telling jokes, and talking of home.

Floodwaters made upriver travel arduous. With the weight of the soldiers, the boat careened at every corner, further compromising the walls of the boilers.

INDIANA HISTORICAL SOCIETY PUBLICATIONS
VOLUME V   NUMBER 3

THE

SULTANA DISASTER

BY

JOSEPH TAYLOR ELLIOTT

INDIANAPOLIS
EDWARD J. HECKER, PRINTER
1913

In 1913 the Indiana Historical Society published The Sultana Disaster *by Joseph Taylor Elliott, a survivor of the explosion.*

On April 27, 1865, just north of Memphis, Tennessee, three of the four boilers exploded, and the soldiers were confronted with a fatal decision: stay on the boat and face the flames, or plunge into the icy Mississippi River. In their emaciated condition, the soldiers did not have a chance. Fewer than 1,000 survived.

Prior to finding my family's letters, I had no interest in the Civil War. Newspapers, books, and stories about the war held no power for me. But after discovering *The Sultana Disaster* by my great-granduncle and reading about the preventable loss of life, my personal *Sultana* obsession began. My collection of Civil War books piled higher and higher—virtually tumbling off the shelves and into my hands.

In *Loss of the Sultana and Reminiscences of Survivors*, edited by Chester D. Berry, I discovered fascinating stories of men croaking like frogs, singing the National Anthem on shore, and riding an alligator crate. Of special interest to me was the story of Isaac Van Nuys, who was among the last to leave the boat, watching 1,700 of his comrades "go down to a watery grave."

I found my Sarah character in "Midland War Sketches" (*Midland Monthly* [January 1895]) by Louise Maertz and *A Woman of Valor: Clara Barton and the Civil War* by Stephen B. Oates. Fodder for the canteen/tunnel story was unearthed from *This Was Andersonville* by John McElroy. I shamelessly plucked true Civil War stories from virtually every book I found, and I lovingly embraced and wove the true stories into mine.

My greatest joy in writing this book was that I wrote alongside the ghost of my great-granduncle more than a century after his death. Although I never met him, I feel as if I knew him well. This story is not just of Joseph Taylor Elliott, it is a careful blend of fact and fiction, and the author's notes will tell the tale.

It still baffles me how such a tragedy as the *Sultana* could have escaped the attention of so many. Was it because most of the victims were soldiers and after four years of bloodshed people were ready to put the war behind them? Or was it because the murder of Lincoln horrified the nation and remained the prevailing story of the day? Whatever the case, these soldiers' lives were not in vain. Retelling the story of this disaster has taught me important things about greed, compassion, courage, and perseverance.

Sarah

Still tasting the honey sweetness of Gabe's lips on mine, I entered his house. He held open the door. "After you." The door latch clicked, leaving Gabe alone with me.

I was a neighbor girl and had been in their home before, but this time was different.

His home looked far different than mine. The rough-hewn table was central to the area. Except for the rifle above the fireplace and the blue calico curtains, the walls were unadorned. His thumb swept across the curtain, pushing the fabric aside. "Thought sure I saw Joseph." His voice was low and deep—almost conspiratorial. "Think he's following us. We won't get caught. I'll make sure of that." He pointed his chin toward the fireplace and challenged me with a lifted eyebrow. "Joseph will never find us there."

The fireplace, made of gray river rock, took up most of the north wall. The chamber was huge. Hiding there was a brilliant idea. I wiped my hands on my skirts. "You want us to hide in there? In the chimney? No one's foolish enough to hide in a chimney."

His eyes flashed green and he smiled. "We're foolish."

I glanced out the window.

"You looking for my brother?" he asked. He held me by the elbow, and my arm heated with his touch. I was of marrying age—seventeen. I shouldn't be alone with Gabe.

"Joseph? No, I'm looking for your father and mother. Where are they?" The road, partially hidden by a maple tree, cut a line between pastureland and a newly sown field. Indianapolis was to the south of us.

I pushed up on my toes. There were no wagons down the road, as far as I could tell.

"Town meeting," Gabe responded, his dimples deepening, as he ran a hand through his brown locks. I couldn't pinpoint the smell of him, but it intrigued me—perhaps the musky odor of charred ashes.

Warmth worked up my neck and into my cheeks and I hesitated. "Umm."

"Ready?" He motioned toward the chimney, his eyes sparkling. "If we don't . . . then we'll never have time alone."

I was too old for games, especially with someone older than me. "I thought we were hiding from Joseph."

He gave me a rakish smile. "We are. I mean, we will." His eyes focused on a small figure down the road. "He's coming!" He ducked and grabbed me by the arm. He swiped me away from the window and tugged me toward the fireplace. "You want him to see you?"

Clasping my skirts with one hand, I stooped into the chamber. My eyes adjusted to the light—the chamber was barely big enough for the both of us. "Impossible," I muttered, grabbing one of the river rocks.

"Not impossible," he shouldered underneath me and boosted me up the flue. My skirts fought against me. Wedging my fingers between the rocks, I worked my way up the chamber. Midway up, I pressed my back against the wall. He clambered up and fixed his back opposite me.

"He'd better not find us," I breathed, certain that Gabe could hear the thump of my heart.

"He'll never think to look up here." His face was inches from mine. I'd never been that close to him and could feel his warmth through his shirt.

I gripped my fingers between the river rocks and adjusted my feet. "I'm going to be covered in soot. And smell!"

Ashes sifted down as he transferred his weight, and his leg brushed against mine.

"I don't know why I listen to you, Gabriel James." I adjusted my back against the chimney wall, and the rocks nudged into my spine.

"You're fond of me, that's why." His hand brushed against my arm. "You have to admit, this is an adventure."

"Well, that's true, but all good things come to an end." My words spilled out like a silly schoolgirl. He laughed, his voice resonating down the chimney.

"Shh!" he said. "He's coming!" The door's latch clicked open.

I tried to quiet my breathing, but it came out in ragged intervals. I swallowed, pinched my mouth together, and tried to breathe through my nose.

The door banged against the frame and footsteps echoed in the room.

I gasped.

"Shh," Gabe said.

The steps marched closer.

A chair scraped across the floorboards by the table. From the sound of it, someone was sitting down.

My fingers ached. Gabe found my hand and rubbed circles between my thumb and forefinger. A small patch of daylight came up from below, highlighting his jaw. I wanted to touch his bristly chin.

I closed my eyes, not because I needed to, but because I wanted to imprint that moment—to savor it. Gabe would be leaving soon, marching to the beat of a Union drum.

And I didn't know how long he would be gone.

Four Years Earlier

1

Joseph

INDIANAPOLIS, SUMMER 1856

My fingers itched for my Green River knife. After finding the perfect piece of basswood, I hid behind our woodpile and sat, hunched over my work. The woodpile, smelling of maple and applewood, was far from the house, tucked behind a row of pines. I was twelve—old enough to know the best spots on our property.

My thumb pushed the knife forward as I attempted to carve a S, Sarah's first initial. I wasn't an artist; that was for sure and my thumb slipped, nicking out a gouge.

"Dad-blame-it," I swore. My carving was ugly. I blew off the shavings and frowned.

Startled by the snap of twigs, I wheeled to my right. It was Gabe. He lifted his cap, raking back his dark curls. "Been tryin' to figure out where you were," he said.

He stood in his indigo blue shirt, looking more like a lumberjack than someone just two years older. He bent down and swiped my carving out of my hands. "Is that a 5?"

Heat rose up my neck. My brother didn't need to point out my mistakes; I was plenty aware of them already.

He toyed with my carving, turning it over in his hand. "Or maybe an S." Tossing my carving on the ground beside me, he adjusted his suspender with his thumb and with a crooked smile crowed, "It's an S, isn't it? For *Sarah*?"

I wasn't sure what to say. "Just c-carvin' a letter. Don't matter which one."

"Good kindling. Not sure what she'll do with a . . . 'five.'"

Sweeping the shavings off my lap, I stood my full height, brushed past him, and marched to the house.

My carving wasn't going to win Sarah's heart, I knew that. Maybe I had a chance with a different kind of letter. I sat down at the table and pen in hand I got to work.

July 19, 1856

Dear Sarah,

I thought that you and your father might be interested in coming over sometime. I don't see you when I walk by your house and I wonder what you've been up to. Maybe, if you come over, we can talk.

Yours,
Joseph

Nothing about my letter was remarkable. I folded it into a small triangle, tucked it into my hand, and started toward the door.

Gabe took his position as my older brother seriously; he stopped me at the front door. "Where are you going? What do you have?"

I wasn't going to give him an honest answer—not then. "Nothing," I said, trying to work my way past him.

He blocked me with his arm. "So what's going on?"

I ducked underneath him. "I'll let you know." Leaving him standing in the doorframe, I ran down the lane.

First produced by John Russell in Green River, Massachusetts, in the 1830s, these knives were of high quality and value. They became very popular with westward-bound Americans in the nineteenth century.

NATIONAL MUSEUM OF AMERICAN HISTORY

To get to Sarah's home, I followed the road toward town. Shoots of corn spiked out of the ground to my right. Up a slight grade on my left, just past the McCartney's pasture, was Mrs. Habernathy's house. I'd have to make it past. Her house was all windows and porch—probably designed with spying in mind—and a white picket fence lined the property.

I edged to the opposite side of the road and walked faster, half trotting. The town of Indianapolis spread out in front of me. Sarah's house was down the hill, just within view.

The sun beat down. The heat was good for corn, I guessed.

"Yoohoo! Joseph!"

Of course, Mrs. Habernathy probably had been waiting for a passerby.

She hurried out of the house, her crinoline snagging on the doorframe. "Humph," she jerked her dress free and crossed the porch.

"Yes, ma'am? Can I help you?" I stuffed the letter in my pocket and unlatched the gate. The delivery would have to wait.

Her beefy arms pumped her forward as she strode toward me, huffing. "Goodness. With the rain and all, I can't keep up with my garden." I could see from the road that her garden was far below her standards. "Come here, Joseph." She gave me her hoe, conveniently resting by the front door. "Start there, by the bee balm. Dig deep. Get the roots. Don't want those weeds up again tomorrow."

I knew the routine. She had roped me into chores before.

With the letter burning in my pocket, I half pulled, half hacked at the weeds until I finished a row. The ground was clumpy and smelled of wet dirt. I stood up to stretch.

Guarding the door, she folded her arms under her bosom. "You hear all the ruckus?"

Her question caught me off-guard, "What do you mean?"

"They're formin' a National Guard." Pursing her lips together, she motioned toward town.

"National Guard? Why?"

"Those Southerners." She tucked her chins to her chest, leaned forward, and whispered, "We're in for a heap of trouble." Her breath smelled of prunes. "They're gathering munitions in town. Stockpilin'. Next thing you know. . . ." She blinked. "Well. Probably shouldn't have said anything. Don't worry." With one last glance toward town, she disappeared inside her house, and I was stuck with her wretched garden.

"Munitions?" I muttered and gripped the hoe.

The garden became my battlefield: bullets spiraling, cannons firing, soldiers tumbling. One by one, the weeds succumbed to my hoe. I finished and walked the hoe to her door.

Her timing was perfect. Holding a glass of water, she charged out of her house. "Here, dear, have some."

I was eager to bring Sarah the letter and gulped down the water, but Mrs. Habernathy, quick with her pitcher, refilled my glass to the brim. "Springwater. Good, eh?" Her eyes flitted toward her garden, "Oh, my word!" She balanced the pitcher on the railing and cut a beeline toward the garden.

When she reached the edge of the plot, she stopped short, her face turning a shade of magenta. "Joseph Elliott! What on God's good earth did you do to my garden?"

I gulped and choked, water dribbling down my arm. Balancing the glass carefully, I stepped up beside her. We both gawked at her garden. Except for the wilted weeds, it looked perfectly fine to me. "I was hoein'. Like you t-told me to."

"W-well," she sputtered, matching my hesitant speech. "How come you hoed my tomato plants? Every. Single. One." She drilled her finger into my arm. "Look now! Not a tomato plant left. You've managed a perfect row of . . . of ragweeds!" With a scalding glare, she waited for my response.

I cleared my throat, searching for an answer. "I guess I don't know the difference between ragweed and t-tomatoes." They looked like tomato plants to me. I gave a hooded glance toward town. Sarah's house was just down the hill, where the dirt road met cobblestone.

Mrs. Habernathy's bosom heaved, and she sucked in air. "Well, you would think . . ."

The gate squawked open and I wheeled around. The last person I expected was Gabe. He clicked impatiently on the latch. "Joe, Father needs you at home."

"Really?"

"You better get there. In a hurry." Gabe shrugged his shoulders, indicating that he had no idea what Father wanted.

Mrs. Habernathy was quick with a response. "What have you done *now*, young man?" She fluttered her chubby fingers, waving me away. "Better skedaddle."

I was at the gate before I realized I still had Mrs. Habernathy's glass. I ran back to the porch, perched it on the railing, and left for home.

The walk back home seemed much longer than the walk to Mrs. Haberna-thy's. I didn't have any idea what Father wanted. Seemed to me, I had spent the whole day in trouble.

I found Father at the back shed, a lean-to really, made of used gray lumber. He and Gabe could have been twins; the only difference was that Father was large and wearing a red-Merino shirt.

"What do you want, sir? Gabe said you needed me."

I stood there, my hands gone sweaty. He squinted at me. "Don't believe I asked for you," he said, reaching in the shed door.

"B-but, Gabe." I pointed toward Mrs. Habernathy's house. Father pulled a hoe out of the shed and pressed it in my outstretched hand.

My brother had sent me home on purpose; he wanted to get rid of me.

"Since you're here," Father continued, "you can help your mother with the garden." He motioned toward our plot.

Our garden was a hellhole, with a blackberry hedge lining one side and two chestnut trees on the other. There was no breeze. I wiped my brow with the back of my hand and trudged to the garden. "Where's Gabe?"

Father shut the door to the shed. "Oh, he went to Sarah's house. Said he might be gone for a while."

A parade of weeds found the blade of my hoe: cocklebur, lamb's quarters, and clover. I knew every weed's name. When I finished, I left the carnage lying on the ground and slammed the hoe in the shed.

Gabe was going to hear it from me.

Time stopped moving forward—my mind filled with images of Sarah and Gabe. Maybe an hour later, he sauntered down our lane, meeting me at the garden. "You got the run on me," I said.

He plucked up a stray weed, tossing it into the grove. "What d' you mean?" He looked back at me, his eyes all doe-like and innocent, shifting his weight to one side.

I gave him an icy glare. "First you trick me into going home. Then you act as if you d-didn't do anything wrong."

He lifted his chin. "Just wanted to save you from yourself." His answer was too quick, as if he had rehearsed it.

"Really?" I balled my hands into fists at my side. Unclenching them again, I worked out my words. "You were t-tryin' to get rid of me."

He picked up a wilted cocklebur and pitched it into the grove. "Why would I want to get rid of you?"

I took a deep breath. Obviously, he was baiting me. "Well, you fancy Sarah and you d-didn't want me hangin' around."

There, I'd said it.

"She's a neighbor girl, Joe. Not like she's the only girl in the world. And, in case you're wondering, you'd never catch her eye." He squinted at me, "She's sweet on someone who has more . . . well . . . charm." He kicked a dirt clod back into the garden and tilted his chin toward me. "Some reason you're so all-fired mad? You *care* about her or something?"

"No," I said, but my stomach burned with the lie.

2

Sarah

At that hour, no one should be awake—not ghosts and not me. I was on my father's schedule, and even early morning hours were not my own.

"Sarah! Get up." Father's muffled voice echoed through the door.

I couldn't remember what day it was. No school. A Saturday. Adjusting the straw underneath me and tugging my wool blanket over my shoulder, I glanced out the window. Not a thread of daylight. At the age of twelve, I should be able to sleep longer.

I thrust one foot out of bed and stomped on the plank floor, hoping Father would think I was up for the day.

"Come on, Sarah. Now," he said.

I sighed and thumped my foot again.

"Sarah!" he said—louder. More impatient.

I stumbled out of bed, got dressed, and wisped my hair into a bun, the golden strands dodging my hold.

"Dr. Sutton!" Our front door vibrated on its frame.

I tripped into the living room. The room smelled of beeswax candles. Evidently, Father had been awake for a while.

The door shuddered again. I couldn't recognize the voice. "Dr. Sutton!"

Father opened the door. Our neighbor, David Lehman, stood outside, his shoelaces untied, his shirt flapping loose.

"What's wrong? What is it?" Father grabbed his medical bag off the shelf.

David's eyes were round, and his words came in gasps. "My wife! She's givin' birth."

Thrusting an arm into his coat sleeve, Father turned to me. "Stay. Here." His voice was gravelly and sharp.

I had no intention of following orders—not with the tone of David's voice. Their voices trailed after them.

"*. . . so much blood. . . not long.*"

David's wagon rattled away and disappeared behind our grove. Without thinking, I sprinted toward the Lehmans' home, my route directed by a pale flicker of light. The air was brisk and smelled of leaves.

A shiver running through me, I slipped into the Lehman house. The click of the latch would have announced my entrance on a normal day, but this was not a normal day.

No one saw me; they all focused on Annie, David's wife.

In her threadbare calico dress Annie looked young and small. Her clothes tangled about her as she clutched the side of the bed, her mousy brown hair twisted in damp clumps, sticking to her forehead, cheeks, and neck. Her eyes were glassy in fear.

I'd never witnessed childbirth, but still I knew: something was wrong. Tearing my eyes from Annie, I glanced at my father's profile, brow furrowed and lips vised in an angular frown. Rooted in the doorway, I couldn't leave.

"A lot of blood," someone said.

Another scream, this one I felt through the floor. Annie's blood collected in the hollows of the sheets and dripped off the side of the bed. A crimson river, it streamed along the plank flooring. I inched forward along the wall. My skin prickled with fear.

A whimper.

My heart racing, I tucked back into the shadows.

"Baby. Baby's coming!" A miracle coming headfirst into the world. Red faced and wrinkled, the baby was matted with a whitish substance. I rolled up on my toes and waited for the first cry.

A floorboard creaked, almost giving me away. The baby took his first breath and his newborn cry pierced the air. Like tiny rose petals, his little hands reached gracefully into the air.

Father handed the baby to someone I couldn't see.

"Annie," Father's voice. "*Annie!*" louder.

She tilted her head toward her son and closed her eyes, letting out a slow sigh. She never held him.

Father checked her pulse, staring at the wall in front of him, his fingers resting on her wrist much longer than necessary. "Sorry, David. So sorry." Father's eyes were glossy and wet.

David gripped the back of a ladder-back chair, his knuckles ringing white, his Adam's apple working in his throat.

I pinched my eyelids shut, trying to erase the images I had seen.

Father hesitated by the bed. "I'm not far away. If you need someone, you can come get me."

"Can you stay awhile?" David's voice had a choking, desperate sound.

My knees shaking, my chest heaving, I slipped out the door.

I took a deep breath, filling my lungs with the brisk autumn air. That was the first time I saw a woman die in childbirth. Had my father's face looked this stricken when I was born? Did my mother have a chance to cradle me in her arms before she died?

Determined to have our home spotless before Father's return, I washed up his breakfast dishes and then dusted my grandfather's walnut hutch. I twisted my cloth through Father's candlestick chair.

The room was void of any feminine touch: no basket of sewing, no indigo yarn. I moved the rocker to the other side of the room, then back again, and shifted the rug to the side. Father didn't believe in clutter; there were no figurines to clean or clocks to wind.

I straightened the portrait of my grandfather and then peered down the road. One wagon, pulled by a team of two work horses, plodded along. Beyond the wagon, nothing. Father wouldn't be back any time soon.

His desk was off-limits. I saved it for last.

I jerked a drawer open, and a clutter of papers spilled out. Bills, receipts, notes, and envelopes fluttered to the floor. I glanced toward the door. Gathering the papers and tapping them into a tidy pile, I noticed a stack of letters still lying in the bottom of the drawer—all tied together with a blue satin ribbon.

Carefully lifting the letters from the drawer, I sat down in my father's chair. I looped my fingers through the ribbon, unbound the stack, and traced the curving nuances of delicate script. Not until I saw my mother's signature did I realize that the letters were from her. My breath quickened. I could almost smell her lavender perfume.

> *Dearest William,*
> *With abundant pleasure I embrace a few moments to write you a brief letter.*
> *Your letters are received by me with the greatest joy and my beating heart aches for your reply . . .*

UNCLE TOM'S CABIN;

OR,

LIFE AMONG THE LOWLY.

BY

HARRIET BEECHER STOWE.

VOL. I.

ONE HUNDRED AND FIFTH THOUSAND.

BOSTON:
JOHN P. JEWETT & COMPANY
CLEVELAND, OHIO:
JEWETT, PROCTOR & WORTHINGTON.
1852.

Uncle Tom's Cabin *by Harriet Beecher Stowe was written in 1852 as a depiction of the cruelties of slavery in the American South. It was immensely popular in its day and helped to fuel the abolitionist cause against slavery. Sarah's father may have been upset if he caught her reading this novel because it was believed that women, especially young girls, should not be exposed to such things.*

I read most of her letters, pausing at the tender thoughts—the sweet turns of phrase displaying the depth of her love. Her missives breathed of intangible things, like joy and hope and dreams.

The letters must have been written when Father and Mother were courting—long before she knew about me. I stuffed them back in the drawer and waited for Father's return.

When Father arrived that evening, his face was drained of all color; tight-lipped, he opened the cupboard and poured himself a large measure of whisky. Then he sat in his wing-backed chair, I on the hearth. The fire's light danced through the room in waves of ochre and gold, flitting and undulating on my grandfather's portrait, our camelback trunk, and my father's grim face.

I tried to ignore the ache that permeated the room and focused on my book. If Father knew that the book that I was reading was *Uncle Tom's Cabin* by Harriet Beecher Stowe, he would be angry. Nevertheless I continued to read:

> Things have got to a pretty pass if a woman can't give a warm supper and a bed to the poor, starving creatures, just because they are slaves, and have been abused and oppressed all their lives, poor things!

I rested the book on my lap. My mind ached dully. The notion of slavery simply wasn't discussed—at least not with Father.

My neighbor, Mrs. Habernathy, had told me plenty; she spoke of walnut-colored children wrenched from their mother's arms, and she whispered of runaway slaves. "Heard some folks in town are housing 'em."

"Why?" I had said.

Then she gave me a solid look, her eyes wet and haunted. "They've been treated poorly." I suspected that she had assisted those slaves somehow.

I would have let those runaways stay with us. I knew that for sure.

I glanced over at Father. Lean and tall, with salt-and-pepper hair and blue-gray eyes, he could capture a woman's heart. He snapped open the paper and worked out the creases with the palm of his hand. His eyes darted above the paper. "The Union's at risk." I listened, because he rarely met my eyes.

"Do you . . ." I started to say.

He rifled through the next pages. "Damn Southerners." He reached for his glass, swishing the whisky in loose amber circles. Weariness filled my frame, my body aching. I wanted to ask him about the runaways, but I didn't dare. I wanted to ask about Annie, her baby, the slaves. Most of all, I wanted to ask about my mother.

I cleared my throat. Normally, I wouldn't have broached the subject, but Father's decanter was half empty and in that more vulnerable moment, I dared. "F-father?"

He crooked his finger between pages and took a deep breath, the sweet smell of whisky crossing the room.

"I know that you loved Mother, but have you ever thought of remarrying?" I sat forward on my chair.

He sighed and set the newspaper on the table beside him. His eyes were sharp and penetrating.

My throat burned. I had done it; I had asked too much. Knotting my fingers in my lap, I tried to make myself as small as I could. The fire popped and crackled—the house shuddered in the wind.

He turned toward the darkened window. "I don't seem to manage very well." His voice sounded chafed. "Not on my own."

I swallowed, searching for words that might make him happy, that might make him less angry. "I think you're managing," I said in a small voice. "Just fine."

We both knew that statement was a lie.

Lifting the glass to his lips, he drained the last of his whisky.

I wanted to tell him, "I'm here. You don't have to be lonely." Instead I sat and gazed out the window, too.

3

Joseph

My fifteen-year-old brother took the shine off whatever I did. And he knew how to get me in trouble—like the time with the gun.

I was thirteen years old, and to me everything in our home was large enough for giants: an oversized door, a massive fireplace, and a hand-hewn table. The only thing hung on our buttermilk walls was my great-grandfather's gun. The muzzle-loading musket, a "Brown Bess," was beautiful, with a polished maple stock; the gun had seen service in the Revolutionary War and was my father's pride and joy.

One evening after supper, my father bragged, "Your great-grandfather had supper at the Black Bear Tavern." He squared his shoulders and turned to each of us, sharing a slice of his shining smile. "He sat right next to Lafayette and George Washington. Never forget that a man of humble Scottish descent can eat supper with the President himself!"

Giving him a half smile, Mother rose from the table. She straightened her shoulders, lengthening her small frame. "I'll let you boys clear the table. Then chores." Wrapping herself in her shawl, she plucked up her sewing basket and walked toward the door. "I'll be down the road. Sarah has mending to do."

Like clockwork, my mother found her way to Sarah's house: she brought eggs on Mondays, she baked bread every Friday, and she brought sewing on Saturday. "A motherless girl needs someone," she often said.

Father stuffed his cap over his curly brown hair and unfolded himself from the table. "I'll start on the cows." As if on cue, he grabbed his jacket and went out the door.

We were supposed to be clearing the table, but Gabe had other things in mind.

"Grab that musket." Gabe squinted up at the gun. "Hurry!" I could count on him for some fun.

I shoved a bench close to the fireplace, clambered up, and stretched to lift the gun off its mountings. I handed the gun to him.

"Nice, eh?" Toying with the mechanism, he gave me a crooked grin.

"Yeah. Nice. Careful." Having second thoughts about my actions, I backed away. "What're you going to do with it?"

Bronzed by the firelight he looked the part of a warrior. "Just wait. You'll see." He crooked his finger against the trigger and pivoted toward me. "Who knows, someday we could be soldiers—maybe sooner than you think. Heard that those Southerners are stirrin' up trouble."

With a cold-steel barrel pointing right at me, I wasn't worried about the Southerners. "D-don't think we're s'posed to play with that gun."

Gabe shifted his stance, squaring one foot on the bench and one foot on the floor. He lifted the barrel parallel to the ground, squeezed his left eye shut, and repositioned his grip. "You're the one who took it off the wall."

I swallowed hard. "You're fifteen," I reminded him as I stared down the gun. "You should know better."

"Know enough." His eyes flitted toward the fire. "Joseph, can you stir the fire? We're going to need more heat."

"I d-don't think I'm s'posed to play with fire, neither."

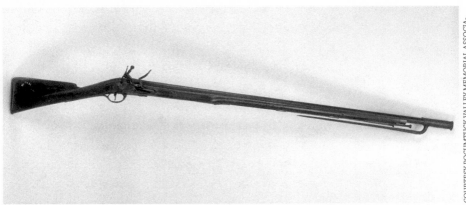

The Brown Bess was a type of musket (a gun loaded from the muzzle) that was popular throughout Europe and America in the eighteenth and early nineteenth centuries. Many who fought in the American Revolution would have used a Brown Bess or a similar type of weapon. The Elliotts would have been proud of their ancestor's service in the American Revolution, and his gun would have been a prized possession.

Gabe's jaw had a determined set. "Not playin' with fire. Mindin' it. Gee willikers, do I have to do everything?" He juggled the gun with one hand and grabbed the poker with his other, prodding the logs and bringing the coals to life. Like screaming ghosts, flames shot up the chimney. Then, twisting toward me, he straightened into his full height and leveled the gun. "Don't tell Father."

"D-don't tell him what? That you're pointing a gun at me?" I clenched and unclenched my hands.

He repositioned the barrel, squaring it on my forehead. "Better not. And don't tell him we're messin' with his gun, neither."

I couldn't think clearly, not with a gun pointing at my head. "And I s'pose you don't want me to tell him about Sarah."

The barrel dropped a few inches. He narrowed his eyes. "Where did that come from? She's a *neighbor* girl."

"You t-take a fancy to her."

He shook his head. "Think what you want. Take this." He tossed a broomstick to me. "You're the Redcoat, and I'm the Minuteman." Just like that, he had brushed off Sarah.

Looking half the soldier as Gabe did, I mustered my broomstick. He tucked back his shoulders and leveled the gun.

I lunged for it. His grip wasn't tight enough, and the musket toppled, its butt smacking the coals.

"Get it!" he clambered for the gun. "Watch out!" As sparks spiraled through the air, he grabbed me by the elbow and jerked me away.

The bench slammed to the ground. A blast went off, the charge echoing through the room and filling the house with the papery smell of dry plaster.

"Joseph!" Gabe's voice cut through the silence. "Now you did it." He plucked up the gun and put it in my hands. Probably for evidence.

"I didn't know it was loaded!" Balancing the gun, I backed away from the wall.

"You're gonna be in So. Much. Trouble." His eyes skated from the wall to the door. "Just *wait* for Father."

I already knew what Father's reaction would be. "You're the one playin' with Father's gun!"

We both looked at each other wide-eyed.

My legs like jelly, I righted the bench, climbed up on it, and fitted the gun back on the mountings. "Get rid of the mess!" We both examined the hole in the north wall. Gabe had blasted right through the plaster laths, leaving a hole the size of a dinner plate.

"The broom!" He waggled his fingers toward the corner.

As quickly as I could, I swept up the dried plaster, laths, and straw. Gabe was going to get what was coming to him. First he would take a trip to the woodshed. Then me.

Knotting our hands, we waited for Father, the next ten minutes stretching on like an eternity. Gabe scraped his shoe back and forth on the floor. "Sure you don't want to run?" He nodded toward the door.

I caught his foot with my shoe. "Better not."

He nudged my foot away. "Now's your chance. Better run while you can."

I sat forward on the bench, waiting.

The door's handle turned, the door opened, and my father filled the frame. Stamping snow off his feet, he first looked at us, and then he looked at the wall.

I swallowed hard and gave Gabe a fierce look. It didn't take a genius to figure out what had happened. "Uh, I," I started.

"You could've been hurt." Father bent down to brush off some loose plaster from the wall. Then he stood to his full six-foot-two height and tugged on Mother's dresser, moving it to cover the damage. His eyes leveled on Gabe's. "Don't do it again."

Gabe nudged me, and said in a voice just loud enough for me to hear: "Coulda told you. Father has a soft spot for us boys."

4

Sarah

INDIANAPOLIS, SUMMER 1857

Patches of red crept up Father's neck. He was seated at the table, elbows guarding his drink, eyes fixed on a half-empty glass.

I looked up from where I sat wrapped in a blanket in a chair where Mrs. Habernathy had positioned me. It was summer, but I was chilled to the bone. My long hair hung tangled and damp around my shoulders.

He dragged his eyes from his whisky and stared unblinking at me. "You're destroying my standing in the community. Permission must be granted before you accept a gentleman caller."

"A n-neighbor," I stammered, my eyes latched on the water ring left by his glass. "Gabe's a neighbor. And I didn't know he would be there." I took a deep breath, my skin prickling. "Y-you told me to gather medicines from the pond. You said—"

"I know what I said." His jaw muscles tightened, forming a rigid line. "I just expected you to have better sense than to keep company with a young man without proper supervision!" Father drained the last of his whisky in one gulp and slammed the glass on the table. He pushed back from the table, the chair's legs scraping against the floorboards. "This morning I hear more about those damn Southerners. Then this afternoon I find out my own daughter—*my thirteen-year-old daughter*—nearly drowned while swimming in the pond with a boy! You're—" Stopping his sentence midstream, he glared at me. Then he replaced the bottle in the cupboard, set his glass in the sink, and stalked from the room.

Like I explained to Father, I had gone to the pond—just as he had instructed me—to collect black-eyed Susan, a remedy for soothing sores, and mother-wort, an antidote for soothing the mind.

I wavered a bit once I got to Hardin's Pond; I remembered stories of a child—Sallie—who had drowned there. She was eleven, I think—and the only girl in a family of eight. She'd been missing for days. The neighbors searched for her, echoing her name through cornfields and woods. Weeks later an elderly gentleman discovered her near the pond. Vultures had eaten her flesh away.

I couldn't escape my gruesome thoughts and was hypnotized by the glimmering pond, distracted by the fermenting smell. I turned around to the crunch of wagon wheels.

"Sarah!" Gabe's voice boomed across the pond, startling me. He was fifteen—and tall. "Whoa!" he called to his horses and leaped to the ground. "Never thought I'd see you here." His voice had a velvety warmth to it.

His image silhouetted dark against the weeds. Squinting against the sun, I tried to see his features. "Who else would be collecting black-eyed Susan and motherwort?" I called.

"You're right." His rich baritone voice closed the distance. "Who would collect herbs on a hot day like this? I mean, who *in their right mind*?"

I giggled. Even though he was across the pond, I could feel his presence. I closed my eyes and willed myself to stay calm. Father would disapprove of our meeting. At thirteen, I shouldn't be alone with Gabe.

Ignoring any premonitions, I projected my voice as loudly as I could. "If you came over here, you wouldn't have to yell."

"You're the one who's yellin'!" He tromped through the brome toward me, his long strides crunching through the grass, brush, and weeds.

His dimples deepened. He walked up to me, and my face warmed. "Where's your brother?" I peered down the road.

"Joseph? Chores. He'll be done soon."

"I'm not supposed to talk to you unsupervised."

One eyebrow shot up. "Really? Well, you just did." He was so disarming—his green eyes, that smile, and those locks of hair curling into his collar. I was out of my element with Gabe, and my pulse quickened.

He took my basket and set it down on the ground, leaving my hands empty. "It's only a matter of time."

It was a furnace outside, stifling hot even at that time of night. The scent of field corn filled my nostrils. I wished for a breath of wind.

I tucked my hands behind my back. "What do you mean? Time 'til what?"

His voice was lower, more serious. "We're headed for war."

"I doubt that will happen," I said, regretting my response as soon as I said it. I didn't mean to discount Gabe.

There was a subtle shift in his eyes. "You want to talk about something else? I mean . . . there's probably other things to talk about." He motioned toward the edge of the pond. "I want to show you something, anyway."

I rolled up on my toes, trying to see past him.

"Have patience," he said. "You'll see soon enough."

My heart was racing; he was so close. I felt his warm breath on my forehead. "I don't have all day," I choked.

His grin reminded me of a cat. "Sure you do."

With a crook of his finger, he beckoned me to follow him. What could the surprise be? We were at Hardin's Pond, after all, and very few things were out of the ordinary. A rare flower? A fledgling bird?

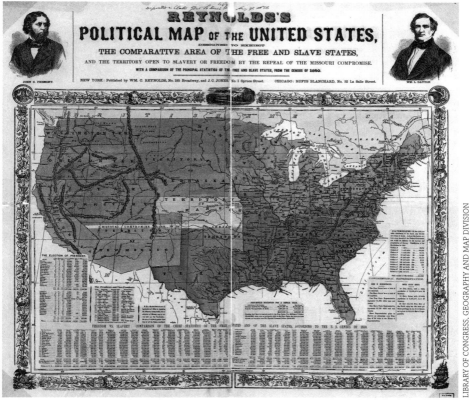

This political map from 1858 reflects Gabe's sentiment when he says that the country is headed for war. Here one can clearly see the huge divisions in the United States in the years before the Civil War. The main divider, of course, was slavery.

The ground was mushy at the pond's edge. I was intent on my feet—and my thoughts. Gabe, well ahead of me, stopped underneath an old oak.

"What is it?" I asked. It was cooler in the shade.

"Put your hands over your eyes." His bluntness surprised me.

I thought about how furious Father would be if he saw me with Gabe. "Why should I close my eyes?"

"Won't be a surprise unless, of course, you're surprised. Hands over eyes," he insisted. "If I wanted you to know, I'd let you peek." Sighing, I pinched shut my eyes. My nose caught the tangy scent of the herbs I'd been collecting as I covered my eyes with my hands.

I sensed him leaving my side. Left alone on the pond's bank, my imagination ran wild.

I heard crunching and scraping noises. A minute later, small branches snapped overhead.

Then I felt it. Something stringy—bristly—rubbed my neck. I swiped at it and opened my eyes, wheeling my arms to push it away. A hemp rope. Why would he think viewing a rope was worth my time?

"A rope." He straddled the limb above me and knotted the rope to the branch. Then he lopped a leg over the branch and shimmied down.

"Obviously," I pushed the rope away. "So you brought me over here to see . . . a rope?"

"Well, actually . . . it's a swing." He toyed with the rope in his hands. "You have to examine something carefully before you recognize its possibilities," he replied, tilting his chin and smiling.

I hadn't expected a rope—much less a swing.

He nodded at me and climbed on the large knotted end, pumping back and forth until the arch of his swing extended well over the pond. Tilting back, he took advantage of the rope's length, his frame paralleling the pond. Two Gabes fought for my attention: the one in the air and his silver reflection.

He swooped gracefully over the pond, and I realized his height in the air. "Get back here!"

He waved on the swing's journey back to the tree.

After a few more trips, he leaped off beside me. The rope, like a pendulum, finally slowed. My breathing slowed, too. He offered me the rope. "Your turn."

"But my skirts," I faltered, trying to think of excuses. The thought of dangling over a pond unnerved me. Half taunt and half dare, his dimples were a reason to try.

"Your skirts will get in the way, but you'll manage." He cocked his head and handed me the rope. "Here, your turn."

I looked at the rope and took a deep breath. Eyeing Gabe, I bunched my skirts in my hand and tentatively placed one foot on the knot. *Rash decision, I'm going to regret this,* I thought.

A cloud shifted in front of the sun, and the pond turned black, the air chilling. Giving a little jump, I pulled my feet up and swept over the water, the coolness of the pond and the freedom of the moment exhilarating me. I whisked over the water, noticing the cattails—and a piece of fabric snagged in the weeds.

Sallie?

I panicked. My hands slipped, and losing my hold, I wheeled backward and tumbled into the water, smacking the surface. My skirts bloomed around me, and then like an anchor their weight pulled me under.

Where was Gabe?

My lungs ached for air. The water churned, and bubbles spiraled to the surface as I sunk lower. Down, down I plunged, the water becoming darker and darker until it turned black. My skirts now twisted around my legs, I lost sight of the pond's silver surface.

Help! cried the voice inside my head. Blindly, I trundled my arms in the water—grasping at anything—fighting for air, choking on pond water, and struggling against weeds.

Was this the way I was going to die? Colder now, the depths of the pond swallowed me. Water churning, thrashing, spinning. Then I saw it. Barely. Gabe's hand.

Silt muddied the waters; his form disappeared. I heard muffled noises, the water still sucking me under.

I swallowed more water, starving for air. Ghostlike shapes floated toward me.

Then a tug, a pull. Someone was pulling me under! Clawing with all my strength, I fought against him. His grip on me tightened.

Panicking now, my lungs choking for air, I grappled against the water. The pond's surface taunted me: scolding, mocking, glittering, shimmering.

A last tug and finally—air.

Somehow we reached the pond's bank. Grasping at weeds for leverage, I struggled against the mud, my calico skirts clinging to me.

Our gasps matched in a ragged rhythm. It took awhile before I had command of my voice. "Y-you almost killed me!"

"Yeah." Panting, he fisted a hand to his chest. "But I saved you too."

The pond was shrouded in a black veil. Did I hear a child crying? Maybe it was me.

5

Joseph

INDIANAPOLIS, SUMMER 1858

When your brother is two years older than you, it's pretty hard to find something that you're better at. I wanted to be better at *something*.

"You wanna fish?" Gabe grabbed our fishing poles from the shed and motioned me down the road. "Bet fish are bitin' today."

You could almost hear the corn grow—it was one of those sweltering summer days. I pulled my sweat-soaked shirt away from my skin. "Too hot for fishin'." Sweat trickled down my back. I was fourteen, old enough to know that the fish wouldn't bite, not in this heat. "We don't have worms," I added.

"Sarah will. We'll stop there on the way, but first I have to get something." He motioned toward the top of the rise—Mrs. Habernathy's house marked the halfway point. He jammed his fishing pole in my hands just as we reached her gate.

Typically she would have noticed us, but she was too intent on her work. She mumbled something, set down her hoe, wiped her gritty hands on her skirts, and went inside.

Gabe took advantage of that moment, strutting across her neat lawn and going straight for her flowers. He nabbed five or six irises from under her windowsill and flashed a glance at her window. Then he ran like lightning.

Me? My jaw flopped open like a catfish's.

The next thing I knew, the old lady opened her window. "My flowers! Half of them are gone!" She waggled her arm at me and gave me a breezing for all she was worth. "Joseph Elliott, how saucy you are! Stealin' flowers!" Gabe was long gone, and she thought that I was the flower thief! I peeled off after Gabe, feeling guilty for spying, not thieving.

I tried to match Gabe's stride. He was yards ahead of me, already on the cobblestones of town. It was easy to guess his next stop—Sarah's. With the spray of flowers behind his back, he knocked at her door. She peeked out, and Gabe swept out the flowers. "Flowers for milady. Hope they brighten your day."

I was halfway down her lane and could see pink flushing up her cheeks. "They're lovely! How thoughtful!"

Thoughtful. She thought he was thoughtful.

She adjusted her blue calico skirts, took the bouquet from Gabe, and buried her nose deep in the blossoms. "Mmm, they smell wonderful."

Gabe looked almost regal—except for his crazy cowlick. He thrust his hands in his pockets. "We came for worms."

"Fine trade." she glanced my way. "Flowers for worms. I'll keep that in mind next time I want flowers."

I stifled a laugh.

Sarah disappeared into her house with the bouquet and came out a moment later with a bucket in her hands. Thrusting it in front of us, she gave him a coy smile. "Thirteen of them. A dozen. An extra just in case one gets away." She hooked one worm with her finger and introduced it to me; the worm didn't look happy. "I keep 'em in the springhouse, next to the turnips." Her delicate hands were a muddy distraction.

Gabe took the bucket from her, the corner of his mouth curling. "Remind me not to eat your turnips."

She threaded a stray hair behind her ear. "Or the yams." She pinched her lips together, containing her smile.

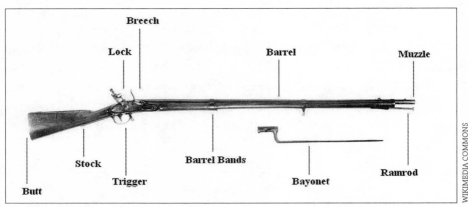

The guns used during the Civil War were very different from the modern rifle. Whereas there were some changes from the Brown Bess, many of the firearms were still muskets or other muzzle-loading guns that could only hold one bullet at a time and had to be reloaded after each shot, a time-consuming task.

He nodded back toward Hardin's Pond. "You want to come with us, Sarah?" I gave him a sharp look. This fishing trip was supposed to be just the two of us.

"I can't. Saturday. Laundry," she glanced back at the string of shirts fluttering on the clothesline behind her. Then she poked in the bucket, disturbing the worms. "Besides, my father."

She didn't have to explain; we had been neighbors for our whole lives, and we knew her father well.

"Another time." Gabe and Sarah's eyes met. Adjusting his cap, he took the bucket and she nodded.

"Why d-did you ask her along?" I started, as soon as we left her yard.

"Knew she'd say 'no.'" He glanced back at her house. His jaw was set. "Just bein' polite. Besides, I want to show you something."

I walked to the pond wondering what was more important than fishing.

We backtracked to Hardin's Pond. It was midway between Sarah's house and ours—just past McCartney's stone bridge and through the hollows. The closer we got to the pond, the longer his strides. Gabe flashed a broad smile. "Wind's shiftin'. Gonna get cooler. Fish are gonna think they're in heaven." We both smiled.

The pond was magical. Oaks ruled the sky; willows drooped branches as if guarding the water; and a medley of mushrooms, moss, and grass carpeted the ground. The moist air was slightly cooler and smelled of sweet clover.

"So, how did you know Sarah's answer before she even said anything?" I took the worm bucket and set it on the ground.

Ignoring me, Gabe plopped down on the shore, his back against the embankment. He dug in the bucket for the liveliest worm and baited his hook, wiping the worm juice on his pants. "Hold on." He cast his line in the water. The pond's mirrored surface scattered and ripples raced to the shore.

I wasn't going to get an answer from him, at least not any time soon. Exhaling, I stretched beside him, as the cool water cupped at my heels. "How come I never catch fish?" I cast my line into the water too.

"You're not very good at it. Plain as that." Gabe bobbed his line in the water.

I lifted my pole to check on my worm.

"If you'd pay attention, you'd be a good fisherman too." He squinted against the water's glare.

"Pay attention to you or pay attention to my line?" I shifted my fishing pole to my left hand and waited for his answer.

Still concentrating on his line, he rolled his eyes. "Both."

I was impatient and bored; I hadn't had a nibble. How could I pay attention when the fish weren't biting? Eyeing Gabe, I sucked in some wind and worked out a belch.

He wasn't to be outdone. His belch was loud and juicy.

"Wish I could belch like you," I muttered.

"I know. Can't help it. I'm a master." Gabe sucked in a deep breath, pulling his chin to his chest. His stomach caved in below his ribs and he proudly belched again. He was good. More than good. He was magnificent.

My next attempt didn't produce a belch, but something else. The smell of rotten eggs permeated the air. "D-did you hear that?"

Gabriel edged away, eyeing me with disgust. "Faugh! Some things you don't want to be an expert at."

I didn't say anything. The evidence spoke loud enough.

We both waited for the air to clear. "So," I finally asked. "What did you want to show me?"

"This letter." Balancing his pole with his right hand, he pulled a letter out of his pocket. "Looks like Father and some neighbors will be leaving for Washington, D.C. They're getting muskets."

"Why?" I loosened the grip on my fishing pole and reached for the letter.

He swiped it away. "Those Southerners. Everybody's worried about those Southerners. They—" Midsentence he jerked on his line, and the rest of his sentence got lost with the catch.

6

Sarah

INDIANAPOLIS, FALL 1860

It was the devil's drug, and our neighbor, David Lehman, couldn't get enough. My father gave me the delivery job. "One bottle." He ran his index finger along the row of bottles, alphabetically arranged on a shelf by the door, stopping at a bottle labeled "Laudanum."

"Why does he need this?" I took the bottle from him and tightened the lid.

Father's eyes drifted toward the cupboard. "His wife gone and all. And his family down south." He picked up the newspaper from the table. "Shouldn't be sparin' laudanum on him."

"What do you mean?" I gave him the bottle and wiped the cinnamon smell off my hands.

"He's a Southern sympathizer." He spat out the words as if he had a bad taste in his mouth and wrapped the bottle in the paper. "Better get going. David will be wanting this." Steadying himself on the table, Father gave me the bottle. Then he went to the cupboard and rummaged for his own.

I was grateful to get out of the house. The air outside was refreshing, crisp, and smelled of leaves. I wasn't planning to ride sidesaddle. Not that day. "It's my sixteenth birthday," I explained to Beulah, my father's horse. "I can even ride through the creek. If I want."

My words were far braver than I felt. I glanced back at the house. Father wouldn't notice—not if I left right away. I cinched up Beulah and departed at a trot, choosing my path carefully.

Beulah was a remarkable horse, a toasty brown bay. She perked one ear forward and flattened the other ear backward, probably wondering why we were heading to McCartney's meadow.

The wind picked up and leaves scuffled across the road. I gave Beulah a nudge and reined her down the hill.

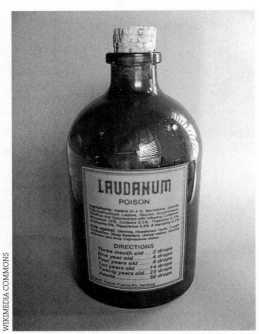

Laudanum was once widely used as a sleeping aid and a way to relieve pain for any number of medical problems. It contained opium and was highly addictive.

Possum Creek beckoned me. Dotted with stepping stones, it meandered lazily just northwest of me. I fit Beulah between two box elders and went down the embankment.

There was nothing menacing about the creek to me, but to Beulah, the creek was a monster. She flattened her ears to her head, edging backward. "Come on, Beulah!" I heeled her, pressing forward. Wild-eyed and sliding sideways in the clay, Beulah whipped in a circle and plowed back up the embankment. "Beulah!" I yelled.

She huffed, her sides heaving. "You're not an easy one," I muttered and sat heavy in the saddle. "It's all right, Beulah. The creek's not going to bite you." I took a deep breath.

In a sweet melody, the water rippled in front of us. Shafts of sunlight dappled the ground, and birds flitted through the branches. I toyed with the stirrups and waited.

I relaxed and—wonder of wonders—Beulah did too.

My mind was set. With or without Beulah, I was going to walk through Possum Creek—preferably with.

I urged her forward. "Come on, Beulah." She bent her neck down, grazing her nose over the water. "Attagirl!" I encouraged her, lifting the reins. She clomped through the water, high-stepping to the creek's edge.

When I got to McCartney's bridge we climbed up the sharp bank and turned for David's house. Built on a rise, it was only twenty yards from the stream.

Dismounting, I walked to the door but couldn't bring myself to knock. I left the laudanum on the doorstep.

* * *

Back home, I tethered Beulah to our hitching post. "Come on. Let me get my things." She pawed her hooves, and I kicked her leg soundly. "Behave!" She sidestepped toward me. I responded with a shove.

"Sarah!" The voice belonged to Joseph.

I jumped half a foot off the ground. "What do you think you're doing, Joseph Elliott? Scaring me to death?"

He looked particularly handsome, the browns in his shirt matching his dark hair. "I came to wish you a happy birthday." Shifting his weight, he gave a hesitant smile. "You talkin' to your horse?"

I grinned at Beulah. "I always do."

She whinnied, baring her teeth.

"She talks back." Joseph scratched under her mane and gave me a shy smile.

I looked past him toward the house.

"Why are you so . . . I d-don't know . . . jumpy?" He followed my gaze.

I had reasons—my transgressions, mostly. "Promise you won't tell anyone?"

"Tell anyone what?" he asked.

"You have to promise first." I cleared my throat. "Not tellin' you anything unless you promise first."

"Sure." He nodded his head solemnly.

I loosened Beulah's cinch. "I stole my horse," I whispered.

He whispered too. "You stole your horse? How can you steal your own horse?"

"Well, not really. I had permission and everything." I tossed the cinch over the saddle. "I'm supposed to take the bridge. Not supposed to ride her through the creek."

The pupils in Joseph's eyes darkened. He glanced toward the house. "Is your father asleep?"

"Yes," I said, but I wasn't entirely sure.

His eyebrows arched. "You didn't ride sidesaddle? Your father won't be happy about that."

"True." My stomach knotted. "Will you help me unsaddle her before Father wakes up?"

"Already am." Joseph pressed down on Beulah's poll and lifted the bit from her mouth. He gave me a cautious smile. "You know what they do with horse thieves."

I tugged off her saddle. "It was my own horse. I'm not a thief if I stole my own horse."

"If you say so." Following me, he reached for the saddle. "Here, let me take that."

"I've got it." I gripped my hand tighter on the cantle. "I'm fine." The saddle awkwardly bumped against my legs. Half tripping on my sodden skirts, I lugged the saddle back to the barn.

His words followed me. "Your father will be angry."

With the saddle under my arm, I barely managed the door. "Angry that I rode through the creek, or angry that I didn't ride sidesaddle?"

"Both."

"He won't find out," I said, putting the saddle away. Except for cracks of light between rough-hewn planks, the barn was dark. Everything was meticulously organized. Bridles, halters, and ropes lined the north wall, each on its own nail. A bin by the door housed brushes and curry combs. Jars of ointment were shelved to my left. The leather smell of the room was comforting.

"Sarah!" Joseph said urgently.

I wiped my hands on my skirts and ran out to the yard. "What's wrong?"

Joseph was intent on Beulah. He ran his hand down her hocks, squatted by her, and traced along her fetlock. He squinted up at me. "Did she walk through clay?"

"I took her through Possum Creek, of course she did." Grabbing my skirts in one hand, I crouched beside him.

Chunks of clay clung to her fetlocks, and her hooves were etched with gray.

He gave me a hard look. "Well, we better get her cleaned off before your father wakes up."

"You're right about that." I primed the pump outside the barn, filled a bucket with water, and drained the bucket on Beulah's back legs. We both scoured her as fast as we could.

The door bounced on its frame, the sound of it echoing across the yard.

"Your father," rasped Joseph, nodding toward the house.

"Father!" My throat was dry as cotton. On Father's best days I didn't want to disobey him, and today wasn't one of his best.

"Quick! Hide the bucket." Joseph grabbed the bucket from me and hurled it in the barn. Father's feet crunched toward us.

"Hurry!" I hastily tossed the cloth into the weeds.

"Sarah?" Father was yards away.

Joseph and I dashed in front of Beulah, our hands behind our backs, frozen in place.

Father rounded the barn. "What are you up to?" He cocked his head, demanding an answer from one of us.

"Grooming Beulah, sir," explained Joseph. I glanced at him, thankful for his quick response.

With a sharp look at me, Father circled Beulah. Then he crouched by her hooves. "Sarah. Where did this clay come from?" His voice was pinched. A ruby flush crept up his neck.

I knotted my fingers behind my back. "Why do you ask?"

"You went through the creek with her, didn't you?" Father scraped his thumbnail on Beulah's hoof. "Clay. Gray clay. That's Possum Creek clay." Standing up, he frowned, his eyes boring straight through me.

I searched for an explanation, but my mind went numb.

Joseph stepped forward. "D-Dr. Sutton, I'm the one who took Beulah. My father was working our horses and our cattle got out."

"He needed something to ride," I added. "And you were asleep. I didn't dare wake you."

Joseph and Father locked eyes.

Father weaved to the side. "Umm, well, if that's the case, just make sure you wake me up next time someone needs to *borrow* Beulah." He strode to the house. I waited for the slam of the door.

Joseph caught my eyes and smiled. He had stepped up for me. I flushed warm with relief and affection for Joseph.

"Sarah?" Joseph swiped off his kepi and knuckled it in front of him. "I wanted to t-tell you. . ." His jaw muscles worked. "Just that, well . . ." Then a slight change crossed his face.

I turned around to see Gabe walking down the hill toward us, his stride determined and long. Self-consciously, I smelled my hands. They smelled like horse.

"Hi, Sarah." His eyes were a shimmering green.

"Hi, Gabe." I wiped my hands on my skirts. My words stuck in my throat.

"You want to go for a walk?" I must have given him a blank stare. He gave me half a smile, motioning down the road. "Care to go for a walk?"

My eyes latched on our house. "A walk? I don't know, I . . ." My cheeks warmed. I thought of my Father. "I shouldn't."

"Just for a little while. I've already asked Mrs. Habernathy to chaperone." His voice was deeper than usual. Gabe looked toward Joseph. "All right if I steal her?"

Joseph's voice was quiet. "It's up to Sarah."

I didn't know what I wanted. I wasn't sure what to say. I looked back at the kitchen window. My father wouldn't know that I was gone. Besides, I was pretty sure that he was sleeping, or would be sleeping in a short time. I could count on the rhythm of his days. "I hope you don't mind," I finally said, pressing my lips together.

The two brothers stood there, arms folded, glaring at each other. Then Joseph backed up a step and nodded his head. "I'm going to stay here and put things away. Go ahead." He turned back to the barn.

The wind shifted and leaves tumbled across the road, as Gabe nodded toward his house. "I have something to show you."

"What's that?" I didn't know what to expect from Gabe. Was it another surprise?

He flashed me a crooked smile as we walked down the road. "You ever drive a wagon?" He shoved his hands in his pockets.

With one hand, I clasped my skirts against the wind and scrambled after him. "We have one, but I've never driven it." I glanced back at the house. Father was still inside.

"Well, today's like a day of harvest," he crowed. "First, I get to spend time with you, and second, I get to watch you handle a wagon!"

He made me feel important, as if his day had turned golden just because I was with him. "I think I'd like to watch you drive it first," I suggested. He flashed a winsome smile and my skin warmed.

We walked up the hill toward Mrs. Habernathy's. Oddly enough, she wasn't on her front porch waiting for us.

"Is she here?" I peered into her backyard.

"Nope." His mouth twisted in a smile.

"I thought you said—" I started. Maybe I had heard Gabe wrong. "I thought she was our chaperone."

"We'll be all right." His shoulders lifted, as if to dismiss her. "We won't be gone long."

Something stirred inside my stomach. His strides lengthened. My heart thumping, I tripped up beside him. I thought he glanced at me, but with the tilt of his kepi, I couldn't be sure.

"Just a short ride. We'll be back in no time." His chin jutted forward.

In a less than twenty minutes we were at the Elliott farm. A maple grove and overgrown hedges lined the huge property. Gray outbuildings surrounded the farmhouse. With its curtained windows and whitewashed siding, this home was a friendly contrast to mine.

I followed Gabe to the barn, my heart pounding in my chest. His hands were rough, strong, and confident as he hitched up his team of roans. Gabe was comfortable with the leather and the horses, and he was comfortable with me.

"All right." He turned to me. "Climb in the driver's seat."

"B-but I was going to watch you drive first."

He offered his hand. "What fun is that?"

I gathered my skirts, climbed on the seat, and tentatively grasped the lines. I didn't want to make a fool of myself. Not in front of Gabe.

He climbed up the other side and edged toward me, repositioning the lines in my hands. The tenderness of his fingers surprised me. "Go ahead," he encouraged. "If you chirrup at Hank and Herm, they'll start at a trot. I know you usually kick Beulah, but if you try kicking the wagon, you'll hurt your toes."

I smiled. "I could kick *you*."

"Yes, but I'd kick back harder." His lips hinted a smile. "Where are we going? Name it. Anywhere you like."

He chuckled and looked enticingly handsome with his wide smile, laugh lines, and strong chin. I redirected my gaze to the road, wondering if he could hear the thump of my heart. "Where would *you* like to go?"

His voice was low and smoky. "Doesn't really matter."

I gave him a sidelong glance. His eyes were such a deep green color, I could have studied them for miles.

There weren't many roads to choose from. We went straight west from the Elliotts' place. The woods were thicker and the country hillier. It was a different world entirely. Perhaps, though, it seemed different because I was with Gabe.

When we got to the first hill, I worried that we wouldn't make it to the top. I didn't have to encourage the horses, though; they clopped right up the hill.

"I'm impressed with Hank and Herm."

He smiled, "Me, too." He edged forward on the seat. "Our horses are triers."

"Triers?"

He leaned closer to me, the warmth of his skin surprising me. "Not the smartest or the fastest, but they're triers. They're good hearted. They don't give up. They're the kind of horses you want to have."

"I'm a trier." I loosened my grip on the team.

His smile lines deepened. "Smart and beautiful too."

I was flattered, but if I had to pick—being smart, being beautiful, or being a trier—I would choose being a trier first.

We spent the whole afternoon riding through the woods, just the two of us. Squirrels spiraled up oaks and chattered their way down. Sunlight teased through the branches, and tiny leaves filtered the sky with a greenish hue.

Every once in awhile Gabe glanced at me. Our eyes connected and he'd nod, sharing half a smile. Then he'd turn to the road and clear his throat. When he thought I wasn't looking, he'd glance at me again. "I'm always going to remember today," he said. "You and me in the woods."

"I'll never forget when you almost fell off the wagon," I teased.

He dropped his jaw in mock surprise. "Never came close!"

"Yes, you did!" I insisted, laughing. "When I jerked to a stop! I never laughed so hard in my life."

"Me, neither. But it would have been funnier if it happened to you."

I loved everything about him, but if I had to pick one physical attribute it would be his fetching smile or perhaps his broad shoulders. He was solid and unpredictable at the same time.

Back home, when he helped me down from the wagon, his hand lingered on mine.

7

Joseph

Our cow Peal was all udder and ribs, cantankerous, and prone to kicking, but she produced more than enough milk for our family. I smiled at the thought of Gabe milking her.

"I need a bucket." My mother waved me toward the door. I knew where I'd find a bucket. In the barn, with Gabe and Pearl.

Dodging between raindrops, I ran to the barn. The smell of moldy hay hit me when I slipped through the door. My plan was to grab the bucket and head straight for the house, but as soon as I entered, I knew I'd have to stay.

Gabe and Father were talking in low, hushed tones. I flattened myself against the wall. A thin lantern light cast a bronze glow against the rough plank walls. Father, milking Pearl, sat on his three-legged stool. Gabe, intent on Father's words, leaned against a stanchion.

Neither of them knew I was there.

"Have you noticed the tension?" I couldn't figure out what Father was talking about—maybe about Gabe and me.

"I have. Don't think Joseph has," answered Gabe. I ducked behind bales. If I was going to catch the gist of the conversation, I wasn't going to let either of them know I was there.

"North or South, which side's right?" asked Father.

"We are," Gabe's voice was clear and strong. I knew what they were talking about. The Southerners. Seemed to me that everyone was talking about them.

"If we don't do anything, there'll be nothing left of the Union," continued Father. "Seven states. Seven of them already seceded."

"Good thing we live in Indiana," answered Gabe.

"If there's war, Indiana boys will fight, too." Father's statement settled in the air.

"There's the question of slaves." Father moved within my vision, his hand reaching toward the lantern. His fingers were shaking. I could always count on his steadiness; the tremor in his hand surprised me.

My chest burned, my stomach knotted.

He took the lantern off the nail. "Those men are being auctioned off, sold away from their children." He turned toward Gabe. "Don't think we've heard the worst of it."

"So Gabe, would you fight?" asked Father.

Thunder cracked, and rain poured from the sky, pounding the roof and muffling the conversation. I took a deep breath, my pulse racing.

Their conversation continued. The rain battered the roof, and I caught pieces of their sentences. My mind leapt from one thought to another—the idea of leaving home, the thought of war. I was thankful for the distraction of a leaky ceiling.

"Wouldn't be easy for Mother." Rain drumming in a regular percussion, the last of Father's sentence was lost, and I was momentarily distracted by

The presidential election of 1860 proved to be one of the last straws for the South. Southerners believed that the Republican candidate, Abraham Lincoln, would forcibly end slavery, so they refused to support his bid for the presidency. Therefore, shortly after his election, Southern states began to secede from the Union.

the droplets that clung to the beams, unlatched their grip, and dropped to the floor.

Eyeing the ceiling, Gabe strategically nested a bucket between two small mounds of hay. "You ask me if I would fight?" He adjusted the pail. Then he looked my way, as if he knew that I was there. "There'd be nothin' holdin' me back," he said.

* * *

The next day I perched on the peak of our barn while Gabe worked below me, fitting the shingles. Clenching two nails between my teeth and pinching them with my lips, I took out a nail and tapped a shingle in place.

"So what's with you and Sarah?" Gabe's question seemed completely random.

"What d-do you mean?" I peered over our grove toward Sarah's house and tightened my grip on the hammer.

"Well, when you were younger you were bringin' her letters. Carvin' her initials." His eyes were laughing. "Now, seems like you're always mopin' about her."

"Not mopin'. Hammerin'." I pummeled a nail for emphasis. Seemed Gabe knew exactly what to say.

He followed my gaze. "By the looks of it, you're sweet on her."

Why couldn't he leave it go? The hammer slipped out of my hand, skittered down the roof, and landed on the ground.

"See what I mean?" Gabe shot me a look. "You can't even concentrate." He climbed down to retrieve the hammer. "So, you gonna get permission to court her? You actually think she *likes* you?" Even from that distance, I could see his eyes laugh.

"Just let it go." There were plenty of other things to talk about like fishing, riding—*shingling*. Why had he pinned the conversation on me?

Gabe paused on the bottom rung, shaking his head. "So," he said. "Question."

"Hmm?" I fitted another shingle.

He climbed up the ladder, stretching to hand me the hammer. "You heard the talk?"

"Talk of what?"

He plucked up a few stray nails. "You know. War."

I dragged shingles down the roofline. "You think it'll be soon?"

"Well, Joseph," his eyes were shining bright. "I think war's days away."

8

Sarah

INDIANAPOLIS, SPRING 1861

A moonlit escapade to McCartney's bridge would work if we all kept the secret. Even though at the age of seventeen, I was old enough to do as I pleased—in fact, I'd been old enough to do as I pleased for quite some time—I would have to avoid getting caught. I wanted time with Joseph and Gabe, because they would be leaving soon.

Gabe had asked me if I could join them for a horse race. I couldn't resist.

Any chance of winning might be lost if I wore skirts, so I pilfered Father's pants and shirt. The thought made me smile: not only had I stolen Father's horse, but I'd also taken the shirt off his back.

I waited for Father's breathing to slow. Then I slipped out of bed.

I knew every creaky board from the kitchen to the porch, so I engineered my footsteps to miss every one. The third floorboard from the door squeaked loudly under my foot. With a furtive glance toward Father's bedroom, I leaped over the threshold and slipped out the door.

The air smelled of lilacs. A gentle breeze lifted my hair. Quickly gathering it into a bun, I went to the barn.

Beulah nickered when she spotted me. She was as eager as I for the ride; she nosed right into her bridle. I left for McCartney's bridge, my heart pounding.

The meadow was pretty—perhaps the prettiest I'd seen. A sliver of moonlight waxed in the sky. In that light, the weeds were almost iridescent. A farmer's field bordered one side of the meadow and woods edged the other; the stars hung like shimmering lanterns in the sky. Both brothers waited for me by the bridge—Joseph on Hank and Gabe riding Herm.

Gabe stood up in his stirrups. "Hi, Sarah."

My throat went dry. "Perhaps we should—I don't know—ask permission." Gabe wasn't managing Herm very well, so I reined Beulah close to Hank.

"A little late for that." Gabe tugged at his reins, tightening his hold on Herm.

"True," I added, trying to quiet my conscience. "Besides, it's just a race among friends." I nodded at Joseph, and he replied with a shy smile.

Gabe's horse was prancing, sidestepping, and eager to run. "You ready to put your horse to the test?" He reined Herm's head to the right, putting a stop to the prancing.

"*You* ready?" I countered. I didn't want to appear overconfident, but I knew Herm and Hank were farm horses, best suited for a plow. Beulah had the heart

Herm and Hank, similar to the team of horses pictured above, were used on the Elliott farm. For centuries before the invention of the tractor, farmers depended on horses to help with pulling carts and plowing fields.

of a racer—her canter was smooth. Furthering my advantage, Joseph and Gabe had never seen Beulah run.

Joseph studied the meadow. "D-do you want to walk our horses through the route first? Just to make sure that there aren't any rabbit holes or anything?"

Gabe adjusted himself in the saddle, readjusting the reins in his hands. "If there's logs to jump or rabbit holes to dodge, the race will be more fun."

That's more like it. His sense of adventure mirrored mine.

Ears forward, eyes widening, our horses anticipated the race. Gabe reined in Herm's energy, tugging hard on his bit. He nodded at both of us. "Ready. Set. Go!"

The three of us were off to an awkward start. After Gabe's initial lead, I had the edge. He slipped a few feet behind me, leaned forward in his saddle, and whipped Herm with the tail of his reins. Obviously, he didn't want to lose to a girl.

I was winning, slightly, "Go, Beulah!" Just then Beulah stumbled over something. I lost my balance, my feet slipping out of the stirrups. Gabe took advantage of my mishap, and Herm's stride matched Beulah's.

My hair loosened from its fastenings and whipped about my face. Beulah huffed, her head bobbing, her gait lengthening, and her neck straining forward. I could hardly stay on. *Probably my last ride with the boys,* I thought. *I'm not going to lose.*

Gabe's eyes focused on the finish line, his mouth firmly set in a frown. Ol' Herm was slick with sweat—his legs fully extended, his nostrils flared. Gabe cracked his reins, and Herm ate up the ground.

I felt a lump in my throat. Tears blurred my eyes and the wind whipped my hair. I wanted to hold onto that moment. That memory of childhood racing away.

Beulah sensed my distraction and drifted toward the right. Hank muscled beside me, and Joseph's voice resonated above the pounding of hooves, "Y'haw!" Reins gathered in one hand and pommel grasped in the other, he leaned forward. Hank pulled ahead.

The finish line—the hickory trees edging the meadow—came into focus. It still was anyone's race.

Herm bobbed ahead, then Beulah, then Hank. I heeled into Beulah. "Come on!"

Neck and neck! Only a few yards left.

A blur of snorting noses and flying hair, we passed the hickories. I gathered up Beulah's reins and looked to each side. Unbelievable. A three-way tie.

"Well, how about that?" Gabe grinned. "We're all winners." He tugged on his reins, backing Herm away from the trees.

"Or all losers." I scratched Beulah under her mane.

Gabe's horse, prancing, followed the tree line toward me. "Can't have a three-way tie. Have to find some way to break it."

Of course, I thought. *He wouldn't be satisfied with a tie. He'd want a clear-cut win.*

"How're we going to do that?" My heart was beating fast, still in the race.

We worked our horses north, Gabe leading us through a network of bushes and stunted trees. "Maybe we could each do something. Maybe a trick with our horses. Best man wins." He smiled broadly at both of us.

"Or woman," I added, smiling too.

"Yes, or woman." Gabe reined Herm away from the bushes.

Nudging Hank's hindquarters, Joseph pulled up beside his brother. "So what trick will you do?"

Gabe sat back on his saddle. "Whoa." He turned toward me. "Think I might hop on the saddle."

I nudged Beulah, and she trotted up beside Gabe. "Anyone can do that!"

"From behind? Jumpin' over his hindquarters?" Gabe patted Herm's neck. Evidently, he had thought through his plan.

A potentially impressive trick. "You can do that?"

Gabe winked at me. "Just watch." He turned to Joseph, daring him to match his challenge. "And what're you going to do for your trick? Stay on your saddle?"

Joseph didn't say anything, and I didn't expect him to. He glanced at me. Then he fixed his gaze on his reins.

Gabe tilted his head toward me. His voice was soft. "How about you, Sarah?"

I wrestled with several plans, but none of them equaled Gabe's. Then it came to me, "I can stand on my saddle!" I was rather pleased with my idea, thinking I might win.

"Anyone can do that." Gabe shifted his weight on the saddle. "Maybe on one foot?"

"I-I'll try." Standing on my saddle with only one foot was something I had never accomplished before, but a stunt I could try.

Joseph looked from Gabe to me. "Who first?"

"I can." Gabe swung his leg over his horse. With his left hand on the pommel and right hand on the cantle, he leaped to the ground. I couldn't wait to see the feat; I knew he would be magnificent.

Backing up to a few feet behind his horse, Gabe ran ahead and gripped his hands firmly on Herm's hindquarters, launching himself forward. As easily as in a game of leapfrog, he split his legs and landed squarely in the middle of the saddle. He adjusted himself in the saddle. "Not bad, eh?" Although it was dark outside, I saw the flash of his white teeth. "Your turn, Joseph."

"I'll go," I offered. "I'm ready." I wasn't really ready, but I wanted my trick behind me.

Gabe sat back on his saddle. "Go right ahead."

Needing some distance from the boys, I reined my horse toward a lone maple; the tree could serve as a prop if I needed it.

To make sure I had enough room to stand, I judged the distance between my saddle and the lowest branches. I slipped my feet out of the stirrups and awkwardly put one knee on the saddle, then the other, wedging both feet underneath me. Then balancing on my haunches I stood up, holding both arms out to steady myself. I nodded at Joseph and Gabe, and both of them grinned.

I centered my right foot on the saddle and lifted my other foot.

Then everything went to pieces.

Beulah trotted forward. I fought to stay on, but I couldn't manage. My feet peddled backward on Beulah's rump. My arms drew circles in the air, and I reached for a branch, nabbing it just in time. A tentative hold, but I was losing my grip. The distance to the ground was farther than I thought.

"H-h-help!" I sputtered, fighting for a better hold. Just then I heard horse hooves behind me and felt hands encircling my waist, pulling me down. I glanced back. Joseph had rescued me.

With one arm, Joseph lowered me gently to the ground. After I felt earth under my feet, I looked up. Hank bobbed his head, as if he knew he'd done some feat. Joseph's eyes sparkled. "It looks like Hank's pretty proud of himself."

I bit my lip, appreciating my rescue.

Beulah had no idea that she had done anything wrong. Without a care in the world, she happily chomped grass ten feet from the tree.

I smiled at Joseph. "I think you won."

After a glance at Gabe, he grinned at me. "I guess I did."

9

Joseph

INDIANAPOLIS, APRIL 1861

Funny, how one moment Gabe and I ate at the table, elbowing for more potatoes and peas, and the next moment our whole world shifted. It started with the arrival of a visitor one April evening.

"Who's knocking at this hour?" Father pushed back from the supper table, and someone banged at the door again.

Mother waved toward the door. "Joseph, will you get that?"

I slid out from the bench and lifted the latch. Our neighbor, Mr. McCartney, stood in the doorframe, huffing for air.

"Mr. McCartney, what's wrong?" I asked.

His face was the color of turnips. Gasping, he knuckled his hands on his knees. "Just heard news. In town." His breathing was ragged. He must have run all the way. He looked up at me, his eyes fastening on mine. "It's war."

"W-what?" I turned back to look at Father. The color had drained from his face.

"Those bloody traitors," Mr. McCartney continued.

My father stood up. "What happened?"

"Fort Sumter. Those Rebels. They attacked Fort Sumter."

* * *

In the next weeks, the war invaded our lives. No one talked of much else. Whenever I went out to the livery or the mercantile, the conversations were all the same: rebel aggression, munitions gathering, troop organization.

I needed to talk to Gabe. "Let's go hunting, Gabe," I said, grabbing my bow and quiver. He nodded vaguely. I thought he'd had enough, too.

He marched down the road ahead of me. The closer we got to White River, the thicker the trees. He pivoted toward me. "Did you hear about Leander? He signed up with the Ninth." He pressed forward, giving me a glance over his shoulder. "Think I'll sign up too."

I could hear the river rushing as we prepared to leave the road and work our way through the weeds and down the embankment to our favorite hunting grounds.

"Come on. We're *hunting*." I stopped short. "The war will be over in months."

"That's what they say." Gabe was strides ahead of me. Suddenly he cut to the other side of the road. "Hey! Look at this, Joe!"

I trotted after him.

"A sign. Read this." I couldn't label the tone in Gabe's voice.

In this great emergency our government wants men. Men with stout hands and willing hearts. Men who will fight manfully for our just and holy cause.

He turned to me, smiling broadly. "A recruitment sign. Our chance."

I leaned my bow on the tree, the letters swimming in front of my eyes. "I'm not even 18."

"Don't matter." He bent down, squinting at the fine print.

I took an arrow out of my quiver and toyed with the feathers. "They won't let me join. Gotta be 18."

He twisted back to me. "Just write the number 18 on a piece of paper and slip it in your shoe."

"What do you mean?" I asked.

"Geesh." Gabe plucked up my bow. His next words came out slow, like he was speaking to a child. "You put it in your shoe. When they ask you if you're over 18, you say 'yes, I'm over 18.'"

I didn't need advice—especially advice that might land me in battle. "I-I think we ought to wait. Mr. McCartney said . . ."

"Don't care what he said. If we wait, it'll be done. We'll miss it. Joseph, this is our chance. It's our chance to . . . see something." I could almost see the world in Gabe's eyes. He tossed his bow over his shoulder and hiked ahead of me. "Just think! We'll go to faraway places. It'll be such a change!" I caught up to him. He wheeled toward me, his eyes glinting with fire. "We'll ride railroads, meet generals . . ."

"B-but," I stammered.

"Joseph." He stopped. "I don't need to shoot anyone. I just want to be there."

ANOTHER CHANCE!

400 DOLLARS **BOUNTY.**

TO AVOID THE DRAFT

ENLIST IN THE

7th IND. CAVALRY

This Regiment has been recently authorized by the Secretary of War, and is to be commanded by

J. P. C. SHANKS,

An able, efficient and experienced officer, having served on the Staff of Major General Fremont, during his Campaign in Missouri and Western Virginia.

$100 BOUNTY TO ALL INEXPERIENCED RECRUITS.

$400 to "Veteran Volunteers" who have served nine months or more in the United States Service and were honorably discharged. $25 of which, and one months' pay, will be Paid in Advance, on the Muster-in of the Regiment.

Recruiting Office, at_____

Or HAMLIN & PROTZMAN'S Office, Indianapolis, Ind. (No. 16 East Washington Street.)

LIEUT. S. M. LAKE,

Recruiting Officer for 7th Ind. Cavalry.

During the Civil War recruitment posters such as this were plastered all over the country, both in the North and the South.

I searched for something to say—something that would show that I understood, that I was in it, too.

"So?" The corner of his mouth twisted. "Are you in?"

"What if we joined the same company?"

His face soured. "What kind of adventure is that? I'd never get away from home."

I stood there stunned, not knowing what to say.

"Joseph." He jabbed me in the arm, "I'm teasing. They'll prob'ly put us in the same company. Don't worry. We'll smell gunpowder soon enough."

That's what I was afraid of.

10

Sarah

INDIANAPOLIS, FALL 1861

Weeds wrecked the order of my well-tended garden. Only a few nasty weeds dared poke their heads above the soil. Their fate? A vicious attack from my hoe. The last thing I wanted was an undisciplined garden. I broke up the clumpy soil, breathing deeply of the earthy smell, the promise of harvest.

The weeds of war were not as easily eradicated. My garden was my refuge. Nestled between the lilac hedge and our stable, my plot had the full benefit of the afternoon sun. I peered past our house. There must have been a town meeting; carriages and wagons had lumbered past our house all day. The garden work kept my mind focused on something positive and productive.

My garden was exquisite this year—a rainbow of color. The yellow and orange squash, pumpkins, and corn all clustered together in one area. The dark purplish eggplant resided in the northwest corner, and the green cucumbers, beans, peas, and herbs in another. The blues and pinks of the evening sky completed my garden's palette.

Sweeping a loose hair from my forehead, I paused to admire my work. A figure strode toward me from the cup of the valley, close to Mrs. Habernathy's house. At that distance, I wasn't sure who it was. Joseph? Gabe? I smoothed down my skirts.

He closed the gap, and I recognized Joseph, the leaner of the two. Joseph walked closer, hesitating at the edge of my garden. "Impressive. You've arranged your plants by color."

His eyes flicked across my garden. "You could alphabetize your plants instead."

"Far too easy!" My heart skipped a beat, and I squinted at my plot. "Actually, I have other plans for my garden."

"What do you mean?" He edged a dirt clod with his foot.

I waved toward the corner of the plot. "Herbs in the shade of tomato plants. Potatoes in the corner over there. Sandier soil."

Joseph nodded and glanced at the house. "D-do I need your father's permission to talk to you?"

I hadn't thought about my father. "He's helping the Mulvanys, I think. He took Beulah."

"I can come back later," suggested Joseph. I read something in his eyes, like maybe he understood.

I hacked an imaginary weed. "No, I mean, yes. I mean . . . you're only going to be a few minutes, right?"

"Well, I was hoping I could talk to you. There's something important." Joseph gently pried the hoe out of my fingers. "I want to show you something."

"What is it?" I tucked my hands behind my back.

"Oh, something." Joseph carried my hoe to the shed and closed the door. Smiling shyly, he started down the road and motioned for me to follow him. I didn't know where he was leading me, but I was curious.

We passed cattle, their pink noses buried in clover. A calf bellowed and pranced to its mother. We crossed the McCartney's stone bridge, the creek glistening silver. When we walked through the hollows, that's when I knew we were on our way to Hardin's Pond. I swatted a mosquito and questioned the wisdom of an evening visit to the pond.

The asters and black-eyed Susans nodded a welcome in flashes of purple and gold. The willows bowed their greeting, and the pond, silent and shimmering, had an expectant air.

My shoes sunk into mushy ground; I excavated one foot, then the other. The mud clung halfway up my shoes. Another mosquito, but this one drew blood. I slapped it and sighed. Was Joseph going to say something? Anything?

His eyes were tinged with something I couldn't describe. Sadness, maybe. Worry.

"I want to show you something." Slowly, he unfolded his hand. In the hollow he held five stones, flawlessly flat and perfectly round. I'm not sure what I anticipated, but I didn't expect stones. The stones gave me pause. "Are you expecting a giant?" I asked.

He shook his head slowly to ward off some thought.

The pond seemed unsettled with our presence, and the reflection of the oak distorted—a blurred vision of grasping fingers. Chilled, I tightened my arm around myself.

Joseph's eyes narrowed. "You're not scared of the water, are you?"

"It's fine," I lied. "I mean . . . I'm fine." I expected demons from the pond's depths to rise and accuse "Liar!" The demons knew.

A weak smile. I could feign joy. Even there.

Joseph crouched down. With a quick check to see if I was watching, he tossed one of his stones across the pond. His stone skipped cheerfully, finally ducking underneath the surface.

"Six times!" I said, clapping, no longer pretending to be happy.

Joseph stood up to full height, his face solemn. He selected a small speckled stone and gave it to me. I flung it across the shimmering pool. Without a single skip, the water swallowed my stone.

"Murderer!" Joseph shook his head, hiding a smile. "You need more patience."

"And technique," I added, watching the ripples race back to shore.

Joseph glanced sideways at me, rolled the stone around in his fingers, adjusting it in his hand. With one smooth motion he tossed it parallel to the pond's surface. His rock skipped seven times before dipping beneath the water.

My skin warming, I put my fingers over my mouth.

Joseph turned to me and grinned. Then a cloud crossed his face. "I have to tell you something."

"That I'm no good at skipping stones?" I rolled back on my heels.

"N-not that." Joseph slipped another stone from his pocket and toyed with it in his hand. "It's just that I'll be leaving in a few months. I'm serving in Lincoln's War."

The demons slid out of the pond. Their clawed fingers crept toward me, their icy breath sifting through me. My fingers felt frozen. "No! Gabe? Is Gabe going too?"

Joseph didn't have to say anything. I knew. *Please let them stay, let both of them stay*, I pleaded silently.

For a while we gazed at the pond watching the water lap at the shore. I struggled for something cheerful to say, but only thought about how lonely I would be. How selfish was I? I was more worried for myself than I was for Joseph and Gabe.

Joseph picked up a stone from the ground. He examined it carefully, then squatted and let that one spin through the air.

I stood there and watched it go.

My words simmered inside, begging to cry out. Finally, I said, "I don't want you to leave. I don't want either of you to go."

"I d-don't think that we have much of a choice." Joseph looked past me.

I drew a breath. "If you had a choice, what would you do?"

Joseph hesitated. I waited for him to say something. Anything.

11

Joseph

INDIANAPOLIS TO LOUISVILLE,
DECEMBER 1861—FEBRUARY 15, 1862

We were called up and had only a week to get ready. I wanted time for Sarah. Father, though, had other plans for us. He had two sons at home and there was work to do, a new outbuilding being his highest priority.

"The McCartneys tore down their old shed and I need your help," he said.

"It's December!" Gabe faked a shiver.

"Doesn't matter if it's twenty degrees below zero. I've got some of their boards. They're chock full of nails." Father motioned to the wagon standing next to the barn, piled high with gray boards. "Need the nails pulled out." He handed each of us a hammer.

Gabe leaned into me. "Got our work cut out for us. Looks like neither of us will have time to see Sarah."

"Seven days," he muttered as soon as Father left for the barn. "We only have seven days of work like this, and then we'll be free."

Going to war wasn't freedom, but Gabe's perception didn't surprise me. I didn't respond. Instead, I glanced toward Sarah's house. Then I got back to work.

Days later, Father was hitching the wagon, and I eyed the road to Sarah's house. Her willowy form surfaced at the top of the hill. Snow, displaced by her footsteps, puffed around her as she walked toward us.

"Sarah?" I trotted up the road to meet her.

Her skirts swirling around her, she quickened her pace. I ran to close the gap.

Her dark woolen cape, a stark contrast to the fields, shimmered in the sunlight. "You're leaving today," she said when she got within hearing distance. Her cheeks flushed red.

"We'll be on our way to Kentucky. Training camp." I didn't mean to sound like I was bragging.

She gave me a basket. "I brought something for both of you." Rolling up on her toes, she peered over my shoulder. I guessed she was looking for Gabe.

Ignoring the lump in my throat, I focused instead on Sarah. "Bread?" I lifted the muslin. The loaf, steaming warm, smelled of molasses.

"For Gabe, too. You're both leaving today, right?" She edged to the right, putting our front door in her direct line of vision.

Just then our door slammed shut. Someone—I was sure it was Gabe—ran up behind me. Sarah stood stiffly, giving him a shy smile.

He tripped up beside me. "Sarah." His voice sounded different somehow.

She tucked her hands behind her, her eyes flickering from Gabe to me. "I don't want you to leave."

Gabe dusted the snow off his pants. "War'll be over in a matter of months."

I had a hard time believing that. Seemed like everyone had been worked up for such a long time, it would take a long while for them to simmer down.

"Boys." Father's voice rang from the yard. "Let's go."

"We better . . ." I started.

Gabe held up his arms, as if to say "What did you expect?" He leaned toward Sarah and whispered something. I thought I heard, "Wish we had more time."

Maybe I heard my own thoughts.

"Gabe! Joseph!" Father's voice was sharp. "Today?"

I memorized her face—the flyaway hair, the tentative smile.

She escorted us to the wagon. Mother was already seated in front, her hands hidden in her lap and a woolen blanket tucked around her feet. Father, seated beside her, held the lines in one hand. "Hello, Sarah."

"Mr. Elliott," she answered, but her eyes remained on us.

Gabe and I climbed into the wagon bed. The axle groaned as the wagon jolted forward, and Sarah disappeared behind the trees.

"Should've taken the sleigh." Father took off his cap and brushed off the flakes. I caught our folks exchanging a look. This would be our last journey as a family, at least for a while.

Mother twisted toward Gabe; her eyes were rimmed dark red.

Gabe gave her an encouraging smile. "It's all right. We'll be fine."

She squeezed his hand. "You two watch out for each other." Her eyes were still focused on Gabe. I tried to catch her eye.

Lifting his chin, Gabe glanced at me. "Joseph won't have to watch out for me, but I'll be watchin' after him."

Mother's voice was raw. "Well, just stay out of harm's way."

"Stay out of harm's way?" Gabe nudged me. "How're we supposed to do that?"

We were off to face the Rebs; we might never come home. She turned my way and mouthed the words, "You watch out for him anyway."

It was my chance to say good-bye, but the words caught in my throat.

* * *

The pungent smell of coal signaled our entrance to the depot; the area consisted of one small whitewashed building and three round bins for coal. A water tower squatted in the corner just to my left. Dozens of people crowded the platform. Children wrenched free of parents, ladies waved handkerchiefs, and a red-faced tuba player blared out "Happy Land of Canaan."

All our families cheered.

I gave Gabe a sideways glance. He was on the balls of his feet, peering above the soldiers in front of him.

We were packed like apples in a crate. Some soldiers were as old as my father, gray-haired and bearded. Others, their chests pressed forward, looked like schoolboys in uniform.

Gabe peered back at Mother and flashed a grin. He leaned toward me. "Think she's going to miss us?"

"Probably." I couldn't say much more. My throat was tight, and my mouth tasted of acid. "Yes, mother will miss us."

He looked at me hard. "No, I mean Sarah. You think she's going to miss us?"

His question took me off guard; I didn't realize that Sarah was topmost on his mind. I shifted the conversation. "What's takin' so long?"

Gabe nodded toward the back of the train. "They're still loadin' cars with supplies. You know, half tents, blankets." I stood on my toes, trying to see beyond the man in front of me; he had grimy, licorice-colored hair and smelled of lard.

"Not long now," continued Gabe, giving me a half smile. "Ready?"

My stomach lurched. Nothing about me was ready.

"Company D!" an officer called. I peered back for a last look at Father, the platform blurring with faces and flags.

"That's ours." Gabe edged forward. "Let's go!" He inched ahead of me. Then the tuba pumped out some song I didn't even know, and we sifted into the train.

The car was dark, crowded, and stifling. Gabe and I elbowed for a spot by the door.

Groaning, the train slowly picked up speed, its wheels clickity-clacking in steady rhythm. We passed a stone bridge that reminded me of home—then cornfields, farm houses, fences, and streams.

I thought about Sarah. There wasn't a "we" in Sarah and me. I had to remember that. If she was going to care about me, I had to be twice the soldier Gabe was. I clutched the door frame and leaned out to get air.

"You all right?" Gabe leaned out too.

"I'm fine," I lied. I didn't want to meet his eyes.

Our train halted. Off balance, I adjusted my grip.

"A town." Gabe motioned ahead. A half-dozen clapboard houses crouched in the valley below. The depot must have been the hub of the town. Seemed to me that the whole town was there—a flurry of white-lace handkerchiefs dotted the air. "They're expecting us." He braced himself on the door.

The brakes squealed, and the train slowed. Suddenly, Gabe yelled, "Time to kiss the ladies, boys!" Legs trundling the air, he launched himself off the coach and pounced onto the decking below. He looked up at me and smiled.

"Gabe!"

Ignoring me, he scanned the crowd and fixed his eyes on a young lady. She was wearing an emerald dress. He rammed through the crowd, reached her, and hollered up to me, "Hey, Joseph!" He interrupted her gasp, covering her mouth with his.

Someone's elbow jarred me in the ribs. "See that? He's bussin' her!"

The lady looked shocked at first, but a smile played on her lips as she pushed Gabe away. She placed her gloved hand on her mouth.

Pivoting toward me, he threw back his shoulders and waved.

The train jerked forward. "Come on, Gabe!" I rooted my feet to the floor.

Pushing through the crowd, bounding over tumbling crates and nail kegs, he leaped back into our car. "Close one!" He cupped his hands on his knees and gasped for breath. "Made it."

Stuck with the image of the emerald dress, I waited for his breath to slow. "D-don't you care for Sarah?"

"'Course I do," Gabe answered, between ragged breaths. "That lady wanted to . . . uh . . . give me her respects."

"Respects," I echoed. I had only one rival in *this* rebellion, and he didn't love Sarah—at least not the way I did.

Our boxcar door grated shut. I barely heard a muffled voice from the other side. "If you can't stay put, we'll *make* you stay put!" I checked for Gabe's reaction.

His grin widened. "Don't think he appreciated my patriotic display."

I guess that made two of us.

* * *

The training camp at Bardstown, Kentucky, seemed like the other side of the world. It was treeless and definitely not home. When I walked through the gate and past the guardhouse, my legs turned to jelly. I wasn't a soldier. At least not yet. I was scared and didn't know what we had gotten ourselves into.

"Not going to be easy here," said Gabe. "Think you're going to make it?"

"D-don't I have to?" I stammered.

"Depends. Depends if you're cut out to be a soldier or not." With his chin held high, the guards could have mistaken him for an officer. "There's our new home." He nodded toward the training grounds, just past some rows of tents. A newly built compound stood to our right.

We entered, the smell of green lumber greeting me. I'd never slept far from the ground and chose the bottom bunk. No sooner had I staked my claim than our order came to get our new uniforms. "Everybody out! Lively, now."

"We'll see if they can make you look like a soldier." Gabe threw me a stabbing glance and marched out the door.

At the edge of the grounds our quartermaster and his assistant stood behind tables stacked with shoes, pants, and jackets. The assistant, a small, scrappy fellow with a large hooked nose and proud cleft chin, plucked a jacket from a pile and shoved it in my hands. His shrill voice made heads turn. "By the looooks of it, this jacket oughta fit your scrawwwwny frame." I glanced around to see if anyone else heard.

When I tried on the jacket, I lost a button and when I bent to pick it up, another popped off. Gabe tugged at my high-water sleeves. "You look like a schoolboy."

Next, the pants—the pants of a Goliath. I rolled up the legs. When I walked, my pants slipped down, and I clutched at the legs to keep them up.

Gabe found me some twine. "Here, tighten this around your waist." I cinched my waist and knotted the twine.

"Better find someone to trade," he hissed. "If you don't, everyone will think you're wearing your father's clothes."

Once we were dressed like soldiers, we lined up on the field. Gabe, always in step, had marching down to the ground.

Me? I was hopeless. Thank God, I wasn't the only soldier without marching skills.

"Stop right where you are!" Our sergeant's voice cracked from the front of the field. "You're a bunch of apple-shakers! Every one of you!"

His paunch belly, overbite, and beady eyes gave him the appearance of a rodent. He rocked forward on his toes. "Don't you know left from right? If you can't march, how the *hell* will you fight?" His eyes scanned across all of us. I wanted to run for home. Instead, he turned on his heels and left us staring at our feet.

I tried to convince myself that things couldn't get worse, that in a few days we would parade in perfect lines, but the second day was miserable.

Piles of hay and straw confronted us when we entered the grounds. "Straw. What's that for?" I asked.

We filed in line. Gabe motioned to our left. "Look there. Twine, too."

Our captain shouted something that put everyone in action. Gabe passed the twine to me. "Tie the hay around your left foot," he hissed. "Didn't you hear the captain? Straw around your right."

"Those orders d-don't even make sense." I fumbled with the twine, tying my left foot in hay.

"Dress the line!" Captain's bark interrupted us. Like scarecrows with misplaced stuffing, we shuffled into place. "Hay foot! Straw foot!" The Captain's voice pierced across the field. "Hay foot! Straw foot!" Soon the ground was littered with hay and straw. "He knows the trick for farmers," someone said behind me. We marched forward in an embarrassing line. "Hay foot! Straw foot!" I skipped into step.

"You're not cut out to be a soldier." Gabe marched forward in perfect parade. "You can't even get your feet right."

Hay and straw was the day's first insult, and, unfortunately, the day wasn't over. A team of workhorses—both muscular and midnight black—pulled up on the grounds, hauling a loaded wagon behind them.

Gabe was up on his toes. "What's that?"

I wasn't sure. "Looks like firewood."

"No, maybe kindling or something," he said. "Broomsticks," he added when we passed the sticks down the line. "Guess they didn't have enough guns to go around." Gabe turned to me and shouldered his broomstick.

"If we don't have practice, how are we going to. . . " I started.

"Dress the line!" the captain ordered, striding down the row.

We scuttled into place. "Not like you haven't used a broomstick before," rasped Gabe, checking himself against the rest of the line.

"Will we ever get to do anything but practice?" I asked.

Gabe replied, "Soon enough."

* * *

Two months later our guns were issued. We didn't have much time to learn how to use them, because we had marching orders—it was time to face the Rebs.

"It'll be easy." Gabe stuffed his ammunition into his bag. "Tear open the bottom of the cartridge, pour in the gunpowder, and ram a bullet into the barrel."

I wiped my hands on my pants. I wasn't ready. Not near.

Given three days' rations of salt pork and hardtack plus sixty rounds of ammunition, I packed, unpacked, and repacked my haversack with everything

BATTLES AND LEADERS OF THE CIVIL WAR, 4 VOLS. (NEW YORK: CENTURY COMPANY, 1887–88), 1.84.

Many of the young soldiers had no prior experience with military procedures. They had to be trained and equipped before they could march off to fight the enemy. Although country boys such as Joseph and Gabe knew how to fire a gun, city boys knew very little about weaponry.

I needed: blanket, canteen, Green River knife, and hemp twine. Then I packed something I didn't need—paper for writing Sarah.

Gabe motioned me toward the gate. "Big day! Time to face the Rebs." Dressed in Union blue, soldiers filed in rows. "Expect our practicin' and drillin' will be put to good use," he added.

I grabbed my sack and gun and joined him. With canteens clanging in time with our step, and our line bunching and stretching like a blacksmith's bellows, we marched forward. I peered over the heads in front of me. "Can you see where we're headed?"

We funneled through the front gate. "My guess is south." His lips curled in a smile.

Soon enough we were marching four wide with uniforms as crisp as sandpaper. A gambler could have predicted I wouldn't find the right step.

"Hay foot!" Gabe rasped. The soldier next to him grinned.

The road wound through pines, then down into a valley, the trees thinning. I could barely see the front of our line—it was maybe a mile ahead. We switched to route step, and the men in front of us slowed down to a snail's pace.

"Think we'll see some Rebs?" asked someone behind us. I tightened my grip on my gun.

"That's what we're lookin' for. Gonna find some?" Gabe gave me a smug look.

From that point on, I scoured the pines. A rabbit zigzagged through the forest floor, turning my knees to liquid.

"Don't worry," said Gabe. "You're not going to be a vulture's treat. Not any time soon."

His consolation didn't help. I couldn't keep my eyes off the trees.

The line balled up. "Looks like it is time for lunch." Gabe dug in his bag. The soldiers around us rummaged through their bags, too.

I was thankful. If Gabe was eating, he couldn't talk about the Rebs.

I bit into the hardtack, so hard I nearly cracked a tooth. Gabe chomped through two days of rations. "Why are you savin' yours?"

I gave him the practical answer. "Aren't three-days' rations supposed to last three days?"

Dousing his cracker in water, he jawed another bite. "Better eat it now, or it'll be full of worms." He nudged the soldier beside him. "Right?" That soldier, his mouth full of crackers, nodded.

"Just tryin' to keep what I've got." I jammed the rest of my hardtack in my bag.

Gabe pitched his last bite into the woods. "Anything else you're tryin' to keep to yourself?" he said, giving me a knowing look. He dusted his pants and stood up.

Thankfully, he didn't finish his line of questioning. The sky darkened, and large plops of rain spotted the dirt. Then the heavens opened up. Soon we were slogging down the road through ankle-deep mud, our whole troop a noisy chorus of squishing.

Gabe crushed through the mud. "Perfect loblolly." Under the brim of his cap, I saw the white of his smile.

I couldn't march on dry ground, much less in the mud. My feet slid sideways. The heels of my shoes flapped and soon came off completely. The cuffs of my pants dragged, weighed down with mud.

That night we took turns replacing stakes or sopping up the tent. I longed for home. As difficult as soldiering was, I stayed hopeful, remembering Sarah's words at Hardin's pond:

I don't want you to leave.

In the early morning hours, when Gabe's breathing steadied, I took paper out of my sack and wrote her a letter.

COOPER HEWITT, SMITHSONIAN DESIGN MUSEUM / ART RESOURCE, NY

As the Union and Confederacy prepared for war, thousands of young men volunteered for service. In the 1860s, although railroads were becoming a common means of transport, marching for miles was still standard practice for soldiers.

February 15, 1862

Dear Sarah,

We had a miserable day. The rain came down in torrents, and I think I had mud up to my ears. We couldn't even hear birds sing.

Gabe and I share our half tent. I wonder why we even bothered setting it up. It's wobbly and leaks like a sieve.

Seven contrabands came to our picket post in the night. We fed them on crackers and sent them on their way. I didn't get a chance to see them, but our guards haven't stopped talking about it. I didn't know at the start of the rebellion what we were really fighting for. Now I know.

There are so many things I wish I had said when we were together. I never had the courage to tell you how much I care about you, but I think I do now. Please don't forget me.

Yours,
Joseph

I pictured Sarah asleep in her home, her hair tangled around her head. Did she ever think about me?

12

Sarah

INDIANAPOLIS, MARCH 1862

The town seemed hollowed out. Empty. A number of young men had left for war, and nearly a year after the war began only a few had returned. I missed Joseph and Gabe.

That particular day I had been tugging out stalks from my garden, and although Father was home, I hadn't seen him all afternoon. With a prickling suspicion, I walked into our house. Father's back was turned to me. His carpet-bag and clothing were laid out in neat piles.

I coughed. He twisted toward me with a silent stare.

"Are you packing? Are you leaving?" I asked, my hands turning cold.

"Been packing all afternoon. Already got the wagon hitched." He stiffly waved toward a letter on the chiffonier. "Read for yourself."

> *STATE OF INDIANA*
> *Executive Department*
> *Indianapolis, Ind. February 2, 1862*
> *Wm. T. Sutton of Marion County, State of Indiana, is hereby appointed a Special Surgeon to visit the Army of the Ohio and will report to the Medical Director.*
>
> *BY THE GOVERNOR*
> *O.P. Morton*

"I'm serving with the Seventh Artillery." He wedged his shaving kit into his carpet bag. "They're in Tennessee or Kentucky right now. The regiment's desperate for doctors."

I didn't say a word. I couldn't. Swallowing hard, I strode to the closet and rummaged for my carpetbag.

Father whipped around. "What're you doing?"

"I'm assuming that I'm going with you." I kept searching for my bag.

His voice was tight. "Women don't serve."

Finding my bag, I flung it down on the bed. I marched to the desk, drew out a newspaper, and spread it on the quilt. Tapping my finger on an article, I read, "No woman under thirty years need apply to serve in government hospitals. All nurses are required to be plain-looking. Their dresses must be brown or black, with no bows, curls, jewelry, or hoop skirts." I gave him a pointed glare. "You see? Women may serve."

Father shot me a glance and returned to his packing. "You're under thirty. You're not plain."

I drew a breath. "Is my dedication to the cause less than yours?"

"Dedication's not what's at issue," he countered. "You can't come along." By the tone of his voice, his position was set. He hadn't even considered me.

Father strode to the medicine shelf. "Mercurous chloride, oil of turpentine, copper sulfate . . ." He opened his medicine kit and fitted each bottle inside. Then he went to the kitchen cupboard, removed his bottle of whisky, and

Sarah and her father were about to face disease, unsanitary conditions, and horrific injuries. Although medicine at the time of the Civil War was far from the standards we have today, doctors and nurses played an active role in the war. Nurses, like the one in this drawing, provided comfort to the dying.

tightened the cap with the palm of his hand. He tucked the bottle in his bag. Giving a last look at the room, he walked out the door.

In a burst of energy, I packed my shoe hook, calico blouses, dark skirts, and petticoats. I was determined to go with Father. Bag in hand, I left for the barn.

I lugged my bag over the side of the wagon. "I need to go. I'd be in more danger left alone here. And if you had me along, you wouldn't need to train an assistant." Then in a flash of inspiration I knew what to say to sway his decision. "Besides," I paused for emphasis, "how would it look to the *community* if I was left alone?"

He looked me square in the eyes. I couldn't read what I saw there—maybe anger, maybe disappointment. He sighed. At that moment, I knew that I had won.

Beulah nosed against her collar, and we moved forward with a jerk. I gripped my hands together on my lap and sat back. I had no idea what I was getting myself into, but I couldn't stay at home. Not if I was going to make a difference. Not if I was going to help our cause.

Stately oaks lined the road like sentries, saluting us as we rode past. I caught momentary flashes of a sweeping valley, a brick farmhouse, pasturing cattle, and apple trees. My throat tightened; I had left my home behind.

13

Joseph

I was no soldier. I couldn't keep up. My shoes fell apart, the sides, tongue, and soles separating. My feet numb with cold, I couldn't keep the pace.

Gabe motioned toward my feet. "We won't be able to keep up. Not with those . . . uh . . . boats." He tugged me out of line. Our troop sloshed forward, and I stopped to retie my shoes.

Snow-flocked trees surrounded us on both sides. With drooping boughs, the trees smelled of wet pine. Swatches of movement flicked between the trees.

"You d-don't think there're savages here?" I squinted between the branches.

"Could be." Gabe set down his gun, leaning it against his leg.

Colors shifted. My voice cracked. "Rebs?"

"Maybe." He rubbed his hands together and tucked them under his arms. "Cold, eh?" he asked, his words huffing in blue clouds.

I saw a flash of color beside me, my mouth going dry as linen.

A soldier, wearing a slouch cap tilted over generous ears, approached us, his grin dominating half of his face. "O'Farrell here." Then eyeing my shoes, he said, "See you got trouble." He was a beanpole: spindly, gangly, all legs.

"I do have trouble." Gabe's eyes shifted toward me. "His name's Joseph."

I coughed and set to work on my other shoe.

Gabe grabbed his gun by the barrel, saddling it on his shoulder. He peered down the road, "Don't see the rest of our company, Joseph. Would you hurry?"

My numb fingers tugged at the twine and gave a furtive glance toward the woods.

"Joseph, hurry." Gabe nudged me with his foot.

Hopeful for sympathy, I looked up for O'Farrell, but he was gone. Just like that, he was gone. "Where'd he go?"

"Should've snubbed him to a tree like a mule." Gathering his sack, Gabe swung it over his shoulder and peered in the woods. "Can't be far. Probably attending to the call of nature." He plowed into the woods. "Come on. Better hunt for him.

"We d-don't even know him." Leaving one of my shoes untied, I stuffed the leftover twine in my pocket.

He waved me forward. "Yeah, but there's Johnny Rebs around. We better look."

Our steps were soundless, cushioned by drifts of snow. Tracking O'Farrell wouldn't be a problem; his footprints were huge. My fingers stung with the cold. I gripped my gun and scanned the woods, expecting a Rebel behind every tree.

Gabe motioned ahead. "O'Farrell!" he called.

Pressing a finger to his mouth, O'Farrell twisted toward us. A deer stood, maybe twenty feet behind him. Her ears quivered. She bolted, slipping through pines on the other side of the clearing.

An uncanny bristling feeling came over me. A faint metallic sound. "W-watch out!" I tugged at Gabe.

Rifles popped behind us and the smell of sulfur, saltpeter, and carbon drifted toward us. Gabe peered through the gray mist and loaded his gun.

O'Farrell clutched his hat over his face. With one smooth motion, my brother swiped it onto the ground. "Come on, O'Farrell. Get your gun and fight!"

A half dozen shapes wove through the trees. Gabe wedged his gun on his shoulder. Gunfire cracked, its smoke filtering through the pines. "This is crazy!" I fumbled with my gunpowder. My heart thumped in rapid rhythm. "We can't see them. They can't see us."

Another volley of gunfire. A maple broke overhead with a deafening noise. Branches crashed to the ground, large chunks narrowly missing us. Ice shattered to the forest floor.

Nudging me, my brother nodded toward the woods. His voice was hushed, "Keep quiet. We can cut through there and make up some time. You ready?" I wasn't ready. Not by a long shot.

O'Farrell eyed the woods and backed away. "*I'm* not going in there!" Gabe glared silently at him, shouldered his gun, and marched into the woods.

"Um. I'll stay here. Just in case. You can come get me after you're sure," O'Farrell replied, setting down his equipment. He dismissed me with a wave of his hand. "Go ahead, I'll be fine."

I trailed Gabe into the quiet woods. Gun smoke hung in the air, transparent like a widow's veil. Looking around, we could see no one else. It seemed like we were the only ones left on the earth.

The trees stood spidery, stark black against white. I crunched through the snow.

"Someone's here," Gabe said, pointing maybe ten yards ahead. "Look!"

From where I stood, I could see something on the ground. I clutched my gun and stepped forward.

A soldier lay between two large oaks, his leg twisted at an odd angle. He lifted his head. "Help me!" His uniform, if you could call it that, was mismatched and threadbare. His pants were a soiled mustard color and his coat a dirty gray.

Gabe looked from the Reb to me.

I placed my canteen in the Johnny's hand.

Then I heard cracking, like gunfire—but louder. I whirred around. Peering through the mist, I watched a giant limb separate from its trunk. "Gabe!" I hooded my head with my arms. The huge branch splintered in a final, deafening crack and tumbled to the ground, landing inches from us.

My heart jumped and I waited for my breathing to steady.

The Reb rolled to his side. "You better leave." He worked onto his elbow and squinted into the trees. "Our men will be here to check on the wounded. You don't want to be caught in the middle."

Footfalls, softened by the distance, sounded to my right. My nerves tingling, I took my canteen and twisted it shut. "Best be going."

"Probably the rest of his company." Gabe nodded in the opposite direction, toward the clearing. "Let's get back." He plowed ahead of me, trenching a path through the snow.

My breath escaped in short puffs of vapor and my shoes suctioned in the snow as I trudged behind him. We worked our way toward the glade. The trees thinned and the air brightened.

No surprise to me, O'Farrell was where we had left him. With a stick in his hand, he was scrawling his name in the snow. He started at our approach and jerked up his head.

"Hello. I'm just . . ." His stick jabbed through the air.

Gabe, in no mood for antics, swatted the stick out of O'Farrell's hand. "Better look for our men." My brother motioned forward with his gun. "Let's go!"

It was easy to follow the direction of our company; the ground was pounded flat. We tripped behind Gabe. Every once in awhile, I bent to retie my shoes.

Half running up to him, I called, "My shoes! Slow down. Why're you in such an all-fired hurry?"

Adjusting the sack on his back, Gabe lengthened his stride. "Pick up the pace." He turned his head toward me and met my eyes. "Stragglers don't have a chance."

* * *

A few days later, our troop marched south and crossed the Tennessee border. For the most part the snow had melted, but rough patches of gray sludge still hid in the shadows.

We spent the evening pitching tents. My brother, wanting to impress our officer, volunteered to scout the area. Somehow, he roped me in too. He slammed my haversack in my hands. "I have an idea. Come along."

"Where're we going?" I didn't want to meet Rebs in broad daylight, so I sure didn't want to meet them at night.

He slung his sack on his back. "You'll see soon enough. Ready for adventure?"

This is a sharpshooter taking aim at the enemy, canteen hanging from a nearby branch. Canteens were the water bottles of the day and carried about a quart of water.

"Seems to me like we've had enough," I grumbled.

Campfire smoke filtered through the pines, filling the air with a thick ashy smell. He marched through the trees. "Better than latrine duty," he said, waving me forward.

I didn't care to be trotting after him on another so-called adventure. Maybe he didn't realize that he was putting us both in jeopardy. I gave a backward glance toward camp. Ridgepole tents dotted the hill, campfires glowing orange.

Gabe found a path of sorts. "Come on, daylight's dying." The sky, all roses and violets, bordered his silhouette as he forked to the left.

I trotted up to him, my sack bouncing on my back. "Do you think we'll find any Rebs?" I took a second look back at camp. "D-don't want to face 'em if we don't have to."

He turned toward me, his teeth flashing white. "That's the beauty of it. Never know."

I couldn't understand his bravado. We weren't far from Confederate territory, and I wanted to come home alive.

Only a mile out of camp, my shoes flapped apart. "Wait!" I ripped off my shoes and shoved them into my sack. The frost, still in the ground, bit my toes. I hobbled behind Gabe. My heels, now raw, were a magnet for every sharp rock.

He pushed forward.

"Slow down," I said, picking up my pace.

We crested a hill, and the countryside spread out around us like a blanket. The sky was on fire. Distant hillocks were planted with cows. Their spindly twig legs barely large enough to hold their hefty frames.

I balanced on one foot, grasped the other, and examined my heel. It was raw and ripped. Dirt and small stones imbedded the sores.

"Here." Gabe tugged at his canteen's strap. Twisting open the lid, he sluiced water on my foot.

"Ouch!" I flinched.

He opened my haversack and rummaged through my things, tossing out my socks and my Green River knife. "Would you use your head?" Taking out a shirt, he clutched the collar in one hand and tugged against the buttons, ripping my shirt in half.

"You crazy?" I grabbed my mangled shirt. "That's my best one!"

Gabe grinned and swiped the shirt from my hands. "Not anymore." He tore another strip. Dropping to one knee, he held my heel and wound the cloth around my ankle and foot. "There, that should get you where we're going."

"Where are we going?" The path disappeared into a hodgepodge of weeds: thistle, wild oat, nettle, and mouse ear. I cupped my heel in my hand, trying to pressure away the sting.

He nodded down the hill. A building stood twenty yards to our south, its painted white spire barely visible above the trees.

"A church? Thought we were scouting for Rebs." I took a deep breath, exhaling slowly.

My brother pushed through the weeds, calling over his shoulder. "Used to be a church. Hospital now." He must have known about this building all along.

Questioning his judgment, I limped behind him. "My foot's not that bad. D-don't need a hospital."

It was Gabe's turn to sigh. "Shoes. We're getting you some shoes." He opened the door to the church, the smell of medicine hitting us as soon as we walked in.

Like cemetery stones, rows upon rows of cots lined the floor while gas lanterns flickered their shadowy images. My eyes adjusted to the light. The windows were boarded shut, the pews gone. The church had no feeling of peace. I followed my brother's gaze. His eyes narrowed toward the front of the sanctuary.

An orderly came out of the shadow. "Need something?"

"Joseph," was Gabe's vague answer. Nodding at the orderly, he strode to the front of the room.

I trailed behind him. Arches, beams, and the altar were the only evidence of the building's former life. Just left of us, a soldier moaned, his voice echoing in the chamber. Most of the soldiers were sick, I guessed. Some wounded.

Motioning to a cot on our right, Gabe waved toward a soldier's shoes. "This one. Take those."

I couldn't see past the sticky crimson on the soldier's belly and reached out to touch his wound. Surprised by the warmth, I jerked back my hand. The soldier was a sleeping giant. He never moved, never winced, never cried out. Frowning, I pulled up a crate and sat down.

"What are you doin'?" asked Gabe.

I focused on the soldier's wound and waved my brother away. "Waiting."

He tugged a crate next to mine. We sat there, hunched forward, watching the soldier's chest rise and fall. "What are you waitin' for?" he asked. He leaned toward me. "He's not gonna give you a fight. Just take his shoes."

Guilt weighing heavily, my answer was slow. "I'm *not* taking his shoes. Not 'til he's d-dead." I was firm on that decision. Wearing a dead man's shoes was bad enough; I wasn't going to wear the shoes of a man half cold.

Gabe sat back on his crate, folding his arms. "So, you're going to sit and watch his shoes 'til he's cold as a wagon tire?"

Exactly. I folded my arms too.

Behind me, something clattered on the floor, temporarily silencing the cries of the sick.

My skin prickled. Watching a man die wasn't what I expected. I focused on the poor soldier's hands—mottled skin, spidery veins, darkened fingernails. "You think . . . " I started. The soldier gurgled; the tightness left his face. Maybe he was dead. He seemed relaxed, at peace.

Muffled footsteps scraped the floor behind me, and a red-headed soldier edged between Gabe and me. He unlaced the soldier's shoes, tucked them under his arm, and turned and walked away.

Gabe stood up, his arms stiff at his side, his hands fisted in a ball. "You see what just happened?" He squinted toward the door. "Why didn't you take those shoes?"

The accusation resonated through the room, taunting me again and again. "Whydidn'tyou? Whydidn'tyou?"

My chest knotted. "The guy wasn't dead." My answer felt weak, even to me.

Gabe retorted, his tone dull, "Well, he's dead now. And his shoes are gone."

He didn't need to tell me what I already knew.

I couldn't drag my eyes from the poor soul in front of me. He had no one—not a preacher, a mother, or a friend. If I sat there, he'd have someone. Even if it was only me.

Behind me, Gabe's voice became background noise. "So why're you still here?"

A burn worked toward my throat. I wasn't ready to leave.

"You need shoes. We'll keep trying," Gabe said, sweeping his arm toward the door.

Finally adjusting to the darkness, I noticed things I hadn't noticed before: orderlies wove through one aisle to the next—filling cups with broth, rebandaging wounds. A baptismal font, wedged in the corner, served as a medicine stand.

Tearing my eyes away from the poor soldier, I turned toward the door.

Gabe worked between the cots, and I limped behind him. "So why are you going through all this? I mean, I'll manage without shoes."

He opened the door and twisted toward me. With the rectangular patch of evening sky framing him, his face was unreadable. He answered in low tones: "If the Rebs are after us, you'll have to run."

That night I wrote Sarah. I decided not to mention my quest for shoes. I didn't tell her about the skirmish in the woods either. I wanted to tell her I loved her.

But I didn't know how.

March 10, 1862
Tennessee

Dear Sarah,

Every time we march along a pond or a lake, I remember us skipping stones together. I think of you often, and I am grateful for ever knowing you. Did you see the moon last night? It was incredibly beautiful. I wondered if you might be look-ing at it, too. As beautiful as the moon is, it will never hold a candle to you.

Yours,
Joseph

I gave my letter to the sutler. He called me by name, taking me by surprise. "Thanks, Joseph. Will she write you back?"

14

Sarah

"We're here." Father jumped off the seat and circled around the back. "And just in time."

"Here?" I surveyed the area. Oaks and maples lined the meadow in an almost perfect circle, serving as a border for three parallel rows of tents. In each row the tents opened into each other, spreading from one side of the meadow to the other. I gathered my skirts. Taking my father's hand, I stiffly climbed down.

My curiosity had the best of me. "What do you mean? Just in time for what?"

"You saw all those troops we passed. Bound to be fighting soon." He grabbed my bag off the wagon.

"Would the Fortieth . . ." I started. With all the troops we had seen, I wondered if there was any chance of finding Joseph or Gabe.

Father's lips whitened, forming an angry line. "This is a regimental hospital for the *Seventh*. Not the Fortieth. We're unpacking. Don't have patience for your—" He silenced me with a sharp glance and lugged his medical kit off the back. "Ready?"

I didn't have time to think. Hobbling toward us was our greeting committee—a lone man. I assumed he was a doctor. He clutched a cane with one hand and extended the other to Father. "Glad you're here. The battle's days away." He had a remarkable face: a bulbous nose, pitted skin, and a scraggly beard. "My name's Byron McIntyre, Assistant Head Surgeon," he announced.

"William. William Sutton. Not easy finding you. Like searching for a needle in a haystack. Your troops have been on the move," Father responded.

"Just got here." Byron waved at the tents behind him. The walls were rolled up, exposing cots and straw pallets. "Our boys have been drillin' and preparin'" for the Rebs." Byron met my eyes, his face twisting. "You a laundress? Cook? Don't need women 'round here. Don't have a place for 'em."

Clearly, I had made a poor decision; I shouldn't have come along. I pressed my lips together. "I won't get in the way."

He gave me a pointed glare. "You won't get in the way," he spat out, drilling his cane into the dirt, "because you won't be stayin'."

Father's jaw muscles tightened. "Sarah's my daughter. Don't worry—she'll be useful. If she's not worth her salt, you can send us both home."

I looked at my father, surprised.

Deep furrows lined Byron's brow. "We'll have to see to her transportation. Maybe someone can escort her home."

Father patted his pocket. "I have papers. Right here."

Father had papers. I didn't. I hid a smile, grateful for the small white lie.

"Humph." Byron studied me. Squinting, he tilted his head to the left. He heaved a sigh and waved his cane toward the grounds. "We'll see. If you're no good, you go home. Simple as that."

I gave Father a furtive glance.

Ignoring my reaction, Byron gave a curt nod to Father. "Best give you a tour. Follow me. Think we have time."

Byron walked with a pronounced limp, his right leg slightly shorter than his left. I caught Father's eye and mouthed, "Polio?" Father shrugged.

Byron stopped short. A canopy covered the central area and shaded the mess dining table. At the other end was a cooking stove. "Food's not that great. Watered down soup, mostly," he said, still frowning. "The cooks sleep in that tent down there." Then he waved behind us. "The medical director's and surgeons' tents." He intended his words for Father. "You'll sleep there. Not sure where we'll put the girl."

"The girl," I repeated under my breath. Did he think I was merely a child?

Father lifted one eyebrow in my direction, his signal to keep my mouth shut and told Byron, "We'll share a tent. We'll be fine." I nodded in agreement, but I was far from fine.

A percussion of gunfire burst from behind the trees. "Skirmish," Byron explained. "Not a battle. Not yet." The sky darkened with a dusky cloud of gray, and I swallowed, my throat paper dry.

Byron nodded toward the hospital tent. "Don't have many soldiers there right now. Just a few with measles. Been treatin' 'em with brandy and quinine, as good a treatment as any. You've had measles already, right?"

"No." My stomach knotted. I had enough to deal with. I didn't need to worry about measles, too.

His eyebrows knitted together and he grumbled, "Don't get 'em. Can hardly deal with a woman, much less a sick one . . . or a dead one." His words trailed off as he slipped into the tent.

I followed Byron. A hand-hewn table stood in the corner. Medicines, bandages, basins, and towels were strewn across it in a disorganized mess. I smiled, itching for order. Finally, something I could do. "I can straighten these, if you wish," I said, my mind's eye already envisioning the table neatly arranged.

"You can leave your hands *off*." His left eye twitched.

In warning, Father's eyes penetrated mine. I clamped my mouth and pressed my hands to my side.

Byron motioned to the rows of cots that lined both sides of the tent. "Mostly empty now, but you can plan on 'em fillin'." He massaged his bristled chin. "S'pose you're tired. Head this way."

The Battle of Pittsburg Landing, more commonly called the Battle of Shiloh, took place in southern Tennessee on April 6 and 7, 1862. On the first day the Confederate troops almost succeeded in breaking the Union lines, but on the second day the Union forces were able to defeat the Southerners with a strong counterattack. It was the bloodiest battle in American history up to that time, and casualties from the two-day battle kept doctors and nurses busy around the clock.

Whipping his cane in front of him, he outpaced me. We filed out of the tent, then worked our way between tents to the north edge of the compound. "You got family involved in this war?" He looked to my father. Clearly, his question wasn't directed to me.

Father threw me a sidelong glance. "Not family. Neighbors, though."

Gabe's half-skewed collar came to mind, and, touching my fingers to my neckline, I squinted his image away.

"Well, the Rebellion should be over in a matter of months. You'll see 'em again," muttered Byron.

"What?" I leaned forward, not certain what I had heard.

Tucking his cane under his arm, he rubbed his eye sockets with the heel of his hand, his eyes making soft squishy sounds. He was going to say something like, "Chances are, they'll come back hurt," or "You never know."

Shifting his weight, Father sighed.

"Never know," I mumbled to myself, the words marking my intangible fear. If only I were a prophetess with a window to the future. I wanted to know when the brothers would come home—or *if* they would come home.

I imagined Gabe knocking on my door, brandishing a crooked smile. He would lift me in the air and twirl me around, my skirts circling and spiraling. When he set me down, my skirts, still spinning, would twist around my legs uncertain of their path and the room would spin. Unbalanced, I'd fall into his arms and bury my nose into his chest, smelling the ashy scent of him.

I swallowed hard, my throat aching. The end of the war was months away, and I couldn't spend all my time pining. I had work to do. I shook my head to clear my thoughts.

A tent, smaller than most, stood behind Father, framing his wiry features. Then, as if God himself sent a distraction, I caught movement behind him. The door flap blew open. A hand hesitantly clutched the fabric and tugged the flap shut. I peered around my father, gaining a better line of sight.

It didn't look like the hand of a soldier. It was muscular and the color of rich dark tea, unlike the color of any hand I had ever seen. "Contraband." The word spilled from my lips, unnoticed by my father.

Byron, though, gave me a burning look. His brows furrowed. Then he turned his back toward me, drilled his cane in the dirt, and pushed toward the opposite end of camp. "Best be on our way," he said brusquely and moved on.

My thoughts churning, I glanced in the direction of the tent and matched Byron's halting stride. The young man was a puzzlement. Perhaps he was a slave. Perhaps Byron had been protecting him and didn't want anyone to know.

Urging me forward, Father waggled his finger toward Byron. I bit my lower lip and tasted blood.

I had to settle down.

The rows of tents flanked my left and my right. Most of them sagged, their ropes misdirected. The soldiers probably didn't know how to properly raise them, I thought, trying to forget about the man.

Byron halted. Turning toward us, he cupped the ball of his cane in both hands. "Here's where you'll be stayin'."

I should have asked Byron about the young man. How I deeply regret my lack of gumption! Giving Byron a nod, I turned to the canvas tent beside us.

It was about the size of our wagon. Father opened the flap and waved me in. "This will be fine. Thank you."

A blanket attached to the tent's ridgepole separated our sleeping quarters; we each had a cot and a mattress. Stakes driven into the ground supported a board and a tin washbasin for us to share.

This wasn't home. Not even close.

I set my carpetbag on the floor and sighed. Father gave me a hollow look and sat stiffly on his cot, rummaging through his bag. I sat down on my cot and shivered—almost as if a gust of wind had sheared straight through our tent.

15

Joseph

"Double-quick!" the captain commanded. His voice pitched an octave high.

Double-quick? The balls of my feet were blistered and sore. How could I march double-quick?

All of us Indiana boys marched, our feet slapping the ground in a steady rhythm, our column narrowing as we snaked through the oaks, every sharp rock sending pain up my legs. "Why . . . we marchin'. . . like the d-devil's . . . on our heels?"

Gabe's words were staccato, too: "'Cuz . . . . we're . . . missin'. . . it."

"Missin' what?" A staccato of gunfire answered my question. Starting and stopping and starting again, the battle was winding down.

The woods opened up into a meadow. Greeted by a rotten-egg stench of sulfur, we stopped in our tracks, washed with a feeling of helplessness. Bullets had sheared the underbrush. Trees were hacked from their roots. Wounded horses pedaled their hooves in the air, their heads drooped and their eyes gummy and sad. Bodies sprawled over the meadow, laced through each other like twigs from a windblown tree.

Lifeless air settled in my lungs.

"Think that's going to happen to us too?" someone asked. I blinked, struggling to grasp my field of vision. I clenched my hands, my fingernails biting the palms.

"That?" Gabe's jaw muscles worked. He gave me a fierce look.

One Union soldier lying nearby was crusted with blood—his walnut-dark hair stuck together in clumps. The poor soldier's face was black as soot, his left cheekbone glaring white against his shredded cheek.

Gabe nudged the soldier's body with his foot. With more nerve than I could muster, he reached into the departed soul's pocket and removed a letter.

"Jeptha," he muttered—more to himself than anyone else. "Jeptha Harover. He's a Wisconsin boy."

"*Was* a Wisconsin boy." I stared into Jeptha's face. His eyes, unseeing, stared back at me.

"Yes. *Was*." Gabe swallowed.

The rest of our troop filtered across the meadow. I guessed they were looking for someone they knew. One of our men plucked up someone's canteen and slipped its strap over his shoulder.

I tried to imagine Jeptha's family, his home. He probably had sisters. Brothers. My throat burned as I blurted out, "If something happens to one of us, Mother won't be the same."

"Father, either." Gabe pressed his fingertips to his eyes and rubbed his temples.

My words bottled inside me. "How will Jeptha's family find out?"

Gabe's face grayed and he cleared his throat. "Probably read it in the newspaper."

I didn't want this to happen to me—to bleed out on a field. I squinted at Jeptha's jacket. His uniform wasn't even frayed—wasn't even *used* really. "Look at his uniform. The Sunday's not worn off it yet."

"Look there." Gabe motioned toward Jeptha's feet. "Somebody's already taken his shoes."

Good thing. I needed shoes, but I couldn't have taken them. Not then.

Smoke wisped toward the sky, like a soft message directed toward heaven. This was wrong—this killing of brothers and sons. My throat hurt. Ached. "You think any Indiana boys are here?" I finally asked.

We stood paralyzed, trying to make sense of it. The field was strewn with limbs and guns, the ground soaked with sticky crimson. The meadow blurred. I knew one thing: this field had been beautiful once.

"Never thought there'd be this much blood." Gabe's voice was miles away. "Will we ever make it back home?"

He had put words to my thoughts.

His lips in a grim line, he shouldered his gun. "It's gonna get worse."

"Worse than *this*?" I tasted bile.

He tightened his grip on his gun. His next statement surprised me. "You don't think Sarah's caught up in this war, do you?"

I hadn't considered that.

* * *

I should have been able to put Pittsburg Landing behind me. After all, I hadn't even lifted my gun. But when I closed my eyes, I witnessed the ruined meadow over and over again.

Things were easier when my eyes were wide open and when my feet were moving to marching orders. We marched southbound, every step taking us farther from home.

Our orders—to find wood—took us near Rebel grounds. A stream, ribboning through black willows and downy poplars, drew a winding line between Confederate territory and us. "Plenty of wood," I said.

"Plenty of Johnnies, too." Gabe motioned farther downstream. There were twenty, maybe thirty Johnny Rebs milling beside the riverbank. Most of them wore butternut or gray; some of them wore farmer's britches, and a few of them wore Union blue. They were a raggedy lot, many of them bearded. They didn't look like enemies.

"We're s'posed to report back," I reminded him. The trees blocked our view, but as we got closer to the stream I realized that a dozen or more Yanks were on our side. Their uniforms were crisp and new.

"Look." Gabe waved toward the stream. "What's going on?"

A motley fleet of handmade boats—made of scrap lumber, bark, and tin— drifted toward us. The boats turned the stream into a floating dry goods store. Each vessel carried curious cargo.

A Billy Yank crouched on one side of the stream, pouring coffee grounds into a small tin cup. He centered his cup on a vessel and shoved it toward the opposite bank. He flicked his eyes toward both of us.

"What're you d-doing?" I asked.

He lifted his chin, as if the answer was obvious. "Sendin' over coffee. Exchangin' for tobacco."

Our eyes fixed on the craft as it dipped downstream. On the other side, a Reb crouched on the bank. When the boat drifted next to him, he snatched it from the water. Then he tied a plug of tobacco on the vessel.

I turned to my brother. "Could I trade something for shoes?"

"Could try." Gabe eyed the boat. "But I don't think there's enough shoes in either camp."

A Union soldier, his belly on the embankment, scowled at us. "What're you two starin' at?" The hair on his face made up for the lack of hair on his balding pate. His sooty face was weathered and lined, but his eyes were a youthful sapphire blue.

My brother was quick to answer, "Just wonderin' if we could use your boat."

The man's boat drifted close. Grabbing the cargo, he clutched the crude ship and walked away. I leaned toward Gabe. "Maybe he didn't hear you." Then, louder, I asked, "May we use your boat?"

Turning toward us, the soldier tucked his cheek full of tobacco. "You can use it, but I'll need more tobacco tomorrow." He wiped the hull of the boat on his pants and gave me the vessel. "Get it back to me before then."

A Reb on the opposite shore strode toward us. He had shoes on his feet and a pair in his hand. I didn't want my chance to walk by. "You, soldier! You got an extra pair of shoes?" I called.

He dangled them in front of me. "Why would I give you these shoes when our Southern boys need 'em?" He wasn't going to give me the shoes. "If I give 'em to you today, you'll chase me with 'em tomorrow," he added.

"If I trade for my knife, tomorrow he might stab me in my back," I whispered.

There was nothing wrong with this man's ears. "Fair trade," he agreed and gave us a tobacco-stained smile. "Ship me your knife."

Part of the reason why the Union was able to turn the tide at the Battle of Pittsburg Landing was the arrival of reinforcements by steamboat late in the day on April 6. Throughout the war the Union army was at an advantage when it came to transportation, especially with access to railroads, steamboats, and ships.

BATTLES AND LEADERS OF THE CIVIL WAR, 4 VOLS. (NEW YORK: CENTURY COMPANY, 1887–88), 1.489.

I couldn't believe it. Shoes. I was going to have shoes. "Didn't pull those shoes off a dead man, did you?" My thoughts spun backward to Pittsburg Landing.

"Sure as hell didn't pry them off a live one." He baited me with the shoes. "You want 'em or not?"

I wasn't going to miss this chance. "Give me a minute." I knotted my Green River knife on the boat and pushed it toward him, watching the vessel cup and dip with the current. In less than a minute the Reb had my knife. His eyes intent on his new weapon, he unthreaded the twine, loosening his purchase. The blade of the knife shimmered in the sunlight, and I half-regretted my trade.

"You gave up your knife?" asked Gabe, a little too late. The knife wasn't in my possession anymore. My stomach lurched.

The Reb wiped the knife across his leg. I wasn't sure if there was going to be a trade after all. This was a fool's game, and I was the loser.

I had given up my knife for nothing.

My eyes riveted on the shoes. They sat at the edge of the water, unlaced. The soles seemed sturdy enough and the leather was polished. Someone had already worn them plenty; the left shoe was scuffed and distinguishable from the right.

I wanted them. "Send 'em over," I called, my voice louder than I expected.

The Reb lifted an eyebrow, making no movement toward my shoes.

"A fair trade." I motioned toward the shoes, urging him.

The Reb balanced my shoes on the craft, wound twine around them, and shoved the boat my way.

Gabe slapped me on the back, his grin a mile wide.

My spirits soaring, I focused on my shoes. The current swept my shoes forward, and they lurched and buckled in the water. "Got 'em!" I tripped into the water.

"Don't lose 'em!" called Gabe.

But, I didn't have them. The shoes were drifting away. I grabbed at them, and they ducked away from me. Mindless of the icy current, I trounced through the water.

"Get 'em!" cried Gabe.

I reached, "Ha!" With the dripping shoes clasped in my hands, I pivoted toward him and smiled. My shoes weren't perfect but they were good enough.

Still breathing hard, I sat at the river's edge. I laced my "new" shoes and tied the last knot.

Something white and round lay on the ground in front of me: a perfectly flat stone. I picked it up and smiled at the thought of Sarah.

"*That* was an adventure," Gabe rocked on his heels.

Returning with a grin, I slipped the stone in my pocket. "We'll have to let Captain know there's wood to be found."

"Best head back to camp," he agreed.

The stone burned in my pocket.

"Would you hurry?" Gabe motioned forward. "Got something on your mind?"

"No, nothing," I lied and traipsed after him. A letter to Sarah was the first thing on my agenda, and Gabe didn't have to know.

We arrived at camp and a stream of birds swarmed from the bushes, announcing our arrival. Raucous crows, murderous black clouds of them, slashed into the sky.

The first thing I did, once Gabe left to talk to the Captain, was take out my pen and paper.

> *Dear Sarah,*
>
> *I take pen in hand to tell you of a bit of excitement I had today. I traded my knife for a pair of shoes. I will probably miss my knife. It has been several months since I saw you last. Although I have a hard time pulling up images of home and our farm, your face is constant. I long to be with you again. I found a stone today.*
>
> *Remembering you at Hardin's Pond.*
>
> *Sometime I will try to write you about Pittsburg Landing. I can't find the words to tell you right now.*
>
> *Yours,*
> *Joseph*

Branches snapped behind me. I wheeled around. "O'Farrell, what d-do you want?" I never knew what to expect with O'Farrell.

He shoveled his hands in his pockets. "Need you to read a letter from my Eliza." O'Farrell had a girl. Unbelievable.

I folded up my letter. "Read it yourself." I was absolutely in no mood for him.

He shifted his weight. Then he dug in his pocket and blinked at the letter. He coughed. It didn't take a genius to figure out his problem.

With a sigh, I sat on a log, stuffed the letter in my jacket, and pitched the jacket on the ground. "You shoulda told me you can't read." I was curious what Eliza saw in him and what kinds of things she wrote him.

He sat beside me and gave me her letter. I scanned through it, glanced at him, and started:

I take pen in hand to tell you of my love.

I gave him a sharp look. I could feel his breath.

My love for you is just as sweet as new-mown grass in summer heat.
Please come to me in a new day and in the violet's bed we'll lay.

O'Farrell edged forward, and I glared him back. The poem was terrible, and I had no choice but to complete it.

I need you in my arms, my dear, so come to me. I want you near.

He leaned even closer. "That's all? Read it again," I could smell onions on his breath.

"No, I've read quite enough." Creasing his letter, I scowled at him.

"That's okay. Got it in my head." His eyes went soft. "'I need you in my arms my dear, so come to me. I want you near.'" He grappled in his bag for a piece of paper and handed it to me, "Write her back. Can you? Please?"

I knew how to write letters—at least according to the sutler. Why would anyone take a shine to O'Farrell? Unable to think of an excuse, I readied my pen. "What d-do you want me to write?"

His eyes took on a faraway look, "Um. Dearest Eliza, You're the love of my life. I miss the scent of your hair."

I felt like an intruder. How could it be? O'Farrell, illiterate and bungling, with breath that could wilt a cornstalk, had a way with words. He also had a girl.

Then he knocked over my ink, and I had to start over. Listening once to his personal business was bad enough, but listening twice was painful.

I stowed my ink and reached for my jacket. It was gone. It was walking away, with Gabe in it. My worries had only begun.

* * *

I sat by the fire and tried to forget my jacket.

Smoke hovered between the hills, the golden glow of campfires dotting the meadow. It was cold. I needed my jacket not only for its warmth but also because of the letter.

Tossing my coat behind him, Gabe added kindling to the fire. My jacket was just past him, wadded in a clump, Sarah's letter half sticking out.

O'Farrell trounced toward us with a pail in hand. All elbows and knees, he tripped and doused our fire.

A thin column of smoke filtered through the pines.

Gabe lifted his hands. "Don't snuff the whole blamed fire. I need coals for cookin'." He picked up a stick and poked at the ashes.

"Didn't mean to. Accident." O'Farrell wafted the smoke with his rawboned hand.

My brother and I exchanged glances.

"Gonna be midnight before we eat," growled Gabe. I peered in the pot. The roast looked edible—it wasn't sticky or blue like our last rations. He had scavenged onions and potatoes, the stew reminding me of Mother's cooking, and of home.

"No belly-achin'," he warned. "Whoever complains is the next cook."

He ladled the stew, and we forked into it. It had an odd taste—the taste of pepper. "Seems to me there's a lot of . . . um . . . spice." I coughed into my arm. I wanted to nab the letter, but I couldn't come up with a plan. If I sauntered over to retrieve it, I would be caught red-handed. If I stayed put I risked Gabe discovering the letter. Either way I was cursed.

Fortunately O'Farrell couldn't read my thoughts. Only focused on Gabe's awful concoction, he gave me a sour glance and then shoved his stew to the far side of his plate. "Can't eat this garbage. Not fit for a sow."

"Our first complaint." Gabe grinned at me. "O'Farrell, you're the next cook."

O'Farrell squirreled up his nose. "Don't want my cooking. Even buzzards would turn up their noses." Using his fork as a plow, he trenched corn rows into his stew. "You know," he muttered, "if you want out of this war, one bite of Gabe's stew would be the ticket."

"There are probably better ways out." I frowned at my stew.

"All I'd need is a kindly bullet," he added. "I'd be sent home for months. I'd gladly welcome it. In fact, I'd consider the Reb a right kind fellow." He jarred me with his bony elbow. I tightened my grip on my plate, wondering where he was going with the conversation.

"Let me shoot a hole in your gut," said Gabe. "Just deep enough so you can go home." He forked up more stew and continued between bites. "My bullets are friendly as any Reb's, and maybe even friendlier." He moved a bit to the left. I saw the blue of my jacket.

"I'd let you take a shot, but you have to promise you wouldn't miss. My luck, you'd aim for my belly and hit my heart instead," said O'Farrell.

Gabe set his plate on the ground behind him. "If Joseph aimed for your belly and missed, he'd probably hit your toe, or maybe that tree. You can't count on Joseph to have an accurate miss."

"If I hit your leg and it had to be amputated," I said, "you could still drive an ambulance. Then you wouldn't have a furlough."

"And if you hit my head?" he asked.

Gabe heaved a log on the fire. The fire popped and sparks spiraled toward the sky. "If Joseph hit your head," he said, "we'd have to amputate it. Then, you still wouldn't get a furlough 'cuz we'd prop your rotting body against a log and use it as a decoy." He laughed, his rich baritone echoing through the camp. O'Farrell giggled like a schoolgirl.

Their laughter gave me the cover I needed to snatch my jacket and tuck it into my haversack. That night, my sack was my pillow; I wouldn't let it out of my sight.

16

Sarah

PITTSBURG LANDING, TENNESSEE, APRIL 6–7, 1862

The next morning I awoke to the rumble of distant thunder, but the noise wasn't thunder at all. I froze at the hospital tent's entrance. Ambulances approached, stretchers filled, and injured soldiers crowded every corner of the tent.

Nothing had prepared me for the horror of men bloodied in battle. Men swarmed from the ambulance wagons. Yelling. Screaming.

Need your help over here!

He's losin' a lot of blood.

This man's hurt bad. Get him to the tent. Fast!

Byron brushed past me. "Get to work."

My hands were ice cold.

"They're pilin' in!" someone yelled. A stream of soldiers poured into our tent—some carried, some walking. Two orderlies brought another soldier inside.

I frantically looked for unused cots. Something had to be done. "Over there!" I motioned toward the back of the tent. "Put the minor injuries there."

An orderly pushed past me. "You s'posed to be orderin' us around?" He tromped to the back of the tent, throwing a glare over his shoulder.

I was able and I was there. Wasn't that clout enough? "I have received my authority from the Lord God Almighty. Have you anything that ranks higher than that?" I retorted.

I turned to find Byron standing feet away, his face flushing beet red. "You plan to stay with the regiment?" He practically spat out the words.

"Y-yes."

Inches away from my face, he leaned hard on his cane, his lips pinched shut. "Then do something useful. If you can't, we'll send you home."

More soldiers filtered in. Escaping Byron, I ran to the supply table, nabbing a basin, bandages, and a rag.

Father waved me toward the back of the room. "Clean wounds. Start over there."

Nodding, I wove between orderlies, soldiers, and cots, and worked my way to the back of the tent. My first soldier's face was gunpowder black. His leg twisted at an odd angle. His thigh was scraped raw, and pieces of flesh draped in loose shreds. Something was imbedded in his wound—maybe gravel or dirt.

The soldier winced. "Oatmeal," he said. "Looks like oatmeal." I pulled up a crate, dabbed at his wound, and looked down the row of soldiers. Like a nightmare, the room telescoped in front of me.

"More on the way!" someone shouted from the door.

Byron hobbled toward me, tossing me a sheet. "When you finish cleaning, tear those linens in strips. Need more bandages. Hurry! And later, if your *highness* has time, you can write letters begging for supplies." He turned. "*That's* how you make yourself useful."

Women participated in the war in various ways. This drawing depicts women sewing clothes for soldiers, washing clothes at army camps, and writing letters for soldiers.

17

Joseph

Our new marching orders came, and we headed south again—even farther from home. "Ready for this?" Gabe pointed to the gray mist above the hill on our right. The ground trembled under our feet, shooting vibrations up my spine. A metallic taste filled my mouth—thirst maybe, or fear.

We trooped past brackish ponds, dry river beds, and parched cornfields. My canteen bounced against my leg, empty. "Need some water."

Gabe popped the cork from his canteen, peered into it and took a swig, wiping his mouth with the back of his hand. His jaw was set in a hard line. "Perryville's going to look like Pittsburg Landing, except we'll be in the thick of it. Just wait and see." Tightening the lid he let the canteen drop to his side.

A soldier up the line started sobbing. Tears burned in my eyes, but my feet kept moving me forward. I lifted my canteen. Empty. My throat was cornhusk dry.

An angry percussion of bullets rang out. My stomach knotted, and I stumbled. My mind couldn't manage my feet. How was I going to manage battle? Smoke billowed above the hill ahead. The closer we marched to Perryville, the louder the rumble.

"Men! Over here!" Captain Dilling waved us men—all fifty or so of us—together at the bottom of the hill. I glanced up the rise.

"The time has come to engage the enemy." Wine-colored blotches blossomed up the Captain's neck. "Fill in the gap. Keep your eye on the Rebs. Aim low, and fire deliberately." Gabe's face was as white as cotton.

A low murmur rumbled in the back of our group. Captain rose to his toes, his voice piercing through us. "If one of our men is down, leave him lyin' there and fight. We'll gather the wounded later. Get in your ranks!"

We Indiana boys dumped our sacks. Gripping my gun, I stumbled into place.

A chill ran through me.

"Get on now!" Captain's face was scarlet. "Run!" He waved up the hill.

To my left, other companies marched forward. To my right, more.

My heart pumping wildly, I half ran, half tripped up the hill, the grass crunching under my feet. Gabe pummeled ahead of me. He turned back and yelled something, his eyes round and white.

A shell burst over my head. Clouds of smoke filtered down, and with it a wicked stench of rotten eggs.

I reached the cusp of the hill, getting my first sights. A ragged line of Union soldiers stretched to our left and to our right. "Fill in the gap," our captain had said.

We stepped through those bodies and filled in the line. I gasped in deep breaths.

Below, Rebs strung out like beads; the field shimmered with steel, bayonets glistening in the sun. A war machine, the Rebs marched forward—hundreds of them, thousands—all marching our way.

"Hold the line!" somebody yelled. The row shifted and straightened, our boys ramming their barrels full.

"Fire!"

Gabe's gun recoiled. He squinted against the smoke. Grabbing another cartridge, he ripped through it with his teeth. "You all right?" he called. I hardly heard him against the noise. Did Gabe think he was on a Sunday stroll? Didn't he know those Rebels were marksmen? They had honed their skills on rabbits and quail. Now they drew a bead on us.

"Look there!" Gabe nodded. "They're layered thicker than hops." Knapsacks and guns littered the ground, along with hundreds of men—and parts of men—cast like rag dolls across the field.

The ground rumbled like thunder. Fire and smoke blazed in one solid sheet, the noise grating around us. I had seen enough at Pittsburg Landing. Here, I was breathing the battle.

"Fire!" someone yelled, his voice tinny against the noise. The ground rattled underneath me.

Pressing my gun to my shoulder, I squeezed one eye and pulled the trigger. Nothing. I rammed in another charge. It still didn't fire.

"Come on!" Gabe yelled over the guns.

Firing a rifle in the Civil War required a soldier to follow a series of steps in a precise order. Remove cartridge from pouch and tear it open with teeth. Pour cartridges down barrel of rifle and drop in minié ball. Withdraw ramrod from gun. Jam ramrod down gun barrel to pack in ball and powder. Return the ramrod to original position with pinky finger. Pick up rifle and pull back hammer. Remove cap from cap box and place on cone of rifle. Make sure hammer is fully cocked. Aim and shoot.

I dropped to my knee and examined my weapon.

"Hold your ground!" someone yelled. My stomach was a stone. An acre away, shoulder to shoulder, they plowed together as one. I glanced to either side. Our Indiana boys, one row behind the other, fired their guns, then loaded and fired again.

I cocked the hammer back and pulled the trigger. Nothing. My gun was suddenly foreign. Fumbling with the mechanism, I glanced at the field. Soldiers falling, flags flying, guns firing—the smoke thick and choking.

Someone went down on my left. Capable soldiers fought beside me while I fussed with a silent gun. Inept. Bungling. Useless.

I jammed my ramrod into the barrel trying to shake the bullets out. Shells screamed overhead. Gabe's voice pitched high, "Hurry!" I'd never heard him sound like that. Scared, almost. His face was granite. He leaned forward, focused on the enemy line. His gun recoiled again.

Minié balls flew past us. I tried the trigger again. Gabe motioned toward a gun lying just in front of us, gripped in a victim's hands. "There's one!" he yelled. "Grab it!" The body, chewed up by gunfire, lay in a dark pool of crimson. My heart beat hard against my chest. I wrenched at the gun—the barrel was slick and warm.

A puff of smoke boiled out of a Rebel cannon. The blast echoed across the field. The Rebels marched closer, maybe ten yards away. I found a Johnny in my sights, aimed slightly above him, and discharged my gun.

Gabe's voice trumpeted, "There you go, Joseph! Bully for you!"

Another puff escaped. The soldier right next to me yelled, "Up goes smoke!" Silence. And then the shell's screaming cry. The blast of shot and canister. The flash of musket fire. Load, lock, and fire. Load, lock, and fire. Rebels hid behind the gray dust of battle. My chest was tight, my mouth wicked dry.

Our front line disintegrated. Rebs cut through us like a scythe through wheat. Bayonets shimmered, steel struck steel, someone to my left toppled backward, and then several soldiers on my right. The Rebs plowed forward, the field blurring gray.

Just then, a musket ball passed through our color-bearer's head. Falling backward, he crumpled on the ground, the ensign of liberty still gripped in his hand. The world turned white, my vision clouded, and my head throbbed.

Gabe bumped me back. I couldn't hear his words. At that moment, his feet collapsed underneath him, and I crouched beside him. "You all right?" My hands shook. I grabbed his jacket and jerked him toward me. "Gabe!" I screamed. His arm moved, slightly. His eyes flickered open.

He rolled to the right and grasped the Minié ball that lay beside him, the one that had hit him, and rotated it in his hand. "Too played out to do much harm," he said rubbing his arm. He smiled slowly. "This bruise will get me sympathy, for sure." Gabe had a twist on the battle I couldn't comprehend. He thought it was some kind of game.

18

Sarah

Barely an hour after we had set up our makeshift hospital, ambulances lined the road, and soldiers staggered through the doors, reeking of sulfur and sweat.

"Slaughter pen," I heard someone say.

I tried to focus but fumbled with bandages, basins, and blood. A roll of bandages streamed out of my hands.

Byron hobbled toward me, "What're you doin'?" He nabbed the bandages with the tip of his cane. "We're short on supplies. These have to last." Lips pruning, he scooped up the bandages and pressed them into my hand.

"More soldiers comin'!" someone yelled by the door. Nodding, Byron shuffled to the back of the tent.

I searched for Father, spotting him in the back of the tent. He wiped his scalpel on his apron and glanced up at me with glassy eyes.

My motions now automatic, I cleaned and wrapped open wounds. Dip cloth in the basin, wring, clean. Dip cloth in the basin, wring, clean. A muffled popping broke into my consciousness; undeniably, I had become accustomed to the ratchet of war.

Someone lit a gas lamp. Its oily smell permeated the tent. The door flap opened and the darkening sky surprised me. Eventide. Fighting had ceased, at least for a while.

My fingers, stuck together with blood, and my rag, already stained crimson, provided little hope of cleanliness. Rinsing my hands in the cool bloodied water and then drying them on my skirts, I looked up at the door.

A young man stood silhouetted in the door like a dark ghostly figure. He shifted to the left and then to the right. I squeezed shut my eyes. When I opened them again, the man was still there, chin jutted forward, spare and lean-visaged. He wore a shirt of faded blue, with the sleeves rolled up to his elbow.

He was real, and very black. My pulse quickened. He was the same man from Pittsburg Landing, of that I was certain.

He flashed me a warm smile, his teeth as straight as could be, and asked, "Can I help you?"

My eyes skated toward the supply table and its small heap of linens.

He nodded toward the table. "I can tear those into bandages."

"Y-yes." My mind raced with questions. Where was he from? Where was his family? What were his plans? Instead, I asked only, "What's your name?"

"Truman."

A cannon blast sent tremors through the tent. The bottles on the supply table quaked, and one clattered to the floor. A man cried out behind me. An orderly, his face ashen gray, popped his head in the door. "Git ready. There's more."

One of the main causes of death during the Civil War was infected wounds. Not only were hospitals unsanitary by today's standards, but also men had to sit and wait for hours or days before seeing a doctor.

Truman, his hands already ripping bandages, turned and locked eyes with me.

Byron's voice trumpeted across the room."Didn't you tell me you knew someone named 'Joseph'?" My skin tingled at the mention of Joseph's name, and I swiveled toward the back of the tent. Byron worked his way up to me, his eyebrows knit together in a frown.

"Yes." Was it possible that Joseph was here? I peered toward the back of the tent.

"Follow me. Think you better see this soldier." Byron tapped his cane toward the back of the tent. "Joseph. You said you knew a Joseph?"

Knew? My mouth turned dry.

Basin in hand, I worked my way between the cots, Byron's hesitant gait slowing us down. "B-but Joseph's in the Fortieth infantry," I said. "He'd be somewhere else."

Planting his cane in the dirt floor, he faced me and frowned. "Big battle. Fortieth could be fighting too."

I drew a sharp breath. Of course. The Fortieth could be out there too. The brothers could be nearby—closer than I thought.

Then I saw him—second cot from the end. My breath caught. Dark haired and slender framed, his face was black as soot. Shredded pieces of cartilage hung where his ear had been.

Byron motioned me closer. "Look here. This soldier tagged himself." He nabbed off a scrap of paper pinned to the soldier's coat. "Says 'Joseph.'"

My mouth went dry. "Joseph?"

The soldier turned toward my voice.

"Is this your Joseph?" Byron's question surprised me—was Joseph mine?

Joseph's eyes blinked open. Green. His eyes were green. I let out a ragged breath. The soldier wasn't Joseph, not the Joseph I knew. "N-not mine."

My heart still thumped wildly. This soldier wasn't mine, but he was someone's. He needed help.

A disturbance broke out at the front of the tent. Byron's feet shuffled away. "More wounded!" he bellowed.

Some of Joseph's hair was stuck to his forehead. I pushed a strand back.

"Miss?" I could barely hear him. "Lookin' for a Joseph or somethin'?"

I leaned forward. "Yes."

He squinted up at me. "That surgeon said so. You thought I was him."

With the start of the Civil War, many slaves in the South realized that if they could make it to Union lines they would stand a better chance of becoming free or even signing up to fight against the slaveholders. Such men were called "contrabands."

From the front of the tent, Byron's voice knifed through our conversation, "Miss Sutton. We've got other wounded soldiers here."

"Hope he's all right," continued Joseph. "I mean, I hope *your* Joseph's all right."

I hadn't gotten any letters from either of the boys. Sighing, I dipped a cloth in my basin and wrung it half dry. "Don't know. Wish I did."

Byron waved me over. "Miss Sutton, get over here. Now!"

Joseph nodded toward Byron. "No way of pleasin' him."

I tried not to smile. Cleaning Joseph's injury the best that I could, I packed his ear with lint and wrapped it.

The tent swarmed with doctors, orderlies, and soldiers. "Sarah!" Byron's sharp command echoed back to me, his face blossoming red.

"I-I have to go." I gathered my cloth and basin.

"You heard from him? I mean, your Joseph?" Joseph adjusted himself on the cot.

My feet were glued to the floor. "No." I wished I had heard from him.

"Soon. You'll hear from him soon." His tone was meant to sound reassuring, but to me it felt like a lie.

"W-was the Fortieth Indiana there? I mean, today?"

"Don't know." He blinked up at me. "Looked like all of Buell's army. Can't say for sure. An iron storm. That's what it was." His Adam's apple bobbed in his throat. I didn't want to press him any further.

Byron waved his arms. "More comin'!" he yelled as another wave of soldiers poured through the door.

Nearly a year had passed since I had seen Joseph or Gabe. I didn't know when I would see them, or even *if* I would see them again.

19

Joseph

STONES RIVER, TENNESSEE,
DECEMBER 31, 1862–JANUARY 2, 1863

A year into the war we were well-seasoned soldiers. Perryville had been like an open wound—ugly and terrifying—but Stones River was a battle fought blind. The fog was so thick we couldn't see much at all. I didn't expect to make it home.

We'd been fighting three hours, maybe four, the sickening smell of sulfur filling my lungs. Our boys rammed their guns full: aiming, firing. Some falling. *It could be me*, I kept thinking, *It could be me*.

"Help!" somebody called. "Help!"

Above the booming cannons, a dozen—maybe more—wounded soldiers cried for water, their voices blending in an aching refrain.

"Is someone going to help them?" I shouted above the roar.

Gabe jammed his ramrod down his gun. "Don't think about it!" Tucking his chin, he gave me a warning glance.

"Water!" A thin cry etched across the field.

"Someone needs water," I whispered, toying with the mechanism on my gun. Bullets splattered around me. I rose to my toes. Then my feet were in action—I tore away from our line of blue and sprinted for enemy gray.

"Joseph! Get back here!"

I pushed forward, my heart beating hard in my chest. Bullets whizzed past me. I couldn't breathe.

My canteen swung on its strap and butted against my leg. Ducking and dodging, running with the stops and starts of a rabbit, I ran toward the Confederate side.

"Fool! What are you doin'?" Gabe yelled from behind our lines. "Get back here!" His voice was yards away.

"Hold your fire!" somebody yelled.

Guns still popping, I leaped over someone. I tripped over a limestone out-cropping, fell, and stumbled forward. The field was a blur of shadows, enemy gray melding with steel-colored fog.

"Hold your fire!" I heard again.

"Help me. Please. Water." The voice came from ten feet away.

Dark gray on gray, the shadows shifted. My legs were possessed.

"Help!" someone cried, four feet to my left.

I glanced back. Vague outlines twisted behind me.

"Hold your fire!" This time from the Confederate side. The fog lifted just enough to see their faces.

Just ahead, an injured soldier struggled to lift himself from the ground. I got closer—an arm's length away. Golden hair spilled out from under his gray slouch cap. His cheeks flushed cherry red. He blinked up at me. "I want to go home."

"I know," I answered, squatting beside him. "M-me, too." I glanced at the Rebel line.

A bullet had penetrated just below his collar bone. I fitted his mouth to the canteen, and he emptied the water in four short gulps.

I tried to lift him and twisted toward our line. "Someone, help!"

The boy's body relaxed in my hands. I grabbed his collar. "You all right? You all right?" In that blink of a moment, he was gone.

He was a child. He had crossed the bar, and he was only a child.

"Get back here!" Someone's voice trumpeted across the meadow. Guns cracked; bullets popped. I left the soldier and staggered back to my line. "Gabe!" I called, hot tears blinding me. Someone grabbed me and pulled me toward the line of blue.

"You some kind of fool?" Gabe tugged me behind him. "Don't. Don't do that again!"

I knew one thing: I would do it again, if I was given half a chance.

Then the shapes distorted, darkened, conjoined. Bayonets surfaced over a hill to our left. "They're flankin' us!" I screamed. "They're flankin' us. Get over here!" I had something to prove: to show Gabe that I was a soldier, that I knew how to fight. "They're comin'! Run!"

An echo of demons emerged from the earth. The Johnnies' shrill yells sent chills up my spine.

"C-come on!" I looked back at our men; their heels barely in motion. Two soldiers, maybe three moved forward. Then the rest of our company charged toward the Rebs. Like angry wasps to a nest, the Johnnies swarmed toward us.

"Come on!" I motioned our men forward.

Enfields spit bullets like fire. A Reb vaulted in front of me. With my bayonet's tip, I sliced him through, his eyes bloodshot and glaring.

Another Reb appeared out of the shadows, headed straight for me. I crouched and plowed for his belly. Jarring against him, I uprooted him from the ground. His gun spiraled through the air. I strained for the weapon, grasped it—just barely—and swiveled it in my hands. Then I slammed the gun on the Johnny's head. The field was a blur of butternut and blue.

* * *

I startled awake the next morning, O'Farrell's face a foot length from mine. "Hey, Joseph, you're wanted in officers' quarters."

In my mind's early morning fog, I wasn't sure if the fighting had been for real. I squinted up at O'Farrell. Our tent was small, and he filled much of the space.

"Officers' quarters? Why?" Scrambling out of my blankets, I grabbed for my shoes. My heart thumped out of my chest.

His knobby shoulders lifted. "Dunno. Think you're in a heap of trouble."

"Huh?" I asked, lacing my shoes. My fingers fumbled. I unlaced everything and started again.

"You're in trouble, and the sun isn't even up yet," he added, his lips twisting like a corkscrew. He backed through the tent flap. Gabe clambered out behind him.

My mind spinning, my thoughts registered nothing.

Unfolding myself from the tent, I squinted down the row of tents. "Who?" I asked.

"Colonel Moorhouse. Glad it's you and not me." O'Farrell folded his arms and bobbed his head, "Go ahead. I'll stay here."

Gabe tugged me toward the colonel's tent. "What'd you do?" His gait slowed to match mine. A line of concern etched between his eyes.

The tents stretched out in front of me. My stomach was in knots. I wasn't sure what I had done wrong. Running through the possibilities and swallowing hard, I ducked into the colonel's tent and took off my kepi. The tent was bare except for a table and an occupied chair. Colonel Moorhouse leaned forward, tapping his fingers in an impatient rhythm.

Officers were expected not only to be good leaders but also to care for and reward their men when they deserved it. Colonel Moorhouse would have been greatly pleased by Joseph's quick action and bravery, rewarding him with a promotion. Some of the bravest men were the vedettes or advance scouts, such the one pictured above, whose job it was to go a head of the army to ensure safety.

What was the protocol for entering an officer's tent? I'd never done it before. "Good morning, sir. You called for me?" I wiped my hands on my pants.

He squinted up at me, his eyes penetrating and dark. I couldn't read his expression; most of his face was camouflaged in hair. I imagined the worst—maybe someone was hurt at home.

Then he thrust out his hand to shake mine. "Congratulations, young man," Colonel Moorhouse said. I stood there dumbfounded. He must have made a mistake.

"You took control of a difficult position. If you hadn't rallied our troops, more of our men would've. . ." He let go of my hand. "Those Rebels flanked us. Your quick reaction saved us some of our men." He pushed corporal stripes across the table. "You earned this, young man."

I had surpassed my brother at last. Gabe didn't have stripes but I did.

Still toying with the chevron, I exited the tent.

Gabe, his elbow against an oak, asked, "You in trouble?" I couldn't read Gabe's expression. Angry, maybe—or hopeful. I shook my head.

"Well, what then?" He shifted his weight.

"St-stripes," I blurted and thrust out my hand.

I waited for Gabe's reaction. He glanced at my chevron and then looked off somewhere behind me. "Bully for you." His voice was flat.

20

Sarah

I picked a shard of glass out of my hand. We were running low on chloroform. Counting the bottles a second time and coming up with the same number, I wiped my hands on my skirts and rifled through another crate. "Four. Never going to be enough."

My stomach churned with the thought that just over the hill were soldiers, guns in hand, and we didn't have enough supplies.

Truman squeezed through the tent door, chilling the hospital with winter's brisk air.

"Better hope no one needs an amputation." Father picked up a broken bottle of whisky. "You were the one who wrapped the bottles?"

He knew very well that I was the one to pack the bottles. He had seen me pack them at Murfreesboro.

"I loaded them on the wagon," offered Truman, the corners of his eyes twinkling. He knew he had rescued me.

Another face appeared in the tent, eyes darting around. "Someone comin'!"

Orderlies snapped open the cots, lining them in straight rows. I emptied a crate of its bandages and thrust blankets and pans on the supply table. "But I don't hear fighting," I said.

A young soldier stumbled in. Skeletal in appearance, he took off his kepi and combed his hand through his hair. I half expected him to give me a rakish grin.

My breath quickened, "Gabe?" I ran toward the door, stopping, starting, stopping again. He turned. I wanted him to be Gabe—so much that I was ready to accept his higher hairline and his cleft chin. He wasn't Gabe, not even close.

He faltered by the first cot and sat down, winced, and unlaced his shoe. Tugging the toe of his sock, he looked up at me with hollow eyes. "Miss?" My heart softened.

I tugged a crate over beside him. "What's your name?" I put pressure on his ankle.

"Kearns, John Kearns." His ankle was puffy and warm.

"My name's Sarah. Miss Sutton. I'll have to ask Byron to look at it." Grabbing his haversack, I wedged it under his ankle. "You don't happen to know the Elliott boys? Gabe? Joseph?" I don't know why I bothered to ask. "They're brothers from Indianapolis," I added, feeling stupid. "Neighbors of mine." I wiped my hands on my dress.

His eyes brightened. "Joseph and Gabe? Fortieth Infantry?"

I hadn't mentioned the Fortieth. He'd only know if. . . My knees turned to jelly.

"Think I might know 'em." Readjusting his foot on the sack, he looked up at me. His eyes were green, like Gabe's. His hair was wavy but light brown, a dimple pocketed in his left cheek.

"You know where they could be now?" My brained ticked fretfully; they could be just miles away.

He glanced toward the door. "Maybe at the hollows, just south of here."

A warm flush worked up my face. "Think they're here? I mean, not far?" They were close. Only miles. I could . . .

John nodded at my excitement. "You'd have to follow this road 'til you get to Overall Creek. Then track the river upstream."

My thoughts tumbled over each other. I hugged myself, trying to imagine Joseph and Gabe—probably bearded, maybe taller. They'd be so surprised to see me! They couldn't possibly think about me as much as I wondered about them.

I surveyed the tent. Cots stood waiting for soldiers, and still there was no noise of battle. No one would miss me. Certainly, I didn't need to worry about my horse. Beulah was capable, after all; she had tracked Possum Creek at home.

"Umm . . . Miss?" John's voice jarred me back. "You can't go by yourself. A girl travelin' alone?" He shook his head. "You'd be askin' for trouble."

For a moment, I thought of finding Truman. It was broad daylight, though, and I was sure that he couldn't risk being outside. According to Truman, his master had been a tough, drinking man, and the mistress of the house was a portly woman with an evil disposition. He had no intention of going back.

"Trouble," I echoed, trying to focus. John was right. It made no sense for me to trail after Joseph and Gabe. Absolutely none. They hadn't written me, and it had been a year since I had seen them. The war had probably changed them. Why was I exhausting my time in worry?

But I couldn't stay, no matter how sensible that would be.

An orderly—a scarecrow, really—hesitated by the door, a dipper in his hand. Two orderlies leaned against the supply table, one toying with the bandages, the other one smoking a pipe. With only one soldier receiving treatment they didn't need my help.

Slipping on my cape, I ran out of the tent, grabbed Beulah's saddle and bridle, and dashed to the corral.

Beulah, though, had her own agenda. She stretched her neck against me. "Beulah!" I stuck my thumb in her mouth and tried to fit her bit. Like an unruly toddler, she jerked her head away. I warmed the bit in my hands and worked it into her mouth. "What's got into you?" I slipped the headstall over her ears.

I tried to remember John's directions about Overall Creek. If I got lost, I'd track the stream. If I met Rebs, I'd . . . I'd figure out something. Wildly confident, I cinched the saddle, fixed my foot in the stirrup, and mounted Beulah. Then I galloped away.

Beulah's hooves slid in the greasy ruts. Slowing to a walk, I moved off center. Travel might be easier on the side of the road. She poled through the pines. The farther I journeyed along the road, the more my confidence flagged. I longed to lift a rein and turn back.

The crisp air whispered of new snow; tiny flakes trailed to the ground. I could barely feel the reins in my stinging fingers.

Beulah's ears cupped forward, and I glanced down the road. An ambulance lumbered toward us. Shuddering, Beulah's muscles tightened, and she side-stepped, whuffed, and flared her nostrils. "Beulah!" I jammed my heels into her—again and again. Stubborn and headstrong, she backed until her hindquarters pressed against a tree.

Branches whipped me as I struggled to dismount and then tugged on the reins and wrenched her from the tree. My shoes suctioning in the mud, I remounted and prodded Beulah back toward the road. The ambulance slowed to a stop.

The driver's tenor, "Whoa," interrupted us. With tousled hair and a slender build, he looked barely fourteen. His team pranced forward. "Whoa, I said!" He yanked on the lines.

"Can you help us?" he asked, urging me toward the back of his wagon.

I already had my hands full, but the driver didn't seem to notice; he was so occupied with his own problems.

"What do you need?" I released Beulah's reins and slid off her.

"Some help in the back. Soldiers. Hurt bad."

My stomach lurched. How could I turn back to the hospital tent? Joseph and Gabe were probably only miles away. "I can't. I mean. I'm going . . ." I motioned weakly down the road. If I went in the ambulance, I'd lose any chance of finding Joseph and Gabe.

The driver, realizing my destination, gaped at me. "You can't go that way. Not the way you're headed. You'll be in the thick of the fighting."

I stood paralyzed by the side of the road. In the distance another ambulance rumbled toward us, silhouetted against the haze of battle. Then, like a ragged line of ants, one after another the ambulances crawled down the hill. There was a blast, and then another. A vibration surged up my spine.

"That's where the battle is, Miss. And if you're lookin' for someone . . ." He shook his head. "Chances are . . ." He looked me solidly in the eyes. "Miss, we need your help here."

I straightened my spine. Beulah, snorting, with white eyes and flattened ears, seconded the driver's request. I couldn't remount and ride her any time soon. Leaving her, I high-stepped over the ruts in the road to the ambulance.

The team pawed the ground and pressed against their collars, eager to leave. "I'm Adam Scheider. Obliged." He gripped at the lines. He had his hands full with his team, so I picked my way to the back of the wagon, scrunched my skirts in my hand, and climbed in. Just as I thought, Beulah was smart enough to follow.

Almost cellar-like, the wagon was a darkened world, heavy with the smell of blood and men's sweat. Two stretchers hung suspended from rubber straps on each side. I tucked my feet beneath me and sidled in between the stretchers.

The wagon jerked forward.

A young soldier beside me, hit in the stomach, stemmed the flow of blood with his hand. Part of his small intestine had escaped the abdominal cavity. His large intestine was mealy and raw. Every time we hit a rut in the road, he cried.

I fought the taste of acid roiling up my throat and into my mouth.

On the other side, a young man—his once handsome face now half gone—blinked down at a photograph clenched in his hands. His eyes were deep, an intoxicating brown, and the right side of his face was smooth beneath the dirt and blood covering it. The left side of his face was a poor parallel. All that remained was a piece of his tongue, his nasal passage, and shreds of muscle hanging from his cheekbone. He clung to life as—like a leaky bellows—air whistled through his mutilated throat.

I squinted at the picture gripped in his hand. "You have a beautiful little girl." The girl's image smiled back at me, her eyes dark and hopeful.

He blinked back a tear.

"She has your eyes." My voice caught, and I waited until I could form my words. "I'm sure she knows you love her dearly."

There was a slight tremor in his hand. I covered his with mine, understanding why I had been asked to help. These men were dying. They needed someone to sit by their side. Beulah trotted behind the limping wagon with no worries whatsoever, as I sat in the human debris and cried.

"I-I have a horse. Ss-she's following right behind us." I was babbling, but I couldn't help myself. "I know I should ride sidesaddle, but it is such a nuisance." The wagon jolted. I grabbed one of the swinging stretchers. Repositioning myself, I planted my palms on the floor. "Her name's Beulah." The wagon hit a dip in the road; I lurched to the right. I was sharing my story to soothe the soldiers, or perhaps to calm myself. "When I was a little girl, I rode with my father, both of us on Beulah. The wind was so fierce. Her ears flattened . . . not a good sign." The wagon jerked again, this time to the left.

I felt foolish, but I continued my story. "Beulah reared. I was young but smart enough to knot my hand in her mane. I jerked the reins to the right and she slowed to a stop. That's when I noticed my father was gone." I smiled at the memory. "He was in the grass. You know what he told me? 'You're quite a rider. Keep your head on your shoulders, and your horse will carry you through.'" My tone was wistful. I swallowed hard. "My horse will carry me through . . ."

The wagon lurched forward and back again, coming to a stop. Adam, his young face void of emotion, helped me out of the wagon. "Lay 'em here." He nodded toward a massive oak, with some papery leaves still hanging on. It was an old tree, solid and beautiful. As a child, I might have swung from such a sprawling giant; I might have watched Joseph and Gabe climb it. I might have been happy—joyful even.

I wasn't a child—not any more.

Adam and I unloaded the soldiers, including the man holding his intes-
tines and the man with half a face. With some difficulty we removed a soldier
who was burly and carried most of his weight in his upper torso. Adam
hooked his arm over one shoulder, and I positioned myself under his other
arm. Together, we half dragged him out of the wagon and sat him under the
tree.

Adam glanced in the wagon, his face turning gray. "There's someone else."

Forgetting my discomfort, I squinted in the ambulance. Someone emerged
from the dark, "W-who?" The soldier unfolded himself from the wagon.

With disheveled blond hair and a lanky build, he couldn't have been more
than eighteen. He crumpled to the ground. "Hurt. Hurt bad," he mumbled. His
arm, shredded and sticky with day-old blood, was a macabre puzzle of cartilage, tendons, and flesh.

I shredded fabric from my petticoat. "Are you hurt anywhere else?"

He was dressed in blue homespun, and his skin carried a clammy sheen.
"Don't know. Don't think so."

My fingers trembled as I wound the fabric around his arm. "Your name?"

"Enoch. Enoch Nation." A strong name. He looked up at me with pleading
blue eyes. This man had a chance.

Leaving Enoch with Adam, I charged back to the tent. Almost every cot
was full. "I need a surgeon," I panted. "A doctor. I'm not sure what this soldier
needs. Something. Quick."

"Surgeons are busy." Byron leaned against the table and reached for his
forceps. "Working on bullets, here."

"You know where my father went?" I scanned the tent. Every cot was full.

Byron nodded toward the door. "Think he's outside. Been there most of the
day." He avoided my eyes.

My heart thumping, I ran outside. "Father?" Soldiers surged toward us,
braiding and twisting in cords of Union blue. The meadow was alive with men.
I was desperate to find Father. Everyone looked the same.

Another ambulance trailed down the road toward us. And another.

I found him by a maple, sitting down with his head between his knees.
"Father?" I ran up to him.

"Yes?" His voice didn't even sound like him. He turned toward me and
blinked. I took a half step toward him, and stopped, my stomach tightening.
His forehead furrowed in cold sweat; his lips formed a gray, grim line.

He was obviously sick, but I needed his help. "Would you help me? Please?"

"What do you need?" he asked, annoyed. His eyelids were half closed, his face gray, lips pinched together.

Carefully I said, "A soldier. Over there." I motioned toward the oak.

Father took off his kepi, wiped the sweat beads off his forehead, and replaced his cap. "I'll do what I can." With an unsteady gait, he followed behind me.

An orderly marched past us carrying a stretcher in one arm.

"Help us. Please," I said to him, and the three of us threaded through the mass of wounded soldiers, horses, and wagons. Surrounded by yells and screams, I focused on the tree ahead.

The three of us lifted Enoch onto the stretcher. "Enoch, you're brave," I said, adjusting his arm. Swallowing hard, I forced myself to slow my breaths, calming my racing heart and tightening chest.

The orderly took one side of the stretcher. My father and I took the other, and we worked our way back to the tent, pausing to redistribute the weight. The orderly opened the door to the tent. Faces turned our way.

We set Enoch on the table. My hands trembling, I searched for a handkerchief, finding one deep in my pocket. I creased the cloth in a fold. "How much chloroform?" I glanced at the supply table and nabbed the last bottle, soaking my cloth with chloroform. I tipped the bottle. The last drops of liquid saturating my handkerchief.

Enoch moaned, and rolled to his side.

"You might need more than that." Father took the bottle from me and pitched it into a crate.

"Will we have enough?" I glanced at my handkerchief. Some of the liquid had already evaporated. I clenched my hand tightly around the cloth, trying to preserve the moisture. What if other soldiers came in, needing this precious liquid?

Father spread his instruments on the table, shifting his eyes toward me, his pupils darkening. "If we have more soldiers, someone will have an amputation *completely awake*." He raised one eyebrow at me. Numb to his statement, I fitted the handkerchief over Enoch's mouth. He pulled away, and I cupped his head with my hand.

Father rubbed his thumb back and forth against his knife's razor edge.

The chloroform was doing its work; Enoch's body relaxed. I clutched underneath his shoulder, and held his arm steady while Father sliced the skin open, exposing the muscles below. Enoch flinched. A guttural noise escaped his lips.

Father's jaw tightened. "Retract the muscle, Sarah. Up. Up as far as possible." A grim undertaking, since Enoch's arm was slick with blood. "Grip tighter." He gave me an icy glare.

Moaning, Enoch's eyelids flicked open. His half-alert state made me queasy. I couldn't stamp the image of broken chloroform bottles from my mind.

"Concentrate!" Father shot me a fierce look. I gripped Enoch's arm tighter. His arm, a stubborn network of muscles and tendons, didn't loosen easily from the bone.

"About done?" somebody yelled. "Another one for you. Outside."

Wounded soldiers poured into the tent.

Father set down his knife and grabbed his saw. He steadied himself against the table and drew a breath. He motioned toward Enoch's arm. "Ready for this?" Oddly enough, I was curious. Father grated off the bone just below Enoch's elbow; the papery smell of bone dust filtered through the air. With the saw's angry bite, I strengthened my grasped on his arm.

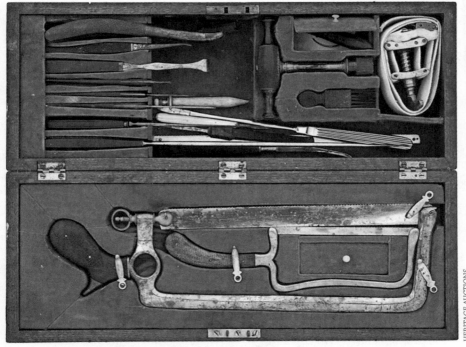

HERITAGE AUCTIONS

The minié balls used during the Civil War caused gaping holes, destroyed muscles, and splintered bones. Faced with such catastrophic wounds, a surgeon's best choice to save a life was amputation. Doctor Sutton's amputation tools would have been similar to those in the kit above.

All at once his hand dropped into the bowl—the fingers curled, the severed tendons, muscles, and veins mashed and useless, the fingernails dirty and crusted with blood. Blood streamed from his arm into the bowl.

Father reached for his pliers, adjusted his grip on the handles, and snipped off the bone's jagged end.

Blood pulsed from Enoch's artery. "Clamp, Sarah. Clamp!" Father yelled. Pinching the artery, Father motioned toward his instruments. "Clamp!" Still holding Enoch, I grappled for the tools. The hooks, probes, pliers, and forceps lay in line on the table, but I couldn't find the clamp. "Sarah!" He grimaced toward the edge of the table.

"There." I jammed the clamp into his hands.

"Lost the vessel. Need the hook." My hands shaking, I reached for the hook and placed it in Father's hand. I wiped my hands on my skirt. With a mechanical certainty, he hooked the end of the leaking vessel and tugged out the end of the artery.

"Ready? Another one!" An orderly called by the door. A wave of soldiers entered the tent.

"These boys are being cut to pieces!" I said, trying to concentrate on my work.

He used a needle next, and then oiled silk thread. Father struggled with the thread. "Can't get it through that damn small eye." Wetting the thread in his mouth, he twisted it with his fingers and worked the strand through the needle. Then he stitched through Enoch's angry skin. The skin puckered under the tightening thread.

"Styptic. Lint." Father motioned toward the supplies. His face turned ashen. At first I thought he was angry at me. Had I done something wrong? He weaved to one side.

"You all right?" I grabbed his elbow.

Fisting his hand on his stomach, an unmistakable shroud of pain clouded Father's face. "I'm going back to my tent. You can finish up here."

With a nervous glance at my father, I generously applied the styptic on Enoch's arm. I wadded some lint in my hands, and spread it out on his wound. "B-but what about . . . " With my lint-covered hands, I waved toward the soldiers still filtering through the door. I steadied myself against the table.

"Can't," he said, small beads of sweat forming on his forehead.

I wrapped Enoch's arm in a bandage. Groaning, Enoch pulled away.

Father staggered to the door.

"My arm," Enoch moaned. His face twisted in pain. His eyes fully open now, he blinked at me. "You—You cut off my hand?" His tone was accusing. Sharp.

"It's all right," I said, numbly.

"All *right*?" Still groggy from the chloroform haze, he looked at his stump, his words slurring into each other. "What am I . . . supposed . . . to do? I can't even hoe."

I didn't know what to say. His hand lay in a bowl by my feet—he wouldn't have use of it again. I was a butcher. We all were.

"You'll be able to do a lot more than you think," I said feebly, brushing some hair from his eyes. "You need to heal first."

His eyes flitted open and then closed, and I wished I hadn't said anything. He lifted his head from the table, his good hand clenched beside him. "Useless."

I didn't have an answer.

Two more orderlies carted in another young soldier. Enoch's jaw muscles worked. "You'll send my sister a letter, won't you? I mean if something happens?" Pressing his lips together, he turned his head away.

"More coming!" someone said. Five more soldiers entered the tent.

I stood frozen. Aching. Uncertain.

* * *

Long past midnight, I finally entered our sleeping quarters. "Father?"

Greeted by the oily smell of candle wax, I found him on the edge of his cot, doubled over in pain. "What's wrong?" His hands, usually holding a scalpel or a knife, were empty, knotted across his stomach.

Eyes filled with pain, he whispered, "Think I have dysentery." He looked up at me. "Don't have long."

At that instant, life slipped even further from my control and almost sucked me under.

I slept fitfully, dark images sifting through my consciousness: the big oak, a severed hand, the blood-soaked ground. I startled awake, feeling more dead than alive.

My thoughts drifted from Gabe to Joseph to Father. If Father died I would be alone.

I fumbled for my shoes, not bothering to button them completely. Father draped his head over the cot's edge and mumbled something.

"You awake?" I whispered. Answered by his regular breathing, I put on my cloak and walked into the brisk morning air.

I stopped short once I entered the hospital, my breaths coming in ragged gasps. Enoch's cot was empty.

I'd never been so alone.

21

Joseph

CHATTANOOGA, TENNESSEE, NOVEMBER 1863

"We'll be lucky if we make it home," O'Farrell said, plopping beside me just outside my tent. He tugged at his collar, drawing it tightly under his chin.

The sky was an overcast gray. Seemed like everybody else had hunkered down in their tents—except for O'Farrell and me.

"What if we don't make it home? You ever think about that?" He wheeled a large tree stump closer to me and sat down.

"Not lately." Gabe and I had drawn patrol duty. He was already yards down the road, while I sat on a stump fumbling with a knot in my shoelaces.

"Can you read this letter from Eliza?" O'Farrell worked out a letter from his pocket. "Think she's worried." Obviously, he was getting mail.

"Gabe's waiting." I nodded down the road. "Captain said to be back before nightfall."

"Short letter." He opened the paper and tapped it. "See. Ten lines."

"Hardly worth sendin'." Eliza must have been quite a girl to put up with him, I figured. I took the letter, my eyes marching down the page. "Says she misses you."

"'Course she misses me. What else?"

I sighed. "All right." I read more carefully, and my voice turned solemn.

> We buried three this week. They were such lovely boys. They died at Chickamauga, and the whole town is in mourning. You remember James McLelland, don't you? He was one of them.
>
> Whatever you do, don't be careless. There are people who love you. One of them is me.
>
> Yours,
> Eliza

O'Farrell swept the letter from my hand and jammed it into his sack. "She doesn't have to worry. I'm not careless." He motioned toward Gabe. "It's *him* we need to watch out for. Look. He's on guard duty and not even carrying a gun." Gabe was a speck down the road.

I grabbed my rifle and peeled off after him. "Gabe!"

He swiveled back to me.

"Your gun," I huffed, catching up to him. "You d-don't have your gun."

He shrugged his shoulders. "Small chance of us runnin' across Rebs." He gave me a lopsided grin. "Besides, you have yours."

Leaves skittered across the road, crunching underneath our feet, both of us walking toward Confederate territory. In a steady rhythm, my gun slapped against my side.

I should have been in good spirits. Gabe and I had the whole afternoon out from under the eyes of our commanders. Then I realized that in my haste to catch up with him, I had forgotten to load my gun.

Whatever you do, don't be careless.

I couldn't tell Gabe, but if we met up with Rebs, we wouldn't stand a chance. My mouth went dry.

He took a swig from his canteen. "You hear about Chickamauga?"

"Uh. A little." Eliza's words paraded through my mind.

"Damn Rebs. Gettin' the best of us. They know how to fight. Who knows what could happen." He gave me a knowing look. Then, both of us heard it at the same time: the crunch of wagon wheels.

Birds flocked out of the bushes.

Crouching, Gabe pointed to the south. A supply wagon trundled toward us, the occupants wearing uniforms of butternut and gray.

"Your gun," he hissed. "Aim your gun." They were only yards away.

Unable to run to camp for powder and stuck with an unloaded gun, I had two choices: tell Gabe that my gun wasn't loaded, or somehow pretend that it was.

The wagon jerked to a stop. I slammed my gun to my shoulder—the grit in my voice startling me, "Hands in the air!"

Widening his stance, Gabe jutted his chin toward me. His tone was lower than its usual pitch. "Better do what he says, or my brother will blow you half-way to hell!"

I glanced at my useless gun.

The driver, more bear than man, nodded toward his wagon bed. His muscular hands shot to the sky. "Got whisky back there." Panting, the cub next to him agreed. "We'll share it."

Gabe leaned into me. "Our day took a turn for the better, but keep your gun ready, just in case."

Like a hell-bent fool, I gripped my gun.

The driver tipped his cap, "Don't shoot." Leading with his stomach, the old bear rolled off the seat, tripped over his feet, and pummeled to the ground. "Gol dang it!" He stood up and wiped the gravel off his hands. Gabe eyed me, and I instantly read his thoughts: the bear's voice was an exact match of Father's.

The Reb lumbered to the back of the wagon and grappled mugs out of a crate. Replacing the stopper with a spigot, he emptied whisky into the mugs and took a swig from his own. "Sweet stuff." He wiped his mouth with the back of his hand. "War's over, far as I'm concerned."

Gabe nodded and raised his mug.

Balancing my rifle in one hand and my mug in the other, I took a draw, savoring the vanilla, caramel, oaky taste.

"Prob'ly the only whisky left in the state," the old bear growled. He drained his mug and leaned against the wagon.

I saluted him with my cup. "If we're in charge of the whisky, there won't be a single drop left."

The smaller Reb returned the salute. "You're country boys, jest like ourselves. Tryin' to survive, best we can."

"Here's to survival." I touched my brother's mug with my own. Gabe nodded and shared a smile with me, the first smile I'd seen in some time.

The ol' bear took a swig. "Sharin' your whisky will ensure our bein' easier on you. You can be sure of that," I said. At that moment if the decision to end the war would have been ours, the four of us would have packed our bags for home.

With a nod to the Rebs, I pulled Gabe aside. "Be less trouble all around if our prisoners would just, I dunno, escape. Easier for all concerned."

"Don't think there's a medal in it. Hate to think of all the explainin' we'd have to do." He set our mugs on the wagon bed and motioned down the road. "You fellas just go. We don't want to, um, trouble our sergeant with a couple of Rebs."

Air whisked leaves across the road, and a cloud darkened the sun.

The ol' bear tipped his kepi. "We'll be off then. Kind of you." He started toward the front of the wagon.

I nudged him with my gun. "Kind. Not stupid. We'll take the whisky. Might need it." I gave Gabe a sideways glance.

The Reb frowned. "Can't rightly do that. Got people to answer to." He set down his mug. "Our cap'n was anticipatin' whisky." With a longing look at his whisky barrel, he heaved a sigh. "But maybe we can come up with some kind of excuse. I mean, if we put our heads together."

Gabe winked at me. "Maybe the barrel coulda rolled off the back."

I couldn't help it, but I chuckled.

The cub nodded. "Or got stolen by Indians." He gave me a sly smile.

As far as my brother was concerned, the party was over. He brushed off his hands. "If you want, we could blast a hole through the whisky barrel. Then we'll be done with it."

"One trip of my trigger and there'd be nothin' left to argue about." My warning tumbled off my tongue.

Gabe leaned toward me. "Huzzah." The corner of his mouth tugged in a grin.

Hoisting the whisky barrel off the back, the ol' bear clambered onto his seat and gathered the lines. "If we're going to eat crow, might as well be a warm one." With a flick of the lines they were on their way.

JAMES I. ROBERTSON JR., *TENTING TONIGHT: THE SOLDIER'S LIFE* (ALEXANDRIA, VA: TIME-LIFE BOOKS, 1984), 64.

Sometimes the army would publically punish soldiers as a way of humiliating them and also preventing others from misbehaving. In this story, Gabe was being punished for fornication with one of the general's favorite ladies.

"Let's get that barrel movin'." Gabe nodded toward camp. "No tellin' when more Rebs could show up." He edged the barrel on its side. "Gotta say," he added. "Those Rebs and us. We differ politically, but we're a unit on the subject of whisky." He jarred the barrel with his heel and nudged it down the road. For the most part, he maneuvered the barrel easily on the slight downhill grade.

"So, how about that!" Gabe gave another shove. "My brother captured a couple Rebs." I heard the shared pride in his voice; the victory was sweet. With my unloaded gun I had captured two Rebs and some whisky too. "Too bad you lost 'em." He heeled the barrel, and it tumbled in front of us, jolting down the road.

Pumping my fists, I slowed my pace.

"Teasing," he said, giving me a backward glance. I kept walking, but his negative words still played in my mind.

We arrived back at camp with the whisky intact. O'Farrell looked happy to see us—or maybe just pleased with the whisky.

* * *

I woke up with the taste of oak in my mouth.

Allowing morning's thin light to enter the tent, I flapped open the door. I rubbed the sleep out of my eyes. Gabe's blankets were nested in a clump beside me, but he wasn't there. My pulse quickening, I staggered out of the tent.

The air, cooler than the day before, was fresh and sweet.

That's when I discovered him. He stood in the middle of the encampment, shrouded in a barrel jacket. I'd seen one soldier drummed out of camp, and I'd seen another tarred and feathered, but I never had seen anyone encased in a barrel.

"Great Scott, Gabe! What're you doin'?" I tripped up to him and squinted at the placard in his hands.

Fornicator.

The woodiness in my brain dulled my speech. "What'd you d-do?"

"Read the sign." Gabe adjusted the strap on the barrel. "Just enjoyed some . . . er . . . horizontal refreshment. Didn't know she was the general's favorite . . . um . . . lady." His face was relaxed—even wistful.

"When'd you have time for that?" Ribbons of pink morning light shone through the trees. The camp was still asleep, but reveille would be playing soon. I glanced up the row of tents. No one awake. Not yet.

Gabe shrugged. "Well, you started snorin' and I left. Knew you weren't going with me." His caustic words echoed, or maybe they just resounded with me. He turned toward the brightening sky. Wood-lined and round, he looked ridiculous.

"Were you smart enough to, you know, to use something to prevent . . ." I followed behind him.

"Conceiving a bastard?" Gabe's chin tilted toward me, and I felt even more uncomfortable. "Kind of a bold question."

Seemed that I wasn't the "bold" one. I drew a deep breath, realizing how awkward the conversation had become. "What d-did she look like?" I knew it was an odd question, but I just wanted to know.

He pivoted toward me, his barrel swinging like a bell. "You mean when I was . . ."

Did I have to clarify? "Yes, when you were. . . " I glanced toward the tents. If anyone saw my brother in that barrel, I didn't want to be a witness. "What did she look like?" I asked again.

"Didn't see her. Well, maybe a little of her back," he answered. His situation was beyond words.

The sun blinked above the horizon, highlighting Gabe's predicament. I was embarrassed for him and embarrassed for me. I shook my head. "So you're in a barrel for fornication, and you d-didn't see her?" It just didn't make sense to me.

"It was worth it." He rested one foot on the other. "And I'm still the one who came up on *top*, if you know what I mean."

I stood there, my thoughts boiling. I'd heard more than enough. Didn't Gabe realize what he had done? To that girl—to Sarah? He treated Sarah as if she were insignificant, and she would never know. I wheeled toward my tent. "You probably got what was comin' to you." Without a backward glance, I left him standing there.

After that, he refused to talk to me. I understood. There were things I couldn't discuss with him either. Gabe and I were no longer the brothers we once were—ones who talked about anything. Having secrets made us enemies, same as we were with the Rebs.

22

Sarah

Oddly enough, Abraham Lincoln had declared an official day of Thanksgiving and Praise. Our nation, a scarlet remnant of its past, was torn. Father was ill, and I wasn't sure that I could manage without him.

For what could I be thankful?

The battle was only moments away. Cooks were hoisting pots, laundresses were carting washboards, and I was unwrapping medicines. Truman removed a crate from the wagon and heaved it over his shoulder. Ambulances came into view as Father and I paused at the hospital's entrance.

Father motioned to the south. "More on the way!" A steady stream of ambulances wheeled toward us. No one needed to tell us the battle had begun.

Two orderlies carted the first soldier inside, setting him on the cot by the door. The young man couldn't have been older than sixteen. Gunpowder covered his face, and his teeth were clenched in pain. He twisted his shoulder for my inspection. "You're *not*. Takin'. My arm."

I examined his wound. "Don't think we'll need to." Just inches above his elbow, a bullet had penetrated his uniform.

"Couldn't see 'em fightin'. So foggy up there." His eyes braced on mine. "Like . . . like . . . we was fightin' ghosts." I gave him a draw of whisky. He wiped his mouth with the back of his hand.

Father clutched his stomach. "You all right?" I asked, grabbing his medical kit from the floor. "Let me. I can do it. Talk me through it." With my father struggling behind me and a soldier needing care, I didn't know what to do first.

Father grasped for his bag and doubled in pain. "I can," he said.

My father was in no condition to serve as a doctor. His face had taken on a grayish hue, and his breath came in short rasps.

I tugged a crate behind him. "Please. Please let me help."

THANKSGIVING-DAY, NOVEMBER 26, 1863.

Surrounded by death in the wake of the bloodiest battle in American history at Gettysburg in July, few Americans found reasons to be thankful. However, President Lincoln encouraged all Americans to reflect on every blessing they still had and give thanks to God for those things.

He unclenched his fist, and his bag dropped to the ground. Weaving slightly, he slumped down.

"You all right? Father?"

Vaguely, I heard Byron's bellow. Soldiers bumped past me, coursing through the doors in a grim ribbon of blue, adding to the chaos inside the tent. Father looked up and said, "Probe the wound with your finger."

I glanced again toward the door. Willing myself to stay calm, I examined the wound. It was flaming red and the size of a large button. I burrowed my finger in the muscle—wet, sinewy, and tough. How imbedded could the bullet be? I dug deeper. Tendons, maybe. The soldier cried out and vised my arm. I wrenched away from his grip.

"Feel anything?" My father edged forward on the crate, his hand heeled against his stomach.

Then I felt something, maybe an inch deep, "Yes. Not sure what it is." I drilled my finger deeper. The soldier moaned.

Father waved toward his kit. "Take that probe. Insert it in the wound."

I grabbed the probe. Someone yelled out from the back of the room.

"Concentrate. Keep your mind on your work." My father's voice had an edge. "Come on. Now. When you hit something hard, rub it with that probe." He leaned forward, gripping his stomach.

My knees were weak. Steadying myself against the table, I inserted the porcelain tip and plunged in the wound. The first layers were easy: soft, spongy. Then my probe hit something solid—deeper than I expected. Bullet? Bone? "Think I found it," I said.

"Good. Retract it. If it's white, you've hit bone. Discolored, the bullet."

Retracting the probe, I examined it. "Kind of gray. Brownish gray." I turned for Father's reaction.

Father's face had turned a mottled, marbly color. "Yes. That's it." He took a ragged breath. "Now, clench it with the forceps and tug. If you need to, probe with your finger too."

I awkwardly clutched the forceps. Twice, the bullet slipped from my grip.

"Come on, Sarah." His voice was firm but almost comforting.

Readjusting my grip on the forceps, I tried again, tugging out the forceps. The bullet, thankfully, was snagged. "There!" Turning to my father, I flaunted the forceps in a celebratory wave.

The soldier slumped against me. "Fainted. He fainted." I set down the forceps. His forehead felt clammy and wet.

"Typical." Father's crate grated behind me. "Saved us some whisky." Then Father said something that caught me off-guard. "If you don't have papers, you won't be able to stay."

"W-what? What do you mean?"

"I mean . . ." His voice was tight. "If something happens to me. Better have authorization. Have someone write Governor Morton."

I couldn't breathe. "If something happens," I whispered.

It wouldn't be long.

* * *

The next few days I tried everything I could think of: castor oil, cold rags, tea I made from dogwood bark. Certain that my father was hungry, I used a spirit lamp and tin cup to warm broth for him. He wouldn't eat anything.

I begged another doctor for help. "Can't you help him? He's a doctor."

"Haven't you noticed?" His voice was cold steel. "People are dyin' all the time."

I tried more blankets, more water, less blankets, less water. Nothing seemed to work. If I thought too hard about his situation, I felt paralyzed—unable to do anything at all.

With every passing day Father became weaker. His eyes were rimmed with dark shadows, his cheeks hollowed, and his face tinged gray. He rarely got out of bed.

He motioned me to come close. "I haven't been the best father, you know."

"Oh, yes, you have." My mind was numb. I sat down on the crate beside him, reeling with the weight of his words. He had been far from the best, but he was all that I had.

Clearing his throat, he smoothed my hair with his hand. "You're going to be all right." I wasn't going to be all right. *Why did people say "you're going to be all right" when nothing was right at all?*

He had healed so many soldiers, but he couldn't heal himself. I didn't know how I would manage without him. It wasn't fair—nothing about his illness was fair. "I love you," I whispered, unsure if he even heard. I wanted to hear him say those words back to me. I wanted him to tell me how capable I was, or how wonderfully I had cared for him. Anything.

The next morning he was gone. I would never hear him say anything again.

* * *

The skies were angry. Gray clouds rolled in from the west, and wind whipped at my skirts. Someone had already buried him. Their duty, I supposed. He had no flowers, the only marker for his grave was a six-by-three-foot mound of dirt.

I should plant flowers, I thought. I closed my eyes, trying to recall where I'd last seen a shovel—the cook's tent. I ran there, grabbed the shovel, and rushed back.

My feet moved forward, but my mind was numb. I stumbled, stopped, and stared at the shovel. I had no father, no mother. I was an orphan. Alone.

Drawing a breath, I closed my eyes. My shovel jarred on the frozen clay. Barely a dent. Useless. Hurling down the shovel, I sat down and sobbed. Joining me, the cold wind howled like a crying child.

I don't know how long I stayed there. The darkening sky surprised me. Somehow—I don't remember how—I retraced my steps to the cook's tent and set down the shovel. A deep breath, a slow exhale. Maybe, if I went back to the hospital tent, where I was needed, where people relied on me, I'd be all right.

I found Byron by the supply table, intent on his work. He was organizing medicines—not his usual task. The muscles in his jaw tightened. He nodded at me. "Just tryin' to do somethin'."

"Me too," I whispered. Truman stood beside me and fitted bottles in a crate.

Struggling with my thoughts, I worked beside them and sorted bottles. Then the three of us stood in the doorway and listened to the wind.

23

Joseph

In a matter of weeks our company constructed a grid of ragged buildings into our winter quarters. Gabe, O'Farrell, and I dug down a foot or so into the frozen ground, laid logs, and chinked them with mud, fashioning a log cabin of sorts. Although our roof was a motley combination of shingles and boards, it served as a barrier against the snow.

The inside of our cabin wasn't much, but we were creative—log ends served as stools, bayonets substituted for candlesticks. Gabe scrawled a sign for the entrance of our cabin: "Buzzard Roost." That title suited us—we became good enough at "roosting." For Gabe, "roosting" was hunting. For me, it was writing letters to Sarah.

January 19, 1864

Dear Sarah,

It has been far too long since I've seen you. I miss home.

It is warmer here in Tennessee than back home, but we still have some snow. Yesterday we had a snowball fight. Our snowballs were more ice than snow, and there were heavy casualties. One of the lieutenants lost two front teeth. At least five men had bloody noses. I have a few scrapes, but turned out all right.

The officers were worse off than the rest of us. The higher the officer, the more he was targeted. We took some of the officers prisoner, and they exchanged whisky for their release. Fine exchange that was! We will have to take them prisoner again.

Hopefully, the new order prohibiting snowballs will be lifted.

I'm not sure if you are getting my letters, but I hope you are.

Yours,
Joseph

Rappahannock Station Va March 14th 1864

I wanted to see Sarah, but first I needed to find her. Maybe something had happened to her. One thing I knew: ideas came easier with a knife in my hand.

I borrowed O'Farrell's pocketknife and settled onto a stump outside our quarters. My masterpiece was nearly complete—a Union soldier with buttoned jacket, slouch cap, and a miniature rifle. I was frustrated because I couldn't get his facial expression right.

So intent on my carving, I didn't notice O'Farrell sidling up beside me. "So what's your girl's name?" he asked. "You've made a hundred trips to the sutler, and you're always carryin' a letter."

"Maybe I'm writing my mother," I said, without looking up.

"Letters to your mother?" He peered over my shoulder. "You wouldn't be sendin' letters to your mother a hundred times. You don't act like a mama's boy." I didn't plan to share information about my letters, especially to O'Farrell.

"Maybe she's not gettin' 'em." He slipped his hands in his pockets. "Haven't gotten any response, have you?" His persistence was annoying, but he was

Wives, parents, friends, and other family members eagerly awaited news about the soldiers, hoping to know they were safe. Soldiers also wanted to know what was going on at home and so countless letters were sent back and forth over the course of the war.

right—I hadn't gotten even one letter. I made a decisive cut with the knife and my wooden man suddenly looked angry.

O'Farrell scooped up gray snow, working it into a ball. "Maybe she's not livin' at home. Your letters could be pilin' up with no one to read 'em. Maybe . . . maybe she got married." Rotating his arm, he whacked his snowball into an old hickory tree. "Bull's eye!" He wiped off the snow from his hands. "Prob'ly a mountain of those letters molderin' somewhere."

It was no use. I blew off the shavings, set my carving down, and turned on him. "O'Farrell, mind your own business." I didn't know how to be clearer than that.

"More fun mindin' yours." O'Farrell rolled a log beside me and plopped down, nabbed my soldier, and studied it.

Had I been that transparent? Then I worried: If O'Farrell seemed to know everything, had Gabe read my mind, too?

I snatched my carving out of his hands and tried to weed out the anger in my voice. "So. Let's pretend I *d-do* have a girl, and she's not getting my letters. What would *you* do? Just s'posin' that was true?" I couldn't believe I was desperate enough to seek advice from O'Farrell.

"Take out an advertisement." His answer was matter of fact. He slipped off his haversack and took out a newspaper, spreading it out on his legs. "See, right here. It says, 'To my girl, just want you to know that I'm fine in Alabama.'" He grinned up at me. "Joe, you could say you were fine in Alabama." He folded the paper in crisp fourths. "But, you're not in Alabama, and you're not fine," he said looking up at me, "from what I can tell."

I grimaced. "Well. I'm not going to take out an advertisement."

"Just a thought. Think you should. Better than sittin' with your head in your hands," O'Farrell replied.

I wasn't sitting with my head in my hands. I was carving. I picked up O'Farrell's knife and got back to work.

He stared over my shoulder. I wheeled around. "Can't you back off? You have to share your opinion on everything?"

His response came slowly, more seriously than before. "You haven't heard from her, right?"

No, I hadn't heard from her. Not once. "No." I turned back to my carving.

Then he asked me a question—a question that got me thinking: "Well, how do you know she's okay?"

24

Sarah

My living situation changed due to my Father's passing. The laundress and I now shared quarters. Louise, a rotund woman with a rat's-nest bun, was soft-spoken and calm and the perfect person with whom to share a tent. She made the offer the night my father died, and I moved right away. I needed somebody.

But the next morning, Louise was anything but calm.

She whipped open the door and silvery morning light flooded our tent. The pitch of her voice higher than her usual tone, she said "Lookee out there! Someone's comin' on horseback. Can't tell for sure, but they don't look like our boys." She wheeled toward me. "Rebs. I think they're Rebs."

I ran out the door to find two bays cantering toward us, with a third following behind. After they ground to a halt, it was apparent that the riders wore gray, the color of our enemy.

My stomach twisted, but I squared my shoulders and stood my full five foot six. "What do you want?"

One of the officers looked no older than I. A bristly mustache raked over his mouth, and a beakish nose overwhelmed his diminutive chin. "My brother, Leonard," his breath came in short rasps, "back at camp." The officer's horse nudged me, jostling the reins. "A bullet wound in his arm," he panted. "We don't have a doctor."

"You have a pass?" I thrust out my hand.

"Showed it to the picket guard back there." He waved toward the north of our camp, mumbled something, then reached in his jacket and handed the pass to me.

Military Pass
No. 254
Ringgold, Georgia. February 19, 1864
Pass bearer Mr. W. H. Munday
through our lines
By order of
Col. Uriah Root

"Um. Mr. Munday, every surgeon's busy . . . " I handed the pass back to him. "But if you need my help . . . "

Louise tugged at my elbow. "Don't get involved." Her breath smelled like rotting potatoes.

The two men talked as if I wasn't there.

"We really need a doctor."

"Will she be any help at all?" one asked. "First of all, she's a Yankee. Second of all, she's a girl."

"We really need a doctor," the first one repeated.

Sighing, they waved me toward the hospital tent. "Get what you need."

I should have been concerned—they were Rebel officers, after all. I ducked into the hospital for my Father's medical kit. Fumbling through the contents, I checked for the forceps, the probe, and the bandages. "Opium. I'll need opium," I muttered to myself, my hands flying over the supply table.

Truman stopped me at the door. "Where are you going?"

My throat aching for air, I looked past him, toward the officers and croaked, "To help this officer."

He pushed open the door flap. "That Rebel?" Deep furrows lined his forehead. "I don't know . . ." His sentence stopped midstream, and he motioned up the hill.

Adjusting the medical kit, I slipped past him. My choice to leave with the Rebels was more of a gut feeling than a clear decision. In my mind, I couldn't deny assistance—Confederate or not.

I was barely out the door when the officer motioned toward his extra mount. "Here, get on ol' Sal. She's saddled and ready to go." I glanced at the corral. Beulah, scruffy with her winter coat, happily chomped hay.

Sal nickered and nudged my arm.

"Um. Don't have a sidesaddle," the officer mumbled. "That all right?"

I tucked my foot in the stirrup, gripped the horn, and hoisted myself into the saddle, my skirts tugging underneath me. Sal shifted when I mounted her, and the officer frowned. "You know how to ride?"

Do I know how to ride? I answered with a "Giddap," circling Sal to the south. I fumed as we trotted down the road, my mind brimming with negative commentary.

* * *

I expected more tents and more soldiers, but the Rebel encampment wasn't much: a few rows of tents, smoldering campfires, some corrals for horses. About a dozen men stood in a willow's shade. They knuckled their hats in front of them. I dismounted. Wiping my hands on my skirt, I strode toward the circle of men, willing myself to stay calm.

"She thinks she can fix 'em," one said. Someone coughed.

I shot him a poisoned glance. I was in Rebel territory in the midst of soldiers armed with only a medical bag. I gripped my bag and entered the ring. Two soldiers were lying on the ground; one in a pool of dark crimson, blood still oozing from his side.

"Not going to make it," I murmured to myself.

Someone's voice rang behind me: "She doesn't know what to do."

Another soldier slumped against a rock, cradling his left arm in his hand. Blood stained his shirt sleeve and laced between his fingers.

"Leonard?" Setting my bag on the ground, I knelt beside him, unwrapped the wound, and checked for an exit wound. Finding none, I used my little finger to determine the depth of the bullet's entry; it was only a finger deep.

He fisted his hands, rings around his knuckles whitening. I expected him to cry out and glanced up at the circle of men. Why was I helping Rebel soldiers, men my late father absolutely despised? My father wouldn't have helped these traitors.

"Is she gonna do something?" I heard someone say.

His forehead drawing beads of sweat, Leonard groaned and rolled to his side. The circle of men tightened.

My breath came in ragged intervals. "Move! Give him room!" I waved them back.

He lifted up slightly. His face graying, he squinted up at me. "You're no surgeon. I'll *wait*." He turned to look for his brother.

I grabbed the probe from my bag. "If you don't take care of your injury now, it'll get worse." I nodded at the circle of soldiers, making sure they heard me too.

"Not a woman," he added, groggily. "Especially not one from the *Union*." Someone behind me chuckled.

"Perhaps you'd rather it *fester*," I intentionally stressed the last word. I wheeled around to the soldiers behind me—"Be quiet! You want him to die? Someone, help. Hold him still." Two soldiers came forward and held Leonard while I searched for the bullet with my finger. I had done this procedure before. In a series of memorized steps, I dug and probed, tugged and pulled, and pinched out the bullet—not an easy task when he writhed like a snake. "There!" I waved the bullet in the air.

The Confederate soldiers hushed. A couple of them said something that I couldn't make out. Lifting his head, Leonard squinted at his arm.

Maybe Gabe was hurt somewhere, too. I imagined his eyes, no longer laughing. Immediately, I tried to erase that thought. It did me no good to think the worst.

A soldier tucked my elbow in his hand and helped me to my feet. "Thank you, ma'am. We'll bandage him up."

Army camps often took up large tracts of land. This watercolor of the Union army's camp at the Cumberland Gap near the intersection of Virginia, Tennessee, and Kentucky shows how a camp might be arranged with headquarters on the left and rows of tents for the men on the right. This image is a depiction of men from the Ninety-first Indiana Volunteer Infantry Regiment.

The sun met the horizon as I left, the countryside washed in golds. My shoulders ached. No matter how fatigued I was, I was satisfied with my work. The day's events, though, made my resolve grow stronger. I needed to find Gabe. I had been more than two years since I had seen either of the brothers, and I didn't know if I would see them again.

* * *

The days spilled from one to the next, and soon a week had passed, each day having its own set of challenges. When I woke up on that particular morning, February 24, 1864, I didn't realize that the day would be my most eventful yet.

We were only a few yards from our hospital when I recognized someone just outside our tent's entrance. His silhouette was familiar. I squinted at his features.

Then his voice made me smile. "Sarah!"

The last time I had seen him he was weak and sick from the amputation my father had performed. His blue eyes shone, his hair a little longer, curling over his ears. "Enoch! What're you doing here? What happened to you?" A shiver tingled up my spine.

"What happened to me? Went home for a while." He whipped off his kepi with his good hand, arcing it in front of him in a grandiose bow.

I dismounted Sal and handed the reins to the officer. With a wave, the Rebels pivoted and rode back to their camp.

"So you're here with your regiment?" I asked, my face flushing hot.

"Not quite yet. Haven't joined up with 'em after my . . . umm . . . respite."

I fought with a strand of hair, pushing it behind my ear. "How are you?"

Widening his stance, he peered in the hospital tent. "Problem is, I need a bed. Just for a few days. Not quite ready to head back to my troop."

It was good to see him. Somehow his presence cheered me. "We've got plenty of empty cots right now. I don't think you'll be putting anyone out."

We talked for a couple hours, maybe more. Our conversation was easy. Comfortable. Relaxed. I missed those kinds of talks I'd had with Joseph. I missed the Elliott brothers—both of them.

Our conversation was interrupted by the clopping of hooves.

Enoch's eyes narrowed. "Know him?" He nodded toward the rider, at that distance a gray shadow.

"Not sure." I rolled up on my toes.

The horse, midnight black and muscular, sat back on his haunches and slid to a stop. The rider wore Union blue. "Rheuben Meeks, messenger for Brigadier General Windhorst." He swung a leg over his horse and slid to the ground. "You're Miss Sarah Sutton? Can you visit with me? Maybe inside?"

I stole a glance at Enoch. "If you state your business quickly." We ducked into the tent, leaving Enoch holding the reins.

"I have a note from the general." Rheuben slipped out a letter from his jacket. "He heard you went to the Rebel camp and cared for soldiers there. He wants to know the strength and position of their forces."

He deposited the letter in my hands and gave me a curt nod. "You know more than us, and your help's appreciated. I'll wait here for your response."

I unwrapped the note and scanned through it.

February 23, 1864

I appreciate your mission of mercy to our brave men and your care for our sick and wounded soldiers. You are loyal to our flag. I know that you will do whatever is within your power to bring an early end to this war.

Recently you traveled across the combat line to aid injured Rebels. I need you to describe the Rebel troop's position, their number of divisions, and their probable intentions. Are you aware of any reinforcements they are expecting?

Resp'y Yours,
Gen'l

Although I had tended the injured at the Rebel camp, I had also been alert and watchful. I vaguely recalled a soldier's bequest: "Keep him alive. We need ev'rybody we've got." I never anticipated subterfuge—nor that I would be capable of it. My hands trembled as I wrote my response:

February 23, 1864

Dear General,
The Rebels are located a half day's ride from the hospital. I would estimate as many as 50 tents. Their infantry was much smaller than I anticipated and they are desperate for reinforcements. They do not expect replacements any time soon; their forces are ragged and weary.

Respectfully,
Sarah

As much as I supported the Union and wanted the war to end, I didn't want soldiers killed or injured because of something I had done. I was a nurse—a healer, not a killer.

Rheuben took my letter, tucking it into his jacket. "Miss? There's something else."

"Something else?" I repeated dully, studying his face.

He sucked his lips in against his teeth. "The general wants you to locate the position of their picket guards."

"The Rebels' guards? Why me?" I couldn't just go to the Rebel camp, brandishing a white flag. The General wanted me to locate the picket guards in the Johnnies' camp—not the simplest nor safest task.

His shoulders lifted. "Probably because the General thinks you're the best one for the job."

I wasn't the best one for the job—I was positive of that—but something inside me burned to make a difference, and I was too foolish to think that I couldn't.

Rheuben mumbled something about coming back for the information and backed out of the tent. Enoch, thankful for freedom from a nose-heavy mare, gave me a tired smile and went inside the tent.

I waited outside for a moment to gather my thoughts.

When I entered the tent, Byron and Enoch had their heads together deep in conversation. They stopped talking when they saw me. The two of them rolled up a section of canvas. Crisp, fresh air replaced the stagnant air inside.

"Can you believe this?" Byron glanced my way. "My brother Samuel—a damn Reb—sent me a package."

"That's good, right?" I asked.

"No. I wrote a letter, askin' for somethin' from his farm." Enoch shouldered the rolled canvas while Byron tied it. Then Byron shuffled to the supply table and reached for something near the back of the table. "I hoped for jam or jelly. Or maybe some damn jerky. But this is what I got." He produced two copper cowbells, held them over his head, and clappered them in the air. "What am I s'posed to do with these hellfire things?"

"Ring 'em when you need help." Enoch gave me a wink.

Byron pitched the bells to Enoch. "You're likely to use 'em more than me, Enoch ol' boy. Maybe *you* better hang on to 'em."

What an odd gift. The image of Byron and his bells made me smile, but when I knitted those thoughts together—the bells and the mission—I knew what I could do. I gasped, and both of the men turned toward me.

"Know if the moon will be out tonight?" I was sure Enoch thought that my question was odd.

"No. A new moon. Dark as dirt." He edged behind a cot toward the next section of canvas and rolled the material, barely managing it one-handed.

I stepped beside him and helped him work the canvas into a tight roll. "I've been asked to locate the position of the Rebel picket guards, but I need help. Can you help me map their location?"

We rolled the canvas to the ceiling, and he balanced the roll on his shoulder. "You plannin' to spy?"

"With your help." I tied the canvas in place.

He stood there, a smile spreading across his face. "Spying?" Enoch arched his eyebrow. "Not a gentlemanly thing to do."

"Not ladylike either." I took a deep breath. "Ready to help?"

He bowed. "At your service."

We were partners, and we both had decided to take the risk.

* * *

Leaving camp with Enoch might be seen as inappropriate. But if I traveled to the Rebel camp alone, I'd be flirting with danger. We'd have to leave unnoticed. Thankfully, I had a simple plan.

I pulled Enoch aside whispering, "Come here." In a minute we were behind the tent, spooning together water and dirt, mushing the mixture into a pasty meal. I dipped my hands in the bowl and smeared the stuff on my face.

He plastered mud on the back of his hands. "How can a girl look so good with mud on her face?" His eyes twinkled. I felt my face flush, unsure how to take a compliment from a man, especially one slopped in mud.

"If you used a little more, you'd look pretty fine yourself," I answered, pleased with my retort.

After we finished masking our faces, we left the safety of the hospital grounds. Twice I caught Enoch glancing at me. I liked his tousled hair and boyish charm.

A silent fog nested in the hollows. I concentrated on the dark unfocused shapes. Trees—I hoped. My stomach lurched and my mouth went dry. We were yards away from the Confederate camp.

"It'll be fine. You'll see," Enoch said. Perhaps he could feel my fear.

The thicket rustled, and I quickened my pace. "Come on." I tripped over my skirts.

"I'm tryin', Sarah!" He trailed behind me. "Would you slow down?"

Stopping in my tracks, I waited for him to catch up. A hawk fluttered from the trees and swept in front of me like a witch's black broom. I grabbed Enoch's elbow. "This trip will kill me."

"I'll take care of you, Sarah." His voice was husky and low. "I'll do everything I can to protect you." Scattered patches of moonlight, feeble though they were, made the treetops appear full of every ogre imaginable.

So many things could go wrong, and our mission was still incomplete. "How will I ever manage walking near the picket guards?"

Enoch's voice was a whisper, "How will *we* manage? *We*." He glared toward the Rebel camp.

Slipping the cowbells out of my bag, I unwrapped the clappers. "Turn around so that I can fasten this around your neck," I rasped. His skin was warm against my chilled hands, and I fumbled nervously with the knot.

He turned to me. "Probably could tie it easier with my one good hand than you can with both of yours."

My plan was to meander past the Rebel pickets, giving the impression that we were pasturing cows. In the absence of moonlight, if we hesitated like cows chewing grass, the illusion would be complete.

The cowbells tinkled as we worked our way down the meadow with the slow, hesitant steps of cattle, my ears attuned to the tiniest sound: a rabbit's movement, a hawk's flight, a shift in the wind. Then I overheard some Johnnies. We were the object of their conversation.

Are those cows out there?

Sure's temptin' to kill one of those bovine. We'd have a first-rate supper.

Did the Rebel guards think of us as dinner? I hadn't considered that possibility, and obviously, Enoch hadn't thought of that idea either. As if on cue, we clasped our bells.

Where d'you suppose those cows are?

Dunno. Don't hear 'em.

Latching my eyes on Enoch's, I felt his fear. I could see the whites of his eyes even in the darkness. Somehow, we had to complete our mission. "Let's go." I motioned toward the Confederate camp.

I was thankful for a second pair of eyes. The guards were easy to spot, their faces lit by their campfires. Enoch was more observant than I, pointing ahead to guards I had missed, "There's two. See?"

I stepped over a rock outcropping and squinted against the fog. "Did we miss any of them?"

"Not so loud. You'll give us away," he hissed. He waved me forward. "Two more up there. See? In the trees." Their faces glowed amber against the dark pines.

"Probably more up ahead." My heart beating hard, I clasped my skirts and crunched through the grass. My next steps were measured and slow.

He caught up to me and scanned the tree line. "Doesn't look like any more. Let's get out of here." We cut across the field, and I marched back to the hospital as fast as my legs could carry me, Enoch barely keeping up. With every step I took, relief flooded over me.

"You don't look anything like a cow," he said.

I turned back without slowing down. "What do you mean?"

"Swingin' your arms like that." He trotted to catch up. I gave him a sideways glance so steely, I was sure he felt it even though he couldn't see it in the dark.

"Most cows *I* know don't have arms," he teased.

"Well, I'm not most cows." I couldn't see his face, but I was sure that he smiled.

We ducked into the hospital. Byron was waiting for us by the supply table. He swiveled toward us. "Where in the blue blazes were you?"

My mind was numb.

Enoch glanced at me. "Sarah and I . . . we were locatin' Rebel pickets." I was thankful for Enoch's honesty. His spirit of helpfulness resonated with me, and his caring nature reminded me of Joseph. With him by my side, I was ready for anything—even Byron's scorn.

Red-faced, Byron exploded with a stream of expletives, "Damn fools! What kind of one-horse operation was that?" He folded his arms over his belly.

I flashed a smile at Enoch. "Actually, it was a *two-cow* operation."

Byron looked first at Enoch and then at me. Evidently, our smiles were contagious. The corner of Byron's mouth twitched and he tossed a rag to me. "Get that stuff off your face. You're a mess."

I had completely forgotten about the mud. I couldn't let the hospital orderlies and patients know about our undertaking. In a minute Enoch and I were both outside, washing the mission off our faces. "We need to report our findings," I said, wiping off the last of the mud.

He dabbed at my chin. "There. You look better." His smile lines deepened.

My face heated with his touch, and I backed away. "We better get inside. We need to write the general."

We went back to the tent. Retrieving his haversack from under his cot, Enoch removed a piece of paper and offered it to me.

February 23, 1864

Dear General,

Please note that there are 12 picket guards surrounding the Rebel camp. A map indicating placement of those guards is on the back of this letter. I hope this information is helpful for our cause.

Respectfully yours,
Sarah

I signed my name and placed the pen in Enoch's hand. "I'm not the best artist. Can you sketch a map?"

"I can try," he said. Hunching over the paper in steady concentration, he scratched out trees, guards, and fields—a remarkable likeness of what we had seen. He drew two cows. One of them looked terrified.

Smiling, I peered at the cows. "Hey, that's me. You're good at drawing."

"At least I can still do something." He raised his stub, rotating it for my inspection. "See this? Pretty limited."

His bitter response surprised us both; he didn't intend to react so harshly. Shrugging his shoulders, he gave me an apologetic glance. "Sorry. Wish I could turn back the clock."

"Yes, but if you turned back time, I wouldn't have met you." I didn't want Enoch to misunderstand. I really cared about him. It was just that—I wasn't sure.

25

Joseph

An owl hooted and swept in front of me, fluttering into the woods. In the moon's pale-blue light, I could barely distinguish the silhouette of the Reb's picket guard, his profile haloed against the cedars. I clamped my fingers around my musket's stock.

His voice echoed across the meadow. He was maybe ten yards away. "Got guard duty, too, eh? You from around here?" He leaned forward, and I guessed that he was squinting at me.

A breeze whisked in from the north. "Way too far from home. You?"

"Just down the road." His voice broke, enough for me to notice. "Don't want to die in this war," he replied, putting down his gun.

"Don't want to d-die either." I gave his gun a solid look. Maybe he put his gun down just to make me think I was safe without mine. "So why're you fightin' then?" I idly fingered my gun.

"Our property. Our homes. What're you fightin' for?"

I didn't know exactly any more. "To preserve the Union," I finally said. I couldn't take my eyes off his gun.

He stifled a cough. "Nothin' much is bein' *preserved*."

There was a drawn-out pause, like he wanted to say something else. Then, as if he realized he had said too much, he said, "My name's Elon. Elon Ragsdale. What's yours?" A cloud wisped in front of the moon.

"Joseph Elliott. Some people call me Joe." My fingers were biting cold, and I tucked them under my arms.

"If we had more time, I'd tell you about my Mary." He slipped on his jacket. I turned up some dead leaves with my foot, releasing their moldy smell.

"She's a jim-dandy." He limped along the tree line. "She has the darkest, shiniest, silkiest hair. Her skin's so smooth. I miss everything about her."

"My Sarah has hair the color of flax. You never saw anyone with a brighter smile." I must have wished she was my sweetheart because I made it sound as if she was.

"Got four letters from Mary. Get me through the night. Think I've reread them thirty, maybe, forty times. Got any letters?"

"Um. No," I mumbled.

"I mean, she's your sweetheart, right?" He reached down to open his haversack. I was sure he was going to take out a letter—just to prove he had one.

Sure enough, he drew out a letter, just as I expected.

> *Dear Elon,*
> *You mean the world to me and I miss you more than you know. Fight hard against those greedy Yankees. Don't let them have our land.*

He paused for effect. "So, you haven't gotten any letters?"

I thought I had made that point clear.

"Well . . ." he put his hands up as if to say I should forget about her.

Guard duty on the picket line was an essential duty of soldiers during the Civil War. The men on this duty had to remain alert so the enemy could not make a surprise attack on the sleeping camp. It was, however, a dull exercise, with countless hours of uneventful quiet.

"She'll write." I stubbornly dug a hole with my heel.

"Have you ever danced with her?" His voice was quiet. "I'm takin' Mary to a barn dance. I mean, soon as I can."

"No. I've never d-danced with her." I imagined Sarah dressed in crinoline and lace, her hair fastened with a pearl strand, holding her hand out to me.

Chuckling, he wrapped his arms around his rifle, and shared a step or two. Even with a limp and heaviness on his left leg, his feet were sure. A slow dip, a bow. He didn't act awkward—or embarrassed—his two-step making me smile.

The moon disappeared behind the trees and darkness enveloped us, the moist smell of woods reminding me of home. Elon sang in low undertones. His notes wafted through the air, pushing the silence away.

For his last number, he sang "Home Sweet Home."

To thee I'll return, overburdened with care:
The heart's dearest solace will smile on me there;
No more from that cottage again will I roam;

With my crow-like voice I joined on the refrain:

'Mid pleasures and palaces though we may roam,
Be it ever so humble, there's no place like home.

My voice didn't work for quite awhile after that.

I put down my gun.

He propped himself in the crook of a tree. "Late, eh?" he finally said. It didn't take long for him to fall asleep. Fighting the hypnotic strum of his steady breathing, my head nodded, my eyelids drooped. Several times I jolted awake.

Ican'tfallasleepIcan'tfallasleep, I said to myself, trying to pry my eyes open. I couldn't afford to get caught, but I guess I fell asleep right then.

In my dream, Sarah was riding Beulah, high-stepping through Possum Creek. Her hair, lit gold from the sun, came unfastened, falling loose at her shoulders. I stood on McCartney's bridge and watched her come my way.

An odd movement startled me awake. Just out of the corner of my eye I saw a gun. Then, the nudge of a cold metal ring prodded my neck.

I wheeled around. Gabe. His face twisted in an angry scowl. I swiped at the barrel and grabbed his gun. "You scared the blue blazes out of me!"

Gabe jerked away his gun. "You're lucky. If anyone else had caught you sleeping, you'd be court-martialed. Shot clean through by your own men."

26

Sarah

The trees hinted of green, their tiny leaves translucent in the sun. In their midst stood a single plum tree adorned with fragrant white blossoms. I, like that tree, was alone. Were Joseph and Gabe still alive? It had been more than two years, and neither of them had contacted me.

And then there was Enoch. . .

Lost in my thoughts, I breathed in the smell of new grass. Then I remembered the buckets swinging in my hand; I was supposed to be fetching water from the stream. I lost my footing on the embankment and tumbled down, grabbing at roots along the way. My pails plummeted to the sandbar below, landing in the silt behind me.

With all the dignity I could muster, I stood up and wiped my hands on my skirt. The hem of my dress had torn. Sweeping my hair off of my face, I plucked up my pails and swooshed them back and forth in the creek water, then tilted them, letting the cool water stream in.

After my buckets were brimmed full, I poked through the weeds. What a treat birds' eggs would be. I stopped short. Just behind a cluster of rocks, I found—not eggs—but the remnants of a campfire. Cautiously, I glanced around. No movement.

Moving forward, where the beach met the embankment, something nestled in a clump of duckweed. A package? No, not a package, but a roll of paper with something inside. I set down the buckets and carefully unrolled the paper. In it was three cigars.

Odd.

A dignified script ran across the document.

Special Orders No. 52
Headquarters
Army of the Tennessee
*This exacompta is given to Gen. R. T. Russell for his own use. He will show it
to no person.*
He will destroy this copy by command of Maj. Gen. Joseph E. Johnston.
Capt. A. J. William D. Stevens

Well, someone hadn't followed orders. General Russell, whoever he was,
obviously hadn't destroyed the document.

I leafed through the papers, tracing my finger down the columns. Listed
on the document were names, locations, and orders for each troop. My skin
prickling, I turned to see if anyone was watching. The bushes shifted. The
wind? Quickly wrapping the cigars in the paper, I tucked them in my pocket
and gripped my buckets. Water sloshed on my skirts as I scaled the bank a
second time.

I hurried back to the hospital tent, the document burning like a hot coal in
my pocket. Those papers were in the wrong hands.

Mine.

Depositing my buckets on the floor, I strode to Enoch's cot.

"Now what have you been up to?" he asked.

"Just getting water, but look what I found." I scrolled open the document.
"What do I do with this? I think I've discovered a hornet's nest."

"A hornet's nest?" His eyes were laughing. "Looks like cigars to me."

"Oh, much more than that. Read the print." Taking the ledger from me,
Enoch read it; I followed the movement of his lips.

"Do you have any idea of this paper's importance?" I asked. "It not only
spells out the Confederate chain of command, but also states their location.
And their orders. Can you believe this?"

Nabbing his sack from underneath his cot, he slipped the document inside
with his good hand. He used his stump to pull the sack over his shoulder, adjusted the strap, and stood up. "Got to get this document to the general right
away. Can't believe that this information fell into our hands."

My face warmed. I couldn't believe how quickly he had taken over. "Those
papers fell into *my* hands. I *placed* them in *yours*."

He gave a quick glance in Byron's direction. "The general should see this
excompta now."

General Joseph Johnston was the commander of the Army of the Tennessee from 1863 to 1864. An experienced commander, he served as a general in the U.S. Army during the Mexican-American War. In fact many Confederate officers had served previously in the Federal army, so many commanders on both sides of the war knew each other and were even friends.

I had found those papers! Seemed he wanted the credit for it. I looked at him with my fiercest eyes. "Those documents. They're mine." I plowed my hand in front of me, demanding them back.

He gave an evasive shrug. "I'd like to borrow your horse. I can bring this document to the general. His brigade's not far. Can I?" His mouth pinched like a shirt buttoned too tight.

"Can you, what?" I couldn't keep the anger out of my voice.

"Can I ride your horse?" He unbuckled his sack.

"May," I answered. "You *may* take my horse. The question is: *can* you ride her?"

The muscles worked on his jaw. "Ridin' a horse is somethin' I can still do." For a moment, I thought I saw Gabe in front of me; he stood there, determined and strong.

"If you can, find out where the Indiana Fortieth is," I said. I fisted my hands behind my back, my fingernails biting into the palms of my hands. "I want to know where they are."

Enoch gave me a stiff glance and heaved the saddle on Beulah's back. "So that's what you want?" One handed, he tightened the cinch. I edged in front of him and adjusted the stirrups to fit his height. Then I slipped on Beulah's headstall.

"Who's in the Fortieth?" he asked. He placed one foot in the stirrup, grabbed the horn, and threw over his leg. I couldn't read his face. Was he angry?

"Neighbors of mine. From back home." My eyes followed the line of his jaw.

Beulah huffed, sidestepped, ready to go. "I thought . . ." Clasping the reins with his teeth he adjusted the saddle underneath him, then he placed the reins in his hand. His voice was like raw vinegar. "Never mind what I thought. Guess this is good-bye."

"Well, you won't be gone long." I gave him a tentative smile. "After all, you have my horse, and I'll want her back."

Enoch squinted at me. His lips formed a hard line. "Yes. I know. You'll want her back." He nudged Beulah and I watched them go.

* * *

I had just made my morning rounds when the hammer of hooves disrupted my work. Sprinting outside, I found Beulah tethered to the messenger's gelding. Dust from their hooves hovered in the air. The messenger tipped his kepi. "Ma'am, are you Miss Sarah Sutton?"

"Yes." I wiped my hands on my skirts.

He slipped his hand in his jacket, removing a parchment. "Got a letter for you."

"From the general?" My hands trembled. I laced them behind my back.

"No." He loosened his grip on the reins. "From Enoch. Enoch Nation."

My mouth went dry as dust.

April 30, 1864

Dear Sarah,

I won't be coming back. The general asked me to assist him as a special agent. I will aid him with map making and reconnaissance work and will work with him as long as I am needed.

The general found the exacompta invaluable; I believe it helped our cause.

Beulah is a fine horse, and I thank you for the use of her. Don't ever let her go. I won't forget you.

Yours,
Enoch

Walking back to my quarters, I folded the letter and tucked it in my bag. I was glad Enoch had found a place that would make him happy, but I had a hollow feeling in the pit of my stomach.

Funny, I didn't realize how special Enoch was—until he was gone.

27

Joseph

Franklin, Tennessee. Those words will haunt me the rest of my life.

After two days of marching and fighting, and weary as I had ever been, we were on the final stretch of road. Marching onward, my imagination ran wild—every branch a gun, every tree a soldier. I wanted to get to Nashville. I longed to go home.

Streaks of light bathed the fields of corn, cotton, and hay. Stubble, mostly. The smell of turned soil still lingered. Father once said he loved the lay of his land, and I understood. Gabe and I were farmers in uniforms, after all, carrying guns instead of hoes.

Rumors spiraled down the line. "They're saying the Rebs may catch up to us at Franklin today."

Gabe snapped to attention. "Nashville. What about Nashville?"

My heart pounded in my chest, my legs turning to lead. I hadn't expected the change of plans.

"Bloodthirsty Johnnies." Gabe motioned forward. "They're fighting for their land."

Like sheep led to slaughter, we massed in the meadow. Our line—the advanced line—formed well ahead of the breastworks along a ridge out in the open field. A few thousand strong, we stood unprotected and exposed to the Rebs.

Turning to me, Gabe's eyes narrowed. "Look how vulnerable we are out here on the edge."

"Feels like we're on our own." I gripped my gun and twisted back to the main line. The rest of our men were maybe half a mile behind us, half hidden by brush and debris. Their heads bobbed above the branches.

Gabe glanced back, his eye twitching ever so slightly. "Maybe we are."

Then I focused ahead on the solid Rebel line that was maybe a mile away. A shimmering row of bayonets lanced toward us, with flags speckling the line.

"Their numbers are twice ours." My hands had gone all sweaty. The land, with a river on one side and a rise on the other, funneled toward us.

Home. I wanted to go home—to see my father, my mother. I wanted to be anywhere, but here. Pinching shut my eyes, I tried to conjure up the smell of corn growing in the field and the scratch of hay in my shirt.

But I couldn't.

Their regimental band played "Dixie," that haunting tune churning with my thoughts. My blood ran cold.

Mounted officers rode down the Reb lines, a cheer rising from their ranks. They arced in front of us like a venomous snake. General Wagner's orders were clear: we weren't to leave our position.

I looked down our line. Not one of our men turned toward the breast-works. They all stood firm, their guns at the ready.

A mounted Union soldier galloped to the rear. Almost prone in his saddle, his eyes were rounded and wide.

Gabe blinked at him.

"D-did he go back to let 'em know what we're in for?" I asked.

"Maybe," Gabe swallowed hard. "We're stuck up here with a Colonel as green as a willow branch." He must have seen the fear in my eyes, because he straightened his spine, his shoulders cupping back. "Don't worry. They've got to come through that field first."

I licked my lips and glanced back toward our troops. We were human shields—far in front of the breastworks, with no protection except our guns.

"We're commanded by idiots." Gabe squinted back too. "We're strung out here to dry."

A Rebel yell started at one end of the Confederate army and swept along to the other, sweeping in waves up and down their line: "Woh-who-ey! who-ey! who-ey!"

I unpried my fingers from my Springfield and repositioned my hands. "They're goin' to run like the devil."

"They're comin'!" Gabe widened his stance.

The entire force charged toward us, the thunder of their feet shooting vibrations up my legs. Their faces flashed in front of me, their guns blazing and bayonets slashing.

Like a mangle, they compressed into a small space.

"Come on, Gabe!" I was rooted to the ground.

The flood of Rebs swelled, swirling toward us. I frantically tugged at Gabe's arm. "Come on! Retreat!" He leaned forward, hypnotized by the surging gray.

Some of our boys wheeled toward the breastworks, tripping over each other, guns flailing. They were yelling, some of them crying.

In a mass, the Johnnies pounded toward us: butternut, gray, and flashing steel. "Woh-who-ey!" The ground rumbled. "They'll slice us in t-two!" I cried, grabbing Gabe by the arm. Closer and closer they came. "Run!" Our blue line unraveled like a worn seam. I jerked Gabe into motion.

We tripped over our feet, hurtling back toward our line of blue. Behind us, a Reb's voice rang out across the field: "Run with 'em! Run into the works with 'em!"

Guns popped and a putrid cloud of sulfur enveloped us. Soldiers plummeted to the ground. A dozen. More. We hurdled over our own men, leaping over legs, arms, torsos, guns. I churned forward. Gabe stumbled, caught himself and staggered forward. "Run!"

We weren't going to make it. I knew it.

Joseph and Gabe were captured at the Battle of Franklin in November 1864. The battle was an overwhelming victory for the Union as the Confederates were not able to break their defenses.

Knifing toward our breastworks, I tripped over the dead, their bodies spongy under my feet, their ribs snapping like twigs. My mouth tasted sour. Shoulder to shoulder we roiled forward—hundreds of us tumbling over ourselves, barely ahead of the Rebs. We pumped toward our main line. "Go!" cried Gabe. "Go!"

Just over the breastworks I caught a glimpse of our own men. They aimed at the Rebs, and we were in the way.

"They're shooting at us!" My voice pitched an octave high.

Someone plunged to the ground. I tripped, landing on him, scrambling to get up again. "They're shooting at us! Our own men! They're shooting at us!" I screamed.

"Run!" cried Gabe, grabbing my sleeve, tugging me up from the ground. A cannon belched a plume of smoke. Two distinct sounds echoed across the valley: first the boom of explosion, then the crack of bones.

The world slowed. My feet were in motion but my mind was numb. I twisted toward the enemy and aimed. The Johnnies had twenty times our numbers. Maybe more.

Off to the left, one Reb soldier was slower than the rest. He limped, heavy on his left leg.

Mid pleasures and palaces though we may roam,
Be it ever so humble, there's no place like home.

My finger tripped the trigger. "No!" Through the gray haze, he was an apparition as he fell. I hesitated—just for a moment. "Elon!" I remembered guard duty, his two-step, and the letter from Mary.

The Rebels poured toward me, a mass of arms and legs. "No!" They grabbed my elbows and jerked me away.

I knew if I didn't escape, I wouldn't be going home. Maybe not ever. Tugging against them I hollered, "Gabe!"

Out of the corner of my eye, I saw Gabe, his hands shooting to the sky.

28

Sarah

We arrived at Chattanooga, the task of unpacking crates far too familiar. Two at a time, orderlies strode in the tent, carrying crates, barrels, and cots. I stood by the supply table and opened one crate at a time, half wishing I could be outside tending horses or unloading wagons.

I was almost finished with my task, when I opened a crate of jellies from the Christian Commission. A newspaper, the *Ringgold Press*, was wedged between bottles.

Perhaps my mother angel put the newspaper in my hands.

I plucked up the newspaper and skimmed through several articles, then leafed to the advertisements at the end. My chest tightened. "Joseph's name," I whispered, the ink blurring in front of me. I blinked at the lines again:

To Sarah,

I don't know if you are getting my letters, but I want you to know that Gabe is safe, I am safe, and I miss you.

Yours, Joseph

Byron peered in the door, probably to inspect our progress. "Byron," I said. "Here! Listen." My voice wavering, I read him the lines. Joseph must have written it. *My* Joseph.

Seeing my hopeful expression, he snatched the paper from my hands. "Lemme look." His eyes flitted across the page. Then he peered over the paper at me, his eyes glistening. "You're not thinking this is about you, are you?"

I didn't *think* the notice was about me. I *knew*. This advertisement couldn't be about a different Gabe, Sarah, and Joseph.

"There's other Josephs in this world. You don't know for sure that this is

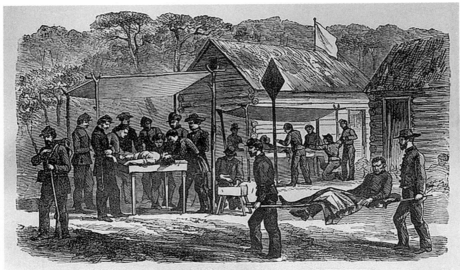

HOSPITAL SCENE.—— BRINGING IN THE WOUNDED AFTER THE BATTLE.

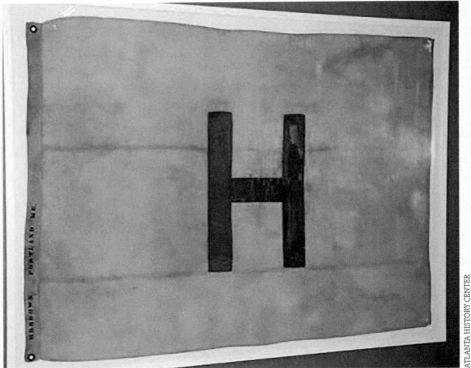

Orderlies were used to bring the wounded from the battlefields or ambulances to field hospitals during the Civil War. Note the flag on the roof of the building. Such flags, often displaying a capital H *(see bottom image), helped mark the makeshift hospitals following battles.*

the one." He scanned through the article again, mouthing the words.

"I know. I just know." I nabbed the paper from him.

"So if this advertisement is from Joseph, where do you think he is?"

I wasn't certain. But I longed to know.

Byron eyed the jam. "You have plans for that?"

"You can have it. Give it away if you like. But do you think we could have some kind of a truce? I would like to mend things."

He humphed, taking the jars from me. "There's probably some soldier who needs this jam worse than I do. Don't think I'll be eating it."

"I won't," I answered, "and going forward, I'll toe the mark."

"And, I hope you find Joseph," he mumbled.

Those were his first kind words to me. I'm not sure if he softened because of the gift of jam or because he knew I was missing someone. Evidently, his gruff exterior was a cover for his soft heart.

The sound of wagon wheels interrupted our conversation. Truman and another orderly approached, carrying a soldier with chestnut hair. I guessed he was probably fourteen.

"What's your name?" I grabbed my basin and cloth and tugged a crate beside him.

"You asked for my name?" My patient blinked up at me. "Seymour. The boys said you'd care for me. M-my ankle . . . "

I rolled up his pants leg, or what was left of it, and examined the wound. His ankle was puffy—mushy almost. A crimson gash sliced down his ankle bone, exposing layers of skin.

"This happened awhile ago." Seymour winced, his face pruning, his eyes squinting with pain. I gently pressed on his ankle, and puss oozed from his wound. "Franklin. It happened at Franklin." He twisted from my touch.

I'd read about that battle somewhere—a newspaper, most likely. I couldn't remember.

He shifted on the cot. "The whole string of us . . . the Fortieth . . ."

"The Fortieth? You were with the Fortieth?" A shiver ran up my frame. "The Fortieth Indiana?" A hundred questions formed in my head, but I only asked, "Was anyone hurt?"

"The Secesh, those dirty Rebels, ripped through us. Bloodbath." He looked up at me with moist eyes.

I sat there with the cloth clenched in my hand, water dripping onto my skirt. "You don't happen to know Joseph and Gabe Elliott? They're Fortieth too." My voice caught. "Neighbors back home."

His eyes grew big as walnuts. "Know 'em. Same company. They're your neighbors?"

"S-same company? You're in the same company?" A tremor ran through my fingers. He knew them! He'd know what they'd been doing, where they were—maybe even if they ever said anything about me.

Before I could say anything else, his hand reached for mine. "Don't know how to tell you this." The pupils of his eyes darkened. He swallowed hard.

My heart lurched. My mind raced. I had to settle down. I drew a deep breath and searched Seymour's face. "Tell me what?"

"Carried away. They were carried away at Franklin."

"Uh." It was as if someone had plowed into me—I couldn't breathe. I set the basin on the ground, crimson water dripping down my wrists and puddling on the dirt floor. "Carried away? W-what do you mean?"

He rolled toward me, his face graying. "Not sure you want to know."

I edged closer to Seymour's cot.

"Not sure if they were hurt," he said. "Captured. Believe they're prisoners now."

"Prisoners?" I let that thought settle. My skin prickled. I had heard about the prisoner of war camps. "Do you know—Do you know where those soldiers were taken?"

Seymour looked up at me, blinking several times. "Don't rightly know where they were taken, Miss." He grabbed my hand, squeezing my fingers too tightly. "Occasionally we get mention of our boys going to Cahaba or Andersonville Prison."

29

Joseph

My first impression of Andersonville came while I was still miles away from the camp—a contaminating smell of sickness and death. The second was of massive wooden gates, iron hinges, and iron bolts.

The dust crept in my shirtsleeves, my collar, and my pants. I tucked up my collar, and Gabe hunkered down in his, as a chilling wind picked up from the North. We poured off the train—some of us without jackets or shoes.

Guards herded us toward a double log cabin just southwest of the stockade. Charging out of the house was a wiry, bearded man. His bushy eyebrows met in a frown. "Get in de ranks!" he yelled. "Got damn you, get in de ranks!" We filed in our lines. "Move it! Now! Or you shan't have a got-damned mouthful to eat." That was our introduction to the camp commander, Captain Henry Wirz.

My arms pressed to my side, I wasn't sure what the protocol was, or what to do. My mind imagined the worst.

"To the stockade. March!"

We filed to the north gate, which swung open, exposing a different world. The smell, a witches' brew of excrement, sweat, and rotting flesh almost sent me to my knees. Blackened hairy creatures swarmed us. "Any news from the front? Any news of exchange?" Elbowing forward, they were a mass of arms and legs.

Gabe's mouth twitched. "Don't rightly know." He pushed forward.

"You have food?" one asked. "Blankets?" They knotted closer.

"D-don't . . . " I muttered, clutching my haversack, my eyes flitting across the grounds. Sentry boxes were positioned strategically about one hundred feet apart atop a pine-log palisade. The tents—hundreds of them—were a hodgepodge of makeshift construction. In front of us, soldiers milled around in rags, their skin stretched drum-tight over their ribs.

The gate swung shut behind me, and my stomach turned.

Gabe and I walked down the main street, of sorts—more of a cow path than a road. We passed a launderer scrubbing a threadbare shirt and a barber scissoring a mangy beard.

"Buttons? You need buttons?" somebody asked. His mouth was all gums and sores.

Someone tugged on my arm. "Pails? Got 'em here." His hair hung down to his shoulders in a knotted nest.

Grim faced, Gabe pressed forward. "Better find shelter."

We hadn't gone far before we reached the heart of the camp. Some Indiana boys—Perkins, Elihue, and Warren—introduced themselves and led us to their tent. With thinning blond hair and lanky builds, the three of them looked like brothers. Perkins, the tallest, waved me forward. "This way."

They had devised a lean-to out of sticks, the sleeve and back linings of a blouse, coffee bags, and the flap of a knapsack. "Doubt you'll find the makings for another. Nothin' much for materials 'round here."

As Joseph and Gabe approached Andersonville they very likely would have smelled it well before they saw it. Andersonville was an infamous prisoner of war camp in Georgia where the Confederates housed thousands of Union prisoners.

"You're Indiana boys." Elihue flapped open the tent. "We'll make room."

I toyed with the strap of my haversack. "Obliged." The air was close, smelling of dirt and stale sweat.

Elihue pushed two haversacks in the corner. "When we line up for roll call, lie low." His eyes turned solemn. "We won't stand up for you there. The commander, Wirtz, is tough." He shook his head. "You don't want to cross him, and we don't want to meet the gallows beside you."

Gabe sat down at the edge of our tent. "Appears we're here to stay."

I sat down too. To the right, the Michigan boys had designed a haphazard shelter—made mostly out of flour bags. To our left were the Illinois boys. From the looks of it, their tent had been there awhile; it was a three-room contraption decorated with pine roots.

"Got something to show you." Gabe unearthed an envelope from his bag. It was bent and dirty, like he had carried it awhile.

"You got a letter? From back home?" I asked, my stomach went sour.

He waved the letter in broad strokes and smiled up at me. "From Sarah."

I couldn't figure out how he got a letter and why I didn't. I peered over his shoulder, "Who's that letter for? You?" The script had a feathery, delicate scroll.

He unfolded the letter and smoothed it out on his leg. "The ink's smeared, but I'm pretty sure Sarah wrote it to me."

"How long h-have you had it?" My heart thumped in my chest. He gave me the letter and leaned back, cupping his knee in his hand.

March 12, 1862

By now you probably know that I'm with the 7th regiment, and assisting in the hospital tent. The sight of injured soldiers worries me, and I can only hope that both of you are all right and that I will see you again once the war is over. Thoughts of you have gotten me through some difficult moments. I can't wait to see you again. Please stay out of harm's way.

Yours,
Sarah Sutton.

"Just one?" I asked. "This was written almost three years ago! You never wrote her back?"

He shrugged in a way that I knew he hadn't.

I imagined Sarah penning it, her delicate hand poised on the page. If I had seen that letter, I would have known where she was.

All at once, it struck me that she had never received any of my letters. Not one. My throat burned. "You should have shown me the letter. Why d-didn't you show me 'til now?"

He rubbed the edge of the paper. "Don't know." Slow and steady, his eyes shifted from the letter to me. "Thought the letter was for me."

He couldn't see past the nose on his face. "You should have let me see it." I glared him back.

"Roll call!" someone yelled. Gabe jammed Sarah's letter back in his sack.

Elihue whisked by us. "Better move it." The whole prison was in motion, soldiers filtering toward the front gate.

"Time to face the music." Gabe gave me a grim smile. Maybe he was apologizing, but I couldn't be sure.

* * *

We stood at the front gate and waited for Wirz. I clenched my hands.

A chain of guards followed him into the compound. He pivoted, his eyes scanning the grounds. He puffed up his shoulders. "First got-damn man who falls out of line, I blow to hell. I'll make every one of you wish you had stayed home." He lifted a corner of his lip. "Stand in your ranks 'til every man's counted!"

I didn't turn my head to check on Gabe, but I knew he stood motionless too.

My stomach was aching for food and a white fog enveloped me. Distorted voices pounded in my ears and rows of men blurred before my eyes. "Plant your feet!" someone rasped. I think it was Gabe. Weaving, I adjusted my stance, gray-black dots blinking in front of me.

Wirz wheeled around. He drew his revolver, the barrel of his gun inches from my forehead. "You got-damned-Yankee-son-of-a-bitch! Why the *hell* do you refuse to obey my orders?"

He pressed the steel barrel on my temple and marched me backwards, bumping me back in line. "I will start de roll call again." His head angled just to the left. "I *will* remember *you*." I stood stiffly, my side aching and my stomach twisting, not daring to move.

Wirz inched around, slowly. His eyes lit on one soldier, then another. "Stay in your ranks. No rations today, you *pitiful* lot of Yankees."

They dismissed us by company, and we scuffled back toward our tent. Gabe turned to me. "Don't 'spect we'll leave here alive." His jaw muscles tightened.

About nineteen feet from the wall, was the "deadline," which Andersonville prisoners were forbidden to cross. Marked by a simple fence, the deadline was intended to prevent prisoners from tunneling under the stockade or climbing over it. Any Andersonville prisoner who approached the deadline was immediately shot. This sketch was drawn by General Lew Wallace during Henry Wirz's trial. Following the war Wirz was tried, convicted, and executed for his treatment of prisoners.

We threaded through the tents, the crowd thickening until we came to a standing halt.

The soldier next to us, his teeth rotting brown, studied my face. "Weren't you the guy at roll call?"

I gave a quick glance at Gabe.

"Better find a way to blend in," he whispered, then tilted his head to the side as if he wanted to say something else. He hunched toward us. "You'll be all right. Look at me. Been a prisoner two years." I gave him a solid look. His hair was knotted in clumps, his scalp crusted with white larvae. His skin was sallow and gray. Didn't seem to me that he'd fared too well.

Soldiers migrated to our left. "What's going on?" I asked.

Our companion lifted to his toes. "Lice race. If you heat the pan, those buggers scuttle like the devil." He nudged me with his bony elbow. "Problem is, you can fry 'em crisp if you don't watch out." The crowd worked loose and we weaved through the maze of tents. Then, like a will-o'-the-wisp, the soldier disappeared, and Gabe and I were on our own.

We passed the tents of the Michigan boys, one of them giving us a grim nod.

"Might never get out." Gabe scanned the prison walls. "Scalin' the walls won't work. Guards will shoot us down."

We worked toward our tent, and I sat down glumly. "If only we could find a way under the walls."

"Ground's pretty tough." He peered at the sentries. The palisade wall was maybe forty feet from our tent.

"If we had something sharp . . ." I milled into the dirt with my heel; the ground was hard as a slab of clay.

Gabe scuffed at the dirt too. "Never going to work." Then the two of us pawed into the earth.

I lifted my head up to watch the guards. "Too risky."

His jaw jutted forward in a determined line. "If we don't do anything, we're just going to rot away. I'd rather do something." He loosened his canteen from his shoulder and sat it on the ground.

We both stared at it. I picked it up, slowly wheeling it in my hand. "I think I know what to d-do."

His eyes brightened. He understood.

"We're splittin' this canteen in half," I said tossing it to him. "A digging tool. Those guards are so busy watching the deadline, they won't notice us."

Breaking into a huge smile, he unfolded himself from the ground. "An instrument of freedom."

30

Sarah

I glanced at the door as Byron and Truman entered the tent. With their features dark against the sun, I couldn't read their faces. I'd heard rumors of the Battle of Selma. Young boys fought beside old men, outnumbered by Wilson's Union boys. I expected to hear more of that battle, but Byron's news was different than I expected.

"Got transfer orders," Byron said, working his way to the supply table.

Truman lifted his hands, palms up, and shrugged.

I dropped my rag in the basin. I hadn't expected Byron to leave me, not when we were so close to the end of the war. For weeks, reports of Union victories all over the South had made their way to the hospital.

"Transfer?" I asked. "When? Where?"

"Needed in Vicksburg. Shortage of doctors there." He cupped the ball of his cane in both hands and leaned toward me. "Gotta care for soldiers passin' through Vicksburg on their way home from Andersonville."

"From Andersonville?" My voice was a whisper. The image of Gabe and Joseph imprisoned there had been burned in my brain.

He nodded, his eyes brightening, "Maybe *you* need to go too." Truman nodded in agreement with Byron's statement.

Suddenly, I couldn't breathe.

* * *

After folding my few articles of clothing and carefully tucking Father's small bag of silver coins in my carpetbag, I hesitated, trying to think what else I needed. Since the beginning of the war, I hadn't accumulated many material goods, but I had inherited my father's medical kit, his wool blanket, and his ring. Those items served as a remembrance—more than a year had passed since his death. Sighing, I inspected Father's medical kit to make sure everything was secure and then gave it to Byron.

It was his idea to travel together. "Smartest thing would be for me to go with you," he said, tossing my bag into the wagon bed and fitting another in the back. "When we get to Vicksburg, we can stay with my brother's family."

"We're going by wagon all the way there?" I asked.

"Train from Chattanooga to Nashville," he said. "Steamboat from Nashville to Vicksburg. *If* we make it to Nashville, that is."

"*If*? What do you mean '*if*'?" I gave him a blank stare.

"Railroads. Not sure if they survived the war." His eyes locked on mine. Then he shook his head, as if to clear his thoughts. "Better check on Beulah." He hunched by the wheels and waved me away.

Beulah. I had forgotten to see if she was roadworthy. I ran to the corral, hoping I'd have time to work with her. Her mane was a witch's bridle of cockleburs; her hooves were rough but serviceable. Gripping her chin, I hooked my thumb

As Sarah and Byron left camp their wagon may have looked similar to this one. Their ride over the hills and dirt roads of Tennessee would likely have been a bumpy one.

in her mouth, pushing against the rubbery corners. "Your teeth look just fine." Good ol' Beulah. I scratched under her mane.

Truman hitched her to the wagon, his brown hands deftly slipping the straps into the buckles. "Can't go with you," his eyes glistened. "Got a job. Gonna be hired help at the Wiggins farm, just down the road."

I blinked at him, unsure what to say. "Thank you for your help in the hospital. I couldn't have done it without you."

He cleared his throat and looked down at his hands. "Anyway, I'm not the only one movin' on. Negroes, loaded with bundles of ol massas' clothing, are flockin' North. Good thing. End of the war's a-comin' soon." His eyes had a faraway look.

"I'll miss you," I said, surprised at the lump in my throat. Truman was a remarkable man and a good friend.

Truman fiddled with a strap while Byron clambered up to his seat.

"I'm drivin'." Byron tossed his cane beside him.

Following the war freed slaves left plantations in droves. Seeking shelter and jobs, many ended up in camps while others headed to the North or into Southern cities. This photo, taken shortly after the fall or Richmond, Virginia, shows what may be a family of freed slaves.

Gathering my skirts, I climbed up beside him.

The wagon jolted forward. Truman lifted his hand in farewell. Beulah took off at a trot and bounced down the road as if she had no load whatsoever. We were on our way, every turn bringing us closer to Vicksburg, closer to Joseph and Gabe. I edged forward on my seat.

Byron tilted his head toward me. "Long trip. Sit back." I adjusted my skirts. Maybe the Elliott boys didn't think about me as much as I thought about them. It would be miles before I knew.

The Tennessee landscape spread out before us in a patchwork of trees and fields, one meadow blending into the next. Beulah jerked to a stop and swung her head toward us.

Byron flopped the lines. "For criminy's sake, you dern mule!" She wouldn't budge. I glanced at him and then frowned at the road—a rutted steep grade. "No wonder," I said. Leaning forward, I willed Beulah to move. "Come on." I placed my tongue against the roof of my mouth and tchicked.

"What's wrong with her?" Byron asked, the lines flopping again.

"The hill. She's got a load, and she's not stupid." I gave Byron a fierce look. "We're never going to get there."

Byron flung his hands in the air.

"Look at the grade," I said, waving up the hill. I clucked again at Beulah. "You can do it." She flicked her ears toward me.

He offered me the lines. "Want these?"

"Encourage her," I said. "Just encourage her." My patience had run dry. I just wanted to find my neighbors.

He *tchicked* awkwardly at my horse and loosened the reins, the wheels slowly ratcheting forward. Beulah strained against her collar and clopped up the hill.

With a deep sigh, I tucked my skirts underneath me and focused on the road. "You're doing just fine, Byron."

"Just fine," he echoed.

I turned my face away so Byron wouldn't see my smile.

We passed a field of clover, the sweet smell reminding me of Hardin's Pond. Beulah slowed at a bridge, and Byron gave her a leather reminder. "Come on," he urged. She bobbed her head and pushed forward.

"Stubborn," I commented, nodding at her.

"You are," Byron answered. "That's why you'll do just fine." He adjusted the lines in his hand.

We clopped over a bridge and passed two farms. "Not sure about Vicksburg." I fussed with a loose thread on my dress.

"What do you mean?" He turned to me with a sour look. "We're on our way."

"I know. I mean, I'm not sure what to do about Joseph and Gabe." I wanted Byron's advice, but I wasn't sure how to ask for it. "It's been such a long time since I've seen either of them."

"They've been through a lot." He toyed with the lines.

"Yes." I wondered if Gabe and Joseph were still the same. Shifting on my seat, I let that thought drift. "I want to know which one of them is best for me. Gabe's handsome. And confident. But Joseph is, well, he's Joseph. I mean . . . he's cautious. But the kindest man you'll ever meet. I guess that's what I want to know. Joseph or Gabe?"

I wasn't sure who Byron would suggest. I loved Gabe's smooth conversations, his grand gestures—his style. But Joseph's thoughtfulness and caring nature made me feel treasured. He put me first. He cared about me. I weighed their hearts in my hands, my heart aching for one of them. I simply wasn't sure which one.

I sat forward on my seat, waiting for his response. He put the lines in his left hand and turned to me. "Well, all I can say is, don't pin your heart to a place that won't stick."

31

Joseph

ANDERSONVILLE PRISON, GEORGIA,
MARCH–APRIL 1865

Once the tunnel was deep enough, I took my turn. I elbowed my way to the tunnel's core, threw dirt behind me, and worked it back with my feet. Perkins, behind me, pushed dirt back to Elihue, and he shoved the dirt out the tunnel's entrance.

"Makin' progress," Gabe said. He scooped the dirt into his pant legs and carried it to the swamp.

For over a month we worked on our tunnel. Our days had a rhythm—roll call, rations, tunnel; roll call, rations, tunnel—each day a mirror of the one before. I peered at the pigeon roosts. The guards looked bored. If they only knew.

We were making progress until the day Perkins buried himself up to his armpits in front of our tent.

Gabe exited our tent, scowling. "What happened?"

Perkins's hair was crusted with gray dust. He broke his shoulders loose and pushed himself out of the hole. "Not sure. Just walked out of our tent and . . ." He looked at me with his hands in the air, as if he couldn't believe what had happened.

"Can't be our tunnel," said Gabe, scuffing dirt back into the hole. "Our tunnel's on the other side of the tent." The three of us stood there, gaping at the hole.

"Well, whose tunnel is it?" I looked down the row of tents toward the Michigan boys. One of them nodded at me. I would have noticed if they had been digging a tunnel.

Perkins shrugged his shoulders and sat down by our tent.

Gabe sat down too. "Don't think it belongs to them," he said. "Think that tunnel's ours."

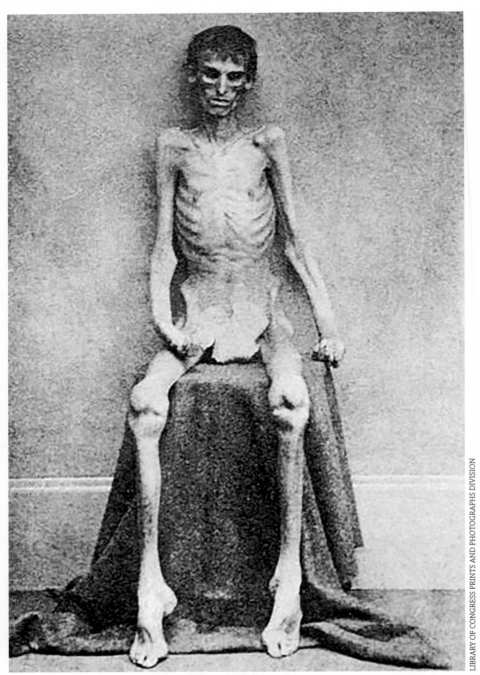

Overcrowding and limited medical care at Southern prison camps led to malnutrition, disease, and overexposure. Many, such as the soldier in this photo, barely survived.

"Can't be." I fidgeted with some of the loose soil. That theory made no sense to me.

Pushing a small hill of dirt with his heel, Gabe shoved some dirt back into the tunnel. "You dig left-handed or right?" His question seemed out of place.

"Right-handed." I took off my shoe and sifted out the dirt.

He pointed his chin toward Perkins. "You right-handed?" Now Gabe had me wondering. He had figured something out; I just wasn't sure what it was.

"Right," Perkins answered, whisking dirt from his pants.

Gabe's face had gone ashen gray. "You get it, don't you?"

I looked at Perkins. His face had turned all loose, his eyes bland and lifeless; there wasn't a hint of recognition.

I must have looked the same way.

"Don't you get it? We're all right-handed," said Gabe. "We're all pushin' dirt the same way. Our tunnel's curved like a blamed horseshoe." Leaning forward, he cupped his legs in his arms. "Our tunnel started behind our tent. Instead of plowing straight toward the fence, it curved back on us."

Then he leaned back, his eyes clouding. His voice went low, "We're never going to make it home."

* * *

Gabe wasn't eating and spent most of the days staring at the palisade walls. All the fight had gone out of him.

"Gabe needs a distraction," Elihue proclaimed, waving some playing cards.

I didn't think cards were enough to pull him out of his sour state. Perkins felt the same way. "You're not going to change Gabe's attitude over a card game." But he swept off some dirt by our tent anyway.

Elihue invited a soldier named Illinois to deal. All legs and knees, he plopped down on the ground by our tent, settling his back against the canvas wall. "So what are we betting for?" He waggled his fingers impatiently and reached for the cards.

Perkins shifted his eyes toward me. "No buttons to wager."

"Have to wager something else." Elihue winked at Gabe. I got the feeling that they had talked this card game over, that they had a plan.

And I was the odd man out.

Humming some tune, Illinois shuffled through the cards, jammed them together, and divvied them out to each of us.

Gabe glanced over his cards. "Got an idea. Illinois, if you have a full house, we'll empty ours. Or at least make room in ours." He lifted one eyebrow at me. "Joseph can find somewhere else to sleep."

Heat rising on my face, I rifled through my cards. I figured out right then the two of them had something planned; I was stuck in a card game and the outcome was fixed.

As if on cue, Illinois plucked out a card from his hand. He laid out a ten and then three kings. Giving me an apologetic smile, he turned the last card. "A ten," he said.

Gabe lowered his eyes. Looked like the cards were rigged.

Still holding my worthless hand, I said, "You're kidding, right?"

"Cards don't lie." My brother motioned toward the prison grounds. "Won't kill you to sleep outside for a few nights. Illinois won your spot. Fair." He turned to Illinois and smiled.

"Where am I supposed to go?" I fidgeted with my cards, then tossed them at Illinois.

Gabe swung his leg in front of him and waved me away. "Just go." I caught a subtle flick of his eyes.

"Fine." I started off toward the front gate. A hawk circled above me in narrowing loops, dipping down toward the camp, the dark image floating through the charcoal-gray sky. I wanted to have that freedom—the freedom to float away. I tightened my jacket. Most of the soldiers had hunkered down in their tents except for me.

When I was twenty, maybe thirty feet from our tent, I twisted back toward it. It didn't make sense to spend the night searching. If I had to sleep anywhere, it would be someplace I knew.

I strode to our campsite and tore open the flap. Illinois, the bastard, was nestling into my spot. "Whatcha doin' here? Git up and git!" Ripping his haversack out of the corner, I tossed it out the door.

Gabe dismissed me with a wave of his hand. "Go now. Clear the coop. Illinois won your spot. Remember?"

I backed away, angry with Gabe for controlling every situation and even angrier with myself. Perryville, Stones River, Franklin. Hell, I'd been through it. I stared at my clutched fingers as if the answer was written there. Then I swooped at Gabe and grabbed him by the arm, yanking him off the ground. "You say he won my spot? No, I think he won yours! Get out. That spot is *mine*."

Gabe just stood there, clenching and unclenching his fists. He mumbled something. I'm not sure exactly what he said, but I thought maybe, "You'll get yours." Then he tugged the tent's flaps aside and disappeared outside.

* * *

Days later, we finally had the news we were waiting for.

"You hear we're going to be exchanged?" Elihue's voice was a whisper, his eyes focused on the front gate. We had been at Andersonville for months. It was hard to believe that our last day was finally here.

"People have said that we'd be exchanged for weeks now." Gabe lifted one shoulder. "Can't be for real."

"Gather your things! Fall in!" someone yelled, putting the whole camp in motion. The Michigan boys were already off toward the gate.

"Get to the gate!" Elihue waved forward. "They're callin' names!"

"Let's go!" I tugged at Gabe's arm. My ears ringing, my feet thumping, I fumbled for my sack and strode to the front. This was the day we had been waiting for.

A guard was already calling our names. "Gabriel Elliott, private, Fortieth Indiana Infantry." The gate swung open. I fidgeted with the strap on my sack.

"Joseph Elliott." My feet were rooted to the ground.

Gabe nudged me. "Joseph!"

Freedom was outside, five yards away.

"Joseph!" He clutched my elbow and pushed me forward. A light breeze buffeted my face, and I swallowed the earthy spring air; the feeling of freedom hit me as soon as we left the grounds. Gabe gave me a solemn nod.

The land was green. I studied the horizon, where the earth meets the sky. Freedom. Its sweetness washed over me. I was going home. I was finally going home.

A few months before we had been robust soldiers who marched for hours. Now we were reduced to walking skin-covered ribcages, collarbones, and knees. My knees wobbling underneath me, I trudged across open fields toward the tracks.

The grave had given up its dead.

32

Sarah

With Vicksburg on my mind, I could think of little else. But first we had to get there. I hoped to see Joseph and Gabe soon.

Chattanooga's livery was first on our agenda. The stable was probably the oldest structure in town: its side walls leaned inward and its roof cupped slightly, shingled with scraps of browns, grays, and blues. The building—if you could call it that—was slipshod at best.

Greeted with a ripe smell of horse dung and fermenting hay, I stepped inside, those scents transporting me to our stable back home. The proprietor gave me a nod. "I'm Jeptha Stephens." Lanky, sinewy, and smooth shaven, his tidy appearance seemed out of place.

"Byron McIntyre. Miss Sutton." Byron motioned toward our wagon outside. "Got a wagon for sale. Wanna take a look?"

We stepped outside, and Jeptha immediately lit his pipe, the sweet smell of tobacco curling in the air.

He clucked, inspecting the wheels and hitch. After a cursory look at the axle, he nodded at me. "Fine wagon. Weathered some. Serviceable. You selling your horse too?" he asked with his eye on Beulah.

I wedged my heel into Byron's foot.

"I'd pay a premium even though the war's nearin' an end." Cupping the bowl of his pipe, Jeptha took another deep draw.

Byron frowned. "Think so? Think the war's almost over?"

"Richmond's fallen, it can't be long now." Jeptha leaned against the wagon. "You wanna sell her? She's a fine horse."

Byron shifted his weight. "Can't sell her. We'll be puttin' her on the train 'long as she loads up good and proper."

I gave Byron a glare. "And even if she doesn't."

"Fine horse," Jeptha said again. "Sure you want to take her along?" Jeptha sucked a deep draw from his pipe. "Want to risk her dying in transport? I've heard of too many . . . um . . . incidents."

I hadn't thought of that.

He moseyed up to the front of the wagon. "How old is she? Twenty-five years old? Thirty? Just sayin' sellin' her might be the kindest thing to do." He stepped back and rubbed his chin. "Like I said . . ."

My father was gone. Beulah was all I had left. I'd miss the rough feel of her mane and her velvety nudge, but I didn't know how I would get her home.

"Train's not going to wait all day," Byron said, bouncing on his heels and glancing toward the station.

I unthreaded a burr from her mane. "What do you think?" Beulah swung her head toward me.

"That we're going to be late for the train," Byron said, shoving his hands in his pockets. He shared an exasperated glance with Jeptha.

"No, I mean . . . Beulah. What should I do?" I toyed with the burr, wheeling it between my finger and my thumb.

"You've had her for your whole life. *I'm* not gonna be the one to tell you what to do."

If I based my decision on personal interest, she'd be first on the train. But if I cared for her—truly cared for her—I would have to let her stay.

The train's impatient whistle broke into my thoughts. I pressed Beulah's poll, and she responded, lowering her head. "Beulah, you're my best friend." She bobbed her head as if she knew. Her ribbed frame and sloped back showed her age, but Beulah was still a beautiful horse to me.

"Hundred twenty-five? Fifty?" Jeptha offered. With one last draw from his pipe, he tapped the ashes against the wagon wheel.

How could I put a number on her worth? I scratched under Beulah's chin and swallowed. "I-I can't sell her. I'd never be able to sell her . . . "

Jeptha tucked the pipe in his pocket. "But?"

I could feel my blood pulsing through my neck—I couldn't breathe. "Not going to accept payment for her." I looked at Jeptha square in the face. "She's too . . ." I stopped. Tears welled up in my eyes. "Mr. Stephens, if you promise that you can give her a good home, you can have her. I want her taken care of. I just don't want her on that train." My words spilled out, and there was no turning back.

Jeptha must have understood. Nodding, he scratched Beulah's neck. His eyes meeting mine.

Byron escorted me to the station, and I focused on the trip ahead. Over the hissing sound of the train's engine, I heard Beulah's neigh. Was that whinny her last good-bye or a plea for my return? Briefly, I closed my eyes stinging with tears, wishing she could come with us.

With a final glance toward the livery, I boarded the train.

Finally, we were on our way to Vicksburg. The meadows blurred by. My first train ride, and all I could think about was Beulah.

Not quite true. I thought about Joseph and Gabe too. I wanted to find them in Vicksburg, and I hoped that they were all right.

For the most part, Byron and I traveled in silence. At times the scenery was breathtaking, the sun lighting a turquoise-blue sky against emerald meadows. Fields sat fallow, wanting for seed. Fuzzy green pastures lay cupped between hills. Spring, my favorite season, had arrived.

Before the war, there were far more railroads in the North than in the South. Because much of the war was fought on Southern ground, most of the tracks there were destroyed by the two armies. However, some trains remained active and were able to transport soldiers and supplies quickly and efficiently. At the time of this photo the Nashville and Chattanooga rail yard was being used as a Union supply depot.

"You all right?" Byron gave me a sideways glance.

"Mmm." I tucked my arm around myself and concentrated on the hills outside.

We passed a small brick house, windows open, curtains fluttering in the breeze. Just behind the house was a young woman hanging a shirt on the line. I couldn't wait to do simple things like that: hang clothes on the line, thin carrots in my garden, or knead rye bread.

I coughed, my chest tightening.

One meadow dipped into another. War had unraveled all human construction: telegraph wire spiraled on the ground and buildings crumbled on their foundations. In contrast to spring's beauty, the countryside was pockmarked with graves. I eyed the sad clumps of earth and wondered how many mothers waited for their sons to come home.

The farther we traveled, the more detached I became. Even though the countryside blossomed with the misty colors of spring, I struggled with a deep-seated ache.

The train rumbled along. I glanced at Byron, his eyes focused on some distant hill. I couldn't read his face. Was he content? Did he have his own struggles?

"How do you suppose they're doing?" I blurted.

"They?" His eyes narrowed against the sun.

I assumed he would guess who I was talking about. "Joseph and Gabe," I answered.

Byron's eyes had no life in them. No spark. No fire. Glassy and somehow dulled, his eyes haunted me. "I don't know." He patted my hand. "You can be sure they're watchin' out for each other."

With a deep sigh, I toyed with the folds of my dress. My chest ached. Coughing, I shifted position, trying to concentrate on the hills outside.

Byron's attention fixed on something, and I leaned to see it too. A solitary horse. The mare's stomach was distended, bloated, and blue, her mouth gaping open in a final sigh. Even in the cool of April, the stench of rotting carcass followed us. I couldn't get Beulah off my mind.

He turned to me and scowled. "Wish you'd stop coughin'." I gave him a half smile—not feeling well enough to extend more than that.

Soon, I fell asleep against his shoulder. My problem was worse than road weariness.

The next days were a hodgepodge of blurred images: a cool cloth on my forehead, a blanket tucked under my chin. "Where are we?" I asked, my voice was thin, hollow, and small.

"Steamboat," Byron answered. "Nashville to Vicksburg." That was the last piece of reality I remembered for a long time.

In a dream I fought a river current, struggling to stay afloat. When I woke, my lungs begged for breath. I fought to keep my eyes open—sleep pulled me back. I tumbled into another nightmare: Joseph stumbled across a field, smears of blood staining his face, his eyes hollow and sad.

* * *

I woke up to a tidy home with hand-hewn chairs, a dirt floor, and white-washed walls. The mellow smell of beeswax permeated the room. A man sat by the table, his mangy beard a match for Byron's. He looked so much like Byron. The man's skin was ruddy and rough, but his hair was whiter and thinner than I remembered. The woman was a lesson in comparisons. Her complexion was porcelain bisque. With an upturned nose, sparkling eyes, and silky black hair spun in a meticulous bun, she looked like a life-size doll.

A muffled sound of voices:

Lee . . . surrendered . . . Appomattox.

The war was over.

I searched for Byron, his profile barely discernible in the dim candlelight.

"Are you better?" Byron's voice echoed as though he spoke through a pipe. "You better?" he repeated, louder that time.

Another dream. A breeze. Leaves chased each other down a forest path, tumbling out of sight.

Voices broke into my consciousness:

"So, is it pneumonia?"

"Pretty sure of it."

"Will she be all right?"

* * *

When I took a breath, pain shot through my side. His words were halting and slow, a kaleidoscope of syllables, sounds, and stops. "Just reminds me of Clara."

A spinning wheel's whirr, or maybe the wind. Someone's bleached voice echoed from the back of the room. "Byron, it's not going to be like Clara. The girl's already on the mend."

My nightgown clung damply to me. The room tilted, or shifted somehow. I was adrift on Hardin's Pond. Floating away.

I must have fallen asleep, carrying my wonderings about Clara with me. I lifted my head from my pillow. Somebody squeezed my hand.

"Clara?" My voice wasn't much more than a croak. Someone stoked the fire and the room warmed. The sound of hissing flames encompassed me. I begged my eyes to open.

Byron stared at his knotted hands. "My daughter." His voice was barely audible. "Clara. She got sick one day. Gone the next." Another log on the fire and the smell of cherry wood filled the room.

My voice came from somewhere outside my body. "Didn't know you had a daughter."

"I had a soft spot for her." Byron took a deep breath. "Just figured she'd grow up, get married, and have a slew of ornery babies."

I adjusted myself on the mattress. A whistle's low moan distracted me. He said something. Pinching my eyes, I tried to concentrate on his words.

"My wife died the same week," I heard him say. "Pneumonia." And then he squeezed my hand.

33

Joseph

After several days' train travel through Alabama and Mississippi, the parole guards informed us that we'd make the rest of our journey on foot. They simply turned us loose and directed us down the road.

Gabe, with more energy than I'd witnessed for months, walked with a mission. "Once we get to Camp Fisk, we'll probably hear word from back home."

When we arrived at the Big Black River, our flag greeted us from the opposite shore. In a snapping salute of red, white, and blue, the flag marked our entrance to freedom.

"Didn't realize how much I missed it." I rubbed my face, feeling the tug of freedom and the sweet draw of home. Someone's hand was at his forehead in salute. The rest of us did the same.

We were so far from home, yet the flag brought us close. I had taken the flag for granted: the freedom that it stood for, the price that soldiers paid. In the back of our group, someone sniffed loudly. My throat burned, and, wiping my nose with the sleeve of my shirt, I walked forward.

In a mass of arms and legs, everyone else churned forward too. Gabe started down the pontoon bridge. "We'll be home soon. Come on," he said, his strides lengthening.

A familiar voice trumpeted behind us, "At that rate, you'll be in Indiana by sunrise!" We whipped around.

"O'Farrell! You old coot! What a sight for sore eyes!" Gabe pumped O'Farrell's hand. "Where've you been?"

"Cahaba Prison," he said. The pupils in his eyes darkened. "We're on our way home."

I didn't have to ask him how bad he had it at Cahaba. There was no meat left to him.

We funneled into line. There were lines for everything: linens, firewood, food.

"Can't wait to see Sarah," said Gabe. His interest in her was alarming.

"Fine time to think of her," I said. "I mean, when we're almost home."

O'Farrell inched up behind us. "What happened to brotherly love?"

Our linens and firewood in hand, Gabe was strides ahead of me, a campfire first on his agenda. He kneeled on the ground, adding kindling to the coals. With his pencil-thin arms, sunken dark eyes, and hollow cheeks, he was a whittled version of his prewar self. The wood crackled and sputtered, as the flames finally caught hold.

O'Farrell, probably seeking attention, chucked a log on the fire.

"Damn it, O'Farrell!" Gabe gave me a frustrated glance. "What'dyou do that for?"

"Needed more wood." His grin was an acre wide.

I propped our new shaving glass on a crate and squinted at it. A stranger stared back at me. My cheekbones protruded, my beard was a wiry nest, and blood vessels showed through my sallow skin. I looked like Rip Van Winkle, just awakened from a twenty-year sleep.

THE LAST EXCHANGE. CAMP FISK, FOUR MILE BRIDGE (VICKSBURG), APRIL 1865

In the spring of 1865, General Robert E. Lee surrendered his Army of Northern Virginia to General Ulysses S. Grant. While this is generally held to be the end of the war, fighting continued for months after the surrender. However, prisoner exchanges such as those at Camp Fisk, Mississippi, increased dramatically as the South began to accept defeat.

"Don't think anyone will recognize me," I said. I imagined Sarah in her garden, carefully planting beans in a meticulous row, her eyes lighting when she saw me walking toward her.

A fellow from a neighboring tent sauntered past Gabe and wormed in front of me.

"Hey, I was using that glass. Who the hell are you?" I gave him a shove.

His nasal voice projected over the camp, "Captain to you. Captain McCoy." He leaned into the mirror, his mouth drawing down like a codfish. "You hear Lee surrendered?"

I gave him a solid look. "Lee surrendered?"

His image nodded.

I glanced back at Gabe. "You hear that? War's over!"

Gabe let out a low whistle. "Hard to believe." He stood up. "Got those Johnnies running with their tails between their legs!"

McCoy fussed with his mustache, twisting the ends into a perfect curl. "They can't keep us here much longer."

In a curious rhythm, Gabe tapped his fingers on his leg. "So Joseph, you ready to go home?"

The thought of home was sweet. "When they finish taking roll, we'll head to Vicksburg and board the first steamboat bound north," I said.

McCoy eyed his image. "I'll be on that boat too." He flicked something off his shoulder. "Just want you to know: As captain, I'll have privileges."

Tipping his kepi, Gabe left our campfire. "Going to see if I can catch news from home," he said with an odd catch to his voice. His timing, of course, was perfect. I was left tending a dying fire. Worse yet, I was stuck listening to McCoy.

First, he shared tales of his battle heroics. Next, he shared his plans for selling his land. At first I nodded politely. Finally, though, I gave up. I tossed the last of the wood on the fire and went to look for Gabe.

Something was wrong. Gabe trudged toward me, the color washed from his face. "You're never going to believe this," he said. His eyes were rimmed and dull.

Had something had happened to Mother or Father? Or Sarah? Gabe tugged a stump close to our campfire and sat down.

"D-did you hear something about Sarah?" I asked.

"Can't believe it took this long for us to hear." He pressed his thumbs together, leaned forward, and gazed into the flames.

Heaviness settled on my chest. I sat down, too. "Tell me! Tell me what happened! Has something happened to Sarah?" No matter how bad the news, I wanted to know. I *needed* to know.

"Don't know how to tell you this." His hollow eyes were a dull slate of green.

"What? Tell me what?" My lungs burned; I was gasping for air.

His voice was barely audible, "Abraham Lincoln . . . "

That was not the name I expected. I took a breath, and air coursed through my lungs. "What happened?"

He turned to look at me. "A steamboat named the *Sultana* just came downriver with news from the North. President Lincoln was shot. Shot by a damn Reb."

34

Sarah

Finally feeling better, I wedged my pillow underneath me and took inventory of my hosts' home. The morning's watercolor light streamed through the windows, bathing the floor in lilac and pink. The home was tidy, fresh, and clean.

"Are we at your brother's house? Vicksburg?" My blanket was itchy. I longed for a bath.

"Samuel." Byron gave me a cup of spring water, folding my fingers around the cool tin.

I drank as greedily as my frail body would let me. "How long have I been sick?" I tried to adjust to the sound of my voice.

"Dunno. Wasn't countin' days." His Adam's apple pumped in his throat. "Didn't know if you were going to make it."

I rolled onto my elbow. "I do remember us talking about your daughter. May I ask you a question?"

"Already asked four. Not that I was counting." Frowning, he leaned back in his chair and looked out the window. "Don't want to talk about it," he replied, wiping his nose with the back of his hand.

Barely able to thread my words together, I continued, "Did she die from measles or from something else?" I should have kept my thoughts to myself.

Byron's chair grated against the floorboards. "Somethin' else. Pneumonia." His eyes latched fiercely on mine.

* * *

I'm not sure how many days it took before I felt like myself. Maybe five. Maybe more.

It was odd—officially meeting Byron's sister-in-law after spending days in her home. Drying her hands in the folds of her skirt, she motioned toward the table. She was every bit a Southern lady. "If you're well enough, join us for pie. My name's Maggie. My husband Samuel's over there. We'd love to hear your plans."

Her statement caught me by surprise. "My plans?" Until that moment I had forgotten about my plans—my plans for finding Joseph and Gabe.

"Sure, my dear." Maggie cupped my elbow and led me to the table. "We'd love to know what you're going to do," she said.

She served me a small portion of shoofly pie. The combined smell of molasses and sugar was too sweet to resist.

"Her famous recipe." Samuel squared his shoulders.

"Pie's too rich for someone just recoverin'." Leaning toward me, Byron forked a bite from my pie.

LIBRARY OF CONGRESS, PRINTS AND PHOTOGRAPHS DIVISION

Although this image shows the Vicksburg riverfront in 1880, it gives an idea of the type of activity that Sarah saw as she approached the Sultana.

I'm sure my jaw dropped. Pinching her mouth like a raisin, Maggie whacked his hand, "Pie's the last thing you need, Mr. Paunch."

"Mr. Paunch? What kind of nickname is that?" I asked. Byron snorted, his reaction generating a fit of laughter from the rest of us. I grasped the table to keep dishes from jiggling.

This home was a happy one. It was the kind of home I wanted—one where I could laugh, where I could be myself.

Maggie lit her lamp, its shadows flickering on the wall, exaggerating our features. Byron pushed back from the table. "Guess I better show up at the hospital tomorrow."

"That's right!" I exclaimed, surprised. "You're supposed to be at the hospital. That's what your transfer orders said."

He shifted on his seat. "S'posed to. But I don't always follow orders." He winked at his brother.

"That's for sure," Samuel retorted. He knew his brother much better than I.

Byron's decisions made no sense to me. "So if you're supposed to be at the hospital, why haven't you been there?"

"First things first. I wasn't going to take care of other people until I was sure you were all right." He patted my hand. "Just prioritizin' my time."

My illness had delayed his care of other patients, and I didn't want to be a burden. Then I realized something that I should have asked long before. "Would Joseph . . ."

He pushed his plate aside. "Dunno. Seems to me Joseph and Gabe should've been mustered out awhile ago. If they're all right. Small chance you'd find 'em now."

My fingers went numb. Tears welled in my eyes. I stared out the window, wishing for some kind of a compass, a star, or a map. How could I find my own way? "But, that's why I came here," I whispered.

Distracted by distant laughter, I caught a glimpse of children playing tag in the grove. One towheaded girl, her hands fisted at her waist, planted herself by a lone oak. Her face was lit up—shimmering with excitement.

I wished I were that child.

My throat tightened. "Home. I need to go home." If I was going to find Joseph or Gabe, I had to be patient and let them find me.

"Well, I think you should stay." He opened the door. Cool air smelling of river water filtered into the room.

I wheeled toward him. "I don't believe I need your permission."

Byron, with his hand still on the doorknob, turned to me. His eyes were soft and kind. "Knew the minute you were well, you'd be headin' home."

A throaty steamboat whistle signaled the new day, heralding my journey home. I packed and repacked my bag: taking out medicines, putting them back in, folding and refolding my clothes. I glanced out the window, hoping to see action on the street below. Byron didn't even notice my angst. He crouched by the fire and prodded the coals. Again, the steamboat's whistle moaned.

"Who needs roosters when you have boats?" Standing up, Byron peered out of Samuel's window too. "Damn steamboats. Wish we were farther from the wharf."

"Beggars can't be choosers." I rolled up on my toes. Just over the rooftops, a half-dozen smokestacks puffed clouds of smoke.

Byron picked up my bag and nodded toward the river. "Guess I better get you there."

I swallowed hard, trying to ward off last-minute doubts; I didn't know how I was going to manage on my own. Angry at myself for my indecision, then frustrated by my anger, my thoughts spiraled as I followed him out the door.

We made good progress until we were closer to the river. The street was jammed with crates, barrels, and kegs. Navigating the maze, we made our way toward the river's edge.

Finally, we arrived at the waterfront, the boat right before my eyes. The *Sultana* was beautiful—a tiered birthday cake on a shimmering platter. With a meticulous construction of fretwork and scrolling, its ornate railings and tiered floors had a majestic air. It was grand, with its freshly painted trim and towering smokestacks.

"You'll be all right." Byron held my elbow and guided me up the ramp. "Don't start bawlin'. Can't tolerate soggy good-byes."

I drew a ragged breath. "Thank you. For everything," I said, tentatively grasping the railing.

He nodded and glanced upriver, deep in thought. "You too." Byron turned and started back down the ramp. The back of his head bounced through the soldiers. My chest tightened like a ball.

Then I noticed the river below. Like a writhing serpent, the water curled and twisted, swirling muddy and dark. A cloud masked the sun. The river darkened and chunks of wood tumbled past.

I was finally going home.

35

Joseph

VICKSBURG, MISSISSIPPI, APRIL 1865

I never saw a city more imposing than Vicksburg. Skirted with rounded hillocks and rested at the bluff's crest, the town bore the ugly scars of battle—crumbled buildings, war-torn hills, and rutted roads. I couldn't see past the destruction to feel the newness of spring.

O'Farrell, Gabe, and I waited on the wharf boat. Burlap bags of coffee beans, drums of cured pork, and barrels of axle grease vied for space. Tarp canopies housed mysterious goods. With boxes, jugs, and crates stacked three-high, the wharf was a temporary warehouse for hemp, brooms, and ale.

"Ready for this?" O'Farrell rocked on his toes.

Gabe squinted toward the front of the line. "Lookin' forward to going home, that's for sure."

Soldiers lined to the street, news of Abraham Lincoln's death trumping all other news.

Heard it was that actor. What was his name?
Think it was Booth. John Wilkes Booth.

A young boy cupped his hands around his mouth and yelled, "Steamboat a-comin'!" Every one of us turned to see the boat. Water foamed at her prow, as she sliced through the river's velvet brown waves.

Gabe whistled under his breath, "Look. She's comin'."

A stern-wheeler churned toward us, her entrance graceful and powerful. Black smoke spiraled out of her smokestacks, water stirring as her paddle wheels reversed.

"Nothin' prettier," I said.

But that stern-wheeler wasn't ours. My attention turned to the boat we were boarding, the name *Sultana* neatly painted in red. Black bunting scrolled her railing, a grim reminder of Lincoln's death.

Soldiers and civilians waited to board: gaunt soldiers boasting crisp new linens, a proud groom escorting his bride, and a portly woman urging ahead her child.

With hundreds of soldiers blocking my view, I could barely see the bow of the boat. For just a moment I caught a glimpse of a young lady; she stood by the flagstaff and glanced my way. She seemed so—familiar. Then everyone bunched together and I lost sight of her.

I pulled up on my toes.

My chest ached and I swallowed hard.

"What are you looking at?" Gabe squinted toward the boat.

She had the same features as Sarah: willowy frame, wheat-colored hair. But it was more the way she stood. Confident—or maybe pretending to be.

It *was* her.

Union soldiers board the Sultana.

LIBRARY OF CONGRESS

36

Sarah

I had privileged information and the facts scared me. As a volunteer nurse on that fine boat and one of the first to board, I had been told that the *Sultana* had been selected as the very last transport steamboat. The boat looked sound enough. From her ornate railings to her decorative trim, no one would deny that she had character. But the minute I set foot on the boat, my bones went cold. Something was wrong.

My ears were keenly attuned to a disturbing noise: A clanking noise from the boiler room. I pushed through the crush of bodies until I found a deckhand. "What's that noise?"

He scowled. "Not sure. Doesn't sound quite right."

If the *Sultana* was the last transport, then why was the steamboat just down the wharf—the *Lady Gay*—leaving with hardly any passengers at all?

Ribbons of mud trailed the *Lady Gay* as she left the wharf on her journey up the Mississippi River. Above her name was an artistic rendition of a beautiful woman—goddess-like with a flowing white gown, porcelain features, and soft wavy hair—appearing to stroll almost regally in an idyllic country landscape. Was that woman smiling or frowning?

With the sun high in the sky and passengers still boarding the boat, I wondered how full it might be before the evening was over.

* * *

The sky's crimson color reflected on the river; half-submerged trees on shore tore a line between earth and sky. The boat was no place for a woman. *Definitely no place for someone afraid of water.*

John Cass Mason, captain of the Sultana

Lines of soldiers, still waiting to board, crowded the wharfboat—more soldiers than I could count. Deckhands and stewards crammed past me shouting, "All dat ain't goin', please git asho!"

I was sorely tempted to follow the deckhands' suggestion. By appearances, the *Sultana* —already jammed full of cargo, soldiers, and horses—didn't have room enough for me.

As if walking through a herd of cattle, I followed the promenade toward the stern. These cattle certainly weren't fit for market; their malnourished frames made me concerned for their travel. The soldiers were cleanly shaven—as if dressed for an occasion. Obviously, the army knew how to tidy up soldiers before sending them home.

Seeing a deckhand attending to the departure of the *Sultana*, I asked, "Where can I find the captain?"

He tipped his cap. "Ah buh-leeve you goin' to need good luck wit dat, Miss! Can't help you."

I was momentarily distracted by a grating noise. Like the roiling stomach of a giant, the floor groaned and vibrated underneath my feet. "What's that noise?" I asked a soldier next to me, "The engine?"

His eyebrows spiked. "Yes, ma'am. Keep walkin' straight and you'll walk right past it."

I hardly made progress down the promenade. "Excuse me, sir." Soldiers parted in front of me. As I moved through a sea of blue I heard mummers and whispers, "*Is she travelin' alone?*" and "*That's not proper.*"

* * *

Clearly the war was over, and those soldiers thought we had returned to prewar conventions. I pressed forward. Another man not far ahead of me, all brass and buttons, called to the First Mate, "Are you sure the freight's distributed evenly?"

The First Mate's response was quick. "Yes, sir."

"When we take on coal, be sure to get as much as we can. We're going up-stream against floodwaters, and we'll need all the power we can get."

"Yes, Captain Mason, sir," he said with a nod.

Now I knew who the captain was, and I approached a clean-shaven man, wearing a neat blue cap, shiny black shoes, and a tailored blue uniform. "Would you have time to address my concerns?" I asked.

He scowled. "Something you need?"

"I'm just a little nervous. Quite a few people on one boat."

Mason wasn't much taller than me, but his commanding voice made up for his lack of physical size. Arching his eyebrows he answered, "You can rest assured. Absolutely no need to be alarmed. This boat has advanced equipment: safety gauges that track steam pressure, a lifeboat, a yawl, fire-fighting pumps, fire-fighting axes, three hundred feet of fire hose, and seventy-six life belts."

A little overwhelmed, I replied, "I hope we won't have cause to use all that 'advanced' equipment."

"No, Miss." He rocked back on his heels. "This is the finest boat on these waters. You'll be safe as a crow in a gutter."

As if on cue, the timbers above us trembled, and a sheer curtain of dust sifted down. "Pardon me, but is that deck . . . Is that deck supposed to be sag-ging like that?" I squinted toward the ceiling. "Perhaps some soldiers should move to a different level?"

Captain Mason took off his cap and slowly revolved it in his hands. "Ah, you're observant, my dear."

I didn't know what to say.

"Get some stanchions," he crowed to his crew. "We need support." Then, with a polite nod, he waved me away.

My skin warming, I plucked up my medical bag and marched down the promenade. As crowded as the deck was, I pressed through until I got to the staircase. The stairs were impossible. "Excuse me," I said to little response.

"Here, let me help you," offered a soldier—more giant than man—at the bottom of the stairs. "Comin' through!" he called and rammed up the stairs with me right behind him.

"Sarah!" someone said. I remembered that voice, the rich timbre and tex-ture of it. My heart ached to see him. The voice belonged to Gabe.

37

Joseph

Gabe, O'Farrell, and I shuffled like old men past the chock and capstan, pushing our way to the stairs. Gabe wormed his way ahead of us. Collecting together, we came to a standstill.

I made it to the top of the stairs and that's when I saw Sarah right beside Gabe—about ten feet away. The air left my lungs.

He curled a strand of hair away from her forehead, neither of them noticing me. He was intent on her face. For a moment I lost sight of them. Then, when there was a gap in the crowd, I watched her toss her head back with laughter, her hair shimmering gold.

O'Farrell was at my heels. "Hey, Joe! You want to see the boat?"

I waved him away. "Can't . . . I . . ."

"You'll never guess." He grabbed my elbow, pulling me toward the stairs.

I tugged my arm from his grip. "Wait." I got up on my toes, trying to see Sarah.

"There's something you need to see." Then he stopped, his jaw flopping open. "Your brother's got a girl?" His bony elbow dug in my ribs. "A pretty one too."

"*Your brother's got a girl?*" I couldn't watch Gabe with Sarah any more. Heat rising on my neck, I plowed toward Sarah.

She tilted her head, and her eyes widened. "Joseph!" she cried, her face brightening. Gabe folded his arms over his chest, looking at me with hooded eyes.

I pushed forward and wrapped my arms around her, lifting her in the air, and the world around us evaporated. The sound of her laughter extinguished every other noise on the boat. After all that time, after all that waiting, I had found her. I tried to breathe her all in—her hair coming down in wisps from her bun, her smooth skin, her shy smile.

Her eyes hinted of sorrow—I wasn't sure. "How did you get here?" I asked, letting her down gently.

She lifted one shoulder. "Oh, *that* would be a long story!" I couldn't look at her hard enough. Her hair was darker and light freckles peppered her nose. She was taller. Thinner.

O'Farrell edged in beside me. "Gabe, you want to see the boat?"

My brother met my eyes. "That's all right, we're *fine* right here."

"Hear there's an alligator aboard. You want to see the alligator?" He pushed up on his toes and glanced toward the stairs.

Gabe chuckled, shaking his head.

"Who's this?" Sarah's eyes shone like stars.

"O'Farrell," he nodded, a grin spreading ear to ear.

Looking from O'Farrell to Sarah I responded, "Sorry. Wasn't thinking."

"Doesn't surprise me," said Gabe, nudging me.

O'Farrell bounced on his toes and motioned toward the stairs. "The alligator. Down by the wheelhouse. Main floor."

"An alligator?" Lifting his chin, Gabe looked toward the stairs. "You're kiddin' me, right? O'Farrell started toward the stairs, tugging Gabe after him. Gabe nodded at Sarah, and he and O'Farrell disappeared in the crowd.

Sarah picked up her medical kit. "Go on with Gabe. I'll find you later."

"Joseph, are you coming or not?" called O'Farrell.

"No," I answered. I wasn't going to leave her.

"It's all right." Sarah waved me forward. "Really."

"Come with me." I wanted to hold her and put my arms around her.

"Joseph!" O'Farrell, maybe ten feet in front of me, motioned wildly toward the stairs.

"Please." I couldn't take my eyes off her. She was thinner and taller, but her smile was the same.

"This is crazy," she said. "An alligator. We're going to work through all these people for an alligator?" Her face flushing pink, she clutched the elbow of my jacket.

"I know." I nodded and pushed forward, working my way toward Gabe and O'Farrell. I gave Sarah a sideways glance, and her cheeks blushed red. She belonged by my side.

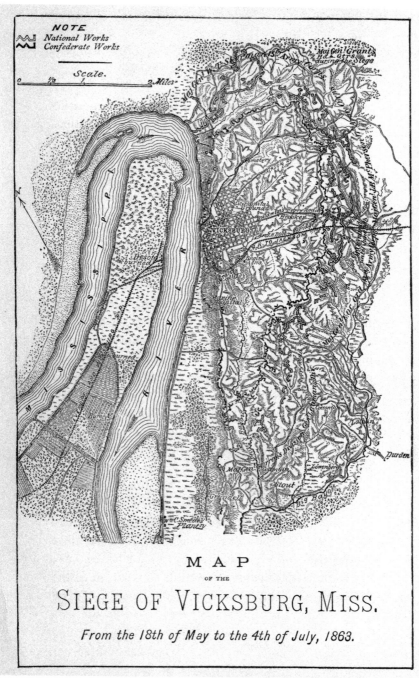

MAP

OF THE

SIEGE OF VICKSBURG, MISS.

From the 18th of May to the 4th of July, 1863.

The *Sultana left Vicksburg, Tennessee (site of the May-July 1863 siege), on April 24, 1865. Its destination was Cairo, Illinois.*

The four of us fought to get down the stairs, shoving our way toward the larboard. All the while, the touch of Sarah's hand warmed me, distracting me.

"Almost there," O'Farrell called back. He ducked into a small room by the wheelhouse, and we followed him in. At first glance the room appeared normal. A workbench lined one wall, strewn with screwdrivers, wrenches, and bolts.

"Looks like someone's in the middle of a project," said Gabe. That's when we noticed the alligator.

The alligator's home, a box about two feet wide and four feet long, covered a section of the floor in the back of the room. The beast wrangled its head out of its crate.

"I'll stay right here." Sarah stood in the doorway, her eyes shining bright.

Gabe grabbed a couple sticks by the door and selected the longest one for himself. "Probably setting here to control the alligator," he said, giving me the other stick.

"So why's an alligator on this boat, anyway?" Sarah set down her medicine kit and laced her fingers in front of her, a faint smile playing on her lips.

I halfheartedly jabbed the beast on his neck. "We hardly have room to breathe, and he's got his own room."

In the fashion of a sword fighter, Gabe tucked one arm behind his back and jousted. The reptile lunged toward him. "Just want him to open his mouth. Show him who's boss." He lifted one eyebrow at Sarah.

The alligator took advantage of Gabe's distraction and swung his head toward him. Lurching forward, it snapped the stick from Gabe's hand, slivering it into pieces.

"He almost took off your fingers." I turned, giving O'Farrell a knowing look.

He chuckled, "That's why I'm in the corner."

"You're addle-brained," Gabe replied, sweeping the floor with his foot. "Anything else to see on the boat?

"Easier to stay put." O'Farrell took my stick and set it by the door.

Sarah lifted up on her toes, catching my eyes.

"Where's your sense of adventure?" Brushing past me, Gabe worked toward the stern, the three of us trailing after him. The swelling river sped past us in a coffee-colored current. "Look at that river," Gabe said. "If you change your mind about going home, O'Farrell, you could dive in and float downstream."

"Might be possible if I knew how to swim. And if the river wasn't flooded," O'Farrell answered. We leaned over, mesmerized by the swirling water below.

Before we took two steps toward the stairs, someone called from the upper deck, "Hey, you got buckets down there? Can you tie a rope on one and pulley water up? We need something to drink."

"Aren't there buckets up there?" I glanced at the fire buckets stored by my feet.

"Yeah. Some. Think they're all bein' used," the caller replied.

"Sure." I found a rope, and arm over arm, I released one of the buckets down to the swirling river below, plunging it into the water and filling it half full. Then Gabe, with a nod at Sarah, threw the rope on the railing above us and hand over hand, he pulleyed the bucket up to the soldier. It caught on the boiler deck railing and dangled just out of his reach.

"More buckets where that one came from, right?" said Gabe.

"Four right here." Sarah wedged one out of the compartment and gave it to me. I pulleyed it up to the men.

"After you're finished up here, I want to show you what's down in the hold." O'Farrell reached into his pocket, then held out his hand, unfolding his fingers. It appeared that he was offering a pyramid of sand. "Sugar. There's a ton of it down below. I'll share. Being there's a long trip ahead."

Little did we know.

38

Sarah

I couldn't always follow my own wishes and consent to the small voice in my heart. I had work to do. My time with Joseph and Gabe couldn't and shouldn't take precedent over my mission on this boat. I had told Joseph as much. So, I moved forward with the work at hand. My first goal was to gain an overall impression of the medical needs, and to accomplish that goal I needed to locate the captain.

I squeezed through a host of soldiers until I found a deckhand. "Where's the captain?"

"Prob'ly here on da boiler deck, Miss. I think he might be talkin' to da clerk." I didn't know how I would manage getting past all those soldiers; they weren't pleased with the idea of letting me through.

"You should stay put," one suggested. "Can't you see there's not enough room to be movin' around? And what business do you have talkin' to the captain, anyway?"

"What business do I have talking to the captain?" I straightened my shoulders. "Mine."

The clerk's office wasn't far. Peeking around the corner, I saw the captain talking with a young man seated inside. The clerk had deep furrows in his brow. Captain Mason squinted over the ledger. "Exactly how many do we have aboard?"

"Too many," the clerk said, leafing through the book. "Hard to keep the numbers straight. There were 398 from the hospital and 570 from the first train. Someone told me there was another train before the second train, so that would mean the second train was actually the third train."

The clerk had a fascination with numbers that I couldn't comprehend, when he looked pointedly at Mason and replied, "There might be 1,996 or maybe 2,142. There could be as many as 2,500. However, there are 97 cases of wine, 250 hogsheads of sugar, 100 hogs, and 100 horses. Of that I'm sure."

"Considerable profit to be made," added Mason, rocking back and forth on his feet.

"Yes, a record trip. A lot of money to be made." The clerk closed his ledger and frowned.

"Just keep in mind that you owe me a great deal," Mason grimaced, bowing out of the room.

He must have been deep in thought, because he didn't even notice my presence.

The captain strode up the promenade on the boiler deck, soldiers parting as if for royalty. I slipped behind him and the gap closed in after me. He elbowed his way down the main staircase and then charged toward the engine room.

Slipping behind him, I followed him into the area, tucking into a corner to listen.

The boiler room wasn't a room really, but more of an area with no walls and just an open fence. It was a fiery netherworld. From my position I could

STARBOARD ENGINE OF "ROBERT F. BRANDT," P0347, INDIANA HISTORICAL SOCIETY

Giant boilers such as these were the driving force behind steamboats. By heating huge amounts of water and forcing the steam through smaller pipes, enough force was created to turn the giant paddles of the boat and propel a vessel forward. Because of the high pressure within the boilers, proper maintenance was critical. Damage could lead to dangerous situations.

see that the area had an enormous coal bin, probably ten feet long with coal chunks the size of a man's head. Behind the furnace stood four tubular boilers with numerous pressure gauges and safety valves.

"So what's the verdict, Winston?" Mason laced his hands behind his back. "How're my boilers?"

"The bulge in the larboard boiler is fixed. Taylor worked all night." Winston motioned toward the left boiler. "Looks pretty good. He riveted on a new piece right there."

Captain Mason gave the patch a cursory glance. "Then we can continue north. Well done." His voice lowered, "Can you imagine the butcher's bill, all the casualties, if we had a faulty boiler?"

Winston shrugged. "A temporary fix. When we reach Saint Louis, we'll make full-scale repairs. Meanwhile, the boilers have their work cut out for 'em."

"That's for sure." Mason looked my way. "We're pushin' over 500 tons of boat and another 140 tons of human cargo."

Winston worked at some dirt in his nails. "Not to mention horses and an ass or two."

"Even a damn alligator," Masson added, and they both laughed.

Captain Mason left the room and I trailed after him. Earlier he told me I was "safe as a crow in the gutter," and I wanted to know how crowding passengers on a boat would keep me safe. After wedging through a wall of soldiers, I caught up to him.

"Captain Mason?" I called.

"What do you want?" He wheeled around. "I have things to do."

"Just wondering, is the boiler all right?" I studied his face.

"All repairs are made." Mason's eyes were glassy. "Boat's sound as the day she launched."

"If you don't mind me asking . . ." I paused, selecting my next words carefully. "How many passengers does this boat hold? I mean, how many does it legally carry?" As crowded as the boat was, I was certain we were over the limit.

Captain Mason looked over my shoulder. Was he uncomfortable? Or nervous? I almost felt sorry for him. "Well, we can legally carry 376 passengers, but we're dealing with unusual circumstances."

"Unusual circumstances?" I asked. "What do you mean?"

"Well, the war's over. We need to get our boys back home," his voice trailed off.

Not willing to accept his justification, I gripped the railing, my knuckles turning white. "I understand wanting to get the soldiers home to their families, sir, but crowding a boat can't be in their best interest." I couldn't keep the emotion out of my voice. "Couldn't you board some of these passengers on other boats?"

"What do you mean?" He tilted his chin toward me.

My cheeks felt hot. "I saw the *Lady Gay* leave the wharf earlier today. I may be wrong, but I didn't see many passengers on her. And," I paused for emphasis, "the *Pauline Carroll* just left. I didn't see many on her either."

Mason's eyes flashed. "Yes, well, the *Pauline Carroll* didn't have many because of the smallpox rumors."

Smallpox rumors? Odd. Perhaps the source for those rumors stood right in front of me. Negative thoughts crept into my tone. "What was the source of those rumors, do you suppose?"

"Are you insinuating that I spread rumors about smallpox? So that I can fill my own boat to capacity?" His voice tightened.

"No, I'm not insinuating anything. I just don't understand. We have over 2,000 people aboard this boat. That's six times her capacity."

"You had better get to your room, Miss." Mason frowned. "This boiler area's no place for a, um, lady."

"I'm on my way. You're correct, this is no place for me. But I want to get home and my only choice is this boat." Once I started, I couldn't stop. "Every inch of the boat is filled. There's no room for these soldiers to lie down or even a place for them to attend to the calls of nature." My face warmed. "I don't believe we'll be comfortable. And I wonder if we'll even be safe." Turning to leave, I realized I had more to say. "Who's your head physician? I'd like to report for service."

He blinked several times. "There's no head physician." Mason widened his stance. "There's some Sisters of Charity, but I'm not sure where . . . "

I peered over Mason's shoulder. "Where are the headquarters for medical personnel?"

"What do you mean?" Blotches of crimson rose on his neck.

My question seemed like an obvious one, at least to me. "I mean, where can people look for help?"

Mason waved his hand in dismissal. "You're free to figure something out, but stay out of trouble."

I'd heard those words before.

39

Joseph

Impossible. It was almost impossible to wedge through the soldiers on the promenade. I found Sarah close to the boiler room. No surprise to me, she was organizing supplies.

She lifted her head to me. Her cheeks glowed a healthy pink.

"How did you end up here?" I asked.

"I went to Vicksburg hoping to find you and your brother. But I got sick." She lowered her eyes. "Just need to get back home." She tucked a loose strand of hair behind her ear. "I saw the newspaper notice."

"I wanted to know you were all right," I said. "You hadn't returned my letters."

"Your letters?" She blinked up at me.

"I wrote you almost every week." The crowd pressed closer.

"Never got any letters." She stubbornly tilted her chin.

Seemed strange, she hadn't got any. "Didn't realize you were with the Seventh until a few months ago."

Her mouth formed a small *o*. She glanced toward the shoreline. "You're here now."

That was all that mattered, really.

The paddle wheel churned us forward, and she nodded toward the river's edge. "Take a look at those trees. They're almost submerged in the water. Can't even see the riverbank."

"All that good land's covered with water." I leaned over the railing, peering into the swirling river. "Look at those eddies. Suppose the high water's to blame. The whirlpools swallow everything drifting nearby."

Captivated, we watched the river braid and swirl below us, the smell of river water filling my nostrils. A snag whirled and disappeared into the black. A huge cypress careened past us through the swollen river, raking against the boat and tumbling downstream.

Just then, Gabe strode toward us. "Hey, Joe." He tipped his kepi at Sarah and motioned toward the stairs. "Come on. If we don't find a place to sleep, we're not going to have one."

I didn't want to leave Sarah. I could have spent all night talking to her, listening to the soft strum of her voice, watching her shining eyes.

"That's all right. Go ahead. I have work to do." She brushed against my arm.

A steamboat churned past us, hugging the bank. "A boat!" someone yelled. "Huzzah! Huzzah!"

"Soon," she said. Sarah reached her hand to me, and I laced her fingers in mine.

Our fingers unlocked. With a glance back at Sarah, I shuffled after Gabe. "Plow the way."

We hadn't gone far when a man, wielding a barrel over his shoulders, crossed in front of my brother.

"Is that whisky?" Gabe followed the soldier through the crowd.

"Yeah. Plannin' to share it with a few of my friends." The soldier shifted the barrel to his other arm. We listed to the right and the barrel toppled to the ground. Whisky pooled beneath our feet.

"Whisky!" someone yelled.

"Have at it!" called someone behind me. A dozen or more men crowded around the whisky and fell prone to the deck, lapping it up like wolves.

"We're turning!" someone cried. The boat swerved again. Like drunken men, we climbed the stairs, elbowing through a wall of soldiers, inching our way back toward the main salon.

A cavernous room in the middle of the boat, the main salon was a beautiful chamber with almost palace-like décor. Long and narrow, with fine carpet and chandeliers, the hall was designed as an after-dinner retreat. It wasn't a retreat now; it was crowded wall-to-wall with soldiers and cots.

There wasn't a cot to be found. "Should have looked earlier," I said.

Ignoring me, Gabe worked toward the edge of the room. "Empty one. Over there."

"Hot as the blue blazes. Think we're above the boiler." I tossed my kepi on the cot. "My spot's saved. Now we need a place for you."

Gabe wedged through the crowd of soldiers. Barely able to see the top of his head, I tracked behind him. "You trying to lose me?" I caught up to him.

"No." He paused midstep. "Don't think there's a spot left." He turned and looked me square in the eyes. "Should have been searching for a spot to sleep instead of talking with Sarah. Think with your head." Tight-lipped, he scanned the area, finishing the conversation.

"Looks like the salon's for officers," I said.

Gabe turned and worked toward the stern. "War's over. What's the worst they could do? Demote us?"

He nodded toward the bow. Maybe half the soldiers were roosted on chairs. Some were on cots too. "Maybe we missed a spot somewhere by yours. Let's get back."

Reversing direction, we pressed our way back to my cot—the one I had saved with my cap. In it was Captain McCoy. With his haversack gaping open, he looked up at us from the coveted spot. Combs, clothes, and letters spilled out. Obviously, he had claimed the area.

Gabe pointed his chin toward me. "So, Joseph, isn't that *your* cap and *your* cot?"

It was my cot. And McCoy had stolen it. "I thought it was."

Gabe swiped my cap off. "We need that, *McCoy*."

"That's 'Captain' to you," McCoy replied with a sardonic grin.

Gabe puffed up his chest and butted up to McCoy. Looked like a fight to me. "Sir, 'captain,' sir. You cabbaged Joe's cot."

The Sultana *was dangerously overloaded when it departed Vicksburg on the journey North.*

"Like a dog marks his spot?" McCoy drilled his finger into Gabe's chest, punctuating every word. "I put my *ass* here to save my spot. My *ass*. Asses trump hats. Now, get your ass and your hat out of here."

I grabbed Gabe by the elbow and backed him away from the cot. "Let that bugger have the damn cot. We'll find a corner somewhere else." Leaving Mc-Coy, we walked toward the stern. I leaned into Gabe. "Asses trump hats," I muttered.

Gabe turned and shot McCoy a final glare. "Hopefully we can find a decent spot to sleep after Memphis."

"That's right. We'll be stopping at Memphis tomorrow." We edged through the crowd.

Leaving the main salon, Gabe scanned the boat's passengers. Right away, I guessed who he was looking for.

He was looking for Sarah.

40

Sarah

I didn't expect to see Gabe, not at that hour. But there he stood, with his elbow in the doorframe.

"You're in the ladies' quarters," I rasped. Peeking out the door past him, I glanced toward Mrs. Woolfolk's room.

"I am," he agreed, almost as if rules weren't his to follow. He took my elbow and tugged me toward the promenade.

Cutting between soldiers like a hot knife through butter, he pushed toward the railing. "Haven't had much chance to talk to you." He made room for both of us. "We're plowing upstream pretty fast." He rested his hand on the banister and rubbed his thumb against the railing. "We'll be home soon."

The boat leaned into the curve and pressed me against the railing. I took a deep breath. The river smelled of dirt. Like writhing black snakes, the water churned and foamed beside us.

His voice was the same. Rich. Full. "How're we going to catch up on nearly four years?" His leg brushed against me, and I warmed with his touch. He curled a lock of hair behind his ear, his mouth crooking in a smile.

I didn't appreciate him pressuring me like this, standing so close. But on this boat, everyone was standing close. I could hardly blame him. Someone stepped on my skirts. I tugged at them, thankful for the diversion. Gabe cupped his hand under my elbow.

Every thought erased. I couldn't conjure up the last day—much less the last four years. I blinked up at him.

The crowd of soldiers pressed in. I could feel Gabe's breath. It smelled sweet, like raw sugar. "So?" he asked. "You miss me?"

I missed him, yes, but he was too close to me.

"You'll have to tell me about the Seventh," he said. "I mean, tell me about what you did."

"I-I had to help locate Rebel guards," I started.

"Sometime I'll have to tell you about the time I captured a couple Rebs. I captured their whisky, too." His grin widened. "That ol' Reb sounded just like my father."

It seemed that he just wanted to tell me about his last four years, not to hear about mine. "Can I tell you about my father?"

He tilted his head, but his eyes were a blank canvas.

"He . . ." My throat closed, and my eyes burned. I brushed a hot tear off of my cheek.

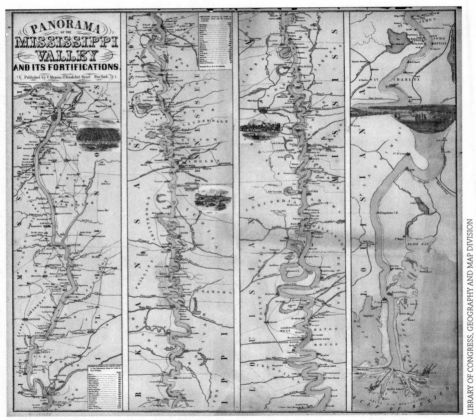

The Mississippi is the longest river in the United States and often considered a division between the East and the West. With its source in northern Minnesota, it flows thousands of miles to empty into the Gulf of Mexico. During the Civil War, controlling the river was an important part of the Union's plan to cut off the South from outside aid and trade.

"That's all right," he said. "You don't have to talk about it now."

But I wanted to. I wanted him to wait for me, to hear what I had to say. Maybe he felt uncomfortable. But I needed to be heard. "I n-need to get back to my room." I pushed toward my cabin.

"Sarah," he said. His eyes were dark mirrors of mine. "Tomorrow. We can talk tomorrow. Think we'll be in Memphis. Not sure. Guessin' Joseph and I will go into town."

"Yes, there's tomorrow." I gave him a weak smile and let him lead me back to my stateroom. He lingered by the door.

"Tomorrow," I said, tugging the door against the frame.

I waited, with the palm of my hand on the door, until I heard him walk away. He was so disarming—he took my breath away.

And now he made me curious. If we were stopping in Memphis tomorrow, how long would the trip last? With the limited supplies under my purview, I had to make sure they would last. Two days? Three days, maybe? I hadn't bothered to ask how many days the trip would take, and its duration was something I wanted to know. What were the stops along the way? We would stop for coal, for sure. I'd overheard the captain say as much.

Perhaps the engineer would entertain a few questions.

I was out of my element, but I entered the boiler room, leaving my medical kit by the entryway. A man sat on a crate, sweat glistening on his forehead. I wasn't sure how to address him. "Mister?" I said.

"What d'you want, Miss? Nathan Wintringer here." He shook my hand—squeezing hard. I could see by his tight smile that he wasn't fond of passengers. This area was clearly his domain.

With a sick feeling, I wiped my hands on my skirt. "Don't let me interrupt you, Mr. Wintringer."

"Too late for that now, isn't it, Miss?" He straightened his shoulders.

Mesmerized by safety valves, shutoff wheels, pumps, and drums, I stood riveted to the spot. My eyes took in each intricate working part, finally resting on the cloth ties on the valves atop the boiler.

"Well, I just wanted to know our schedule," I said as I edged into the area. The smell of oil and coal was so thick I could almost taste it.

"Schedule?" With his index finger and thumb, he rubbed between his eyes.

I took a half-step back. "Yes, what's our next stop?"

Pinching his lips together, he glared down at me. "Our next stop will be right now. That is, if you don't let me get back to work."

The cloth ties seemed out of place. I clenched my skirt in my fists. "If you don't mind my asking:—I started.

"Yes, I mind!" he said, his eye twitching. "But speak your business." He took a rag out of his pocket and wiped his forehead.

I politely pointed to the top of the boiler. "Why are those valves tied down?"

Mr. Wintringer cleared his throat and shifted his stance. "That's none of your business," he said avoiding my question. "And now, Miss, I've got a question for you."

"Yes?" I asked.

He nodded toward the door, "Where are *you* supposed to be?"

I hesitated.

"You with family?" His eyes were small slits.

I didn't want to explain about my father—or the fact that I was on my own. "I'm a nurse. I've been helping soldiers," I answered. I picked up my medical kit. I just wished I was home.

"Got medicine in there?" He tilted his head to the side. "Heard someone needs help. Back toward the stern."

Perhaps Wintringer presented me with an excuse. I left the room and wedged through the crowd. When I rounded the corner I found maybe a hundred men in the stern area. My eyes flitted from one soldier to the next. Then I found him. A dark-haired soldier—about my age—leaned with his back against the wall, his face scrunched in pain.

"What's wrong?" I opened my kit.

"Was in a fight. Got shoved against this wall. My arm. Can't move it." He gripped his left arm.

"I think I can help. May I?" I touched the side of his shoulder. It was mushy as if there were no underlying bone. Lower, I felt a ridge—the ball joint. The bone was loose and wobbly in his arm, "I think your shoulder's dislocated. I could try to fix it. It'll be painful."

"More painful than what it already is?" Clutching his elbow, he leveraged his back against the wall.

I remembered the contents of Father's medical kit. I still had some supplies. After pilfering through the kit, I drew out two bottles. "I have whisky or opium."

"Both?" He forced a smile.

"You still have your sense of humor," I said, measuring some Old Crow.

He swallowed the whisky in one gulp, and I went to work. I bent his elbow so that his lower arm was vertical, and I brought his elbow to his chest. Immediately, I rotated his lower arm outward and jerked as hard as I could. A crunch. He cried out, then he stopped and blinked at me. I smiled. I brought his arm back to his chest and tucked his fingers between his shirt buttons. "Keep it immobile so it has time to heal."

He rubbed on his arm. "How can I repay you?"

I repacked the whisky in my bag. "Don't reinjure it. And don't move your arm."

"Promise. You wait and see. I'll mend in no time." Then he looked me square in the eyes. "You're the one, aren't you?"

"The one?" I was baffled.

"Everyone's been talking about you. 'The girl that's helpin' everyone on the boat.' They're calling you an angel."

I didn't feel like an angel. My shoulders ached, my skirts were torn, and my medicine supply was low. I longed for my mother angel, more than ever.

41

Joseph

The wharf had a ghostly appearance. Gas lamps flickered, their waffling light reflecting on the water. Barrels, crates, horses, and men crowded the space serving as a barrier between Memphis and us.

O'Farrell met us on the gangplank. "You two go ahead. Gonna help with unloading."

"We can't get into the city if we can't get off the wharf." I motioned toward the guards.

Gabe eyed the traffic. "All we have to do is roll one of those hogsheads of sugar to the edge over there and slip away. Easy as that." He shifted his weight. "Want to get into the city or not?"

"I haven't told Sarah we're leaving for town." I looked back.

"I've told her." He shouldered into the hogshead.

I wondered when he had talked to her, but I shouldered the hogshead, too.

With the help of several other soldiers we delivered the hogshead and slipped past the guards. Our destination: an area of town called the Whisky Chute.

Tobacco smoke wafted out a tavern door, thick as the cannon's plume. Laughter bubbled onto the cobbled street. "This is the place," Gabe grinned, opening the door.

Greeted by the sweet smells of whisky, rum, and tobacco, we entered the pub. A good-sized crowd was inside, and by the looks of it, most were Union soldiers. The room was shaded and dark.

We made our way to the front of the room. Behind the barkeep, a system of grid work pocketed pewter steins.

"Ale?" I requested, retrieving a coin from my pocket and placing it on the bar.

The barkeep poured drinks for Gabe and me. The foam flowed over the lip of my mug and pooled onto the bar.

"Enjoy," he said, snapping a rag off his shoulder and mopping up the overflow.

Gabe lifted his mug. "To the end of the war!"

"Hear, hear!" I raised mine.

"Hear, hear!" echoed a soldier to the left of us. He raised his mug too. "Name's Wyman Holmes," he said. His hand left his mug long enough to shake mine.

"Joseph," I answered.

"Goin' home?"

"Finally." Gabe took swig and grinned.

Wyman leaned into the bar. "They're still lookin' for Booth, you know." Gabe and I exchanged a glance. "John Wilkes Booth. You know? The Johnny who shot Lincoln."

Everyone probably knew about Booth, except for some soldiers like me. "There're probably other things I've missed," I answered vaguely.

I didn't know what to say. So much had happened since we were released from Andersonville. I felt like an outsider—like a ghost in the room.

Gabe looked at his hands, folded together on the bar. "You wonder what Sarah's been up to? I mean, this whole time we've been gone?"

"You would have known if you had written her." My answer was caustic, but it was true.

"Too busy watchin' out for you," he grumbled. I let his words sink. He drained the last of his ale in a quick series of gulps. Gabe thought I couldn't watch out for myself—that it was his job to watch out for me.

The bartender took my mug. "You want more?"

"No, I've had enough," I said, nodding at Gabe, making my point clear.

Wyman, his tongue thick with alcohol, mumbled something.

"What? What did you say?" I leaned toward him.

He wheeled his mug at the bartender, motioning for another drink. "He your brother?" Funny, how he knew Gabe was my brother. "Says he's watchin' out for you," he said with a syrupy smile.

Gabe leaned forward, his elbows protecting his ale. "I surrendered to those damn Rebs for him."

"What?" My face burned red and my jaw clenched as I turned toward him. "Not like you had much of a choice."

He shrugged his shoulders and stared into his mug.

"You surrendered so you could watch out for me. Is that what you think?"

"Well . . ." Gabe said, wiping the bar with the palm of his hand.

"You're going to carry the war along with you?" I pushed my mug to the edge of the counter. "You think you saved me? That you went to Andersonville for me? Well, go right ahead and think that." I stood up.

"I'd be with our troop in Tennessee, if it wasn't for you." Those words slipped off Gabe's tongue as easily as if they had been rehearsed.

I pumped my fists by my side. "Go ahead and believe that. Truth is, you watch out for one person. And that person is you." I survived marching through snow, going without food, watching soldiers bleed out on a field. I'd seen Perryville, Franklin, Andersonville, but Gabe thought he had to take care of me.

Wyman pushed money toward the bartender. "Get these boys another drink."

My brother stood up and walked toward the door.

Wyman chuckled into his drink. "Better watch after him."

"Wait a minute, Gabe." I caught up with him at the door. He turned to me, his hands palms up. He didn't say he was sorry, and I didn't expect him too. I knew that the conversation was over.

Memphis, Tennessee, was a major riverboat port. Steamboat travel was much quicker than other modes of transportation, thus a very popular means of moving people and commercial goods. Farmers would bring their produce to the rivers. That produce was then taken to distant markets and sold. In the South the major export was cotton.

"Have a safe trip," yelled Wyman as he bellied closer to the bar, intent on his ale.

Gabe was already outside. I swiveled toward the door, fighting against the door latch. Then, I was out in the night's crisp air, using the feeble light of the gas lamp to look for Gabe.

He wasn't down the street.

"Gabe?" I called. There was a quick movement by the alley. His silhouette disappeared around the corner. "Gabe?"

I walked to the backstreet and found him leaning against the pub's rough siding. He wore a crooked grin. "Shh," he whispered.

Following the direction of his gaze, I squinted down the backstreet. Two people—two lovers—were caught in an embrace.

"Would you look at that?" rasped Gabe. "Think he's going to shag that woman." He cupped a hand and yelled toward the couple, "Hey you! Get on the boat!"

"Come on!" he motioned to me, the soles of his feet flying ahead of me. He tossed a grin over his shoulder. His smugness was motivation enough. I charged forward, and soon I was at his heels.

The steamboat's whistle echoed its throaty tones. "Hurry, boat's leavin'." Another whistle. "Cut a little dirt, Joe!" Like children, we ran side by side.

He sprinted ahead. The mud clerk had his hands on the rope, ready to draw up the plank. We leaped on board. "Made it!"

A deckhand unwound the rope from the chock. "You lucky fellows," he said. "Just in time." With a grind of the paddles, we slushed away from the shore, leaving the gas lamps of Memphis behind us.

We fought our way up the steps and peered in the main salon, where most of the soldiers had already claimed their cots.

So intent on finding a place to sleep, we at first didn't notice the captain of our boat standing along the railing. I could have picked him out anywhere. He looked proud and polished, but also a little nervous.

"How are you gentlemen doing?" Mason's eyes shifted toward the mass of men.

"Lookin' forward to bein' home." I nodded at Gabe. Gabe returned the favor, and nodded back at me.

Mason rubbed the back of his neck. "Got to get there first," he said. That seemed like an odd thing for a captain to say. "You have a place to sleep?" he continued, giving us a half-twisted smile.

"Not yet," I said.

"Doubt I'll sleep. Perhaps when we're safe in Cairo. I'd give all I have to be there now." Then Captain Mason shrugged, tipped his hat, and left us, climbing along the railing to the stern of the boat.

"You hear what he said?" asked Gabe.

I kept my eye on Mason. "He doesn't sound confident."

Gabe pushed through the crowd. "We ought to get some rest," he said. "Shouldn't have gone into Memphis."

"Cots as scarce as hen's teeth," I said pushing forward. "But it doesn't matter. We can sleep on the floor."

Gabe wedged ahead into the main salon. "Let's just find a spot that'll work."

From where we stood, every space looked taken. The room was crowded with soldiers. Some had knapsacks as pillows and were lying on the floor. Some were draped over chairs, and the lucky ones had a cot.

He marched forward, heading toward an empty chair. He plopped down and patted the chair beside him. "Good spot as any. Let's get some sleep."

The splashing sound of the paddlewheel and the muted breathing of the men played a low backdrop to the echo of Mason's words: *I'd give all I have to be there now.* Then my mind shifted. Of course, I also thought about Sarah. Maybe if we could just talk, if she could just see how much she meant to me. She deserved better than Gabe, and even though I wasn't good enough for her either, I'd try to be. For her, I'd try every day of my life.

When Gabe's breathing slowed into a steady rhythm, I decided to look for her.

She was in a stateroom, in the ladies' area—off limits for me. There wasn't a clear path to the stern. I recalled Captain Mason's crawl along the railing and decided to use the banister myself.

I crossed the salon, sneaked out the door, and picked my way toward the railing. Then, tucking my feet between each post, I scissored my legs through the spokes of the banister, working toward the stern. Intent on my feet, I almost bumped into Sarah as she edged toward me.

She looked beautiful. Wisps of hair spiraled on her forehead, her bright eyes shone in the dim light, and her cheeks flushed pink.

"What're you doing out here?" I asked.

She gripped the rail. "Couldn't sleep. Don't know. The river." She peered into the water. "Too many people. Too much time until we get home."

My gut clenched. "Anything else?" I wanted to know why she couldn't sleep—if she was thinking of Gabe or maybe thinking about me.

Chewing on her bottom lip, she looked behind me. "Well, I . . ."

I took her hand. She looked me in the eyes, the color of her pupils deepening. My heart leaped out of my chest.

"Yes," she said, her eyes turning solemn. "I was thinking about you."

I wanted to tell her how I fought battles for her, how I marched through the rain for her, and how I wanted to spend my life *with* her. I didn't know where to start. "It was hard to . . ." I started. "It was hard to be without you. I thought of you every day."

"I know! Me, too. I don't ever want to be separated from you again."

* * *

I have no idea how long we talked—long enough to hear stories about Byron and Enoch, of cowbells and cigars, of bullets and Rebs. In hushed tones she told me about her father too.

Then I told her about the Rebel guard and his strains of "Home Sweet Home."

A soft rain fell, slowly soaking my skin, drops of it glistening in her hair. I could have spent the whole night listening to her stories, listening to her plans for the future, with the paddlewheel slushing in the background.

I pushed a strand of wet hair from her forehead. "It's late," I said.

She lifted her chin. "Yes, we should get some sleep."

I didn't want to leave her. Not then. Not when four years stretched between us. I wanted time with her, just to look at her and to breathe her in. But she nodded and turned, smiling over her shoulder. She retraced her steps to the stern. I waited for her to disappear into the cabins and then I worked my way back to the main salon.

In my dreams I heard her voice—but I heard Gabe's voice too.

42

Sarah

Joseph listened to me; he cared about me. I never expected to feel so deeply about anyone, especially someone I'd grown up with. Sleep wouldn't come easily—not when I had so much to think about.

Whenever I rode Beulah, I could sort my thoughts. I needed her. Perhaps if I spent time with the horses I had seen by the afterguard.

Animals don't ask questions. They listen, or at least appear to. They don't require decisions or have expectations. They serve—not asking for much in return. And I was looking for that the kind of company.

It was perhaps one o'clock or later when I left my room and edged down the promenade. Tiptoeing past some sleeping soldiers, I bumped into a deckhand. He was a rough-looking fellow, with droopy eyelids and a sandpaper chin. "Is there somethin' you need, Miss?" With his push pole, he shoved a snag away from the boat.

"I'm fine," I lied, as I edged past.

"Watch out for da alligator," he nodded toward the stairs, his grin revealing two missing front teeth. "Underneath da stairs. She's da boat's mascot, Miss. We had her near da wheelhouse, but some soldiers wouldn't leave her alone," he informed me. I wasn't about to tell him that I was one of those "soldiers," or at least that I had watched them.

Pushing against another snag in the water, he continued, "She's in a crate. In the closet underneath da stairs."

My nose discovered the horses before my eyes did. The stern area smelled of day-old manure, ripe hay, and sweaty horse. No wonder—there were dozens of horses snubbed to the afterguard, and by the looks of it, most of them had seen their share of service in the war.

A steel-colored mare whinnied her greeting. All ribcage, she rocked back on her haunches and strained against her rope. Then, glistening with sweat, she furiously pawed the floor, tussling her head away from the railing.

"There, there." I loosened her knot and stroked her mane. "You'll be all right."

Next to her was a beautiful bay, who bore a striking resemblance to Beulah. I rubbed my fingers through her forelock, and she burrowed her nose in my side.

With the patter of a soft rain the only sound, I peeked into the cargo hold. A number of horses shared that space too. Oddly, sleeping with the horses was far better than sleeping alone. I had tripped over soldiers on my way to the cargo hold. I didn't want to disturb them again.

Blinking in the dark, I tried to focus. The dank hold housed at least eighty horses, and numerous soldiers occupied every corner. I stepped carefully

Deckhands, such as the one Sarah encountered, performed many tasks, including housekeeping, rigging, maintenance, and watching for snags.

across the plank flooring until I finally found an open place in a small area behind some hay bales. Making a nest for myself, I settled in for the night.

My thoughts took me under the stars with Joseph. He let me think for myself. He was patient and careful and *safe*. He listened to me. More than that, he was a friend. He was somebody who could stand at my side. Somebody who cared.

Finally I drifted off to asleep. But not for long.

43

Joseph

I jolted awake to a thunderous noise and oppressive heat. The deck underneath me trembled and rolled, with a second blast following the first. The whole boat shuddered. Gabe woke up with a start. "We're being fired on. Man your guns!"

"What happened?" I looked toward the bow of the boat. The floor of the cabin deck was shattered in a thousand pieces; much of the main cabin had simply disappeared. The main salon, or what was left of it, was filled with steam, and the chandeliers still glowed with an eerie light. The middle of the boat was a cavernous hole.

Soldiers gaped at each other, unknotting themselves from the floor, as the boat folded into itself. Wood splintered and the decks above us collapsed like a house of cards. Shards of wood pummeled us, and the wall lurched to the right. Boiler fragments blasted from below. Pipes and bricks sliced through the air. Timber cracked, glass shattered, and the wall ripped open.

"Down!" Gabe grabbed my arm, jerking me toward the deck. Chunks of coal and charred wood whizzed past my ear. A plank speared past me and impaled a man, ripping through his stomach and exiting through his back.

"We've got to get out of here!" I tugged at Gabe. We trundled over shattered limbs, legs, and feet.

Many of the injured were scalded, their faces distorted, almost liquefied by the steam. I no longer distinguished the acrid smell of boiled and charred flesh from the pungent odor of burning pitch.

"Come on!" Gabe pushed me ahead.

"Help!" someone called.

Gabe wedged in front of me, but I jerked him back. "We need to find Sarah!"

The cabin floor dropped down in front of me and made an inclined plane to the lower deck. I lost my footing and gripped Gabe's arm.

"The boat's disintegrating!" Gabe cried.

Screams of soldiers echoed around me. Smoke rose out the chasm. I was sure McCoy, who had stolen my cot, must have already slid into the gaping hole.

We made our way through the carnage toward the ladies' cabins. I pushed back the curtain and barged through. A lady, matronly and round, her hair

An 1865 newspaper printed this image of the Sultana *boiler explosion.*

matted around her face, confronted us. "What do you want in here?" Her eyes skirted from Gabe to me.

"Sarah. Where's Sarah?"

She peered over my shoulder. Eyes widening, she stuttered, "S-something's wrong with the boat!" Mouth gaping open, she backed away, wagging her finger toward Sarah's room. I shouldered open the door.

"Not here!" The berth was empty. No one was there.

The boat shuddered. "There's a fire!" Gabe cried.

A dying choir of souls echoed, "Put out that fire! Put out that fire!"

"Get a bucket!" someone called.

We scrambled over the remains of the main salon to the railing and looked around. "I think they all blew off the boat!" I yelled. Compared to the screams around me, my voice was reedy and thin.

Then I saw it. The bucket Gabe had raised earlier was dangling on the railing just below me. I wished I had my knife.

Every time I grasped for the bucket, it flew from my fingertips. Flames, tentative at first, built on each other, curling and spiraling toward the sky, the flame's reflection lighting Gabe's eyes.

"We've got to get off!" Gabe cried.

"O'Farrell," I yelled. "We have to find O'Farrell! This way!" Grabbing Gabe's arm, I tugged him through the mass of men and debris. The cries of injured men, as if shrieking from the grave, filled the air. I stumbled over a beam lying diagonally across the deck. "Someone's pinned! It's O'Farrell! We've got to help him!"

We planted our feet on the deck, grasped the beam, and pulled.

"Pull!" I yelled. The beam wouldn't budge. "Pull!" The beam lifted a few inches off the deck and then sprang out of our hands. "Come on! Pull!"

We both leveraged ourselves against the plank and, with one hellacious pull, the beam lifted a few inches. Gabe grabbed O'Farrell's arm and wrenched him free.

O'Farrell's knee gaped open, the white of bone glistening through torn tissue.

I focused on his eyes. "You've got to swim."

After a glance at the water, O'Farrell turned toward me. "Can't swim. I'll drown."

"You won't," I assured him, handing him a small board. "Hang on to this. You'll be all right."

O'Farrell clutched the board and examined it. While he stood rooted to the spot another soldier ran up to him, grabbed the board away, and dove off the boat.

Gabe wrenched off a door casing and shoved it in O'Farrell's face. "Here, tuck this under your chin."

"I can't swim a stitch. Will this casing work?" O'Farrell gave me a blank stare.

"Not if you're standing here," I interrupted. "Once you're in the water, you've gotta get away from the boat."

We helped O'Farrell to the railing. He turned to look at us with watery eyes. "Help me over." I couldn't do it. He didn't stand a chance. Gabe gave me a fierce look, then helped O'Farrell over the railing. His legs and arms trundled through the air.

Gripping the railing, I stretched to find him. The water was a mass of men and horses. "O'Farrell!" I called. Then I saw him. His head bobbed above the surface yards away. I yelled as loud as I could, "Swim with all the mettle you've got!"

Chaos reigned as the fire churned from the center of the boat, warping and braiding, in a twisted path to the sky. Mutilated flesh peeled off men's bones, and their awful wails grated toward heaven. Everyone on board grasped for life, the light of the fire flushed on their faces. Twenty or thirty jumped off at a time. The river was black with men, heads bobbing like corks.

O'Farrell flailed in the water, gasping. Gabe clutched the rail and peered into the water, "He's not going to make it. Not a chance."

Underneath me, soldiers thrashed in the churning water, reaching out for anything to keep them afloat.

"Throw barrels. Wood. Anything!" O'Farrell said. We both looked at each other.

"The alligator box!" I sprinted to the closet under the stairway.

Someone had thought of the alligator box already. A soldier sliced his bayonet through the beast and dragged it out of the box by its tail. Slogging the box to the larboard side of the boat, he vaulted the crate overboard and leaped after it. Soldiers grabbed the bobbing crate, climbing over it, fighting for it. Men grasped each other, pulling others off the prize.

Smoke stung my eyes. The fire's flaming tongue lapped at the edges of the boat; its burning fingers ran up my legs. I grasped the railing and peered into the flooded river, peppered with men. How could I leave the boat without knowing Sarah was safe? I had just found her; I couldn't lose her all over again. If she was still on the boat, she needed me, and there was nothing I could do about it. Hemmed in by a wall of fire and the crush of soldiers, all I could do was jump, and hope that she had jumped too.

I looked back at Gabe, his face illuminated by the fire. Flames and smoke billowed behind him. I knew what we had to do.

I stepped to the edge of the boat. Dozens of men bobbed in the water below me. I crawled on the railing and jumped off, slamming into the water, plummeting deep below the surface. My lungs starved for air. I clawed my way to the top and kicked off my shoes—the shoes that had been so difficult for me to obtain.

Gabe, a silhouette against the sky and the flames, stood completely still. Then he dove off. I waited an eternity for him to rise to the surface.

44

Sarah

A vibration surged up my body, the boat trembling under my feet. Someone burst into the cargo hold. His eyes were wide and white. "The boiler exploded! The boat is going to sink!"

The boat jolted. I clawed up the hay bales and looked toward the door. Horses, screaming, tugged against their ropes. One broke away and skidded around a pole toward me, his ears flattened and his eyes wide.

My pulse racing, I bolted out of the cargo area. The splintered remains of the decks above were piled toward the middle of the boat like kindling. I fisted my hands at my side, willing myself to stay calm. Soldiers rushed past me, jarring against me. I could barely see over their heads. Where were Joseph and Gabe?

Where had I met Joseph the previous evening? Where had we been? Joseph and Gabe might not have survived the blast. Maybe they were in the water. Maybe they were fighting for their lives.

The railing was cracked but still intact. A clutching mass—hundreds of soldiers—struggled in the river. Hundreds of them were still on the boat, yelling, screaming, crying.

"Help!" someone called. Soldiers flowed around me.

He was on the plank flooring beside me—the young man that I had helped earlier. "You all right?" I asked.

"Think so. Not sure." He grasped the railing. "We're going to drown! Or burn. Not going to make it." The boat shuddered, listing to one side.

"Don't say that. You're fine." I bent down and helped him to his feet. "Once you're in the water, find something to hang on to."

He looked blankly at his arm. "Don't know if I can do it. Can't manage in the water. Not with my arm, and not when the shore's so far." He stood like a permanent fixture.

"You've got to try," I coaxed.

Glassy fear imprinted his eyes.

"Go!" I cried. "Please. Go."

He focused on the churning water. Then, with his lips clenched, he hoisted himself over the banister.

I leaned over. The wretched water knotted and warped below me. Please, God, let him break the surface.

I waited, searching for him. Moments later, his head popped above the water. He grappled at a plank floating past him. Throwing his good arm around it and keeping his other arm stiffly at his side, he kicked away from the boat.

The water, alive with men, whipped and churned past me. I couldn't tear my eyes away. Men were treading water, grasping for boards, casings, or shingles and then kicking and thrashing at each other for possession.

The weaker ones—the poorer swimmers—were left with nothing to hold. They gasped for air, slipped under the surface, and released themselves to the river's angry grip.

I heard a crackling noise, and the stench of burning pitch filled my nostrils. Turning toward the noise, I gasped as flames spiraled from the heart of the boat. At first, the fire was no taller than I. Then it hungrily fed on itself, devouring kindling, pitch, and everything in its path. I backed toward the railing. In a minute the fire had doubled its size, growing into a roaring monster. Finally, a boiling maelstrom shot toward the sky.

The air filled with screams.

"Fire, there's a fire!"
"Get off the boat!"

* * *

Men poured off the side, like a flock of sheep to the field. Groans of the dying echoed above the roar of the flames. I glanced back to the billowing fire and frantically looked for Joseph and Gabe.

"Help!"

A young man stood ten feet away from me grasping his leg. His eyes squinted in pain. His femur bone, splintered like a young branch, protruded through his leg—a bloody mass of tissue and blood. He had twisted his suspenders around his leg, a tourniquet of sorts. Rivulets of blood traced down his shin. "Please! Throw me over!"

"You can't swim that way!" I looked frantically for someone to help. Men rushed past me.

"No. Can't swim." His face burnished gold from the flames. "Rather die in the river. Please." I scanned the boat, my eyes begging for help.

Somehow, I edged him up the railing. In a burst of energy, I wedged myself underneath him and pushed him over. The railing splintered. He tumbled over and barreled into the water. I waited for him to rise to the surface.

I never saw him again.

I gaped at the water, my lungs pleading for air. My mind ceased its function.

Clawing through a dream, I reeled back to the horses. Choking smoke gripped the ceiling and filtered through the cargo hold. Wild-eyed horses pawed the deck, rearing, backing into each other; their shrill neighs echoed around me.

In order to escape being burnt alive, even those who could not swim jumped into the river's cold and swirling water.

Flames leaped from one crosspiece to another like a lizard running along a fence. Heat singed the hair on my arms. The smell of burning wood and burning flesh filled my nostrils.

A soldier ran past me, his eyes glaring and wide. "Get the horses out of here!"

"Trying!" Another soldier untied a chestnut and a roan. Horses, still roped to the post, panicked and reared. "Not safe in here! Get out!"

Just as I turned, a hatch door bounced and shuddered underneath me. I yanked the hatch handle. The door was stuck.

"Soldier, help me!" Both of us leveraged our full weight against the hatch and jerked on the door. "One, two, three, PULL!" The hatch opened. Like bees smoked from a tree, a dozen soldiers escaped, steam and smoke curling after them.

"Get off the boat!"

I glanced back at a mare still hitched to the railing. She rocked back on her haunches. Pulling the post from its moorings, she uprooted it, flailing the timber around her. The smoke twisted around me. A blast of heat. I jammed the heels of my palms against my eyes and blindly escaped the cargo hold.

The boat was being consumed in a hellish grasp of flames; its gnarling fire pummeled toward the sky.

I had to jump, now or never. If only I could close my mind to the image of the river.

The river curled and foamed underneath me. Once crowded with men, it now carried only dozens on its surface, their screams fading and weak. My eyes now wide open, I tore off my petticoat and crawled over the railing, tumbling over. My dress snagged as I plummeted to the water below. The river hit me like a cold fist, and I plunged beneath the waves.

Thinking I would never emerge, I grasped for the surface, my shredded skirts wrapping around my legs. Panic. I reached out, but my fingers found nothing to hold. In one desperate attempt, I lunged at the water, plunging, grasping. "P-please. S-save me."

There was a small shingle, just out of my reach. I lunged again, fighting against the current. My skirts—what was left of them—spiraled around me, weighing me down. Every fiber of my body strained against the river. Finally, I snagged the shingle.

The shingle barely held me. Frantically, I searched for a scrap of wood—anything to hold—and saw another shingle. I grabbed it and clutched both of the shingles in my arms. Someone gripped my arm.

"Get off!" I wrenched myself from his grasp.

Distance. Could I get away from the boat? Horses thrashed through the water. Men clawed past me, the water churning like an angry beast.

The blaze shot up, a fantastical bonfire forming in the middle of the river. The flames mingled with smoke and spiraled toward the sky. In that peculiar light, I saw both sides of the river distinctly: bluffs on one side and timber on the other.

My legs felt frozen—numb—but the heat of the fire warmed my face. The shingles barely held me. I fought for a better grasp, but plunged under the surface again, chugging huge gulps of water.

"Help!" I sputtered, clawing through the water, grasping for something bigger to hold. Small chards of wood drifted beside me, but nothing was large enough to be of any use.

The water was a wild scramble with hands reaching out, grabbing at me and grasping toward the sky. As scared as I was, I separated myself from the surrounding tragedy.

Calm—stay calm.

Mesmerized by the inferno, I couldn't control my thoughts. Flames trundled toward the stern, fire popped and crackled, and screams echoed across the water. Ash drifted from the sky.

One man hesitated on the wheelhouse, caught in a fatal moment of indecision. He waited too long. The wheelhouse wrenched off the hurricane deck with the poor soldier snagged in its framework. He was gripped in the steel housing with gnarling flames twisting around him, his piercing screams tearing through the air.

My eyes riveted on that surreal spectacle. I couldn't turn away. The curling flame devoured the soldier. His screams faded, swallowed by the inferno's triumphant roar.

The wheelhouse thundered down. Water heaved and surged. The stern turned, and the flames reversed; like great wheels, fire swept toward the bow. In a ghastly exodus, more than a dozen men leaped into the water. I waited in a breathless pause while only a few soldiers rose to the surface.

Men clinging to the sides of the boat were singed off like flies.

I hoped that I didn't know any of those men. What of Joseph and Gabe? Were they all right? My body shaking in the frigid water, I gagged on the nausea that surged through me. My childhood friends, the boys I'd grown up with—they had to be all right. I should have searched harder for them. I should have stayed with Joseph through the night. I should have told him everything I'd been trying to figure out how to say for the last four years.

I floated downstream and searched for Joseph, recognizing his features in almost every man I saw.

I drifted farther from the boat, the hull of the *Sultana* following me like a wretched shadow. Its embers glowed crystal shades of orange, yellow, and crimson. A ghostly mirror, the water was a warped reflection mimicking the boat's gloomy carcass. Perhaps a dozen men still clung to ropes tied to the hull of the boat. Their cries echoed across the water.

A huge column of steam and smoke rose in the air, finally obscuring my view.

I struggled to keep my head above water. Coughing and sputtering, my energy dissipated. I needed something more substantial to hold. The entrails of the boat surrounded me, and chunks of debris nudged against me, the river a refuse of railings, decking, barrels, and crates. I couldn't cut the distance. Couldn't fight the current.

My arms were lead weights and my fingers were turning blue. The river roiled and churned, and one of my shingles slipped out of my grip. I flailed—grasping, crying, swallowing the river water. The current was pulling me under.

Then something sleek slipped past my legs. A horse. A dead horse.

Wrapping my frozen fingers in the horse's mangled mane and fighting the tug of my skirts, I struggled to mount her. Black mane. Mottled fur.

Clear and strong, I heard my father's voice.

You're quite a rider. Always keep your head on your shoulders and your horse will carry you through.

That's what I need to do. Stay calm. Think straight.

My vision was limited, the ship's fire no longer illuminating the shore. Two young soldiers drifted past me, clinging to a horse trough. "Oh God, have mercy!" one cried. "Please, Lord, save me!" begged the other. I ached with their cries.

Just then a man passed me, bobbing up and down on a barrel. He came within a few feet of me. "Damn this thing! It'll drown me," he said. Like a waterwheel, he churned underneath the water then clambered back on top, sputtering for air. "My God, I can't hold out any longer!" His eyes widened, his mouth gaped, and his expression was an odd combination of victory and fear.

I, like the man on the barrel, had the same feeling of triumph and terror. Frightened, yet strangely confident, I had escaped the inferno, fought the river, and found a raft of sorts. However, I wasn't safe yet.

45

Joseph

MISSISSIPPI RIVER, APRIL 27, 1865

Gabe speared through the water and clawed over to me. Grabbing me by the hair, he dragged me under. The water swirled around me, choking me. I pushed away and fought my way to the surface. Then I lurched at him, grasped him by his shirt, and lugged him toward the surface. "Gabe, come on!" I yelled.

He had always been so self-assured in the water; his panic surprised me. He doused me a second time.

"You'll drown us!" I sputtered. Small wood fragments floated past. There was nothing large enough to grab. Then just ten feet ahead of us, a large shape came into view—a small section of a staircase.

"Look! Grab that! Swim!"

"Can't! My side. I can't swim!"

He went under. I nabbed him by his shirt, tugging against the weight of the water. Half carrying, half dragging him to the steps, I scrambled on and wrenched him up after me.

Choking on water, he struggled for air.

"Gabe! You all right?" I panicked, waiting for him to breathe.

He shifted his weight, clutching the stairs with both hands. His smile was thin. "A little wet. Fine."

I caught a glimpse of his side. The skin was sheared off, the muscle shredded, mealy, and raw. When he bobbed above the surface, blood oozed from his side. "We'll get to shore. We'll be all right," I said encouragingly.

He was shaking. His eyes were glassy and white. Every sinew straining, he tugged himself up on the stairs.

I dragged us through the slushy water, every pump of my legs shooting pain up my spine. My eyes still stung from the smoke. Grasping Gabe's arm, I pushed forward. Would he go under again?

We drifted with the current, and I couldn't see either shore. Thankfully, I had found something to carry my weight. My worries about Sarah rode along with me: maybe she didn't make it off the boat. Maybe she wasn't even alive.

I tried to relax and reserve my energy.

The black river shivered past us, littered with men, animals, and debris. A lady clutched her baby, barely managing a screaming child and a wooden plank. A poor fellow drifted with a sock in his hands, muttering to himself on his downriver course. One man clutched his valise, first with one hand then the other.

Strange became normal.

Then, riding a faster current, a soldier passed us, yelling, "Have tobacco? Sure could use a chew. If I had some, I could make it to shore."

I expected my brother, usually quick-tongued, to say something. Nothing. I cupped my hand around my mouth and yelled, "Do I have tobacco? No. Check with me tomorrow." I gave a half smile and looked for Gabe's reaction. His skin

Joseph describes a scene much like the painting above as he struggled to stay afloat in the rapidly flowing Mississippi River after the Sultana *explosion. During spring floods, branches, other debris, and even entire trees could be swept away in the mighty Mississippi, making travel difficult and swimming dangerous.*

KARL BODMER FF29-C041, INDIANA HISTORICAL SOCIETY

was a grayish tinge and his eyes stared unseeing. I put my hand on his, guarding his hold on the boards.

I kicked, dragging him along. He barely hung on. Then faintly, above the roar of the river, sounds echoed across the water.

We rounded a bend in the river. Six men or so—scarecrows, really—stood on the opposite shore singing "The Star Spangled Banner." Belting it out, they sang without reserve.

They'd made it. They had escaped the river and made it to shore.

My throat grew tight and my eyes burned. Longing to join them, I clenched my teeth, leaned forward, and strained every muscle, desperate against the current and the distance. My prison-weakened muscles couldn't make headway in the water. With every fiber fighting for shore, I floated past the makeshift choir, the song's sweet lyrics taunting me with their lingering notes.

Jostled by the water, the staircase lurched back and forth. I chugged water. The river had a mind of its own, whipping the staircase away from me. My legs swept along with the current. I grasped and regrasped the staircase in a fight to stay on.

Others were in the water too. "Help, someone help!" I heard a cry. Enveloped in graying darkness, Gabe and I bumped into a submerged tree. Branches ripped at my legs. The steps were slippery; it was hard to stay on.

Gabe stared straight ahead, his eyes unfocused. I grabbed his hand. It had the cold feel of death. "Stay with me, Gabe! Hear me?"

He was played out. Would we both be buried in this watery grave? "Hold on. Got to be a boat downstream. It'll take us aboard. You . . ."

The river picked up speed, swirling and writhing in gnarled fists.

We struck a crosscurrent. When the main current and the crosscurrent collided, an angry whirlpool formed.

"Watch out, a whirlpool!" I clawed against the current, but I needed Gabe's help. "Come on, Gabe!"

Twigs and charred boards were being sucked into the vortex, and we headed straight for it. I gulped in water. The steps weaved through the river.

"Help!" My cry was in vain. No one was within hearing distance; we were on our own.

Terror enveloped me, and I harnessed all my muscle. Gabe's feet dragged in the river. I couldn't keep my grip.

"Gabe!" The whirlpool was just a few feet away. "Hold on!" Twisting and turning, we were swept into the chasm.

I grasped the steps with a strength that surprised me. We spun in circles, branches and twigs bumping against me.

"Hang on!" I yelled. Momentarily I lost Gabe's hand, grabbed at it, and kicked like I never had before, plowing against the circling waves.

Our makeshift raft shot out into the current and on down the river.

"We made it, Gabe!" I cried, turning toward him to share our victory. Only he wasn't there.

Blindly, I clawed at the water. "Gabe!" The river surged, roiling and tumbling over me. Desperate to find him, and desperate to hang on, I clung to the stairs. The river pushed me farther downstream. I fought to stay on.

"Gabe!"

Something brushed against me. I grabbed for it and grasped nothing.

Burning energy, I clawed against the water, ducking underneath, and then gasping for breath. Every time I came up, I filled my lungs with air and dove underneath again. Desperate to find him, I plunged again and again. My lungs bursting, I fought against the current. "Someone! Help!"

I had lost the staircase. With all my strength I worked against the water, not knowing if I was swimming upstream or downstream. I swallowed huge gulps of water.

"Help!" I called again.

The smell of clover. I was back at Hardin's Pond.

I fought against the pitching current, trying to stay afloat. Finally, bone tired and freezing, I let the current carry me.

My brother was gone. "You two watch out for each other," my mother had said.

Ice water penetrated my bones and I couldn't feel my fingers. My mind fixed on images of home—my father filling the doorway, my mother's soft eyes. She was waving. Maybe she was waving good-bye.

I drifted past the lights of Memphis, the gas lamps flickering in the streets. No one was going to pick me up.

Then all was blank.

I dreamed I saw Sarah on McCartney's stone bridge. I couldn't read her face. Her eyes glittered with tears. Maybe she was crying. Maybe she was happy.

Then I heard voices and the splash of an oar. I called for help, like I was crying my way out of a nightmare.

A large, dark image loomed in front of me—a gunboat maybe. A man called, "Is that someone? Fish him out of there!"

I was floating past. I screamed, but no sound came out.

Hands reached down and nabbed my shirt, the current tugging me forward. Someone grabbed me under my arm, and I trolled along with the boat.

"Get him!" Someone wrenched me from the water. Finally, I tumbled into the boat. Like a wet rag, I went down.

"You all right?" my rescuer asked.

"Think so." I couldn't feel my fingers or my feet.

"You almost took me down with you. My name's Neil. Let me help you." He tugged off my remaining sock, tossing it behind him. "Can you walk?" He rolled me up in a wool blanket and carried me close to the boilers.

The ghostly river glided past. I tightened the blanket around me. Alone. I was alone.

Neil grabbed a bottle of whisky, uncorked it with his teeth, and raised it to my lips. "Try some of this." The whisky flamed down my throat. "Pretty remarkable you made it, ol' boy," Neil commented, shaking his head.

I put my head in my hands and ached with a confusing combination of loss and relief.

Would morning never dawn?

* * *

Finally, the river turned yellow-brown, and the sky greeted me with its pale morning tint. The shoreline—at first shapeless and dark——formed jagged silhouettes of trees and bushes and fields. The water shimmered beside us, and the morning light revealed surreal images. A man perched on a snag. Another clung to the top of a half-submerged tree.

I had grown deaf to the cries of soldiers. How many soldiers had we already fished out? A dozen? More? Just when I thought there couldn't possibly be anyone else, Neil ran to the back of the boat and shouted, "Pull her up!"

Her?

I stumbled to the side of the boat and peered over. "Sarah?" I called. She was in the water, her ragged skirts flaming around her, her hair in wet clumps. My heart ached with the sight of her. I wanted to wrap my arms around her, to hold her. I wanted her by my side.

Neal gripped her hand and I grabbed her other hand. "Pull!" We both threw our weight against her, tugging her into the boat. "Pull!"

"J-Joseph?" she sputtered.

Until that instant, I hadn't realized my heart needed rescue as surely as my body. "I-I never thought I-I'd find you," I said.

Sarah, a soggy dripping Sarah, looked up at me, gasping for breath. "Actually, I found you."

Epilogue

Joseph

INDIANAPOLIS, MAY 1865

Our return to Indiana took almost a week. The quickest way north was by steamboat, my hands clutching the railing most of the trip. Then we took the train home.

From the station I walked home to see my parents, remembering a conversation I'd had with Gabe.

If somethin' happens to one of us, Mother wouldn't be the same.

Father either.

Home looked different somehow—maybe smaller. The grove was thicker and tangled with underbrush. The outbuildings were shabbier and needing paint. A new shed stood at the back edge of the property. I half expected to see Gabe.

He wasn't there.

My mother ran out of the house, wiping her hands on her apron. Her eyes were expectant, hopeful, shimmering. My father came out of the barn, dropping the bucket from his hand.

I couldn't look at my parents' faces—their blank shock when they realized that only one young man, not two, walked toward them. Before I reached her, my mother's head was down, her shoulders shaking. I'd heard my mother cry before, but never like that.

Father's arms were around Mother. He looked over her head, his eyes glassy and penetrating. "Gabe? Where's Gabe?"

I shook my head and stood stiffly, not knowing what to say.

Her hands over her face, my mother turned away. When she turned back to me, her eyes were rimmed and wet.

Father let me into his arms, and the three of us held each other. "I didn't think either of you would be coming home," Father finally said. I caught my mother's glance at him. She cleared her throat, her voice etched with pain. "We're glad you're home."

Their tears were for Gabe, but just as much, their tears were for my return.

We made our way into the house. "I need to show you something," Father said, lifting an envelope from the top of the mantel. The script on the letter was angular, with long, heavy strokes.

About twenty-five years after the end of the Civil War, construction began in Indianapolis on the Soldiers and Sailors Monument in honor of those who fought and died in that war. It also honors those who fought in the American Revolution, the War of 1812, the Mexican-American War, the Frontier (Indian) Wars, and the Spanish-American War. Completed in 1901, the memorial stands nearly three hundred feet high and is said to be the first monument in the United States dedicated to the common soldier, men such as Joseph and Gabe.

April 1, 1865
Camp Fisk

Dear Father and Mother,

We'll be coming home soon. When I get home, Mother, I'm going to have some of your fried chicken, first thing.

Just want you to know that I'm watching out for Joseph. I'll make sure he returns home safe to you.

See you in time for planting.

Yours, Gabe

Mother placed Gabe's letter on the mantel and turned to look at me. Her eyes were teary, like the day we left for war.

I stood there stiffly. The house was empty without Gabe. I wanted him to walk through the front door, to take off his kepi and fling it at me, to reach for his bow and go hunting, to gather wood, to milk the cows, to plow the fields. I didn't know how I could do all those things without him.

There was no return to "normal" life. My mother avoided my eyes. My father barely talked.

I told them what happened on the boat. Then they made me tell them again. Like the hesitant tick of a watch, I repeated the story over and over.

Somehow, I needed to find time with Sarah, because—well, she already knew.

Two days after returning home, I found her sitting on her front porch, her hair twisted in a bun. Golden wisps framed her face. With her feet barely touching the floor, she seemed small on that wicker bench.

As if we had an unspoken agreement, neither of us talked of the *Sultana*. The disaster was an ever-present guest, but we didn't give the visitor our time.

Sitting on the bench beside her, I leaned back and smiled for the first time in days. "So, will you be living here on your own?"

"Father left me enough money to stay here." Leaning back on the bench, Sarah rested the back of her hand on her forehead and closed her eyes. "I'll be all right."

I struggled for something to say. "You're going to miss him. Some things will be hard to manage. I mean on your own."

She sighed, "I know. I'll just have to manage." Obviously, she would be alright. She had a strength I hadn't seen in anyone else.

"How are you planning to plant your garden next year?" I finally asked. "I mean, how will you organize it?"

She smiled. "Probably with help from a friend." She took hold of my hand and squeezed it. "Hopefully you can manage a hoe."

"Well, I've watched Mrs. Habernathy enough. I should know how."

"Speak of the devil!" Sarah nodded down the road. "See who's coming?"

Mrs. Habernathy waddled toward us, her jiggling arms keeping time with her legs. Waving her arm as she neared us, I was surprised to see letters in her hand.

"Got somethin' for you, Miss Sarah." Mrs. Habernathy plopped the letters in the middle of Sarah's lap. "The postmaster's been deliverin' these, but you weren't home. It's been a nuisance to collect 'em while you were gone, but I think these are all of 'em." Mrs. Habernathy folded her arms, waiting for a response.

"Thank you, Mrs. Habernathy." Sarah thumbed through the letters. "How kind of you."

"I don't quite understand two young folks sittin' together without a chaperone." Mrs. Habernathy turned toward home. Sarah and I shared a smile.

I nodded toward Sarah's letters. The handwriting was familiar. "May I have those?"

"Umm. . . " She tapped them in a neat pile and gave them to me. I picked the top one:

> Dear Sarah,
> I take pen in hand to tell you of a bit of excitement I had today. I traded my knife for a pair of shoes. I will probably miss my knife.

"You have no idea how much I missed you." I looked up from my letter. "Thought of you every day."

I felt so strongly about her because we had always been friends, because we had spent so much time apart, because we had both survived together.

"You were always in my thoughts too." Her eyes became shiny. "I've got to get something."

"What do you need?"

"Oh, something."

She let the door bang on its frame as she entered the house. A minute later the door banged again. She walked down the porch toward me, carrying a blue satin ribbon.

Taking the letter from my hands, Sarah wrapped the bundle with the ribbon, binding it with a tidy bow. She clasped them on her lap and tilted her head toward me, a small smile playing on her lips.

"I've got something for you." I edged forward in my chair.

Biting her lower lip, she leaned toward me. "What?"

I had to smile. "Patience," I said. She had never been a patient person and probably never would be.

"Oh, I'm patient. I mean, I've learned patience," she countered.

"Really?" I asked, opening my fingers. In the hollow of my hand I held the stone—the smooth, flat stone I had found in Tennessee. Placing it in her palm, I curved her fingers around it. "I've been saving this for you."

"So thoughtful." She gave me a shy glance.

"It survived the . . . " I knotted and unknotted my hands. "Most girls wouldn't want a pebble."

Her smile was warm. "I'm not 'most girls.'"

"Definitely." I cleared my throat. "I want to come calling. I mean, if that's all right with you."

"Isn't that what you're doing?" She tilted her chin toward me, a smile playing on her lips.

I wasn't sure if she was teasing. "Well. Yes. I mean, I guess so."

"You're here," she added.

"I am." And I always would be, if she would have me. "Can I read you the rest of my letters?"

Sarah tightened her fingers around mine and looked up at me through her long lashes. "There'll be plenty of time for that."

Acknowledgments

Many thanks to my dear husband, Les, and to our daughters, Heidi, Jenni, and Casey. They not only endured my captivation with family history and my nonstop chatter about the *Sultana*, but they also loved me for it. A special thanks to my sister, Charissa, who believed in me since the beginning. I've always believed in her.

Thanks to others who lent me their eyes and ears, helping me to refine my work. Ashlee Koedam, my mentor and guide, inspired me and tolerated my bellyaching. Kim Van Es, a self-proclaimed grammar nerd, carefully edited this book. Her extremely picky and often annoying suggestions gave this book the polish it required. Finally, I understand semicolons. Kate Brauning, Rachel Hibma, and Kent Westphal also shared advice, making this story a finer piece. Susan Jongewaard Stanley also shared some remarkable insights. Not only did she pluck out historical inaccuracies, but she also made some really fine tea. My colleagues and students at Northwestern College supported me, inspiring my work and uplifting me in prayer.

Sometimes writing historical fiction is like altering a pair of britches into a jacket. Not everything aligns exactly, no matter how hard you try. My team of scholars greatly assisted my intent for historical accuracy. Any remaining errors are solely mine. My gratitude goes to Gene Saleker, author of *Disaster on the Mississippi: The Sultana Explosion*; David J. Meagher, designer of *Sultana* blueprints; Kathleen S. Hanson, RN, PhD, author of *Turn Backward, O Time: The Civil War Diary of Amanda Shelton*; James Knight, author of *The Battle of Franklin*; and Kevin Frye, Andersonville historian. Thanks to my publisher the Indiana Historical Society Press, especially Teresa Baer, managing editor; Kathleen Breen, Ray Boomhower, and Geneil Breeze, editors; and Patrick Hanlon, intern.

Without my dear mom, Anona (Elliott) Boone, this book would have not been possible. Lastly, thank you to the Association of *Sultana* Descendants and Friends. Their ancestors' accounts are woven lovingly throughout these pages. This story is *Yours*.

Author's Notes

As I noted in the preface, this story is a blend of fact and fiction. In these pages, I included historic figures such as President Abraham Lincoln, Governor Oliver Morton, and the Marques de Lafayette. Other than actual historical persons, portrayed according to my understanding and interpretation, all characters appearing in this story are fictional.

For the most part, character names were selected from a list of those who perished on the *Sultana*. My intention was to recognize both those who survived and those who perished. Enoch Nation, for example, Ninth Indiana Calvary, was captured at Sulphur Branch Trestle. He perished in the explosion and his body was never found. He was not able to tell his story. When his ancestors asked me to include him in my tale, I did, and he became Sarah's companion on her spy mission.

The settings are also a product of my imagination. To my knowledge, Hardin's Pond does not exist anywhere near Indianapolis, nor are there hills too steep to climb. However, the basic landscape of Indianapolis and the surrounding area are accurate for the period.

I hope when you've read this story, you will understand my intent—not only to tell *Sultana's* story, but also to express the power of love.

Some of the many historical facts that have been incorporated into the story appear below. **(Full citations for references can be found in the Selected Bibliography)**

[Page 13] Your letters are received by me with the greatest joy and my beating heart aches for your reply. "Once more with great pleasure I embrace a few moments to write you a short letter. . . . Your letters are received by me with the greatest pleasure, and a beating heart always waits a reply." *My Precious Loulie.*

[Page 15] Things have got to a pretty pass if a woman can't give a warm supper and a bed to the poor, starving creatures, just because they are slaves, and have been abused and oppressed all their lives, poor things! "Things have got to a pretty pass if a woman can't give a warm supper and a bed to the poor, starving creatures." Stowe, *Uncle Tom's Cabin*, 264

[Page 17] Your great-grandfather had supper at the Black Bear Tavern.
"The citizens gave him dinner at the Black Bear." Carpenter, *Genealogical Notes of the Carpenter Family*, 30

[Page 50] "In this great emergency our government wants men. Men with stout hands and willing hearts. Men who will fight manfully for our just and holy cause." Civil War recruitment poster

[Page 50] Just write the number 18 on a piece of paper. Slip it in your shoe. "He would take a bit of paper, scribble the number 18 on it, and put it in the sole of his shoe." Catton, "Hay Foot! Straw Foot!"

[Page 62] We entered, the smell of green lumber greeting me. "The new sheds were built of green lumber . . . soon the soldiers were complaining heartily about their drafty, leaking quarters." Winslow and Moore, *Camp Morton*, 241

[Page 62] You look like a schoolboy. "Trousers and sleeves were too long or too short, and coats were cut on too skimpy a scale. 'We all look like a set of school boys.'" Wiley, *Life of Billy Yank*, 112

[Page 63] Hay foot! Straw foot!" Soon the ground was littered with hay. "He knows the trick for farmers," someone said behind me. "To teach these lads how to march, the sergeants would tie a wisp of hay to the left foot and a wisp of straw to the right." Catton, "Hay Foot! Straw Foot," 1

[Page 65] Better eat it now, or it'll be full of worms. "They had become infested with maggots and weevils." Billings, *Hardtack and Coffee*, 115

[Page 65] Gabe crushed through the mud. "Perfect loblolly." "The roads were awful perfect loblolly all the way and we had to wade through like hogs." Beller, *Billy Yank and Johnny Reb*, 44

[Page 66] Seven contrabands came to our picket post in the night. We fed them on crackers and sent them on their way. "Seven came to our picket post in the night. We fed them on crackers and sent them on their way. McSpadden, *A Leaf of Voices*, 307

[Page 68] No woman under thirty years need apply to serve in government hospitals. All nurses are required to be plain-looking. Their dresses

must be brown or black, with no bows, curls, jewelry, or hoop skirts. "No woman under thirty years need apply to serve in government hospitals. All nurses are required to be plain-looking. Their dresses must be brown or black, with no bows, curls, jewelry, or hoop skirts." Brown, *Dorothea Dix*, 303

[Page 73] The huge branch splintered in a final, deafening crack and tumbled to the ground, landing inches from us. "Artillery fire comes in such force as to shatter good-sized trees, and men are actually killed by falling limbs." Wiley, *The Life of Johnny Reb*, 72

[Page 75] Only a mile out of camp, my shoes flapped apart. "There are men in my company who have been barefooted the last month, having to march all the way from Winchester to Culpepper (sixty miles) in that situation—cold and frosty mornings at that. "Wiley, *The Life of Johnny Reb*, 120

[Page 79] In each row, the tents opened into each other, spreading from one side of the meadow to the other. "The Corps Hospital is formed by three-parallel rows of tents opening one into the other." Maertz, "Midland War Sketches," 83

[Page 83] Stakes driven into the ground supported a board and a tin washbasin for us to share. "A cot, a mattress, a mosquito net, a stake driven into the ground with a board nailed on top supporting a tin wash-basin." Maertz, "Midland War Sketches," 83

[Page 87] Made of scrap lumber, bark, and tin—drifted towards us. The boats turned the stream into a floating dry goods store. Rebs and Yanks separated by narrow rivers developed an ingenious device for carrying on trade." Wiley, *The Life of Johnny Reb*, 320

[Page 89] I knotted my Green River knife on the boat and pushed it toward him, watching the vessel cup and dip with the current. "Facing each other across a river, enemy pickets sometimes sent little hand-carved sailboats to the opposite shore." Robertson, *Tenting Tonight*, 158

[Page 92] The roast looked edible—it wasn't sticky or blue like our last rations. "The Beef is so poor it is Sticky and Blue." Wiley, *The Life of Johnny Reb*, 98

[Page 95] I have received my authority from the Lord God Almighty. Have you anything that ranks higher than that? "I have received my authority from the Lord God Almighty. Have you anything that ranks higher than that?" Denney, *Civil War Medicine*, 91

[Page 98] Did Gabe think he was on a Sunday stroll? "It was not uncommon to see a Reb walking around in a hail of bullets with the apparent unconcern of a man taking a relaxing stroll in the cool of the day." Wiley, *The Story of Johnny Reb*, 34

[Page 100] Pressing my gun to my shoulder, I squeezed one eye and pulled the trigger. Nothing. I rammed in another charge. My gun was still silent. "But Johnny, with utter unawareness of the failure of his piece to fire, continued to ram in charge upon charge. With intermittent though quite futile aiming and trigger pulling, until the barrel refused to receive further ammunition." Wiley, *The Story of Johnny Reb*, 30

[Page 116] His master had been a tough, drinking man, and the mistress of the house was a large portly woman with an evil disposition. "She was a tough, portly woman, with an evil disposition." Still, *The Underground Railroad*, 495

[Page 119] Like leaky bellows—air whistled through his mutilated throat. "Poor fellow, every time he drew breath the air whistled through his mutilated throat like a leaky bellow." Hyde, *A Captive of War*, 3

[Page 119] He nodded toward a massive oak, with some papery leaves still hanging on. It was an old tree, solid and beautiful. "The ground around that tree for several acres in extent was literally drenched with human blood." Edmonds, *Nurse and Spy in the Union Army*, 191

[Page 123] The fingers curled, the severed tendons, muscles, and veins mashed and useless, the fingernails were dirty and crusted with blood. Blood streamed from his arm into the bowl. "A stream of blood ran from the table into a tub in which was the arm." *A Journal of Hospital Life in the Confederate Army of Tennessee*, 19

[Page 131] We differ politically, but we're a unit on the subject of whisky. "However much we differed politically, we were a unit on the subject of fluids." Carpenter, *Genealogical Notes of the Carpenter Family*, 144

[Page 139] Log ends served as stools, bayonets substituted for candlesticks. "Bayonets driven into the walls became candlesticks." Robertson, *Tenting Tonight*, 47

[Page 142] Take out an advertisement. O' Farrell's answer was matter of fact. "Many people placed messages in Southern newspapers, hoping Northern newspapers would print the notices, and their friends in the Union would see them." Wright, *What They Didn't Teach You about the Civil War*, 59

[Page 148] He wants to know the strength and position of their forces. "He immediately told me he had a note from General Sheridan, who wanted me to tell him of the strength and position of the Rebel forces." Holland, *Our Army Nurses*, 58

[Page 151] Scattered patches of moonlight, feeble though they were, made the treetops appear full of every variety of ogre. "Few scattering patches of moonlight, feeble though they were, made the tree-tops appear to be full of every variety of ogre." McSpadden, *A Leaf of Voices*, 313

[Page 155] His voice echoed across the meadow. He was maybe ten yards away. "Got guard duty, too, eh? "A Delaware lieutenant who made a 'hollering' acquaintance with a group of Confederates on picket." Wiley, *The Life of Johnny Reb*, 321

[Page 155] Our property. Our homes. What're you fightin' for? "We are fighting for matters real and tangible . . . our property and our homes." *What They Fought For*, 18

[Page 155] She's a jim-dandy. He limped along the tree line. She has the darkest, shiniest, silkiest hair. Her skin's so smooth. I miss everything about her. "More frequently, however, gabfests were . . . about such matters of common interest as rations, pay, the weather, lice, officers, home, and peace." Wiley, *The Life of Billy Yank*, 353

[Page 163] Franklin, Tennessee. Those words will haunt me the rest of my life. "Franklin Tennessee: These are words that will haunt me the rest of my life." Knight, *The Battle of Franklin*, 7

[Page 164] Their regimental band played "Dixie." "Flags were unfurled and several regimental bands struck up 'Dixie'" Knight, *The Battle of Franklin*, 65

[Page 166] Two distinct sounds echoed across the valley: first the boom of explosion, then the crack of bones. "At every discharge of the guns, there were two sounds—first the explosion and then the crack of the bones." Knight, *The Battle of Franklin*, 74

[Page 174] First got-damn man who falls out of line, I blow to hell. I'll make every one of you wish you had stayed home. "First got-damn man that falls out of line, I blow him to hell." Robertson, *Tenting Tonight*, 132

[Page 174] Wirz inched around, slowly. His eyes lit on one soldier, then another. "Stay in your ranks. No rations today, you pitiful lot of Yankees." "That is the way I get rid of you damned sons of bitches." Meredith, ed., *This Was Andersonville*, 329

[Page 177] "We're splittin' this canteen in half." The great tunneling tool was the indispensable half-canteen. Meredith, ed., *This Was Andersonville*, 44

[Page 181] Negroes loaded with bundles of ol massa's clothing, are flockin' North. "The negroes are flocking in across the broad plantations, loaded with bundles of 'missus's' and 'massa's' clothing." McSpadden, *A Leaf of Voices*, 327

[Page 187] We're all pushin' dirt the same way. Our tunnel's curved like a blamed horseshoe. "Our tunnel was shaped like a horseshoe, and the beginning and end were not fifteen feet apart." Meredith, ed., *This Was Andersonville*, 45

[Page 194] In contrast to spring's beauty, the countryside was pockmarked with graves. I eyed the sad clumps of earth and wondered how many mothers waited for their sons to come home. "Many of the mounds were unmarked or designated simply by a stake bearing a number." Robertson, *Tenting Tonight*, 98

[Page 214] In the fashion of a sword fighter, Gabe tucked one arm behind his back and jousted. "We would punch him with sticks to see him open his mouth." Berry, *Loss of the* Sultana *and Reminiscences of Survivors*, 225

[Page 234] Two people—two lovers—were caught in an embrace. Nine months after the *Sultana* disaster a son was born to Margaret McGhee (possibly a product of the rendezvous in Memphis). Family Lore of Thomas William Wilson, *Sultana* Survivor

[Page 235] Captain Mason shrugged, tipped his hat, and left us, climbing along the railing to the stern of the boat. "I remember, just before I fell asleep, Captain Mason . . . was compelled to crawl around on the rail." Berry, *Loss of the* Sultana *and Reminiscences of Survivors*, 126

[Page 241] Gabe woke up with a start. "We're being fired on. Man your guns!" "I thought at first a Rebel battery had fired on us and that a shell had exploded on board." Berry, *Loss of the* Sultana *and Reminiscences of Survivor*, 374

[Page 241] Wood splintering, the decks above us collapsed like a house of cards. Boiler fragments blasted from below. "Hot coals, boiling hot water and steam, and the debris of the ruptured boilers and furnace shot through the area behind the main stairway." Salecker, *Disaster on the Mississippi*, 82

[Page 241] A plank speared past me and impaled a man, ripping through his stomach and exiting through his back. "A piece of timber ran through his body, killing him almost instantly." Berry, *Loss of the* Sultana *and Reminiscences of Survivors*, 225

[Page 241] We trundled over shattered limbs, legs, and feet. "I was nearly buried with dead and wounded comrades, legs, arms, heads, and all parts of human bodies, and fragments of the wrecked upper decks." Berry, *Loss of the* Sultana *and Reminiscences of Survivors*, p. 319

[Page 244] "I can't swim a stitch. Will this casing work?" "Lewis, I can't swim a lick, do you think this will be of any good?" Berry, *Loss of the* Sultana *and Reminiscences of Survivors*, 108

[Page 244] The water was a mass of men and horses. "The water was a mass of men, some trying to make their escape and others drowning." Berry, *Loss of the* Sultana *and Reminiscences of Survivors*, 205

[Page 244] Mutilated flesh peeled off men's bone, and their awful wails grated toward heaven. "Some were so badly scalded by the hot water and steam from the exploded boiler that the flesh was falling from their bones." Berry, *Loss of the* Sultana *and Reminiscences of Survivors*, 320. "I stood for a few minutes and listened to that awful wail of hundreds of human beings burning alive." *Loss of the* Sultana *and Reminiscences of Survivors*, 275

[Page 247] A clutching mass—hundreds of soldiers—struggled in the river. Hundreds of them still on the boat, yelling, screaming, crying. "No matter how good a swimmer a man might be if he got into one of those crowds his doom was sealed and he would go down with the clutching mass." Berry, *Loss of the* Sultana *and Reminiscences of Survivors*, 235

[Page 248] Groans of the dying echoed above the roar of the flames. "I could hear the groans of the dying above the roar of the flames." Berry, *Loss of the* Sultana *and Reminiscences of Survivors*, 249

[Page 248] He had twisted his suspenders around his leg, a tourniquet, of sorts. "With his suspenders he had improvised tourniquets for both legs, to prevent bleeding to death." Berry, *Loss of the* Sultana *and Reminiscences of Survivors*, 117

[Page 251] In that peculiar light, I saw both sides of the river distinctly: bluffs on one side and timber on the other. "As the flames ascended, mingled with smoke, and shed their peculiar light on the water, we could see both sides distinctly; bluffs on one side, and timber on the other, and with no sensation as to the moving current." Elliott, *The Sultana Disaster*, 173

[Page 251] My legs felt frozen—numb—but the heat of the fire warmed my face. "I was so close to the burning boat that I had to let myself down in the water to keep from being burned." Berry, *Loss of the* Sultana *and Reminiscences of Survivors*, 363

[Page 252] Perhaps a dozen men still clung to ropes tied to the hull of the boat. Their cries echoed across the water. "A rope had been thrown over and was hanging by the side of the boat to which two or three poor fellows were hanging." Berry, *Loss of the* Sultana *and Reminiscences of Survivors*, 207

[Page 252] Wrapping my frozen fingers in the horse's mangled mane and fighting the tug of my skirts, I struggled to mount her. "It was a mule that saved my life and a dead one at that." Berry, *Loss of the* Sultana *and Reminiscences of Survivor*, 302

[Page 252] "Oh God, have mercy!" one cried. "Please, Lord, save me!" begged the other. "As he had been doing a good deal of praying, I have no doubt he is in the better world." Elliott, *The Sultana Disaster*, 175

[Page 256] One man clutched his valise, first with one hand then the other. "I had hung on to my valise all this time, changing it from one hand to the other as either arm grew tired." Berry, *Loss of the* Sultana *and Reminiscences of Survivors*, 245

[Page 257] Six men or so—scarecrows, really—stood on the opposite shore singing "The Star Spangled Banner." Belting it out, they sang without reserve. "There was a large tree floating down the river and on the roots were three or four men. They were singing the "Star Spangled Banner." Berry, *Loss of the* Sultana *and Reminiscences of Survivors*, 327

[Page 259] Would morning never dawn? "Would morning never dawn on a night so hideous?" Berry, *Loss of the* Sultana *and Reminiscences of Survivors*, 120

Appendix 1

The real Joseph Taylor Elliott, a *Sultana* survivor, fought with the Indiana Eleventh and 124th Indiana Infantry Regiments. Three of his family members also served as Union soldiers: his father, General William Johnston Elliott, and his brothers, Adjutant General Byron Kascrusko Elliott (132nd Indiana Infantry Regiment), and Samuel Wilson Elliott (Fifty-Second Indiana Infantry Regiment).

Joseph's time line not only shows some fascinating comparisons but also provides a window to the life of an Indiana Civil War family.

THE EARLY YEARS

1849

Soon after the death of his wife Mary Littel Taylor (1813–1849), William Johnston moves to Indianapolis with his children: Byron Kascrusko (1835–1913); Joseph Taylor (1837–1916); Margaret Ann (1840–); Samuel Wilson (1840–); Emma Martha (1842–); Florence (Flora) (1845–1909); and William Dalrymple (1848–1930). William Johnston's second marriage was to Charlotte (Tuttle) White (1822–1913). Either out of regard for him or at his insistence, his children called him "General." He was a hotelier until 1863.

1856

William Johnston runs on the Democratic ticket for the Indiana State Senate but is defeated.

ORGANIZING TROOPS AND GATHERING MUNITIONS

1856

William Johnston serves as a captain in the newly formed National Guard of Indianapolis.

1857

William Johnston forms the Indianapolis City Greys, a unit of older volunteers who wished to serve the Union. On August 19, with an introductory letter from former governor Ashbel P. Willard, William Johnston procures one hundred muskets needed to equip the new company.

LILA SYBESMA

Joseph Taylor Elliott

CIVIL WAR

1860

While working as a hotel clerk in Montgomery, Alabama, Joseph Taylor experiences animosity toward the North.

November 6: Abraham Lincoln is elected the sixteenth president of the United States.

December 20: South Carolina secedes from the Union.

1861

Charlotte gives birth to Julia (April 12, 1861). The Confederates fire on Fort Sumter, Charleston, South Carolina.

April 19: Joseph Taylor enlists as a private in the Eleventh Indiana Infantry Regiment for three-months service.

April 21–25: Joseph Taylor has picket duty on the Ohio River, near Evansville and marches to Bunker Hill with his regiment, joining Patterson's command.

August 2: Joseph Taylor is mustered out.

1862

February 1: Samuel Wilson joins the Fifty-Second Indiana Infantry Regiment. The regiment captures Fort Donelson, is involved in the Meridian campaign, and fights in the battles of Pleasant Hill, Nashville, and the siege of Fort Blakely.

May 8: Governor Oliver P. Morton requests that William Johnston serve as a special agent of the state of Indiana in the mustering out of Indiana Regiments in Washington, DC. William Johnston is to procure funds so that the troops are paid and to locate the sick and wounded Hoosier soldiers to have them furloughed and sent home.

May 10: William Johnston receives overlooked rosters and notification from Adjutant General Lazarus Noble that Governor Morton will visit the wounded at Pittsburg Landing (Battle of Shiloh).

June 17: Doctor Luther D. Waterman, surgeon for the Thirty-Ninth Indiana Infantry Regiment, writes to William Johnston regarding the conditions of Indiana soldiers in Corinth, Mississippi, who were "exhausted by disease, exposure, climate and labor." Waterman also reports that "all who were able to march" had left for the railroad station in Corinth.

July 9: William Johnston receives a military pass: "Transportation is hereby ordered for William J. Elliott from Nashville to Huntsville, Alabama." He is to visit hospitals "as often as he desires."

December 13: Governor Morton requests that William Johnston visit Indiana regiments in the South "for the purpose of looking after the wants and necessities of the sick and wounded" and that he receive "such facilities as he may need to enable him to get through safely."

December 18: William Johnston receives passes to assist the wounded in Prairie Grove, Arkansas, and Camp Chase, Ohio.

1863
March 14: William Johnston receives an exacompta that documents the organization of troops. Because of the document's sensitive nature, he was "to show it to no person [and] when he has finished his business . . . [he] will destroy this copy." The exacompta was not destroyed.

March 18: Governor Morton requests that William Johnston visit regiments in the Department of the Cumberland to check on conditions, give assistance, visit hospitals, and list the battles in which the regiments fought.

In addition to his military duties William Johnston serves as the Marion County Recorder.

1864
January 5: Joseph Taylor enlists in the 124th Indiana Infantry Regiment and sees action in the Battles of Resaca, Franklin, and Nashville, as well as the siege of Atlanta.

May: Byron Kascrusko serves in the 132nd Indiana, rising to the rank of adjutant general.

September 1: Joseph Taylor is promoted to second lieutenant.

September 7: Byron Kascrusko is mustered out of the 132nd Regiment.

1865

February 6: While his son Joseph Taylor is held captive in Andersonville Prison, William Johnston visits Indiana parolees at Camp Chase, Ohio, and ministers to their needs.

April 9: The Civil War ends.

April 15: President Lincoln dies.

April 24: Joseph Taylor is on his journey home.

April 27: William Johnston is invited to meet Lincoln's funeral train on its stop in Indianapolis. That same day, Joseph Taylor battles for his life following the *Sultana* explosion and subsequent sinking.

August 31: Joseph Taylor receives an honorable discharge and is mustered out of the army.

POST-CIVIL WAR

After his service in the Civil War Joseph Taylor worked in the abstract business in Indianapolis and later established Joseph T. Elliott & Sons, a stocks and bonds company. In 1899 Joseph was elected president of the Marion Trust Company. He began a four-year term on the Indianapolis Board of Public Works on January 1, 1906, and served as its president. On April 27, 1902, his account of the *Sultana* disaster appeared in the *Indianapolis Sentinel* and it was published by the Indiana Historical Society in 1913. Joseph and Annetta (Nettie) Langsdale Elliott had two sons, Joseph Taylor Jr. and George. Joseph Taylor was laid to rest in 1916 at the age of seventy-nine.

Appendix 2

SULTANA BLUEPRINTS

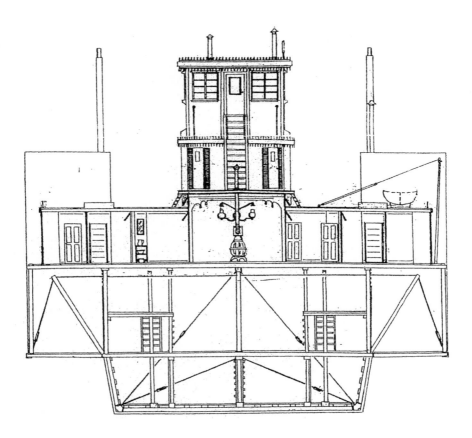

1. Pilothouse
2. Texas Roof
3. Texas
4. Main Saloon
5. Stateroom
6. Passageway
7. Hurricane Roof
8. Hurricane Deck
9. Boiler Deck
10. Main Deck
11. Cross Chains
12. Wheelhouse Support Brace
13. Hog Chain Brace
14. Engine / Wheel Crank Support Timbers
15. Hold

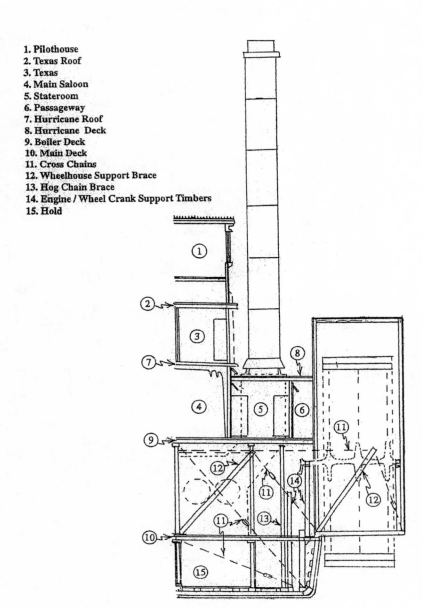

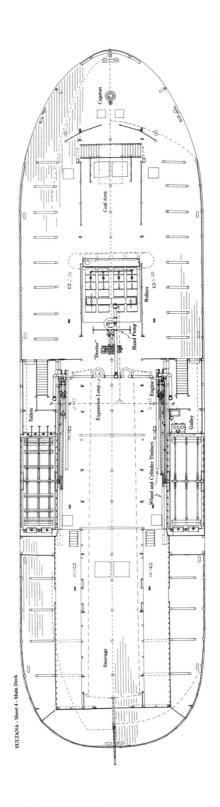

SULTANA · Sheet 4 · Main Deck

Capstan

Coal Area

Boilers

Hand Pump

"Doctor"

Expansion Loop

Engine

Toilets

Galley

Wheel and Cylinder Timbers

Steerage

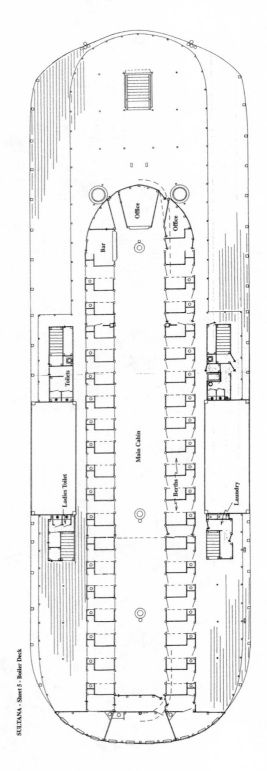

SULTANA - Sheet 5 - Boiler Deck

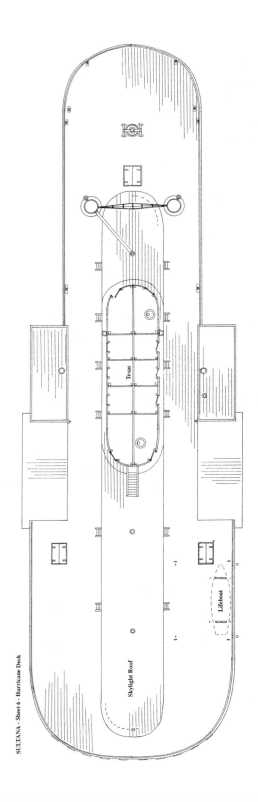

SULTANA - Sheet 6 - Hurricane Deck

Texas

Skylight Roof

Lifeboat

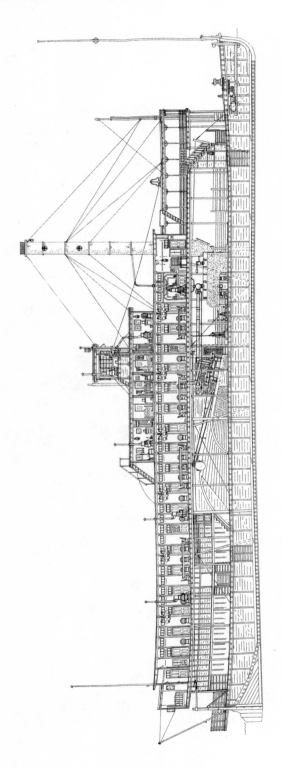

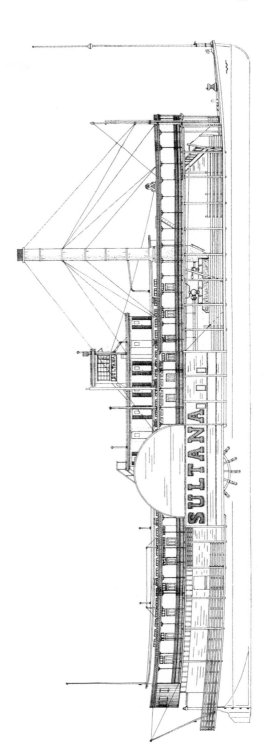

Sultana

April 27, 1865

Glossary

a breezing: a disturbance, especially a lively quarrel

addle-brained: having a muddled or confused mind; foolish, silly, or illogical

afterguard: a structure on a steamboat's main deck extending out from the hull as a means of protecting the paddlewheels. The space created by the afterguard was sometimes used to store freight

Andersonville: a Confederate prison in southwest Georgia where more than 12,000 Union soldiers died

apple-shakers: rural, unsophisticated people

Appomattox Court House: the Virginia town where General Robert E. Lee surrendered to General Ulysses S. Grant on April 9, 1865, ending the Civil War

axle: the rod passing through the center of a wheel or group of wheels

balls of his feet: the bottom part of the feet just behind the toes

baring her teeth: showing the teeth, indicating hostility or readiness to fight

baritone: a male singing voice of medium range between bass and tenor; also, a person having this voice

barkeep: a person who owns or serves drinks in a bar

basswood: any of several linden trees; the straight-grained soft white wood of a basswood

bay: a reddish-brown horse, with a black mane and tail and black on the lower legs

bayonet: a sword-like stabbing blade that may be fixed to the muzzle of a rifle for use in hand-to-hand combat

berth: a fixed bed or bunk on a ship, train, or other means of transport

Billy Yank: a soldier in the Union army (North)

bisque: unglazed china; a pale pinkish-brown color

bit: a metal mouthpiece that is attached to a bridle and used to control a horse

Black-eyed Susan: a flower with yellowish petals and a dark center

blacksmith's bellows: a device for producing a strong current of air, used for stoking a fire

blared out: announced loudly

boiler deck: the second deck one a ship, the one over the boilers

boiler room: a compartment in a ship containing a boiler and related heating or steam-generating equipment

bovine: relating to or resembling cows

bow: the front end of a ship

box elder: a maple tree native to North America

braced: prepare for something difficult or unpleasant

braid/braiding: to weave together three or more strands

bravado: a show of boldness intended to impress or intimidate

bridle: the headgear used to control a horse, consisting of buckled straps to which a bit and reins are attached

brome: an oat-like grass

Brown Bess: a nickname for the British army's muzzle-loading smoothbore musket, used between 1722 and 1838

Buell: Don Carlos Buell was a Union general who led troops at Shiloh and Perryville.

bulbous: fat, round, or bulging

bully: very good or first rate

burlap: coarse canvas woven from jute, hemp, or a similar fiber; used especially for sacking and sometimes dressmaking

bussin'/bussing: kiss

buttermilk walls: pale yellow color walls

cabbaged: to steal

Cahaba: a prisoner-of-war camp in Alabama

camelback trunk: a travel trunk with a domed top used to hold clothes and personal belongings; most commonly used for long trips

candlestick chair: a chair fashioned with cylinder-shaped columns, bearing a resemblance to candlesticks

capstan: a device for pulling on a line (rope). Poles are placed in the square sockets around the top and crewmen walk around it, pushing on the poles.

Captain Mason: James Cass Mason was the captain of the *Sultana*

carbon: an ingredient in gun powder

careened: moved swiftly and in an uncontrolled way

carpetbag: a kind of bag made with a carpet-like material. They were very common in nineteenth-century America.

cellar: a basement, usually filled with food supplies

chafed: to feel irritation, dissatisfaction, or impatience; to rub so as to wear away or make sore

chestnut: gray to reddish brown in color. A type of tree common in eastern North America, producing red nuts

chevron: a 'V' shaped patch, usually upside-down. In the military, emblems that indicate the rank of a noncommissioned officer

chiffonier: a tall narrow chest with drawers

chirrup: a short, sharp, high-pitched sound like that a bird makes. Chirp

chloroform: a colorless, toxic liquid that acts as an anesthesia

chock: a metal loop used for towing or mooring a boat at the dock.

cinch: a strap used to attach the saddle or pack to a horse

cinched: to fasten, as in a belt or strap

clambered: climb awkwardly

clappered: make a loud noise

clout: influence, pull, or importance. Reputation.

clucked: a clicking noise made with the tongue

cocked the hammer: pulling the hammer back on a gun, preparing it to fire

color-bearer: a soldier who carries the colors or flag during battle or drilling

contrabands: during the Civil War, a term for runaway slaves who escaped to Union lines

court-martialed: the result of a trial conducted by the military separate from civil authorities

cowlick: a lock or tuft of hair growing in a different direction than the rest of someone's hair

criminy: a mild swear

crinoline: an open-weave fabric, often in a skirt or underskirt

crosscurrent: a current moving against the flow's main direction

crossed the bar: metaphor for dying

crosspiece: horizontal beams

cupping: forming into an arched shape; forming into a cup or bowl shape

cursory: quick, often superficial

cypress: a type of evergreen/coniferous tree

Day of Thanksgiving and Praise: Thanksgiving had been an informal holiday since the first one with the Pilgrims in the 1620s, but in 1863 President Lincoln mandated that the fourth Thursday in November be an official day of Thanksgiving and Praise. Today, that holiday is named—more simply—Thanksgiving.

deadline: a line drawn around a prison that if crossed by one of the prisoners they risked being shot by a guard

deckhand: a common sailor who performs manual labor

dipper: something resembling a cup with a long handle; like a ladle

disarming: causing someone to lower their guard; win someone over

discount: to lessen the importance of something or disregard it

divvied: divide or share

"Dixie": a popular Rebel song and the unofficial anthem of the Confederate States

doused: to pour a liquid (usually water) onto something

dress the line: a command to reform or straighten up a line of soldiers in an orderly fashion

drew a bead: to take aim with one's gun

drummed out of camp: to be kicked out or expelled in a disgraceful way

duckweed: a small plant with green weeds that grows and floats in the water.

dysentery: a disease common in army camps that causes severe diarrhea and dehydration

eddies: a current of water in a stream or river running contrary to the main current, usually in a spinning fashion

Enfield: a British made rifle-musket commonly used by Civil War soldiers

ensign: a flag, usually denoting national origin and possibly flown with a different emblem sown in (such as a regimental insignia) to further identify a group

exacompta: a type of notepad/notebook.

exodus: a large group of people leaving a place at once

faugh: an expression of contempt, disgust, or abhorrence

fetlock: a tuft of hair above a horse's back hooves

first mate: the second in command on a ship or boat

flagstaff: a staff on which a flag is flown; like a flagpole

forelock: a lock of hair grown over the forehead of a person or animal, especially a horse.

fornicator: an unmarried person who engages in sexual intercourse

fretwork: decorative design, usually consisting of intersecting lines

gas lamp: an old style of lamp fueled by gas

gee willikers: a phrase used to indicate excitement or surprise

gelding: a castrated male horse

General Wagner: General George D. Wagner was present at many battles in the Civil War. At the Battle of Franklin, however, he disobeyed orders to have his troops withdraw from their forward position. As a result, the Confederates were able to penetrate the Union position and many were captured.

glassy eyes: a glazed over look in the eyes when someone is tired or perhaps about to cry

glistening: a sparking or shiny appearance, often because of moisture

Governor Morton: Oliver P. Morton, the governor or Indiana during the Civil War

Green River knife: knives produced in Green River, Massachusetts, from the 1830s to the 1860s, these knives were of high quality and value and became very popular with westward-bound Americans in the nineteenth century

half tent: each soldier was issued half a tent, which could be buttoned together to form a whole tent.

hollows: a small valley

"Happy Land of Canaan": a popular Civil War song

hardtack: a saltless, hard, dry biscuit or bread; good for traveling long distances

haversack: a type of bag that is carried over one's shoulder

headstall: part of a horse's bridle (reins) that goes over the head

hellacious: exceptionally powerful or violent

Hellhole: an extremely miserable or filthy place

hemp: a tall plant whose fibers are strong and good for making cord and rope

Henry Wirz: the commandant of Andersonville prison camp. Eventually he was executed for war crimes because of the horrible state in which he forced prisoners to live.

hillocks: small hills

hocks: similar to the human ankle, the joint on four-legged animals connecting the foot (hoof) and leg

hodgepodge: a mixture of different things, usually in a particularly messy way

hogsheads: a large barrel holding about sixty-three gallons

horn: a piece on a Western (American) saddle that the rider can grab and help pull him or herself up into the saddle

hurricane deck: on a steamboat, the third deck up counting from the water

imposing: having great size or importance

imprinted: made a mark by pressing against a surface, stamp; to fix firmly in the mind or memory

Inferno: a place or state that resembles Hell

insinuating: subtly implying an idea or thought

iridescent: a lustrous or attractive appearance, usually caused by the way a light reflects off the object

Jim-Dandy: something excellent or exciting

John Wilkes Booth: the man who assassinated President Lincoln in April 1865, just shortly after General Lee surrendered his army to General Grant

Johnny/Johnnies: a common nickname for Southern/Confederate troops

kepi: a type of military hat, usually round on top, sloping down towards a visor over the eyes

knapsacks: a two-strapped bag similar to a backpack that is worn over the shoulders

knitted: tied or moved so closely together so as to appear attached.

ladder-back chair: a chair with two upright rods connected with horizontal rods to form the back

larboard: left side of a boat when looking toward the front; port

Laudanum: an opium-based drug commonly used in the nineteenth century as a sedative

livery: a place to feed, stable, and care for horses for pay

loblolly: a thick muddy area, mire, mud hole; a thick gruel; a lout

macabre: a gruesome scene, usually to do with death

maelstrom: a powerful and violent whirlpool

magenta: a deep purplish red color

main deck: the lowest deck on a ship. It is the deck that holds the boilers and where the heaviest freight is carried.

Major General Joseph E. Johnston: General Johnston was the Confederate commander of the Army of the Tennessee from 1863 to 1864.

mangle: spoil, ruin; injure with disfiguring wounds

mangy: having many bare or worn out spots

marbly: having the appearance of marble

mealy: pale, pallid

mercantile: a place of business such as a general store

Mercurous chloride: a medicine containing mercury used to treat irritations on the skin. Though it was common in the eighteenth and nineteenth century, mercury has since been discovered to be poisonous.

merino: a soft wool fabric

mettle: strength of heart; courage

Milady: a fashionable woman

milled: to grind in a spinning fashion; move around in a circular manner

minié balls: an elongated soft-lead bullet with a cone-shaped base common in the Civil War. The bullets exploded on impact, shattering limbs and splintering bones. Arm or leg wounds almost always led to amputation.

Minuteman: a man of the Revolutionary War era, who was ready to take up arms at a minute's notice

missives: written notes or letters

moseyed: move in a slow, easy manner

motherwort: a type of weed that can be consumed to relax a person

Mud Clerk: a crewman on a steamboat

munitions: material such as guns, gunpowder, bullets, etc.

mushing: smashing or squishing

mustered: brought together or formally enrolled

muzzle-loading musket: a type of gun loaded by pouring power and a bullet in the muzzle

Negroes: a term not often used today, this was a common word in the nineteenth century for a person of African descent

nestling: a young bird not yet able to leave the nest

Netherworld: the world of the dead, similar to Hell

orderlies: a soldier or hospital worker usually assigned to carry patients from place to place

ornery: cranky, cantankerous

paddlewheel: a giant wheel with paddles on the side or back of steamboats that spins to propel it through the water

palette: a large and varied collection of colors

palisade: a fence made of wooded stakes usually for defense

pallets: a flat wooden surface for sleeping on that can be easily moved

parole: a prisoner released from prison under certain conditions and promises to do certain things before full freedom is granted

pate: top of the head

paunch: a large belly

pendulum: something that swings back and forth

percussion: a beating or taping, usually in reference to a rhythm or music

Perryville: a town in central Kentucky that was the site of a battle in October 1862. One of the bloodiest battles of the war, it resulted in a victory for the Union as the Confederates lost control of Kentucky.

Pittsburg Landing: a small town in southern Tennessee where a battle took place in April 1862. Also called the Battle of Shiloh, this conflict was a victory for the Union army under General Grant.

plaster and laths: an old style of making interior walls where plaster (a mud-like substance) is spread over wooden slats

plummeted: fell quickly

pneumonia: a disease that affects the lungs resulting in much coughing, fever, and difficulty breathing

poised: composed, balanced

polio: a disease that affects the nerves and legs making walking difficult

poll: the name of the part of an animal's head, referencing a point immediately behind the ears

pounced: swooped or jumped down onto quickly

probe: a skinny stick-like instrument used usually by doctors for searching inside the human body

promenade: the deck of a passenger ship where passengers are able to walk about freely

prone: fall forward; lay flat

prow: front of a boat; bow

puddling: making a puddle by dripping or pouring a liquid onto dirt

pulley: a system where a rope is pulled over a wheel that can assist in lifting heavy objects

purview: the range or scope of authority

push pole: a long thick pole used to push debris away from a boat or to push it off from shore

quiver: a case for carrying or holding arrows; shaking or trembling motion

ramrod: a slender metal or hardwood shaft used to ram a charge into to bore of a musket or rifle

ratchet/ratcheting: to cause to move by steps or degrees—usually used with up or down

rebellion: open fighting against authority (as one's government)

Rebs: slang for Confederate soldiers or Southerners during the Civil War

Redcoat: a British soldier especially during the American Revolution

retorted: to reply usually angrily or sharply

retrieving: getting and bringing back

reveille: a signal sounded at about sunrise on a bugle to call soldiers or sailors to duty

Revolutionary War: The Revolutionary War (1775–83), also known as the War of Independence, was a war between England and the thirteen American colonies.

Rip Van Winkle: the title character in a story by Washington Irving about a man who sleeps for twenty years and does not recognize the world when he awakens

rivulets: small streams

roans: horses with a coat of a dark color (as black or brown) mixed with white

roiled: stirred up; riled

route step: a style of marching in which troops maintain prescribed intervals but are not required to keep in step or maintain silence

safe as a crow in a gutter: secure

saltpeter: a white powder that exists naturally in some soils and that is used especially as a fertilizer, in medicine, and to make gunpowder.

sardonic: scornful, mocking

saucy: being rude and disrespectful; sassy

scalding: burning with or as if with hot liquid or steam

scarce as hen's teeth: very rare; to be extremely difficult or impossible to find

scarlet remnant: bloody evidence

scissored: moved (one's legs) back and forth in a way resembling the action of scissors

scrambling: moving with urgency or panic; moving or climbing hastily on all fours

scrolling: (of an ornamental design or carving) made to resemble a partly unrolled scroll of parchment

scythe: a tool that has a curved blade on a long curved handle and is used for mowing grass or grain by hand

Secesh: Northern slang for Confederate civilians as well as soldiers

settled: came to rest; made a home; made quiet; decided

shag: to have sexual intercourse with

shaving glass: shaving mirror

shimmied: moved effortlessly, with a swaying motion

shoofly pie: a molasses pie or cake

sidesaddle: a saddle for women in which the rider sits with both legs on one side of the horse; to ride using a sidesaddle

sieve: a utensil with meshes or holes to separate finer particles from coarser ones or solids from liquids

silt: particles of small size left as sediment from water

sinewy: full of sinews, stringy; strong

skirmish: light combat involving few men

slew: to kill violently, wantonly, or in great numbers; to strike down

slipshod: very careless

slouch cap: a soft usually felt hat with a wide flexible brim

slushing: making a squelching or splashing sound

smallpox: a sometimes deadly disease in which fever and skin rash occur and which is believed to have been wiped out worldwide by vaccination

snag: a tree or branch when stuck underwater and not visible from the surface

snubbed: tied or roped (to a tree or post)

speckling: a small mark (as of color)

spirit lamp: a lamp in which a volatile liquid fuel (such as alcohol) is burned

Springfield: The model 1861 .58-caliber percussion shoulder arm was the most widely used rifle in the Union army. The rifle was fifty-six-inches long, had a forty-inch barrel, a walnut stock, held an eighteen-inch bayonet, and weighed less ten than pounds.

staccato: music cut short so as not to sound connected; played or sung with breaks between notes

stanchion: a strong, upright pole that is used to support something

stateroom: a private room on a ship or a train

steins: large mugs for beer

stern: the rear end of a boat

stern-wheeler: a steamboat driven by a single paddle wheel at the stern (rear)

stirrup: either of a pair of small light frames or loops often of metal hung by straps from a saddle and used as a support for the foot of a horseback rider

Stones River: the Battle of Stones River, also called the Battle of Murfreesboro (December 31, 1862–January 2, 1863)

styptic: linen scraped into a soft substance and used for dressing wounds and sores

subterfuge: the use of tricks, especially to hide, avoid, or get something

sulfur: a yellow chemical element that is found widely in nature and is used in making chemicals and paper, and in medicine for treating skin diseases

surreal: very strange or unusual; having the quality of a dream

sutler: a civilian licensed to operate a shop on a military post or camp, offering foodstuffs that were not included in the official rations

tchicked: a click made with the tongue and used to urge on a horse

tendons: a band of tough white fiber connecting a muscle to another part (as a bone)

tourniquet: a device (as a bandage twisted tight) for stopping bleeding or blood flow

towheaded: having very light, blond hair

transgressions: violations of a command or law

trenching: digging a long narrow ditch

triers: someone who tries

trolled: to fish with a hook and line pulled along through the water

trundling: rolling along

two-step: a ballroom dance in $^2/_4$ or $^4/_4$ time having a basic pattern of step-close-step

visaged: having a face, countenance, or appearance of a specified kind

waffling: being unable or unwilling to make a clear decision about what to do; to talk or write a lot without saying anything important or interesting

Wagner, General: George D. Wagner did not follow his orders to withdraw at the Battle of Franklin and had his forces hold firm. Two of his brigades were routed and while in retreat became intermixed with Confederate troops, causing the Union forces to hold their fire for fear of killing friendly troops. He was relieved of duty after the battle.

warping: moving in a distorted fashion

waterwheel: a wheel turned by a flow of water against it

waxed: grow larger or stronger

wharf boat: a boat moored and used for a wharf at a bank of a river or in a like situation where the height of the water is so variable that a fixed wharf is impracticable

wheelhouse: the casing around the paddlewheel on a sidewheel boat

whisking: moving suddenly and quickly

whitewashed: covered with a mixture that whitens

whuffed: blew noisily

will-o'-the-wisp: a goal that cannot be reached; a light that sometimes appears at night over wet ground

winsome: cheerful, pleasant, and appealing

witch's bridle: a tangle in a horse's mane

witches' brew: a mixture of dangerous or unpleasant things

wobbling: moving from side to side in a shaky manner

wrangled: argued angrily

writhed: twist (the body or a bodily part) in pain

Selected Bibliography

Bailey, Ronald H. *The Bloodiest Day: The Battle of Antietam*. Alexandria, VA: Time-Life, 1984.

Beller, Susan Provost. *Billy Yank and Johnny Reb: Soldiering in the Civil War*. Minneapolis: Twenty-First Century, 1943.

Berry, Chester D., ed. *Loss of the* Sultana *and Reminiscences of Survivors*. Knoxville: University of Tennessee Press, 2005.

Billings, John D. *Hardtack and Coffee*. 2nd ed. Lincoln: University of Nebraska Press, 1993.

Bonner, Robert E. *The Soldier's Pen*. New York: Hill and Wang, 2006.

Brown, Thomas J. *Dorothea Dix: New England Reformer*. Cambridge, MA: Harvard University Press, 1998.

Carpenter, Seymour David. *Genealogical Notes of the Carpenter Family: Including the Autobiography, and Personal Reminiscences*. Springfield: Illinois State Journal, 1907.

Catton, Bruce. "Hay Foot! Straw Foot!" *American Heritage* 8, no. 3 (April 1957).

Coggins, Jack. *Arms and Equipment of the Civil War*. Garden City, NJ: Doubleday, 1962.

Cumming, Kate. *A Journal of Hospital Life in the Confederate Army of Tennessee*. Louisville: John P. Morton, 1866.

Daniel, Larry J. *Battle of Stones River: The Forgotten Conflict between the Confederate Army of Tennessee and the Union Army of the Cumberland*. Baton Rouge: Louisiana State University, 2012.

———. *Shiloh: The Battle That Changed the Civil War*. New York: Simon, 1997.

Davis, William C. *Brother against Brother*. Alexandria, VA: Time-Life, 1983.

Denney, Robert E. *Civil War Medicine: Care and Comfort of the Wounded*. New York: Sterling Press, 1994.

Dunn, Jacob Piatt. *Greater Indianapolis: The History, the Industries, the Institutions, and the People of a City of Homes*. Chicago: Lewis Publishing Company, 1910.

———. *Indiana and Indianans: A History of Aboriginal and Territorial Indiana and the Century of Statehood*. New York: American Historical Society, 1919.

Eckerman, Nancy P. *Indiana in the Civil War: Doctors, Hospitals, and Medical Care*. Mount Pleasant, SC: Arcadia, 2002.

Edmonds, Emma E. *Nurse and Spy in the Union Army*. Hartford, CT: W. S. Williams and Company, 1865.

Elliott, James W. *Transport to Disaster*. New York: Holt, Rinehart, and Winston, 1962.

Elliott, Joseph Taylor. *The Sultana Disaster*. Vol. 5, n. 3, Indiana Historical Society Publications (Indianapolis: Edward J. Hecker, Printer, 1913): 163–99.

Fletcher, William A. *Rebel Private: Front and Rear*. 2nd ed. New York: Meridian, 1997.

Fraustein, Rebah Morgan. *The Elliott Family of Indianapolis: Descendants of Captain James Elliott Revolutionary War Soldier*. Indianapolis, 1976.

Gandy, Joan W., and Thomas H. Gandy. *The Mississippi Steamboat Era in Historic Photographs*. New York: Dover, 1987.

Garrison, Webb, Sr. *Webb Garrison's Civil War Dictionary*. Nashville, TN: Cumberland House, 2008.

Groom, Winston. *Shiloh: 1862*. Washington DC: National Geographic, 2012.

Hanson, Kathleen S. "A Network of Service: Female Nurses in the Civil War." *Caduceus* 11, no. 1 (1995): 11–22.

———. "Down to Vicksburg: The Nurses' Experience." *Journal of the Illinois State Historical Society* 97, no. 4 (Winter 2004): 286–309.

———. *Turn Backward, O Time: The Civil War Diary of Amanda Shelton*. Chicago: Edinborough Press, 2006.

Holland, Mary A. Gardner. *Our Army Nurses: Interesting Sketches, Addresses, and Photographs*. Boston: B. Wilkins, 1895.

Hyde, Solon. *A Captive of War*. Shippensburg, PA: Burd Street Press, 1996.

Jackson, Henry. *The Civil War Diaries of Henry Jackson Dodson: 40th Indiana Volunteer Infantry Regiment*. [Crystal Lake, IL]: S. E. Bowen, 1999.

Kantor, MacKinlay. *Andersonville*. Cleveland: World, 1955.

Knight, James R. *The Battle of Franklin*. Charleston, SC: History Press, 2009.

Meagher, David J. *Sultana Blueprint* (2004).

Maertz, Louise. "Midland War Sketches." *Midland Monthly* 3, no. 1 (January 1895): 79–85.

Marvel, William. *Andersonville: The Last Depot*. Chapel Hill: University of North Carolina Press, 1994.

McCutcheon, Marc. *Everyday Life in the 1800s*. Cincinnati: Writer's Digest, 1993.

McPherson, James M. *What They Fought For*. New York: Anchor Books, 1995.

McSpadden, Jennifer *A Leaf of Voices: Stories of the American Civil War in the Words of Those Who Lived and Died, 1861–65*. Indianapolis: Indiana Historical Society Press, 2014.

Meredith, Roy, ed. *This Was Andersonville*. New York: Fairfax Press, 1957.

Moore, Frank, comp. *Anecdotes, Poetry, and Incidents of the War*. New York: Boston Stereotype Foundry, 1866.

My Precious Loulie: Love Letters of the Civil War. http://spec.lib.vt.edu/cwlove/.

Noe, Kenneth W. *Perryville: This Grand Havoc of Battle*. Lexington: University of Kentucky Press, 2001.

Oates, Stephen B. *A Woman of Valor: Clara Barton and the Civil War*. New York: Free Press, 1994.

Pettit, Eber M. *Sketches in the History of the Underground Railroad*. Freeport, NY: Books for Library Press, 1971.

Potter, Jerry O. *The Sultana Tragedy*. Gretna, LA: Pelican Publishing Company, 1992.

Pryor, Elizabeth Brown. *Clara Barton: Professional Angel*. Philadelphia: University of Pennsylvania Press, 1987.

Ray, Delia. *Behind the Blue and Gray*. New York: Puffin, 1991.

Rensink, Iva A., *The Girl That Was I*. Self Published, 1983.

Robertson, James I., Jr. *Tenting Tonight: The Soldier's Life*. Alexandria, VA: Time-Life, 1984.

————. *The Untold Civil War*. Washington DC: National Geographic Society, 2011.

Salecker, Gene Eric. *Disaster on the Mississippi: The* Sultana *Explosion*. Annapolis, MD: Naval Institute Press, 1996.

Sandlin, Lee. *Wicked River: The Mississippi When It Last Ran Wild*. New York: Pantheon, 2010.

Schultz, Jane E. *Women at the Front: Hospital Workers in Civil War America*. Chapel Hill: University of North Carolina Press, 2004.

Stein, Gloria Sananes. *Civil War Camp Life: Sutlers, Sex and Scoundrels*. Xlibris, 2008.

Still, William. *The Underground Railroad*. Chicago: Johnson Publishing Company, 1970.

Stowe, Harriet Beecher. *Uncle Tom's Cabin*. Boston: John P. Jewett and Company, 1952.

Varhola, Michael O. *Life in Civil War America*. Cincinnati: Family Tree, 1999.

Watkins, Sam. *Company Aytch*. New York: Plume, 1999.

Wiley, Bell Irvin. *The Life of Billy Yank*. 2nd ed. Baton Rouge: Louisiana State University Press, 1952.

————. *The Life of Johnny Reb*. 2nd ed. Baton Rouge: Louisiana State University Press, 2008.

Winslow, Hattie Lou, and Joseph R. H. Moore. *Camp Morton 1861–1865: Indianapolis Prison Camp*. Indianapolis: Indiana Historical Society, 1940.

Winters, Erastus. *The Civil War Memoirs of Erastus Winters: Serving Uncle Sam in the 50th Ohio, 1861–1865*. Nashville, TN: Gold River Studio, 2011.

Wright, John D. *The Language of the Civil War*. Westport, CT: Oryx, 2001.

Wright, Mike. *What They Didn't Teach You about the Civil War*. New York: Ballentine, 1996.